About the Springfield Writers Group

Established in 2016, the Springfield Writers Group (SWG) is based in Brisbane, Australia. This group of emerging and established writers meet monthly over coffee and too many muffins to support each other's work and efforts towards becoming better writers. There is probably too much time spent laughing and enjoying each other's company, but we do get some work done as well. This anthology represents many months of work, learning, frustration, and joy.

Anyone wishing to contact the SWG can connect through the Queensland Writers Centre, who will forward information.

Return

Anthology of short stories
By members of the
Springfield Writers Group

To all the authors out there – both published and aspiring – don't give up.

The SWG gratefully acknowledge the traditional owners – the Jagera, Yuggera and Ugarapul peoples of Ipswich and Springfield – as the keepers of ancient knowledge and whose cultures and customs continue to nurture this land. The SWG also pays respect to Elders – past, present and future.

We had hoped to include a story from the traditional mythos of the Jagera, Yuggera or Ugarapul peoples in this anthology. Unfortunately, even with extensive research and academic assistance, we were unable to find a story suitable for the theme.

RETURN edited by The Springfield Writers Group. (Chief Editor Aiki Flinthart)

Cover artwork by Croco Designs

All stories are original to this collection

A Cataloging-in-Publications entry for this title is available from the National Library of Australia.

ISBN-13: 978-0-9945660-1-0 (Trade Paperback)
ISBN-13: 978-0-9945660-8-9 (e-book)
Computing Advantages & Training P/L
PO Box 3388, Darra
QLD 4076, Australia

Heartfelt thanks goes to all the authors in the Springfield Writers Group, for their enthusiasm, support, dedication and hard work. Also to our families, for their patience with our hiding away for hours on end as we tried desperately to scribble a few thousand words down. Thanks to Bookface bookstore, for hosting our monthly meetings and the launch.

Contents

467BCE

And When We Return

Pt I

Aiki Flinthart

Incinerating in the belly of a star a hundred light-years from home was not the end I anticipated. I'd hoped to choose my method of death. At home, surrounded by people I loved. Perhaps on a new colony-world I'd discovered. But, today, the choice might not be mine.

Dren, if you don't lock down that regulator, we'll lose the starboard engine! Vanin's thought reached me as I hurtled through the tiny sleeping section and slapped a breather over my face. I thumbed the control for the iris separating the front of the ship from the back and leapt into the airlock.

On it now. Just keep us out of the star's gravity well.

I will if you get me control of that engine, Vanin snapped. *I told you we took damage in the debris cloud outside this system. We should have checked.*

I did *check,* I shot back. *All the diagnostics came back clean.*

Vanin didn't reply and I had to concentrate on repairing the damaged regulator. The ship juddered and flung me against the curved wall. I staggered to my feet.

Hurry up, Dren! We're heading right for the star.

My shoulder ached where it'd taken the brunt of my fall. I hooked both thumbs of my left hand around a handhold and braced myself. The regulator panel ripped easily off the wall and clattered to the metal walkway. The ship shook and spiralled towards flaming death. The floor tilted. My chin cracked on the wall, but I clung doggedly to the handhold.

Turn off grav back here. I can't work when I'm being hurled around the place like a jonball.

The artificial gravity nullified and I drifted, peaceful. Purple blood from my chin formed a sphere and floated away. I yanked out the faulty regulator control circuit and jimmied a temporary bypass. The ship steadied its headlong pace through the solar system and levelled out. I sighed. My skin's stress-grey subsided and returned to resting-green.

Grav, please. I hauled my feet back to the floor and took the renewed weight with flexed knees, then leaned against the wall. Blood splatted onto the walkway by my boot.

It's a temporary fix, Van, I warned. *I'll need to get the replacement out of stores before we try using the skip-drive. But we're out of danger. A few minutes more and the fault would have fed back into the engine and blown us to cosmic dust.*

A claxon blared beside my ear. I jumped and swore. A swift diagnostic through the biocom neural interface told an unpleasant story: I'd fixed the regulator, but revealed a deeper issue. I checked three times, swore again and retreated to the sleeping quarters, sealing the airlock irises.

I slapped a med seal on my chin and arrived back in the cockpit just as Vanin finished inputting new navigational directions. Vanin looked up and the holo-nav display vanished.

'Good news and bad,' I said brightly, checking the engine performance one more time through my neural link to the biocom.

Vanin grimaced and ran a hand over sleek scales on a bare head. 'Dren, last time you gave me bad news we had to bypass a perfectly good planet and eat recycled waste for a month.'

'That planet was inhabited by sentients,' I said. 'We're supposed to find colony sites, not commit genocide.'

Vanin curled a lip. 'We've been searching for over a year. We have to return to Haos soon and report. I don't want to go back empty-handed. Our people are depending on us.'

'I know, Van,' I said quietly. 'But we're not the only search team. I won't be responsible for destroying sentient races because we wrecked our own planet out of stupid shortsightedness.'

'I don't understand why you took this mission if you're not prepared to do whatever it takes to save our people.' Vanin sent me a glare.

I grinned wryly. 'I know you don't.'

'So, what's your good and bad news, then?'

'Two lots of good news. Starboard engine's functioning fine now. We're in no danger of fiery oblivion in the heart of the star.'

'I know that!'

'And,' I said, pretending the interruption hadn't occurred, 'just before the regulator alarm went, the biocom showed the third planet in this system supports life. Gravity's a little higher than we're used to, but not much. Year's a little longer and days are shorter, but well within tolerances.'

'That's excellent. I'll take us in for a look.' The holonav appeared again as Vanin's thoughts altered our course.

'The bad news,' I finished, 'is that we have a small fuel problem.'

Vanin turned wide black eyes on me, the gold vertical pupils their only colour.

'Well, maybe not so small,' I admitted. 'We have plenty of water-fuel in the tow-tank behind the ship, but we're leaking crion particles. The damaged regulator was feeding false readings to the biocom.'

'Can we repair the damage and stop the leak?'

I shook my head. 'Looks like a meteor's punctured the crion reactor tank in two places. To repair it outside, I'd be exposed to more radiation than the exosuit can handle.'

'Can we get home?' Vanin's hands twisted together. The sixth digits and the resting-green of Vanin's smooth-scaled arms flushed ash-grey.

'No,' I said. 'We're alright at sublight speeds. But if we switch on the skip drive, the crion emissions will ignite and blow the starboard engine. We're safe in here and we have time to work out a solution. But, until we do, we can't go home.'

'So, what now?' Vanin's facial skin colours and textures fluxed, changing to match the grey biocom console then shifting back to a sick shade of resting-green.

I ignored the bad manners of shifting in front of me. Vanin was new to recon missions and under stress. This was my twentieth. The Council of Colours supposedly matched recon partners for compatibility, but they'd messed up with our pairing. Van coloured me the wrong way, as much as I tried to hide it.

'Now the engine's stable, the easiest solution is to land. Then we can shut down the reactor and do the repairs.' I pulled up the solar system specs on the holo and enlarged the third rocky planet. The biocom ran a closer analysis and downloaded details into our minds through the neural link. Breathable atmo, seasonal weather changes due to axial tilt. Nothing too extreme that our bodies couldn't cope with – especially if we stayed closer to the equator, in habitats more like Haos used to be. High water to land ratios and massive carbon readings, which usually meant abundant life.

'But we can't take this ship into atmo,' Vanin said, frowning. 'The crion leak would contaminate the whole world and it's the first suitable planet we've seen for months. What about the fourth planet? It's the only other potential. Can we land there for the repairs?'

'You're right.' I ran a few calculations in my head and re-checked as the computations appeared on the holo. 'No, the fourth planet's out. If we can't restart the reactor we'd be stuck there and there's no breathable atmo. We'll have to take the escape pod to the third planet and set the ship into long orbit around this star. On the planet we can gather what we need to contain the crion leak without endangering ourselves, and return later to repair the ship in orbit.'

'For how long?'

'The orbit?' I did the math. 'Maybe seventy-five of that planet's years. That way it won't dump too many crions in the immediate area.'

'No, crad you, Dren!' Vanin snapped. 'Not the orbit. How long until we can fix the ship and get home?'

I stared at the holo-image of the blue-green third planet. 'Hard to say. We're not close enough to tell if there are any sentients or any civilisations. The biocom hasn't picked up any transmissions or evidence of space flight, though. If there's no advanced civ then repairing the ship might be impossible.'

'Gred it!' Vanin wrenched off the piloting visor and threw it aside. 'I need to get home! This was only meant to be a one year mission. Two, at the most.'

'So? What's the problem?' I stood and faced my mission partner. Vanin was never the calmest, but this seemed excessive. Van paced a few steps to the back of the cockpit, then returned.

'You might think we have time to sort this out, but *I* don't. I'm transitioning. Early,' Vanin said, shoulders sagging. The grey flush now covered every visible inch of skin. 'I was meant to be home before it happened. I'm supposed to start a family.'

'Ah,' I said. 'Sorry. This is your first time in the female phase?'

'Yes,' she whispered.

'Don't give up hope yet. We might get home in time. How long will you be female? What's your family history?'

Vanin shrugged. 'Hard to say. My birth parent stayed in phase for over three centuries the first time. Five, the second time. Could be affected by the planetary conditions, though. But that's not the real issue.'

'So what is?' I thought I knew her pretty well after a year in this cramped ship, but the rapid shifts of skin colour and texture flashing across her body spoke of deep inner stress. What was she hiding?

'I...' She lifted her chin and straightened. 'I'll be First Female amongst my family. The responsibility of producing the Heir will be mine.'

'Congratulations.' I smiled wryly. 'Well, I can't guarantee we'll get back in time for you to fulfil that, but we'll certainly try.'

'No!' She gripped my wrist so tightly the thin bones ground together. 'You don't understand. I'll be First Female – and my family is Primary Blue. I *have* to get back to Haos.'

I gaped at her. 'Are you *serious?* What the crad were your family thinking, letting you come offworld? You should be sitting safely in Council of Colour, with your parents, running the gredding world, not endangering your life out here. You should've told me who you were.'

'I wasn't allowed to tell anyone. I'm not even supposed to be First.' She glared. 'I have two older sibs who were meant to transition before me. One of them was to produce the Heir.' She stared out into the star-speckled darkness. 'The Prime Blue insisted I join Exploration. I didn't understand why. But if I'm in trans, it means…something's happened to them.'

Brilliant cobalt suffused her skin. The urge to shift my colour to complementary orange and kneel in subservience almost seduced me. I fought to keep my usual resting-green.

'My Colour is in danger and I'm the next Heir-Mother. You *must* help me get home, Dren. I order it!' Her righteous certainty battered on my thoughts.

I closed her out. Not an easy thing to achieve against a Blue, but I'd had many years of experience. I'd left Haos to escape the politics and do something active to save our people. Mindlessly obeying our planet's hereditary Primaries is what got Haos into trouble in the first place.

I laid a hand on her shoulder. 'Van, I know this is tough for you, but we have to prioritise. We can't get home yet. We'll send the distress call. First, we need to set the orbit and get down to the planet. Then we can work out how to handle your transition. I'll be with you every step, I promise. I've been through it twice.' The hormonal changes transitioning from neutral to female could be pretty brutal. If the Prime Blue had sent her off planet so close to her time then things were worse at home than I'd suspected.

She glared at me, her skin flushing the indigo of rage, then she seemed to regain control. Her skin subsided to resting-green and the gold pupils in her black eyes narrowed to slits. 'Did you have offspring?'

I shook my head. 'Too busy trying to save the planet.' I said lightly. The ache in my chest never got easier, even after four hundred and twenty years. Perhaps it never would. But I'd made my choice; missed my chance. Our world didn't need more inhabitants, it needed fewer. And that was my job. We needed somewhere new to live, or we'd die.

'You're neutral now. When will you trans back to male?' she asked abruptly.

I sent her weary look. 'Probably not soon enough and I doubt your Prime would be thrilled if you produced an heir from an orange, rather than another primary.'

She cleared her throat in the awkward silence that followed and scrubbed a hand over her sharp cheekbones. 'Well, I guess we'd better get organised. We'll need to use all the heavy-water-fuel to create an ice coating on the ship. That orbit you've calculated'll bring it close to the star and the ice will keep it cool.'

'Good thinking.' I squeezed her shoulder. 'The ship's already dragged a tail of ice and rock from the debris cloud. And each orbit will add to it. So the ice'll thicken and protect the ship from damage, too.'

'There won't be time,' Van snapped. 'We'll have it repaired and be on our way home before the ship circles through the cloud again.'

I said nothing. We took our places again, sinking into the bodyform seats and activating the neural link. It was the work of minutes to instruct the biocom to sluice our fuel over the hull, keeping only the escape pod hatch and engine nozzles clear. The water froze into a thick shell.

What about the crion emissions? Vanin asked as she nudged the ship into the correct orbital path and cut the engines. *The planet will pass right through our debris trail in this orbit.*

But the concentration should only be at dangerous levels for a few days each orbit, when the ship's right in the planet's path. So the planet will only be exposed once every seventy-some years. Hopefully the dose won't have any effect on the native life forms.

That's a big hope, she said. *Crions cause mutations in our species. What happened to not destroying sentients?*

We don't even know if the planet has any, yet.

I switched off the integrated biosystems, one at a time, powering down the ship piece by piece until only life support, comms, and the escape pod were fully operational. Then I sent a distress call, switched off the life support and locked down the biocom with a final order to maintain orbit and eject the pod once we were in.

As I ushered Van towards the escape pod, a purple light flashed on the blank comms console.

'Crad!' I hesitated, then stepped out of the cockpit and thumbed the iris control closed.

'What happened?' Van opened the emergency pod iris and climbed in.

'Emergency beacon didn't work. We're too close to the star. Solar interference. Ship needs to be outside the system's debris cloud to tap into the skip-space relays.'

Her eyes widened. 'But that means…'

'Yeah,' I said, sealing the pod iris behind us. 'The biocom'll try again when the ship orbits far enough out – in thirty or so years. But the Council won't get our call for a while.' I grimaced and squeezed her hand. 'Sorry, Van.'

Her jaw hardened. 'No, it's not over. I'm not giving up that easily – not while my family's in danger. They'll hear it. They'll get us. I'll get home. It's my duty to my family and my people. My child will be Prime Blue. I'll make sure of it.' Her dark eyes glittered.

I said nothing as the pod biocom enveloped us in gel-tanks to cushion against atmo descent, and launched into space. In the past, the ancient urge to produce offspring had resulted in borderline insane behaviour in our Primary Colour females. I was in for a rough ride, no matter what we found on the planet.

*

'Atmospheric oxygen content a little higher than home.' I took off the breather and sniffed, then coughed and closed my nasal slits against the onslaught of unfamiliar scents. 'Whew. I can definitely smell animal life of some sort.'

'How can you tell?' Van stared, wide-eyed, at the vast grasslands surrounding the escape pod.

I'd instructed the biocom to search for evidence of habitations and set us down close enough to observe a settlement, but far enough away to be discreet. I didn't want to terrify the sentients.

I grinned at Van. 'Been to fifty planets now. You get to know the smell of animal crap in all its forms. Carbon-based life is similar everywhere, from what I can tell. Bio's your speciality, not mine, but you pick things up in this job.'

The escape pod biocom pinged me and I downloaded the report through the neurals. 'You getting this, Van? Wow, this place has some serious diversity of single-celled and low-level multi-celled organisms.'

'I'm seeing a lot of potential disease-carriers,' she responded. She hadn't taken off her breather.

I grinned. Typical new reconner – never trusting the full spectrum anti-bios the medics gave us before we left home. We had boosters in the med kit and we'd need them if we stayed any longer than a year or two. After that, we'd adapt or die. Luckily, we were a resilient species; long-lived and tough. Our DNA was different enough that local diseases shouldn't be able to get a foothold. If I could get Van safely through her first neutral-to-female transition she should be fine.

Right now, the priority had to be blending in with the natives. The escape pod had its own camo shielding. Once we decided our next action, it would bury itself and run on low power until we called it. The neural link would operate and send updates no matter where we were on the planet.

'Settlement was about an hour that way,' I said, pointing in the direction of the afternoon sun. 'We should get there and check out the locals before we decide where to go.'

Van nodded and shivered, wrapping her arms around herself. I felt it too: a cooler temperature than we were used to shipboard.

'Let's get our biosuits on,' I suggested. 'The adaptive fabric will make it easier to shift and match local physiques and colours. And they'll keep us warmer. Maybe we should have come down closer to the equator.'

Van shook her head. 'No, you were right. Too hard to travel through the vegetation and way more settlements. We'll check out the inhabitants here. Shift to blend in. Then travel south if it gets too cold.' Her gaze became abstracted. 'Biocom says we've got half a year at least until the coldest weather sets in.' She removed her breather and promptly fell into a coughing fit.

We changed into the biosuits and hiked for an hour – long enough for my muscles to tell me I'd been lazy in my onboard exercise routine. The geo-scientist in me was tempted to stop and study every rock, every landform, and every pile of dirt. And Van kept getting distracted by the variety of life to be found in even this bleak-seeming landscape.

Between us and the distant horizon rolled broad, sweeping hills covered in grey-green grasses. In the distance, a cloud of dust and shifting dark forms suggested some sort of herdbeast. I laid a hand on the met-gun holstered at my hip. Predators followed herdbeasts.

Overhead, the yellow sun yielded little warmth in a sky blue enough to rival Van's family colour. I smiled wryly. The Prime would love this place. Anything that reinforced the Blue family's dominance over the other colours.

We topped a rise and I grabbed Van's shoulder. We dropped to our stomachs on the stiff grass and stared in fascination at the little group of bipeds in the valley. I activated the neural-visuals link and zoomed in for a closer look at the circle of skin tents. Some sort of animal roasted on a spit over a central fire. Several bipeds rode on the backs of quadrupeds and shot a basic wooden projectile into a target. They were excellent shots.

'It's a small settlement,' Van said, doubtfully. 'We can't mimic any of them and be unnoticed.'

'No,' I said. 'But we can take them as a template and go to another settlement. We just need to learn the language. They're obviously speaking to each other. Can you link with one of them and download? You're better at it than I am.'

She smiled for the first time in hours and her dark eyes glazed as she merged thoughts with theirs. She frowned, shook her head, then her expression cleared.

'Got it. Fairly primitive culture but there's potential. It's possible we've just found a backwards tribe and there are more advanced civilisations in other areas.'

I picked the language out of the biocom and considered it. 'Linguistically complex. Tonal inflexions. Suggests a long evolutionary period. You could be right. Likely to be more advanced cultures in areas with more resources.' I glanced at her. 'Not sure now is the best time to be traipsing across huge distances, though.'

She glared at me. 'We have to get the ship repaired. I can't stay here. I must get back to my family. They're in danger and Haos needs me. Needs a Blue Heir.'

'I know, Van, it needs both of us. But have you checked your bioreadings in the last hour?' She'd already changed. Her face was rounder, her skin colour more vivid. Under the closefitting biosuit, her body had lost the sharp muscularity of a neutral gender and taken on the sleekness of a breeding female.

'Crad!' She looked at her hands and felt her face. Her eyes widened. 'I thought the transition would take longer.'

'Me too,' I said. 'Planetary effect, maybe. We should get back to the pod. The worst is yet to come. You're going to do some screaming and we don't want to scare the natives.' My wry grin and attempt at humour fell flat and Vanin turned away.

We returned to the pod in silence, with the shadows of afternoon lengthening before us in purple and grey streaks across the grasslands.

The screaming started before we'd made it all the way. I carried her the rest.

Her transition, which would normally take a month or more, lasted thirty-six hours. We stayed, cocooned and protected, in the escape pod. I plugged Van into the on-board medic in the hopes it would slow down the process and make it more bearable for her. But the pod biocom wasn't designed to cope with extreme medical situations. After twelve hours the sedatives ran out and Van woke screaming again.

I had to snap on restraints after her new claws sliced gouges in my arm. My blood spattered the inside of the pod and soaked my biosuit.

Shortly before the dawn of our second full day on the planet, Van calmed down. Her inner eyelids retracted, revealing eyes now brilliant green; the vertical gold pupils luminescent. Her transition looked to be complete.

I crouched before her and brushed back the shoulder-length crop of blue hair that hid her face.

'How're you feeling?'

'Like utter crad,' she said. 'But better than I was. Is it over?'

I grinned. 'Yep, you look to be fully transitioned.' I unlocked the restraints and she groaned, stretching muscles until tendons crackled.

'Everything hurts.'

'Well, a lot's changed. The question is, how long will you stay in female form?'

She sent me a dark look. 'If this transition is any indication, not long. Greddit!'

'Here.' I handed her a nutrition pack. 'Eat. You need it.'

She sucked it and a second pack dry. I mentally counted how many days rations we had left. Not many. I'd need to hunt in a day or so and hope our bodies could digest the native wildlife.

Van drank a full sack of water and sighed. 'Better. Thanks.'

She stood and opened the pod iris. We stepped outside into the cold pre-dawn and looked up at the glittering sky. To the north, shimmering, sweeping lights in green, yellow, and white arced and slipped along the horizon, creating a mesmerising display.

'I can't stay here, Dren,' Van said quietly, staring at the eastern horizon.

I followed her gaze. A handspan above a low range of mountains in the east, a fuzzy star shone brighter than the rest. A long tail glowed behind it.

'That has to be the ship,' Van said, pointing.

'Yep,' I said. 'Pod biocom confirms. Right on track in its orbit. Should be visible for sixty days or so.'

Van's claws extended then retracted. Her skin flushed sparkling sapphire and she drew herself up, regal and beautiful in her new appearance; every inch the Prime Blue's First Female. Again, I fought an ages-old conditioning to kneel before her and offer colour-shift obeisance. Instead, I lifted my chin and met her gaze straight on.

'We will travel south. Now,' she stated. 'I have no time to waste on these primitives. We must find a civilisation that has the technology to repair our ship. I *will* get home before I transition back. If my other sibs are dead...' Her hands clenched into fists and she lifted her head. 'Then I'm the last Blue young enough to produce an Heir.'

'So, what do we do if none of the civilisations are advanced enough?' I laid a hand on her arm but she shook me off. 'Van, I know your position – your family's position – on Haos is important. But my mission is vital. My job is to find planets ready for colonisation. Our people can't survive much longer on Haos. But this planet already has sentient life. We can't interfere. We have to wait for our message to get through. They'll send someone for us.'

'And if they don't?' She turned on me, claws out and new incisors bared. 'I refuse to be stuck on this mudhole while my younger sib becomes next Prime Blue, or my whole family is wiped out by rebels. My rightful place is at the forefront of my family; my people. And if I have to drag these animals into a technological state that can get me home, then that's what I'll do. Whether you help me or not.'

Van's shape shimmered and changed. I recoiled. She stood before me in shifted form and it was all I could do to suppress a spurt of revulsion. Her skin was now smooth and gold-brown; her eyes narrow in a broad face. Her hands had only five digits, with just one opposable thumb. Her glorious blue hair now hung lank, straight and black. She'd instructed the biosuit to copy the clothing of the natives we'd seen: furs and rough cloth, beads, laced animal skin shoes, and all.

Only her green eyes, with their gold vertical pupils, belonged to our people.

'I'm going to get home, Dren. No matter how long it takes, or what I have to do. Don't get in my way.'

She strode away, lit by the first rays of the rising sun.

I had no choice but to follow.

467BCE

Eleusis, Greece

Long-Haired Star

Megan Badger

Bread making is a meditative act. The dough moved under my
hands, springing back when I released and turned it. I looked at
Mother and smiled as she sang the first refrain of the kneading song.
Her deep voice resonated between us and our efforts became as
rhythmic as breathing.

Then you burst through the door like a whirlwind. The dust in
the air danced and twinkled as though you were the light and they
the stars.

'The Archon has come. His horse is white and tall, and his party
is so smartly dressed, and, and...' You plonked down on the stool
and sent flour puffing up to join the dust.

'Astra! Slow down.' Mother brushed off her hands and held
your face between her palms. 'Now, what is it you wanted to tell us
with such urgency?'

You took a deep breath. It was hard not to smile when you tried.

'The Archon and his party have arrived from Athens.'

'Go on.' Mother released your face and the words rushed out, freed from the calm prison of her touch.

'They're all so glamourous, the ladies with hair coiled like snakes, and the horse shining white like the sand, and the men like statues all stiff and respectable, and two youths with copper skin, and the whole town is buzzing like a hive.'

Mother laughed. 'Enough. With such a wild menagerie, we might be best to stay indoors. What do you think, Danica?'

I played along with the jest, rubbing my chin. 'Hmm.'

You looked between Mother and me and your mouth dropped open with an audible pop. 'But, Mother. No.'

'She's teasing you,' I said.

Mother's face lit with a mischievous smile.

You plonked your chin down on your hands. 'That's not funny.'

'Oh, Astra, just look at yourself,' I said. 'How can you possibly meet the Athenian delegation in such a state?'

Your hair was a cloud of tangles and a twig poked out on one side. Grass stains marked your fine wool dress, and your arms, hands, and face were smudged with flour.

'Your sister and I will finish our loaves. Why don't you clean yourself up?' Mother said.

And you were out the door in a flurry, most likely headed to the stream to wash, and I felt sorry for the orchard maids who would have to listen to your chatter while they worked.

Mother took up the breadmaking song again and we sang together. I turned and pressed the dough into a flat circle. Mother poured the oil and rubbed the loaves, her fingers glistening. I sprinkled herbs and seeds from an earthen dish.

*

You were glorious in your best dress, your hair pinned in curls. You walked beside us with awkward composure as we made our way to the town square. The festival for Demeter brought people from across the county and we passed many strangers on our way.

You were right. The Archon and his party were elegant, dressed in blindingly-white robes. They stood like moving statues; animated stone. Your eyes wandered to one of the youths. His comely features lit with a roguish grin and I frowned. He looked like trouble. But the day was bright, the wind whipped up swirls of dust, and the assembled crowd thrilled with the start of the festival season. Who could hold on to worry on such a day?

You were not the only one who struggled to stay still as each party member was introduced. When the first wine was shared the crowd erupted and all was motion again. Friend greeted friend and the strangers were led through the throng and introduced to each family. Our turn came and Mother and I were presented in high regard as ephori, priestesses of the temple of Demeter. You stood, with your head down, looking up through pale lashes as you were introduced as a mystce, a new initiate. In a few days, at the end of the festival, you would learn the secret meaning of the rites and become a seer, like Mother and me.

Your eyes followed the youth, Nestor, as he was introduced to the seers. He was intended to become the next Hierophant, but in training was only a mystce, like you. Many times, I saw the delegates scold him when he drifted off during important meetings, or when he made a face at the back of a solemn elder. One even grabbed his arm to prevent him from touching a sacred talisman.

Perhaps you didn't see. Or did you think it brave rather than discourteous? You were like a hawk, eyes never leaving your prey. And, when at last he was left to his musings, you swooped in. I watched over you with concern, but the square thrummed with music carried on the breath of incense. Caught up in the atmosphere, and tipsy from the overflowing of wine, I lost you from my sight

But later, the wine went to my head and carried with it your image. The world spun as I leaned against the wall of the council building, and a vision erupted into my mind. A bright light; a star with long strands flowing from it like hair. Pain shot through my head. A body struggled, twisted among the star threads. Then it turned and I saw the face. It was you, sister, tangled with the star. You were speeding away into darkness and I was stuck fast to the earth. I could make no sound though I longed to cry out to you.

The vision ended. I vomited. Fire light flickered and I made my way towards it. I knew seers were sometimes overcome by a vision but not usually outside the temple, and it had never happened to me. I went looking to tell Mother, but she was talking with the Archon. As I waited, my unease slipped away. Surely the vision was just a fancy brought on by too much wine. I turned aside and was once again caught up in the dance and rhythm of the music.

*

How many hours passed, sister, before I found you, nestled on a bench with Nestor, deep in each other's confidence? Your face was lit with some inner light, visible even in shadow. I watched in secret for a while but, as you were only talking, I saw no need to intervene.

The festivities were called to a close as the night air rolled down from the mountain. You emerged from darkness to join Mother and me as we walked home. You were quiet. As Mother and I spoke about the day, I watched you from the corner of my eye. You looked without seeing, your mind showing you more pleasant pictures than the moonlit path ahead. Now and then, the corners of your mouth lifted in a smile.

What did you dream of? Where did your mind go when sleep took you? In our bed, with your warm body curled against mine, I watched your eyelids flutter.

*

You rose late, drunk on sleep.

Mother sat quietly. She sipped her morning watered-wine and stared absently at the table. The tracks of tears marked her cheeks; ribbons of salt, though her eyes were now dry.

'Mother?'

She looked up and smiled but it didn't reach her eyes.

'What's wrong, Mother?' I hoped you hadn't been caught up in more trouble.

'It was this day, seven years ago, that your father...' She swallowed the word as though it were bitter poison. 'Died. I know you were younger then, and in the excitement of the festival I didn't expect you to remember. It's fine.'

'Mother, I'm sorry.' With all the preparations I had forgotten how difficult this time was for her. I remembered when it happened, but not how. He was there one day and gone the next. Mother had cut off all her hair and I had hugged her and stroked the uneven stubble while she cried. I had carried you and fed you and played with you, and – so many days – taken you out of the house to escape the darkness that filled it. We had laughed in the sun and I played Mother to you to protect you from her grief.

Mother stood. 'Let's not talk of such things today. The festival is an important time and our Astra will soon be a seer.' She wiped her eyes and moved to the fire.

'Is there any bread, mama?'

'Sweet Astra,' Mother kissed the top of your head. 'Not on the day of purification.' She ladled wine into your cup.

'Why can't we eat just a little? Surely no one would mind?'

Mother sighed. 'You know why. It's more than a rule to be broken, it is part of the sacred rite.'

'But aren't there other things that are more important? Nestor says that the surface rites can be a bit more flexible, as long as the temple rites remain true.'

Mother and I exchanged a look.

'Astra, Nestor shouldn't be discussing the rites with you. Please tell me you haven't been talking about them?'

You looked from Mother to me, then back again, and a frown creased your brow. 'I didn't think there was anything wrong with it. We were just talking. He knows so much more than me and I wanted to know what would happen and you wouldn't tell me anything, so what was I supposed to do?'

'Astra, promise me you won't say a word to anyone about this.'

'Why not?'

'Astra!' Mother grabbed your shoulders and you winced.

'Ow, Mama, all right. I promise.'

She scrutinized your face for a long time before letting you go. 'I have to address the delegation this morning. No food.' She pointed at you. 'Make sure you're ready for the purification.' With that, the conversation was over.

We drank our wine in silence, an uncomfortable tension filling the space between us.

*

We stood barefoot on rough sand. A tumult of clouds wrapped the sky and painted the ocean a sombre grey. Hair whipped across my face and stung. I could see you straining to hear as the Archon's speech droned on, carried over the water away from our hearing. Then his final cry went up and was echoed by the crowd.

'To the sea, initiates. To the sea.'

All rushed to the water, the youngest swimming out past the breakers while the elders were helped to the sheltered shallows behind the sandstone rocks. The water roiled with bodies in motion, transforming the sea into a serpentine beast. The saltwater's chill sent a shock through me as I waded deeper and plunged under a wave. The sounds of joyful squealing and laughter carried over the shore and resounded back from the cliffs. I spread my arms and floated, lifting and falling with the waves. Above me, the wind tore apart the clouds and bright sun pierced through with blades of light.

Something glinted in the corner of my eye. Light gleamed off wet skin. A couple were entwined, limbs like octopi in twisting caresses. They were too far away to recognise. Her hair, darkened by water, clung to her back as her body moved counter to the waves which lapped at them; ocean kisses for kisses. I felt a pulse and a spreading warmth. Heat rose in my cheeks. I swam to shore.

Mid-afternoon you walked through the door smelling of the sea and something else.

'Have you been in the water all this time?' Mother took your hand, turning it over to reveal skin puckered with wrinkles. 'You could catch a chill being wet for so long.'

'Sorry, Mama.'

A smile pulled at your mouth and your downcast eyes sparkled. Mother handed you a bowl of broth.

'You've been away too long. I hope you've been behaving honourably?'

'Of course, Mother.' You wouldn't meet her eye. 'I've been spending time with Thalia. Her mother is busy preparing for the rites, so I've been helping with the babies.'

'Hmm. I thought Petrina, Thalia's aunt, had been tasked with watching her nephews.'

'Well, she was, but she had to go.' Your eyes slid away from hers. 'Yes, she had to go and run errands. There was an accident in the fields, one of the harvesters cut himself, she went to help.'

'And did the harvester report to the healer?'

'I'm sure he must have, but it's so busy with the preparations that maybe he didn't. I don't know.' Your eyes were wide; your hand covered your throat.

'Are you telling me the truth, Astra?'

'Of course I am, Mama.'

'Nevertheless, I'd like you to stay close to your sister from now on.'

'But, Mama.'

'No buts. You will do as you're told.'

'But I—'

'Astra!'

'Alright.' You sat staring into your bowl but didn't drink.

'Are you finished?' Mother asked.

'I'm not hungry.' Your stomach growled. You pushed your stool back and, without looking at either of us, walked out the door. Mother watched the place where you left and sighed.

'Danica, you must keep watch over your sister. She has no idea the danger she's in.'

'What danger?'

She stared at her hands.

'Mother, what danger?'

'Every act, every rite, is sacred. Anyone found revealing them will be put to death. So too any uninitiated person who happened to be present.' She scrutinised my face.

'The boy,' I whispered. 'The boy who was telling her about the rites. But he's part of the delegation. Surely his lapse will be overlooked?'

'I don't know.'

A shadow crossed the window. I turned too late and saw nothing there.

*

You were quiet as we drank our broth at supper, and you kissed Mother's cheek without meeting her eyes when we went to bed. Under the covers, you held your body too rigid, too stiff.

'Astra, what's wrong?' I whispered in the dark.

'Can I trust you?'

'What? Why?'

'Can I trust you?'

I tried to see your face in the dark. 'You're my sister. Of course you can trust me.'

You were quiet for a long time.

'Astra, please talk to me. Maybe I can help.' I waited for you to speak.

'I'm worried about Nestor. I heard you and Mother talking.'

'Astra!'

'I didn't mean to overhear but I can't pretend I didn't and I need to warn him and I was waiting for you to go to sleep but you didn't and I'm running out of time.'

'Slow down. It's late. Why not wait until morning and tell him then?'

'You don't understand.'

'What don't I understand?'

You held your breath.

'What aren't you telling me, Astra?

'I'm supposed to be meeting him tonight, in secret. We've been spending all our time together. He's kind and shy and please don't tell Mother.'

I'd seen the boy's behaviour during the festivities over the last few days. He certainly didn't seem shy to me.

'Mother just wants you to be safe.'

'I'm not a child.' The sulk in your voice said differently.

'Is this boy really worth getting into trouble for?'

'I think I'm in love with him. I didn't mean for it to happen, but it did and I need to see him. I need to know he's safe.' You held my hands, your skin cold. 'Please, Danica.'

'Alright, but I'm coming with you.'

'What? No, you can't!'

'Yes, I can. You're in enough danger as it is because of this boy. I'm not letting you out of my sight.'

'Dani, please?'

'No. Either I go with you or we both stay here.'

You growled. 'You're ruining everything.'

'No matter. You can wait and see him in the morning.' I rolled over and pretended to sleep. You made a move to leave the bed and I grabbed your arm.

'Ow! Let go. You're hurting me.'

I tightened my grip.

'Alright! Come if you must. But we have to go now.'

*

Stars twinkled above the fields as we crept to the meeting place. My cloak did little to repel the cold and soon I was shivering.

'You'll raise the dead with your teeth chattering like that,' you said. An owl took flight from a nearby tree and we both jumped and giggled.

'Do you remember when we were small and Da used to tell us stories about monsters?' I whispered. 'You used to squeal and laugh and we'd lie awake at night waiting for something to jump out and eat us or take us away to some faraway place?'

'I don't remember.' You screwed up your nose and shook your head vigorously, like a child.

'You would ask me to sing the same lullaby again and again.'

'I know the song, but I can't remember the stories.' Leaves rustled beside the path and you started. 'Nestor?'

You leaned in closer. A cat leapt out and hissed at you before speeding back into the dark. We waited without talking, our ears straining for any sound of approach. There were several more false alarms, when small foraging creatures crossed our path, but no sign of the boy. When I heard the yapping howl of wild dogs I decided it was time to go home.

'But he still might come,' you pleaded.

'And he might not.'

We reached the house in the darkest part of the pre-dawn wearing the shadows like a cowl. We climbed into bed and huddled together for warmth.

'He didn't come. What if something happened to him? What if he's dead?' You sobbed.

'Shh, it's okay. I'm sure he's alright. He must have fallen asleep.' Or been otherwise detained. I stroked your hair and hummed Da's lullaby.

'Dani?'

'Hm?'

'You'd remember me, wouldn't you?' You drew a shaky breath.

'Of course I would.' A shudder passed through my body. 'Now go to sleep.'

I hoped the morning would bring comforting news.

*

I dreamed of you wrapped in starlight. Star-strands became your hair. You grew pale and cold and faded into darkness and, no matter how hard I strained my eyes, I could only see specks of you remaining. When I woke, tears wet my cheeks. I reached to hold you and you curled into me and mumbled my name sleepily.

*

The day of offerings dawned and you were tired, but restless. Despite the fasting of the day before, you barely touched your breakfast. You rushed to get ready, your hands so clumsy that I took the comb from you. You didn't flinch as I worked out the tangles, but sat tensed, ready to spring from your seat. I tied your hair back in a bun, wrapping the leather thong around and pushing in bronze pins to hold it in place.

Mother moved sluggishly. I saw her looking at Da's cup where it sat in its crevice in the wall. She took down the cup and wiped it clean of dust with the corner of her dress. She held it to her chest and cried.

'Mother.' I put my arms around her. 'What can I do? Can I help?'

'I miss him so much.' She leaned into my shoulder. I stroked her hair like a child until she calmed.

'Do you want to stay here, Mother? I can do the official duties in your absence.'

'There are more important things today.' She touched my cheek gently.

She patted your head but you pulled away.

'Mama, my hair.'

She rolled her eyes and some of the pain seemed to leave, or did she swallow it?

'Come along then. The offering is today and we must pay obeisance to our goddess.'

*

In the field, the gathering was subdued. People spoke in hushed tones, their voices sighing like wind through the pines. Your eyes darted with such intensity that it seemed you could pierce their flesh. Sharing your concern, I scanned the crowd but saw no sign of the fair-haired boy.

In the fields, lambs were slaughtered. Their bleating cries rang out and were cut short. The men came forward carrying sheaths of barley and mullet. Silence fell, broken only by the rustle of grain stalks shifting in the breeze. The grain was presented to a cloaked figure. We held our breath. Then, down came the scythe in a smooth motion, clipping a single stalk, which dropped to the ground. The sacrifice was accepted. The crowd dispersed and the grain was carried to the temple.

A peal of giggling erupted from the unharvested grain and the blond youth tripped out, his hand holding that of Alyssa, one of the village girls. You froze. Did the scene move slowly for you? I watched your face as it passed from confusion, to realisation, to pain. You looked so much like Mother in that moment that my breath rushed out. He looked over and his face showed nothing. No recognition or shame. He grinned roguishly at his new conquest and they ran laughing away.

You stood so still I feared you had been struck by Medusa and turned to stone. Then you shook your head. A single tear trickled down your cheek but, as you brushed it away, more flooded from your eyes. You looked at me and blushed, then turned and ran the other way.

*

Mother and I ate of the sacrificial lamb, and you weren't there.

We knelt before the temple of Demeter, and you weren't there.

We drank wine with our neighbours, and you weren't there.

You came home when the night air was chill, and you smelled of damp earth. Had the earth held you? Had you wept together? I didn't ask you any questions when you climbed into bed. I held back when you cringed away from my touch. I lay awake, aware of you lying awake in the dark beside me. I did nothing. I just lay there, awake.

*

Before dawn we were called to assembly at the border gates; all the women of the village and surrounding regions. The high priestess and her assistants carried the sacred basket aloft and we followed in a solemn procession. You walked with your head held high and I was proud of your composure. You responded to friendly conversation with a smile. And I stayed with you, just as Mother had asked. When you excused yourself to run an errand, I gave you some distance then followed.

You walked along the stream for a long way, through the orchard, to the edge of the woods and into the shadows of the trees. And I followed, at a distance at first, but closer once you were among the trees.

You walked to a clearing and knelt on the ground. There was something in front of you. I couldn't see, and your back was turned to me. I stepped forwards. My heart raced. I looked over your shoulder and tasted bile.

On a bed of leaves in front of you lay a clay figure, still damp. On the limbs were carved the words of a curse and the name Nestor.

You mumbled under your breath. I didn't want to hear that blackness coming from your mouth, which had so often lit the world with laughter. Then you moved quickly and stabbed the figure with a hair pin.

I gasped and fell back. You were on your feet. You moved like a serpent.

'Danica?'

But I couldn't speak. My head reeled.

'Danica, what are you doing here?' You looked over your shoulder at the poppet with the pin jutting out of its chest. 'Dani, it's not what it looks like. I can explain.'

'How dare you! You can explain? Really? Explain this?' I pointed at the figure. 'That's witchcraft!' Spit flew from my lips. I had never felt such rage. 'Do you know what you've done?'

'Dani, please.'

The pet name stabbed at me.

'Don't call me that. Don't ever again. No sister of mine…'

'Dani, please,' you sobbed.

'Do you know what this means? You can't be initiated, you can't know the secrets. You could be put to death. And the shame! The shame on our family. You've destroyed everything.' And I shook you; holding your arms tight and shaking with all my strength.

'Dani…stop…Dani.' Your teeth clashed together.

I let you go and slapped you so hard you collapsed to the ground. A red welt rose on your face. I marched over to the clay, stomping on it and screaming my anger. The pin scratched my foot but I couldn't stop. I stomped and smashed until there was nothing but a mess of mud and leaves.

'I'm sorry, I'm sorry, I'm sorry,' you sobbed between hacking breaths.

'Get up.' I couldn't look at you. You walked just behind me as I made my way to the house. My anger started to dim and I was afraid. The penalty for witchcraft was death. And you were already marked if anyone discovered Nestor had told you the secret rites before your initiation. You were doubly cursed. I wanted to bundle you up and run far away. I looked back at you and the red mark of my hand was still on your cheek.

*

In the afternoon, the alarm gong rang out. You sat at the table, your eyes wide with fright.

'Don't move,' I said. 'Stay right here. If anyone comes, run to the clearing, I'll meet you there.'

'Are you sure, Dani?'

But I couldn't answer. I was obligated to report her to the high council, but how could I deliver my sister to death? I rushed to the square. Mother was already there and I made my way to her.

'What's happening?'

'No one knows. The delegates have an announcement.'

The waiting was horrible. I wanted to run back to you, but a small pit of disgust had seeded in my stomach. The delegates emerged from the council hall with two bound prisoners. I gasped. Nestor and Alyssa stood with bowed heads.

'I stand before you as a representative of the Elyssian Faith and bring to your attention the betrayal of our sacred rites by these two persons.' The Archon gestured to them. 'The youth, Nestor Katsaros, is guilty of revealing the secrets of the ancient rites to the uninitiated youth, Alyssa Sanna. He has been sentenced to death.'

A shocked murmur passed through the crowd. They all knew the law, but the sentence had never before been carried out.

The delegate continued, 'The maid, Alyssa Sanna, is guilty of receiving secret knowledge of the sacred rites. The sentence for this crime is also death.'

The crowd roared. The boy was an outsider and we had all seen his indiscretions, but the girl was one of us. It wasn't fair that she should suffer for his crime.

'Silence.' The delegate's voice bellowed across the square. 'Both persons were aware of the penalty for their crimes. Sentence will be carried out tomorrow at mid-morning. This is my final word.' The gong rang once and the party returned to the council building.

Mother and I walked home too quickly. Did anyone wonder at our haste? When we arrived you jumped up from the chair.

'What's happened?' 'Did anyone come?' We spoke over each other and I hugged you.

'That boy is to be put to death, along with the girl he was discovered talking to.' Mother's voice sounded tired. You looked at me for confirmation and I nodded.

'Maybe I should—'

'You will stay here and keep your mouth shut.' Mother's eyes blazed. 'Your rashness could get us all killed.' She paced back and forth. 'Danica, have you told anyone about the boy talking to your sister?'

'Of course not. Should I have?' I glanced at you, but you were staring out the window, pale and soul-shadowed with fear.

Mother considered my face and whatever she saw there convinced her.

'No, no, you did the right thing keeping your sister safe.' She looked at you. 'Astra, oh Astra.' She pressed you tight against her. 'I can't lose you, not my Astra, not you too.'

*

The night was long and full of terror. You lay still, staring up at the ceiling. By the sound of your breathing I know you didn't sleep. I quaked at every shadow. Every noise carried the fear that you were discovered, that the morning would bring your doom. But morning brought something worse. As I looked out the window, startled by the peeping of the dawn bird, I saw a new star, skirting the horizon in the early morning light: the long-haired star.

*

The prisoners were led into a field spiked with golden stubble. There was no crowd. Mother and I attended as representatives of the order. The Archon spoke a few words then, with light glinting on metal, drew a blade across their throats. Their blood pooled and clotted on the ground and the barred shadows of trees retreated. The new star peeped above the horizon, barely visible.

You weren't at the house when we got home but I thought I knew where you might be. I followed the creek back to the clearing from the day before. I found you there, on the ground, trying to scrub mud from your hands. Somehow, you had managed to smear it all over your face. The look of you, messy and awry, was so familiar that I felt a wave of relief. Maybe everything would be all right now. I knelt beside you and tried to help clean your hands.

'It's because of me, isn't it? It's my fault.' Your shoulders slumped. You looked so helpless.

'Don't be silly.' I tried to lighten the mood but my voice was hollow.

'I did it. I cursed him with death. I was so angry and now it's too late, I can't take it back, I can't undo it.'

'No, you can't.' I took your hand, 'But you can put it behind you for a day, then another, until it's just a distant memory. Come on...' I let go of your hand and, searching through the aconite which grew plentiful here, picked up some broad leaves and twigs from the ground.

'What are you doing?'

'Making leaf boats, you always loved making them. We'll make today better, you'll see. One good memory…'

You knelt in the mud beside me and took up a leaf, poking in a twig for the mast and attaching another leaf for a sail. We sailed our boats down the stream until the light turned golden and the water ran clear. The last boat got snagged on the river bend and I stood to fix it back on course.

'Leave it Dani. It'll come free on its own.'

'Do you want to go home?'

'You go. I'll follow along soon.'

And I left. I left you kneeling in the mud watching the last boat. I walked away. I was tired and worried and I just wanted things to go back to the way they were.

*

You didn't come home. It was almost dusk when Mother and I began to search, she in the village while I once again trod the path to that dreaded clearing. I was angry and practiced the hard words I would say when I found you. Selfish, uncaring, irresponsible. But you weren't there. The mud on the bank had stiffened. I marched back to the house, fuming, assuming you would be there with Mother; that you would be unconcerned I had walked all that way for nothing.

The torches were being lit when I rounded the corner for home. I had forgotten the festival. I wanted to look for you, but I was angry. You had thought nothing of your responsibilities to me, or to Mother, or to our status in the temple rites. So, I went to the square instead and took a torch from the vendor. I followed the line winding its serpentine way through the village and into the orchard. The leader chanted a prayer to Hecate, she who guides us through darkness, and we echoed the words, raising our torches.

Ahead, a discordant cry cut through the chant and was followed by a long drawn out wail. People rushed forward. I pushed through. There was something too familiar about that wail. Mother's voice. You were lying under the sacred olive tree. Your body was curled into a ball, knees to chest. Your face was a blank mask and vomit stained your dress. Our Mother was hunched over your body. She made an ugly croaking noise as she sobbed.

I looked down at you both. I felt nothing. You could have been strangers. Two men lifted you and carried you like a child to the house. Mother was supported by another woman. I walked alone.

You were laid on the table. The elder women came and washed your body with water fragrant with herbs. As I folded your dress a small pouch fell out. I opened the leather thong. Aconite flowers tumbled free, bruised petals purple-black where they had been crushed into the bag.

*

People stayed in the house late into the night, speaking softly, touching each other. I went to bed. It was cold were you were supposed to be. And I slept.

I woke to find you wrapped from head to toe in fine cloth. I looked at the shapeless parcel you had become and I felt nothing. Mother sat in her chair, still as a statue. Her eyes were too wide.

Your body took up the table so I poured my breakfast of kykeon gruel and sat in the sun to drink. The same birds sang as yesterday, but it seemed like I heard them for the first time. The sun on my face felt brand new. The trees whispered secrets and I listened.

Today was the greatest day of the festival. The statue of Lachus would be carried from Athens and everyone would sing and dance and beat kettles. I went back inside to prepare.

*

I laughed. Not too much, but people stared. And I danced, and twirled, and raised my voice in song, and people stared. And they frowned, though not in anger. They frowned the way an old man would frown at a clear sky right before a storm blew in. I frowned at the sky too, at the star brazenly twinkling in the daytime. Didn't it know stars were for the night?

But still, I danced. I danced through all the sacred sites, through the sacred gate, along the sacred way, and halted by the sacred fig-tree. The women dropped to their knees and pounded their heads, crying in mock grief in honour of Demeter, who grieved for her lost daughter. I looked at them; at their backs rolling, bellowing up and down like sea lions mating on the coast.

I choked on my laugh. It filled my throat and I couldn't breathe. I fell to my knees beside them and hiccoughed, and retched. A long string of spittle dangled from my lip and I tasted bile. Everything roared. The wailing women sounded demented, demonic. My chest was crushed under the force of the roaring.

A knife stabbed my stomach. But it wasn't a knife, it was a seed. Its roots spread through my limbs and they trembled. The stems swelled and filled me up. Leaves curled and my skin crawled. A rotten bud opened and gave birth to a demon that rode into the world on a primal scream, ripping its way out of my body.

*

I don't know where I am.

My body is shaking and, no matter what I do, I can't make it stop. My face is wet. I didn't know I was crying. Someone is touching me and it hurts. They're humming and shushing. Is it supposed to be comforting? It hurts.

*

I'm in a bed. It's not my bed, our bed, it's Mother's. I don't know if it's night or day, but if I lay still things don't hurt as much. She is beside me and then she's not. I would stay here if I could but I need…something. I need.

In the kitchen you are still on the table, wrapped and covered. Someone has embroidered a ribbon with narcissus flowers and covered the place where your eyes would be.

'Would you like some wine?' Mother asks, her voice crackling like autumn leaves.

I nod.

The watered wine is warm and fragrant.

'You slept through the games.'

'I'm sorry.'

I sip my wine. We sit in silence for a while. Mothers hands are shaking and she spills wine on her dress.

'I'm sorry,' she says. She dabs the mark with a rag. 'I'm sorry…' She is still shaking. 'It's all been taken care of. They'll come.' She plucks at a thread on the seam of her dress.

The silence between us is a screaming void. The noise of life outside the door is distant and hollow. The silence roars. I sip my wine. I follow the path of warmth until it too is torn away. My thirst is insatiable, my appetite gone.

*

They come for us when the shadows have moved. A solemn party in dark shades, the women with covered faces. Mother begins the chant, her voice rising into a wail. She beats her chest and pulls her hair. The women mimic her, a false idolatry to sorrow. I beat my chest, too. At first without effort, then harder and harder. I beat until it hurts. The pain shoots through me. Pain is like spears of lightning and it feels good. I scream in triumph. I scream in pain.

*

Today is the day of healing. Today is your funeral. You are carried away and I follow. The procession moves like a meandering stream. The women at the back are nattering. They think I can't hear. They whisper and I catch their drifting words: *mourning fields...wasted life...unrequited love.* Is that what they think of you, my sister? That you will forever mourn for that boy? That you will be trapped in an afterlife of longing, without love? I love you. That is real. That is requited. I turn and scowl at them and they shush each other.

We round a bend in the road. Your funeral pyre squats, monstrous in the harsh light. It is jagged and full of dark crevasses. You are laid on top, with aromatic herbs brought in bunches by mourners. I take a small blade and crop off a lock of my hair, laying it under your hands. I take the ewer and pour wine onto the earth. Dust crusts on top as it soaks, like blood, into the ground. I pour every drop for you.

Mother is passed a torch and lights the tinder at the base of the pyre. The wind gushes and the flames roar into life. A different roaring; cackling and sparking and hissing. An orange glow flares on the faces of the watchers. Tendrils of smoke cross the path of the long-haired star. I spit at my feet for its uncaring face.

The old women wash Mother and me in sea-water and hyssop, which is warmed by the fire. The gentle stroking of their hands is soothing. We dress in fresh robes and sit for the perideipnom, your feast. Honey cakes were your favourite. I allow myself to think only of the sweetness. Sticky crumbs cling to my lips. You were the sweetest child. You were like star flowers in summer greens; the relief from bitterness.

Mother sips her wine and hums the song you loved when you were small. The old women smile and rock. I hum along. The music lifts me up and the room feels lighter.

The evening is stretching out when the first women leave. They depart with fragrant embraces and tickly kisses from unplucked chin whiskers. You would have giggled. Mother would have scolded you. But she would have smiled, and you would have known that everything was alright.

*

The night of the initiation is here. Mother and I walk to the temple. You should have walked with us.

The mystces are gathered outside the door. Some of them crane their necks, trying to see into the darkness beyond. Others are talking with friends, trying to guess what will happen. You would have told them some horrific tale about human sacrifice and laughed at their reaction. You were so quick to laughter.

The attendants emerge and lead us into the entry hall. Mother and I lead the first ritual oath and the initiates repeat.

'A year ago, we were introduced into the lesser mysteries. Now let us enter the mystic temple and be initiated. We must be veiled before we can become seers.'

Mother and I carry bowls of water to each one and continue with the second oath,

'But first we must wash in this holy water; for it is with pure hands and pure heart that we are bidden to enter the most sacred enclosure.'

The attendants lead the party down a steep path under the ground and the air cools the further we go. We enter a small room carved out of stone. Oil lamps cast a dim light and the Hierophant swings a censer of incense. One of the initiates sneezes and another one titters and is shushed.

The Hierophant ensnares us with his gaze and leads us around the room. On the walls are symbols etched in stone. When I was first initiated I didn't pay close attention to them. I was too nervous about making a mistake. Now I see the sacred stories. Pictures and words tell the history of Demeter and her daughter; the heartbreak of the Mother, the awakening of the daughter.

The images swim before my eyes. The Hierophant's voice resonates in the cavern and my body vibrates with the sound. My head fills with the smell of incense and something else. The oil in the lamps has a resin burning. I'm finding it hard to look at anything directly.

The Hierophant speaks of the afterlife, about the joyousness we will find. A light fills the cavern. I hear a rush: the sigh of some, one, or many, breaths released in surprise. The light bathes everything. I can't see. The throbbing voice is joined by another, deep and feminine.

Through the light I see you.

You are perfect; beautiful. Your long hair flows behind you. Your lips don't move. You speak into my mind and my heart. I feel what you tell me: you are safe. You will not spend eternity in grief. You have always had a greater purpose. You are a child of the stars, and to the stars you will return. And I see it: the long-haired star, like a white horse of light, carrying you into the heavens.

My body is warm with the certainty that you are here. You speak to me as a goddess. My sister, rising to eminence among the constellations. You will watch over me. And I laugh. You? Watch over me? That was never how it was supposed to be. You turn from me and I reach for you, but you merge with the star and fade away.

Mother stands beside the Hierophant. She is glowing and slick with sweat. I hear the last words she utters,

'…the revealer of all things; the sun is but her torch bearer, the moon her attendant at the altar, and Hermes her mystic herald. The final word has been uttered.'

The initiates respond, 'The rite is complete. We are seers forever.'

And I see, too. I see the path before me clearly. I am filled with divine wisdom.

*

Mother sleeps as soon as she reaches her bed, tired from the exertions of the ritual.

I watch her sleeping, watch her chest rise and fall with each breath. I climb in beside her and wrap her in my arms.

*

In the pre-dawn light we make bread. Tears stream down Mother's cheeks, but not mine. Through the window I see the long-haired star winging you to your place in the heavens. And, one day, when my life is at an end, it will return for me.

I look at our mother, her face weary with pain, and I sing the first refrain of the kneading song.

Van, these people are just not ready. They're still worshipping deities and they haven't even mastered the use of iron for anything beyond basic weapons and pots.

You think I don't know that, Dren? But they have potential. Their short lifespans mean they're hungry for change. I've given these Greeks the basic mathematics to set them on the road to decent science.

But at what cost?

What does it matter, Dren? We must keep the end in mind. Our people are more important. You must see that? I must get home.

I know...I just—

Enough. We've done what we can, here. We'll keep moving. There's sure to be more advanced cultures elsewhere.

164BCE
Babylon

The Boy King

Ted Johnson

For those who had given up on their deliverer, hope was yesterday's forgotten dream.

For others who had only hope left, he was all they held onto.

A legend...

The boy king,
Left as a newborn on the temple steps;
Born of water and of earth;
Brings fire from the heavens.
Banished, but returns with death at his side,
To destroy our keepers with fire and wind and earth and sky.
Our salvation.
Chosen to restore our people, the world, and the stars to order.
*

Hope dreamed for the blessed hopeful.
And she yearned for the dreamers lost.

Apok held his breath as he edged sideways. He clutched his kite and spool close. Steadily. Methodically. Small even for his nine years. Nimbleness his only gift, he moved lightly. He passed each orphan brother as they slumbered in the temple darkness with just a woven reed mat between them and the cool clay floor. His grey wall-shadow melded with theirs one by one as he crept past.

'Apok? Where are you going?' A sleepy voice whispered in the dark.

Frozen mid-step, Apok quietly responded, 'Out. Go back to sleep, Ezra.'

Ezra stretched his neck back and upwards, making eye contact. 'But what about the curfew? You know that nobody's seen Rostam since he snuck out last week. Aren't you fearful of capture and what the Parthian King might do to you?'

Ezra was two summers younger than Apok and easily influenced. Apok crouched and stoked the boy's tousled hair. He gazed into Ezra's brown eyes. 'There is no curfew. There is no Parthian King. And I...I am no more than a dream to you, my young sleepy friend.' Apok thought for a moment. 'Close your eyes, Ezra, and wait with gladness for your next dream. For it shall be of your mother, arriving here to collect you, to bundle you home and cradle you to sleep in her warm, loving arms.'

Ezra turned on his side and, with a smile, closed his eyes. 'Good night, Apok-dream.'

To wake a sleeping boy was a warning that Apok's vigilance was lax. Once outside, he must move quickly and silently. Hide in the shadows close to the city wall and remain watchful for the Parthian guards who patrolled the night streets. Any citizen who may have looked up at the night sky and gazed upon the broken star would be exiled, along with their family. For an orphan slave boy, with no family, the consequences would be infinitely more severe.

Apok did not stop again until he reached the temple steps outside. He gulped in the night air and exhaled jubilantly. He closed his eyes in wonder; shared the sweetness of his getaway with the taste of the night sky, drenched crisp by the stars but heavy with midnight shadows. This, of all nights, was his time. The eve before his name day. A time to celebrate. A custom long forbidden, but the wind had called to him and, in the immense darkness, he dreamed it was already tomorrow.

Apok opened his eyes to the grey dark. A smile chased his lips and his feet chased the wind's whispers. The burnt-brown street dust warmed and sprayed from his bare soles as he ran into the night.

The wind had not visited him for many weeks. Not since the day he had finished building his new kite. The wind longed to see her take flight but, on that bright blue-skyed day, he hid his kite instead. Terrified the king's guards would capture his wondrous flying toy. They feared anything new and different.

This night she came to him once more. She charmed him. Her noiseless laughter echoed from every corner of the room. Whispering in his sleep, *'Come fly with me.'* Her breath sultry and dry from the sun-bleached desert sand. She cupped his heart as she spoke and smiled. He followed gladly.

Her warmth kissed his cheeks as he ran.

Blinking into the forbidden night sky, he found the broken star, many times brighter than her largest rival. His feet staggered to a standstill and he gazed upward in wonder at the resplendent silver, gold and blue tail cascading behind.

Apok drowned in her perfection.

Fixed on her beauty, he ran once more. The broken star whispered to his heart. As he watched her glide silently across the night sky, she watched him too.

She led him.

He followed.

He danced.

To see his new kite take to the sky was all that mattered to Apok. After all, his kite was a story from the wind.

He'd fashioned the kite from the thinnest and straightest bamboo, draped with sheer, white fabric from old laundry. A black dragon's head adorned the sail, painted with a brush and ink secretly borrowed from the high priest. With found arrow heads to weight the tail, this kite was more balanced and more perfect than any before. Apok admired his handiwork many times every day. Tonight, he smiled as it gleamed and fluttered alongside him.

The wind and his kite – both of them restless – both of them longing for flight.

Apok found the vine-covered trellis. He slung his kite over his shoulder and scrambled upwards. Atop the city wall, he tied a thin rope to the highest trellis rung before lowering himself over the other side. His rope fell short, Apok hung for a moment before plummeting the final drop. The thud of his feet landing on the rich, damp soil seemed to fill the darkness. He held his breath, crouched still, and awaited an outcry, but none followed. Not even the bark of a sleepless dog.

He left the rope behind in anticipation of his return and ran onto the freshly-ploughed field, staying on the firm soil between the furrows. As the wind ensnared his long brown hair, he raised his kite high above his head and let the string tug and flow through a loosened grip. She took flight.

Thick, black storm clouds loomed above, obscuring the broken star. Apok was left with the full moon and the run and skip of the wild desert wind. She revelled with him. She danced with him. She loved him.

The wind was perfect, drawing his kite high into the night sky. Higher than the city walls. Higher than the tallest rooftop. The string spooled through his fingers until his kite frisked amongst the clouds. Her form shone in the moonlight until that too was concealed by boiling, black clouds.

Lighting flashed. Apok counted until each flash turned to thunder's bellow. One, two, three, four, five, six, BANG! One, two, three, four, CRACK! The wind picked up; so did his spirits. His string reached its end and his kite flew higher than any before. It was perfect beyond any dream. His eyes misted with joy. He squinted, desperate for a glimpse of his kite, but the clouds swarmed. The string heaved and swayed in his hand.

FLASH-BOOM! Ribbons of light twisted through the darkness; clawed at his kite's tail. The force knocked Apok to the ground and ripped the spindle from his hand.

Up as quickly as floored, he ran back towards the wall, dashing to reclaim his wayward spindle. His kite burst into flames and hurtled earthward. Apok sprinted. Faster than he thought possible. As if his life depended on it. His spindle danced, only visible through fragments of lightning. He leapt and stretched to catch it.

Missed.

The spindle bounced and tossed along the rocky ground. Defying him. Mocking him.

Heart pounding, Apok watched, helpless as his fiery toy disappeared over the wall and into Babylon city.

He lay still, ears pricked, trying to slow his panting.

Between the rolling thunderclaps, there was only silence urging him on.

Up again, he ran to the wall. Scrambled for his rope; reached high and grabbed the feathery end. He pulled himself skyward and scaled the wall. His kite lay in the street below, its flames casting an eerie glow all around.

As the yellow flames intensified, street oil lanterns popped and dimmed. Some fell from their high sconces along the city wall. Household hearths glowed bright then snuffed themselves black. From where Apok sat, it seemed every flame in the city went cold. The only fire that remained was a lonely light from a small boy's bamboo and cloth toy.

Apok clawed his way back down the trellis and ran to extinguish the flames. As he reached his burning kite, shouts and the stomp of galloping horses echoed off the buildings around him.

And the rain fell.

*

'There he is!'

The first blow cracked and bloodied the side of his head. The next struck the middle of his back. Winded, Apok collapsed into the dust. A phalanx of guards launched upon him. The beatings intensified. He gasped for air. A crushing strike to his ribs curled him into a ball around the pain.

The rain became a freezing torrent.

The guards retreated.

Maybe they'd had enough beating him. Maybe they'd had enough of the icy rain. Through the hail, they dragged Apok's beaten body to the watch tower. They left him on the steps.

Apok curled up once again and looked around with his one good eye. He had his breath back but could barely move. It was easier to just lie there in the cold mud and wait for death to take away the agonising pain.

Death did not come to him.

Not yet.

A rattling of keys came, instead. And a lifting. A flood of yellow torch light as strong arms took him inside and laid him face up on a hardwood table. Apok could not summon speech. Barely winced as the old jailer cleaned his wounds with warm water and cloth. The jailor's hands pressed every part of Apok's aching body.

'Nothing broken,' was just a distant murmur through the ringing in Apok's ears.

A clamouring as two king's guards entered. The old jailer turned to the ruckus.

'Oh. Evening greetings, Bahraam. Greetings also, Keyvann.'

The wide-shouldered Bahraam towered over his offsider. They summoned the old jailer and spoke with him in hushed tones.

Bahraam offered the old jailer a vial of liquid and smirked. 'Orders from King Angra himself. You know the law. None may be out at night. None may look upon the broken star.'

The old jailer looked back at the child, limp on his table. He shook his head, eyes wide and lips quivering, his weathered face begged forgiveness. 'He's just a small boy...I cannot do this.'

'You defy your king?' Bahraam spat upon the old man and shoved him to the floor. 'I shall deal with you later. If you cannot do this, I shall.'

Sympathy flickered through Keyvann's eyes as he looked down upon the jailer.

'The king is not one for leniency. Especially when it comes to disloyalty. Disobedience is treason.'

As the deafening hail crescendoed outside, both guards approached Apok. Bahraam motioned to Kevyaan, who pinned the boy's arms. Bahraam prised the boy's black and puffy left eyelid open. Bahraam paused as he gazed almost lovingly into Apok's eyes,

'Welcome to your purification, boy-king. And the first day – and just maybe the last – of the rest of your miserable life.'

Keyvaan turned away as Bahraam poured half of the liquid onto Apok's open eye.

It was thick and cool, icy at first contact; blurring the guard's faces. The guard then poured the remainder into Apok's right eye. Again, cool and then warmer, both eyes stinging…burning. Initially Apok did not struggle, he knew it was pointless and he barely had any strength. Then his nostrils flared with the stench of burning flesh. He squirmed and blinked in agony.

Bahraam laughed through thick tainted teeth. 'Isn't it just so comforting that my beautiful smiling face is the last thing your big brown eyes shall ever see?'

*

Keyvaan lifted the boy's feet. Bahraam held Apok's wrists. They threw him into a vacant cell and locked the door. Bahraam slid open the small viewing panel. Inside, the boy's tiny, broken frame lay, wracked with shudders. Orders were given to be obeyed, not questioned. If he hadn't done this, the king would've found somebody else who would. Bahraam's resolve strengthened.

'And you, orphan dog, shall be tried for your treachery at first light.' He slid the panel closed and turned his back on the door. Bahraam waited as the hail softened to rain and then eased, then he took the old jailer's arm and escorted him to his doom. Keyvaan remained behind.

*

Left alone in the dark, Apok sobbed. Wet and sore and hopeless. His fists moved to rub his stinging eyes, but two hands gently stopped him.

'Rubbing will just make it worse. Please. Let me.'

Apok started. Was he not alone in this cell? The voice was deep, masculine and seemed centuries old. Soft and comforting; almost familiar. The coolness of wrinkled, leathery hands soothed his burning skin. As they touched his closed eyes the pain eased. His tears subsided.

The old man removed his hands and sat silently for a while before he spoke again.

'So, you're the boy they all speak of. The one who brought fire from the sky. That was very brave of you.'

Apok, painless, dreamlike, floating, replied, 'Brave? I am far from brave. I am afraid but grateful for your magic.'

'Magic?' The old man cleared his throat. 'When you're as old as I you'll know that love is more powerful than any magic. To love one another from the brightest joys of our beating hearts, to the darkest depths of our souls... it is a realisation of a great truth. To take away another's pain honours that truth. It's not magic. It is our purpose.'

The old man continued, 'And fear also serves a purpose. As there cannot be night without day, there cannot be fear without courage. Courage soaked the earth with your mother's tears the night she left you on the temple steps. And that same courage shall call upon you soon. To fight for those you love.'

Apok whimpered. 'I'm just a boy. A small...a small weak boy. I'm blinded now and useless. You speak of things I don't understand. You speak to me of love and courage. Why?'

The old man's response seemed measured and pensive. 'You may think you are small and weak and blind. But I know you are brave...I too was once scarred with blindness. And I carry many other scars.'

He paused. Cloth rustled and his voice moved closer. 'Neither love nor courage judge their deliverer by size or strength. Search your heart, young Apok. You'll find the answers to your questions already there. In what I have shared with you.' He paused once more. 'Maybe I'm here to sow a seed in your heart. Maybe I just wanted to meet you. The boy-king of legends. Who brought fire from the heavens.' The wry amusement that crept into his tone confounded Apok.

'I am not that boy,' Apok blurted, his fingers curling into fists. 'My kite caught fire that's all...and...and we are forbidden to speak of these stories. So, I beg of you, stop.'

The visitor waited patiently, until the boy could stand the silence no longer.

Apok leaned in with a whisper, 'They say he will be a giant and still more. The bravest of all men to face the monster king. But I am small and weak and afraid. I am not a giant. I am not brave. I am not that man of legend. And I...I am blind.' Tears clawed at his throat, squeezing it shut. 'I shall never see my kite again. I shall never see my friends...the sun...the blue sky. And even if I live tomorrow what will become of me?' Apok hung his head and shared his doom with the dust at his feet. 'A beggar in the street...most likely... starving and desperate.'

'Ah...You speak true, young Apok.' The old man paused. 'Blindness. A curse to some...To others, a blessing.'

Apok sat in dark silence. Despondent, he hoped for more. He heard the old man shift closer.

'Yes.' The old man's tone softened. 'Your sight has been taken but you could choose to accept this as a blessing. For now you have the gift of true sight. Now, you can see your true path – from your heart. And that path that will lead you where you need to go, even if it may not be where you want to go.'

Apok waved his hands before his face. Still nothing. 'A blessing? A gift?' he said bitterly.

The old man gently took the boy's hand and placed it on his own chest, over his own heart. He held it there for a while before speaking. 'Can you feel my heartbeat?'

Apok sensed a slowing ebb. 'Yes…yes I can.'

The old man placed Apok's hand on Apok's chest. 'Now, search your heart for mine.'

In his mind's eye, Apok saw a glow before him. Somehow it had always been there but invisible until it touched his heart. Now it shone into every corner of the room.

The old man whispered, 'And now you can see into men's hearts. You are truly blessed without the distraction of your eyes to betray you. See with your heart and you will uncover men's true intent, their goodness, their purity.' He paused. 'And these stories we are forbidden to speak of? I speak of no story. I speak of a truth. A prophecy that is about to manifest.'

The old man fell silent. Apok said nothing, afraid the guard might hear their forbidden talk.

The old man spoke softly. 'Do you remember why you made your first kite?'

'It came to me in a dream when I was very young.' Apok wasn't sure if he should continue but the old man touched his shoulder with warm encouragement. 'The wind. She begged me to make it. And she sailed it for me.'

'Ah yes. The wind. Such a beautiful scapegoat for so many childhood follies. You are still so very young.' Weariness edged his voice when he spoke again. 'But...back to the prophecy...Were you not found as a newborn on the temple steps? Did you not just bring fire from the broken star? From the heavens?'

'I guess.' Apok shook his head firmly. 'But I'm not this boy you speak of. I'm an orphan. Cursed by the great war that brought upon us the Parthian rule.'

'So, you know of your mother and father?'

Apok fought to contain a swell of tears. 'Yes...I have been told that they loved me very much but were both lost in the...You speak to me of a fate that cannot be mine! I don't possess the courage to fight even my own shadow right now...or ever.' The boy hung his head once more.

'Courage is not about fighting, or even knowing how to fight. Or even when.' The tone of old man's words hinted at a calm, knowing smile. 'Sometimes courage is about knowing when to run. Sometimes it's about being brave enough to call upon the help of others. And sometimes, it's about facing an enemy you know you cannot defeat. But you still stand. Defiant. That, my young friend, is courage.'

Tears clearing, the boy contemplated the old man's words. 'But why would anyone fight an enemy they know they cannot defeat?'

The old man drew a long breath. His heartfelt sigh slowly drifted down. 'Because of love. When you know, deep in your heart of hearts, your actions – even, perhaps, your death – brings hope to others.'

'Hope? To others? Death? False hope. What good is that? What hope have any of us against the Parthian king?'

'Your words are wise beyond your years.' A fluttering whimper escaped the old man. 'But when you're as old as I am you'll understand. In a world of suffering and despair... Hope – even false hope – can give people the will to live. And, to the lost and the suffering, hope is most precious gift you could ever offer.'

Keyvaan banged on the thick oak cell door. 'If you know what's good for you, I'd shut up you two.'

Silence.

For just a moment.

The old man spoke quietly, 'Oh, Apok. One more thing.'

A reluctant whisper, 'Yes?'

'Your mother gave you a name…and it is not Apok.'

'It's not? How would you know? What…what is the name she gave me?'

'She named you Apokatasta. An ancient word from an ancient tongue. The prince who was promised to restore what was lost.'

The boy was afraid to ask, because in his heart he already knew the answer, but his curiosity whispered the question for him, 'Why do you tell me this?'

The old man gently squeezed Apok's shoulder. 'Because your true name is your calling. The name of the one destined to deliver his people salvation. With the help of the stars and of the earth and of the elements. You truly *are* the boy king. And together, young man, we have much to prepare for.'

*

The entrance filled with pre-dawn glow as the watch tower door swung open.

'Get up you lazy swine!'

Keyvaan winced awake as the back of Bahraam's huge hand lashed his cheek.

'How is the wretched boy?' Bahraam's tone softened slightly. 'Did he make it through the night?'

'What?' Keyvaan reeled from his sudden awakening. Bahraam sounded almost concerned.

'The boy,' Keyvaan said. 'He spent the entire night talking with the old man. I roused on them more than a few times but—'

'What? What old man? You're a fool Keyvaan. The boy was in that cell alone.' Bahraam lifted the heavy bar across the door. Morning light found the boy hunched, quiet, and alone.

Bahraam peered into every corner. Nothing. 'You truly are a fool, Keyvaan. All I see is a stupid wretched dog here cowering in the shadows.'

Keyvaan cautiously peeked inside. 'I'm sure I heard voices. An old man who spoke like a nobleman.' He shivered. 'Do you think there's something…special about this boy?'

'Shut up! You'll soon be hearing voices of Hell *daewas,* if you don't help me get him onto the wagon and off to trial right now! The King is waiting. He insists on trying the boy himself and he's drawn a crowd of thousands.'

*

Apok welcomed the soft, warm morning sunlight. It quenched his skin's fire and his soul's thirst as it awakened him. It filled his emptiness. It honoured him and whispered tenderly just to him, in a perfect tongue that he had never heard before. And on his special name day, his very soul yearned to understand those lilting words.

Apok looked towards the door. Through closed eyes, his heart illuminated the guard's wide-shouldered figure, haloed in the bright morning sunlight. But Bahraam's heart was sullied, broken by years of death and violence. It called out to be whole again. The old man's words were of truth. Apok's purpose was foretold.

The journey to the city square was short, but jarring. Apok winced as the wooden wheels clunked over broken cobbles. Every muscle and bone in his body ached. Hundreds of feet shuffled as bystanders moved aside.

Once inside the square, Apok's blindness shielded from him the sight of a dozen pale, limp corpses hanging from the gallows. But Apok's heart saw them clearly – the old jailer amongst them, too. Good people. His people. Husks hanging there. They were always there. More every day since the Parthian King's arrival. Their lives stolen and their hearts crying for justice. Precious lives taken for the pettiest of crimes; the king's way of suppressing the conquered people of Babylon.

Apok's heart swelled with sadness. He hung his head in silent protest as he passed by.

But Apok's crime was more severe. His punishment would be far worse.

The cart rattled to a halt in the open city centre. Guards dragged Apok from the wagon and threw him into the dust. There he crouched, shivering in the long morning shadow of the city wall.

*

The Parthian king sat above the gathering crowd and waited. Ignoring them, he focussed on the wretched boy cowering on the ground. Angra Mainyu, god-king, sneered and checked his guards. Well over a hundred royal soldiers, archers, and advisers flanked his golden throne on either side, rendering him untouchable.

And countless shrunken skulls adorned his chair. A macabre testament of the fate of any king who ever dared stand against him. His pale skin glimmered in the morning sun. With his diamond blue eyes and platinum hair, King Angra knew himself to be the epitome of man, pure, divine. A demi-god.

Angra looked down upon the boy in disgust. He looked out upon his slaves; his subjects. In defiance of his laws, they whispered their heathen stories and beliefs in secret. Indoctrination through strength and merciless punishment was his rule. Consistent and unwavering. A regime infinitely stronger than the covenants of his spineless father, and the weak Parthian kings who ruled Babylon before him.

Why did these scum still defy him? Did they not know they were conquered? They moaned about justified taxation. They broke his laws. They hid their defiance behind small boys. Infuriated by their insolence, the god-king surveyed the rabble. It was time to show these Babylonians his true power. They *would* break before him today.

Angra arose gloriously from his throne. Trumpets sounded for all to prostrate before him. As the crowd of thousands looked to dust, the limp boy forced his battered limbs to comply. Two slaves either side of Angra draped an enormous lion's skin and mane over his shoulders. It rested perfectly upon his giant frame and cascaded down either side of his huge chest. Standing proud, Angra towered an imposing full head and shoulders above any man in Babylon.

'My people, I ask of you just one thing.' The king's booming voice pierced the crowd's rising din. 'Who? Who is this boy you bring before me?'

Angra knew exactly who the boy was, and what he represented. Although bruised and beaten, the boy could be a great threat to the throne. Angra had heard of tales that his wisest advisors referred to as children's bedtime stories. But tales had power; the power of hope. And hope led to revolution under a foolish leader. Angra smiled. He was not foolish. He would kill hope here and now.

Apok remained still, face pressed to the cool brown dust. Trembling. Silent.

Bahraam replied to the king's question. 'He is the boy who broke curfew my lord. He is the one who has brought shame among his people. And he shall now face the king's judgement for treason.'

King Angra looked upon the pitiful husk of a child before him. Perhaps he should show compassion to his subjects? To prove he was a virtuous ruler. Not that he cared about these snivelling miscreants, but taking the city of Babylon had provided profitable trade, generous taxes and his deific right to take and be pleasured by any woman that pleased his eye.

No. Angra straightened. This puny boy was no threat. But the legend was.

'Boy. Do you hear me?' His godlike tone commanded obedience. The boy cowered. 'You shall answer each question I ask you with a single word and a salutation to my divinity.'

Apok froze. And a moment passed.

'Boy...Do you hear me!'

Apok slowly drew his face from the dust. 'Yes, my lord.'

'Do not dare look upon your king again, slave.' King Angra saw the boy's sunken eyes and hid his smirk. 'But I see you cannot look upon me. You have gazed upon the broken star and it rewarded you with blindness. Stand now, boy, and show my people what fate that daemon star wrought upon your eyes.' The king turned to his closest confidante and grinned mirthlessly.

The boy struggled to his feet. He turned around for all to see his suffering. In whispers, like the wind, the crowd spoke their astonishment of his closed, sunken eyes. In whispers, they decried the horrendous curse upon such a small, frail child. In whispers, they grieved until the king's foul glare fell upon them. The crowd then hushed, as fear silenced hope.

Angra smiled.

Some dispirited onlookers turned homeward but stopped as the whispering began once more. The whispers built to a murmur until a single voice finally cried out above the growing din.

'How can he be tried? He's just a boy!'

The king gestured for the speaker's removal, but the question swept through the crowd like fire, leaping from tongue to tongue. Angra raised his arms, commanding silence. The crowd disobeyed. The murmurs built to a conflagration.

Angra hesitated. The boy was not yet a man. As a minor, only his parents could stand trial for his treason.

Yet he had none.

A few short words from his wise man and the king again raised his hands high to quiet the din. This time the horde responded.

'Babylonians,' Angra bellowed, 'you speak true. This boy cannot be tried. He is not yet a man.' Angra looked down upon the small boy. 'How old are you slave boy?'

Apok was slow to answer but shouted his response for all to hear. 'I have not yet seen ten summers, my lord.'

The king smiled as he addressed the crowd. 'Well then, it is simple. He must submit to the manhood rite of passage before his trial.'

*

The passage to manhood was the most anticipated event of the year. A gathering held after the fifteenth summer of each boy's life. Dozens of challengers came together on one sacred day. A single archer fired sharp, wooden arrows randomly into the air. The boys sought out the shafts and braced themselves as the arrows approached. The most treasured sign of bravery was a scar upon body, arms, legs, torso and even face. Especially the face. Multiple scars were a sign of great bravery and highly respected.

But now, sightless…Apok's shoulders slumped. A gasp rippled through the onlookers.

The king's impatient voice summoned forth his finest archer. Then the king summoned the archer's apprentice to join his master. The crowd murmured once again. Two archers and one small, blind boy. Someone in the watchers near to Apok cried out that the arrows were longbow hunting arrows: barbed and fatal.

The king laughed.

Apok straightened and gritted his teeth. He stood, accepting his fate. The first arrow tore deep into the dust just a sideways pace to his left. A warning shot. The second much closer. Apok did not move.

He turned his face towards the king. For the first time, he saw into the king's heart; blackened with loathing, spite and a hatred of all things. Including himself. But there was a deep-hidden glimmer. A yearning. To be loved. Apok's heart reached out in wonder and he took pity on the Parthian King.

The king hissed a command to both archers, 'Kill him.'

The next arrows hit the sand and crept closer. The third. The fourth. The fifth just shy of his left foot.

The king sniggered.

Then Apok heard another voice…with softer words. The voice of the old man, and it prickled his spine.

'Run! Your heart will show you the way.'

Apok turned away and sprinted. Light rain caressed his sun-scorched skin and a distant rumble of thunder rolled overhead.

Apok dodged left. An arrow-tip sliced into his right arm. He slipped left again and another arrow drew blood. The archer's aim was perfect, but Apok ducked with astonishing dexterity. Every arrow touched him but none found their intended mark. The crowd roared, cheering him on. Arrows sliced into him, Apok ran faster. As if the wind carried him. The old man had coached him well. His heart guided him, placing his feet safely at each step. And, as he ran, the raindrops thickened and turned cold.

The king screamed at his archers. 'Did I not make myself clear? I want this slave boy dead! Kill him now or you shall both suffer my wrath.'

When the crowd's cheers were far behind, barely audible through the pounding rain, Apok finally stopped. He panted, bloody hands on trembling knees, lungs afire, heart exploding in his chest. His trial was far from over. To live, he must keep moving.

'Run!' came the old man's voice again.

As he staggered forward, Apok recalled the old man's instructions. Find the stairs at the city wall that would lead him upwards. They were exactly where he said they would be and Apok took them two at a time. Escape was close. Freedom called. He could taste it. At a scraping noise, he ducked. Someone squawked in surprise.

'You won't make it, boy!' a mocking voice called. A tower guard, perhaps.

Apok pictured the drop below the stone parapet – ten times his own height.

The sound of galloping hooves stopped short at the steps behind.

'Stop him! Kill him! Kill the boy!' The king's voice.

Apok jumped into blackness.

*

The tower guard snatched his bow, nocked an arrow, and drew.

Angra grinned fiercely as he raced up the steps.

A downward shot at this close range, even at a moving target, even with the rain pelting down, would be impossible to miss.

Breathless, Angra arrived atop the tower in time to witness the fall. The guard released his arrow. Somehow it skewed off target but buried deep inside Apok's calf. The boy collapsed into the mud. Angra leaned against the parapet and cast an approving grin at the tower guard. The crippled boy lay still for a moment in the rain and mud. A blood-soaked arm scrabbled in the muck dragging his battered form onwards.

The king held out his left hand, demanding the guard's longbow. He nocked a fresh arrow.

'And we end this here...and now.' The king drew back, steady as he aimed high, held his breath, and released. His arrow flew swift; its impact sudden and lethal. Apok shrieked and slumped, motionless, the shaft embedded between heart and lungs. Blood, thick and crimson stained the desert sand. The torrential rain washed it away. Apok lay askew, his vacant eyes blurring into a vast hopelessness.

Angra laughed at the heavy sky. The hope Apok had stirred in Babylon's people washed away with the boy's blood.

*

A sniff at Apok's hand and a push against his cheek. A lone desert lioness came upon his body. Had she come to answer his prayers? He desperately wanted to speak with her but lacked the strength. As she moved alongside him, Apok saw her heart glow, so he pleaded from his, *'Please tell me you are here to kill me; to feed me to your cubs.'*

She replied without speaking, *'No. I have been sent by your mother to warm you, to protect you, to speak to you of her love.'* Her voice was soft and full of grief. *'My cubs have no need of your flesh. They were taken from me...as was my entire family... murdered for their pelts by the king's hunters.'*

But there was a hunger in her shallow sniffs. Apok summoned all his strength to show that he was not afraid and spoke aloud. 'How do I know you are not here to trick me? To watch me die and then eat my body?'

The lioness placed her paws together above his head and lay down in the soaking rain. She lay in the cold mud alongside the boy, cradling him with her body. Her thick fur blanketed his bare skin, her head rested next to his.

'*I haven't eaten for many days. I have not had the will to eat, and I may be as close to death as you. I am afraid and alone. But each night, as I slept, your mother spoke to me.*' She licked his cheek, her tongue's rasp waking him. '*She sent me to tell you the things you must know.*'

The warm beating glow of her heart engulfed him and Apok spoke to her from inside a dream. 'Why? Are these things I need to know before I pass into the next life?

'*You know already that she named you Apokatasta, The Deliverer. And she told me why. My name is Mitra, and I bring you only truth and love.*' The lioness nestled closer.

Apok's tears mixed with the rain on his cheeks. 'I'm ashamed for doubting you, Mitra. And I am sorry for the loss of your cubs.'

'*Do not pity me as I live now to avenge my family.*'

'And I am afraid I shall die before—'

'*Hush now, little one, you are simply moving from this life into the next. Your mother grieves now for your suffering, but she told me you need not be afraid.*'

'My mother…I ache for you to speak of her. Is she as beautiful as I see her in my dreams?'

'*Oh, she is more beautiful than any dream could imagine her to be.*'

Apok drifted between consciousness and slumber. He mustered a half smile as Mitra continued.

'When I tell you of her, open your heart and you shall know I speak truth.'

Her words comforted him. As his heart opened, Mitra's heart melded with his, sharing her life and her strength. Sharing his pain, and sharing his fate. Her words fell into him like feathers.

'Your mother, Sahira. She is the moon. You were not expected to enter this world as a man child. It broke her heart to give you up but she could not keep you. She placed you on the temple steps where she knew you would be safe. She grieved. Her despair turned to a great and terrible storm. Your father, Farshid, he is the sun. He watches over you by day. Their parting gift was to name you Apokatasta in the hope that one day you would rise up to fulfil your destiny and deliver your people, the world, the moon, and the stars to order.'

The lioness continued, *'The wind is your sister, Zeka. She came to you last night and begged you to play. And your brother, Asha, he is fire. He also came to you last night and did what he was foretold to do. He is ashamed and sulking now. Awaiting your forgiveness.'*

Mitra paused as a small fire appeared behind Apok. It burned unwavering, bright, even with the rain pelting and only mud below; bright enough that Apok saw it through his blindness and his heart warmed.

'Who am I to forgive him?' he whispered aloud. 'All I ask is that he may forgive himself.' The flames spread and grew, warming his body and Mitra's. Somehow, he knew, the city street lanterns relit themselves; the home hearths rekindled; the entire city of Babylon was bathed once again in a soft, yellow glow.

Apok called to his brother, 'Asha.' The flames seared high above making Apok smile once more. Then, with a wordless thank you, the flames receded to a soothing warmth.

Mitra nuzzled Apok's shoulder. Her heart fluttered and slowed in time with his own.

'Your love and wisdom shines through, little Apokatasta. But there is more for you to know and I feel you slipping away.'

'I feel no pain, only love. And all I see is a beautiful white fading to grey. Please tell me everything and I shall carry it with me into the darkness with joy.'

Their hearts dwindled with the dusk.

'You need to know that your mother's mother...' The lioness laboured a deep breath. *'She is the earth. The same earth that cradles us now. Her love for you is beyond measure. She soaks away your lifeblood and takes with it your pain and despair.'* Mitra paused and her breathing shallowed. *'And the broken star is the mother of her. She is the mother of us all. She is the goddess Anahita...I can see her now behind the clouds. Her silver, blue and gold tail smiles upon you...with great joy.'* Her breath rattled. *'And. Great. Hope.'*

Apok smiled into the encroaching blackness. 'And now I know she is a goddess. I see her... above us...smiling...beau...ti...ful. Thank you...Mitra...'

The last sliver of sunlight spread across the dull horizon as Farshid, the sun, slipped away, taking Apok and Mitra with him.

Their bodies lay there still and wasted.

And the rain.

Ceased.

*

As the floodwaters subsided, Apok's arrows were drawn into the earth with them. The shafts descended and the receding waters dragged them through his lifeless body, into the mud. The watery earth gave way and gently took the boy and the lioness down inside her. Only sand and silt covered the site of their death.

Sahira's pain turned to mourning. She watched, full-bodied but hidden behind the stormy shadows of her grief. As the clouds cleared she bathed her celestial mother and her earthly man-son's grave in her silvery moonlight.

*

Displeased with his filthy task, Bahraam trudged through the cold mud towards where the boy's body had lain. The king had sent him out to check on rumours the boy had vanished; his body taken by a desert lion. With every cautious step, Bahraam reminded himself once more, that orders were orders. He ignored Keyvaan's under-his-breath complaints. Bahraam didn't want to be reminded of the boy's blinding, trial and death. Memories that ate at his heart.

Bahraam stopped short. The brilliant full moon revealed a room-sized depression in the soil. The place where Apok had perished. Bahraam's eyes misted. He turned away and his gaze was drawn to the night sky. To the broken star. Pensively, he pondered the boy's demise, hoping his eyes would clear.

They didn't.

Both guards returned with nothing to report.

*

King Angra Mainyu slept soundly that night. The child was dead and gone. With his demise, hope would also die and his destruction would twist that bedtime story into one sure to frighten wistful slaves.

*

Deep inside the earth. No longer suffering but not passing through, not yet, just still and dreaming in the warm darkness. There Apok learned of his birth and his intimate bond with his brother and sister. In a single night he learned and lived as much as any young man may have done in twenty summers. His grandmother nurtured him.

The goddess Anahita watched over him. When he was ready, her blue and gold threads silently offered him just one wish. The boy who had grown into a man gave thanks and spoke his wish. She smiled upon him and promised to honour it.

As his time inside his grandmother's embrace came to an end, Apok dreamed again. His mother's final words wove inside his perfect dream.

'Apokatasta. The Goddess Anahita has blessed you to be reborn. My mother has granted you the strength, the foresight and the courage you shall need to become the king you are destined to be. Use these blessings wisely. But you must still overcome the Parthian king and grant your people freedom. He is mighty and he shall not give up his kingdom easily.'

*

In the pre-dawn glow a wisp-tailed desert mouse scurried across the cool golden sand, inspired by the whiff of crickets burrowing, escaping from their post-storm watery depths. A small mound of sand rose before her, glowing golden in the sun's first rays. She froze on her haunches, pricked her ears, ready to take her prize.

The sand continued to rise high above her, casting a shadow. She hopped back. Human fingers scrambled to claim solid ground. The sand fell away revealing a hand the size of a soldier's shield. A second hand burst through the sand nearby. The mouse disappeared as a third, much larger dome arose, sand cascading.

An enormous head, with dark hair and sunken eyes, gulped for air. A huge lion's paw emerged beside the head; and then another.

Feline head and shoulders broke through. A gigantic lioness launched herself from the earth and into the early dawn.

Apokatasta emerged beside Mitra. He stood twice the height and girth of any ordinary man. His muscular chest expanded as his lungs drew in the warm desert air. The lioness shook sand from her fur and rubbed against his shoulder.

As they walked, the earth shuddered. They paused just two hundred paces from the city gates. Mitra unleashed a deafening roar across the desert, shaking the city walls.

The giant turned to the gates and bellowed. 'I am Apokatasta. King Angra Mainyu hear me now.' He awaited some response but there was none. His deep voice boomed again, 'I have a single demand of you. Take your people away, back to whence you came.'

Still no response.

'If you leave now it shall be with my blessing of peace and protection.'

He waited with his lioness but there was no response.

'But if you choose not to leave I cannot promise either.'

Still nothing.

An arrow struck the ground nearby. And then a dozen more. Each one successively closer. The shadow of an uncountable flight of arrows darkened the earth.

Apokatasta spoke a single word under his breath, 'Zeka.'

A whirlwind sprang up, turning the onslaught awry. Down they spiralled. A thousand arrows scattered across the sand.

The city gates ground open. The king's infantry marched out, weapons glittering in the sun. Apokatasta and Mitra stood their ground as two thousand armoured soldiers fell into formation. A front line one hundred and twenty men deep. Five hundred mounted soldiers galloped around them and formed at the front. A thousand archers ran out and took a low position at the foot of the cavalry.

Three monstrous stallions emerged, carrying the king, his commanding general, and his high priest counsel. The royal entourage took their place at the head of the army, just a hundred paces from Apokatasta and the lioness.

Suited in gilded battle armour and golden crown, the king brandished his ceremonial golden spear, tipped with star-iron. Steely-eyed, the king broke formation and cantered forward, his stallion prancing to a halt just twenty paces shy of the titan.

The king's words fell, sneering, and full of scorn, 'Boy-king. Are you so foolish you do not know you are dead? So brazen you would dare provoke me?' But sweat beaded his brow and doubt flickered in his blue eyes as they stole over Apokatasta's huge, scarred body.

Apokatasta saw inside the king's blackened heart; the kernel deep within yearned for redemption. 'I offer you safe passage from here, my king. Please take your army and leave us to restore what is rightfully ours.'

The king spat his fury. 'You call me your king yet you do not bow before me!'

'I do not bow because none should bow to your tyranny. Your father and your mother, and the nobles who ruled in peace before them, would be ashamed of your treatment of your people.'

The king's knuckles whitened on his spear. His jaw clenched. 'You dare to judge me boy?'

His high priest threw him a restraining frown.

'No, my king.' Apokatasta lowered his head. 'I humbly ask that you judge yourself.'

'You sicken me, boy,' the king sneered. His priest touched Angra's arm and the king ground his teeth. 'But I shall humour you, boy. How, exactly, should I judge myself? Should I question my rightful place as your king? Should I question my purity?'

The boy's head remained low as he spoke. 'You should question nothing of yourself, my lord. You will be judged only by your own gods, by your own people, and by your own laws.'

The king shifted in his saddle, visibly trying to quell the anger flashing in his eyes.

But he could not.

His rage savaged the air. 'AS I ALREADY AM, BOY!' Every word rang with loathing. 'I am bound to every law I have decreed. Nobody is spared. Peasant, slave, mother, father, brother, sister, soldier, king. Even the gods themselves! All must revere my rule. From my divinity to your filthy...' A cocktail of spite and fear frothed the corners of his lips. '...pestilence. All of us are judged equally in the eyes of the law. All. Equally!'

'Caution, I beg of you, my lord.' A low whisper from his chief counsellor made Angra growl.

The king shrugged him off and charged forward. A small blue flame appeared at the iron tip of his golden spear. His lips curled into a contemptuous snarl. Angra thrust his spear towards his adversary.

Mitra responded with a deafening roar but her warning came too late.

The surge of liquid fire struck Apokatasta's chest. He fell with a cry of pain. Rain deluged from dark clouds, dowsing the flames. Blistered and in agony, Apokatasta writhed on the ground.

'Now burn and die, boy, as I should have finished you yesterday,' Angra snarled.

Apokatasta rasped a single word. 'Ahsa.'

A second blast of blue fire burst from the king's spear. But yellow flames sprang from the earth, surrounding Apokatasta and Mitra.

Blue flame melted into yellow. Yellow flickered and vanished, leaving the giant and his lioness untouched.

The king's face darkened and his voice shook. 'You, boy, have tasted just a glimpse of my power.' He pulled on his stallion's reins, showed his back, and cantered to his army and his city. He raised one gloved hand high, and dropped it as he spoke, just loud enough for both man and beast behind him to hear.

'And now, boy, you shall finally meet your fate.'

The sky darkened once more as the king launched his entire army toward Apokatasta. An immense cloud of battle arrows screamed high and then arced downwards. Aimed at just two distant targets.

Apokatasta rose to his knees. Pain slowed his scorched body. He knew, from the old man, this was a time to call for help.

'Brother. Sister. Ahsa! Zeka! Show us your might!'

A fearsome desert sand storm engulfed the two thousand strong army, blinding infantry and sending horses into panic and disarray. The highest airborne sand ignited into a roaring inferno and turned a thousand flying arrows to ash. Terrified horses balked and trampled over foot soldiers. Fighting broke out, soldier upon soldier.

The king roared, 'STOP THIS INSANITY!'

The time had come, Apokatasta needed to show both courage and compassion. Pain tore through him as he struggled upright. He raised both arms high and lowered them slightly. The sand storm began to abate.

'Mitra,' he whispered, 'go to the city.' Haste sped his words. 'The storm will hide you. Warn my people to stay indoors.'

She ran. Fragments of Mitra broke away, took flight and transformed into perfect replicas of her. A thousand majestic copies of the lioness patrolled the city streets, but the last of her returned and sat proudly beside her master.

Apokatasta rose above his pain and stood tall. His voice pierced through the settling dust, and he repeated the king's own words.

'All must be judged equally. Peasants, slaves, kings, and even the gods themselves. By your own laws, just or not.' Apokatasta fell to his knees once more.

The king galloped towards his assailant, halting abruptly, just beyond striking distance. 'You dare mock me with my words, my laws and my power?' The king smirked. 'You, boy, have fled from a death sentence. You, boy, know in your very soul that your desert tricks are no match for my divine power. And so therefore you, boy, are doomed.'

Still kneeling, Apokatasta straightened and braced himself. The king held his spear at the ready. A high wall of yellow flame surged and surrounded Apokatasta and his lioness. Asha's protection.

Apokatasta raised his head to the sky. His mother and father were there above him. Watching. Waiting. The storm had subsided and the sky had cleared. He called to the moon and the sun.

Darkness crept across the sand.

All eyes turned skyward.

The sun turned to black as the moon ate him and obliterated all but the fiery halo of his light.

The day turned to night and the broken star became visible to all; its magnificent blue and golden tail trailing across the sky. The sun's halo was too bright to look upon but the broken star drew awed gazes. Even the king turned and saw her.

Apokatasta's words pierced through their wonder. 'It is a good omen you see here. Honour her presence and let it be with gladness as you gaze upon the mother of all of us. She is beautiful is she not? The Goddess Anahita.'

Asha's yellow flames subsided. The king turned from the goddess, his face crimson. His words spat once more but this time they came laced with a hint of dread.

'What trickery have you brought upon us boy? You have taken the sun. How do we make this right?'

Apokatasta gave silent thanks to his mother and father before responding. 'Fear not, my lord. The sky shall right itself soon enough. But as darkness fell, you gazed upon what you call the broken star…and by your own laws, none shall gaze upon that star. You and your army are now banished from the city.'

The king's booming voice filled with anger. 'How dare you deem yourself worthy to sentence me? How dare you even consider yourself worthy to speak to me?' The king stepped back, aimed true and hurled his golden spear at the boy.

Mitra jumped. The king's spear pierced her heart. Apokatasta cried out. A thousand city lions turned to dust. Her body skidded across the sand, halting at Apokatasta's feet. Apokatasta withdrew the spear. With tears welling, he knelt beside his lioness.

'I have asked too much of her love and her life.' He trembled as he spoke. 'Who will help me honour her death?'

The sky above slowly returned to its natural self. Father sun beamed his warmth upon the lioness.

All of those who could hear and see him exchanged sidelong glances but not a single Parthian soldier broke formation.

Apokatasta sighed. 'Then I beg of you to let me give due honour as she returns to her creator.' He leaned in to collect his beautiful Mitra.

The king snatched a dagger from his belt and threw it.

Apokatasta knocked the dagger aside with the golden spear. He left his lioness for the moment and stood once more. He faced the king. Truly, the darkness in the king's heart had strangled the last glimmer of light there.

Anger and bitter disappointment tasted of bile in his mouth. Mitra had sacrificed herself for nothing. The king would not be redeemed. Judgement must be passed.

Tears tracked through the dust on his face as he looked up and screamed to the heavens.

'Oh, Goddess. Oh, Earth-mother. LET THERE BE JUSTICE!' Apokatasta thrust the star-iron-tipped spear into the ground. His booming voice channelled a rift in the sand from the tip of the spear. The rift crackled towards his adversary. It deepened into a chasm and spread across the sand. The army shoved and pushed, trying to escape the Earth-mother's wrath. The rift opened to an abyss; a mouth in the earth. Men and horses screamed as they were swallowed by the desert sand. King Angra's gilded armour flashed in the sun. His scream echoed off the city walls. His pale arm clawed at the sky as he, too, vanished into the earth's maw.

Apokatasta watched in horror as two thousand men and a hundred horses disappeared into the gaping hole. He knelt and wept at the edge of a sunken desert. His anger had caused this atrocity. His compassion would never recompense for his grandmother's resolution.

As his father, the sun, Farshid, returned to full glory, the people of Babylon poured from the city gates to celebrate their redeemer. Apokatasta wiped away his tears and stood to greet them.

He pushed through his pain and smiled.

For sometimes, courage is about facing an enemy that you know you cannot defeat. Because that gives hope to others.

And hope is the most precious gift you can offer.

*

Apokatasta lay peacefully in his bed, facing his open window, seeing all with an open heart. A breeze crept into his room bringing warm kisses to his cheeks. Lanterns burned dim and cast long, soft shadows of love high across his ceiling.

A crescendo of heavy footsteps preceded excited knocking on the huge oak doors leading to his chambers. Apokatasta had to raise his voice to be heard above the clamour.

'Oh, please! Shahram. Enter!'

Both doors swung wide as the young king of Babylon strode into the room, bringing with him the yellow torchlight of the passage landing. The soft glow reminded Apokatasta of a night he had spent in a nearby watch tower so many years ago.

The king stopped at his grandfather's bedside and bowed low. Warm and alive with joy, Shahram spoke breathlessly.

'I come with great news, my lord. The goddess has returned as you predicted. People are dancing in the streets. The whole city, I think. They beg you to come join in the celebration.

Apokatasta rested a weathered hand upon the young man's shoulder. The young king's eyes misted with love and understanding. Apokatasta lay still. Smiling too, but only to himself. His unnaturally-extended life would be taken soon. As king, his rule of compassion and wisdom had brought many seasons of prosperity and peace to Babylon.

'Thank you, my beloved grandson. My king. Go to them please. Tell my people that I shall not be joining them tonight. Tell them I shall honour this wondrous blessing from afar.'

King Shahram frowned. 'But grandfather, why would you not join your people on such a joyous occasion?'

'Tonight.' Apokatasta sighed, hollow and spent. 'Tonight, I depart my earthy husk, for she has come to collect me.'

Shahram's eyes misted once more. 'I don't understand. Who has come to collect you my lord?'

'You can see her through my window. The Goddess Anahita. She shall take me back to my grandmother, and back to dust.'

King Shahram swallowed hard. He kissed Apokatasta's cheek, bowed low and pulled both doors to a dignified final close.

The room dimmed and a tiny sliver of moonlight peeked inside. The sliver grew as she slowly moved across the sky, flooding his room with her silvery light. Her light touched Apokatasta's face. His eyes opened wide for the first time since he was a young child. He wiped them in disbelief. He could see once more. And the first vision they encountered was his moon-mother's beauty. Alongside her was the Goddess Anahita, with her ancient silver and blue tail. Holding close the memories of a magnificent lioness; of fire and wind, earth and sun and of the most beautiful moon, Apokatasta closed his eyes for the last time and let his thoughts drift into a wish that had been granted long ago.

To meet with a boy.

A small blind boy, lying in a prison cell. About to be tried for an unjust crime in an unjust world.

Vanin, I can't countenance this. By backing that Parthian king you caused the wholesale slaughter of thousands of innocents.

You're soft, Dren. He had the drive and ambition we need to foster in these people if we're going to drag them into a technological age.

When are you going to stop this? We've been on this planet for half a millennia and—

And I'm still in the female phase. There's time. I can save our people and my heir will rule them on a colony. As long as I'm female, none of my younger sibs will change sex. Don't you see, Dren? If I don't get home, the Prime Blue family will die out completely. There will be no Heir!

And is it worth sacrificing the people of this world for that?

Yes, gred you! You're blinded by emotion, Dren. I've seen you with that...woman.

Leave her out of this, Van. This is about you.

Yes. It's about me and our people. You're forgetting you're not human.

No, unfortunately I'm not.

451CE

ÉRIU (Ireland)

Fire Rain

DA Kelly

'She's shedding her skin, Sneath!' Clutter elbowed his brother. 'Making herself beautiful.'

'She's bright, I'll say that. Brighter than she's been in centuries.'

The two goblins stood in the doorway of their mountain cave and stared at a streak of light blazing across the evening sky. They grinned at each other, flashing tiny sharp teeth.

Clutter rubbed his bony, green hands together. He kissed a small clay tablet pinned to their front door. 'I told you this amulet was lucky! Just like the twins said! I can feel the luck oozing from it like the guts of a well-cooked frog. All delicious and delightful. Makes my lips tingle.'

'It's just a disc of fired clay with a few squiggles cut in it.'

'Then why are my lips tingling?'

'I doubt it's your lips that are tingling.' Sneath snorted a rough laugh.' If we could bottle that night with those twins, brother, we'd be rich.'

Clutter blushed, his skin turning a dusky, forest green. He ran his fingers through his wiry, dark hair, causing it to stick up, all bristles and curls. 'Now, now! Just saying, the amulet is finally working. No need to tease.'

'You know what I see up there?' Sneath turned his attention back to the comet. 'It's got naught to do with luck and nubile faeries, and everything to do with destiny.' His amber eyes widened, his catlike pupils catching the light of the fire star.

'A business opportunity!' Clutter did a little jig. 'I can feel it in me bones. Reeks of plague and omens this one, and you know what that means.'

'Gold!'

'Exactly!'

'Reckon they'll be as gullible as last time?' Sneath hooked his thumbs in the rope holding up his breeches, admiring the feathered glow trailing the fire star.

'They're humans.' Clutter shrugged.

'It won't be like it used to. We'll have to play to the Sky Gods and the Christians. Danu and the Goddess Bridgid. That Jesus lord so many are praying to these days.'

'Good thinking. Spread the love. It'll take a while to get everything ready.'

'Not to worry.' Sneath glanced skyward. 'From the looks of the big, brushy tail and how she shines so promising up there, the real riches won't start for years yet.'

'What'll we spin them this time?'

'Go with doom and gloom. End of days stuff.'

'An oldie but a goodie.'

'If it ain't broke don't fiddle with it.'

'Exactly!'

*

After a rough winter, months of work and wistful chats about their bright, and wealthy future.

*

'Now, you got all the amulets and talismans?' Sneath stood beside their two-wheeled cart, jamming a trunk of small, rough-hewn crucifixes into the back. He hefted the last trunk of wax-sealed pots and shoved it between baskets of vials, scrolls, candles, and dried bones adorned with motley white feathers.

'I left that special one pinned on our front door,' Clutter said, tossing three satchels on top of the pots. 'You know, for luck. Keep our home safe.'

'What good is a slab of dry clay with a few scratches and squiggles on it gonna do? That's worth a few extra coppers, that is.'

'But it's from those twins up north. You know the ones!'

'Course I know them! Still got the bite mark on my bum from that night.'

'On your where?'

'Never mind! Get the amulet and be done with it.'

'They said never to scorn or ridicule the amulet or it'll bring us misfortune.'

'Faeries! Drama queens the lot of them.' Sneath snorted. 'A flutter of wings and you're all gooey and fumbling for your coin purse.'

'A flutter of wings and you're reaching for something else.'

The two goblins wiggled their hips, and sniggered.

Clutter ran to the cave and returned with the palm-sized disc. He handed it up to Sneath who sat perched on a narrow wooden seat at the front of the cart, reins in hand ready to make their fortune.

'I packed a tub of blue fire,' Sneath said. 'Best be prepared. Them trolls will be rumbling about now it's spring. Nothing worse than a hungry troll after hibernation.'

'You're smart like that, brother. Shall I lock the door?' Clutter asked.

'Nah, we'll have a palace soon enough. Just look at that dismal sky. Haven't seen the sun clear for weeks. Humans will be falling over themselves with fear.'

'First thing I'm gonna buy is a warm coat and some new boots.' Clutter tugged his threadbare jacket about his bony shoulders. 'Hasn't been this cold in ages.'

'Always whinging! Remember, no sun means no heat and that means no crops. No food makes humans desperate.' Sneath yanked Clutter up beside him. 'And that means—'

'Gold!' they crowed.

'And hungry trolls!' Clutter added.

'There you go again. Misery on legs.' Sneath flicked the reins. 'On yay!' he called to the mule, and the cart lurched forward, its wheels clattering over dirt and stone.

*

After many bewildered chats about their not so glorious future.

*

Sneath and Clutter huddled beneath their cart. They had been on the road for what seemed an eternity and still no palace. Still no shiny fortune. A small campfire burned in a ring of mossy stones, the rain hissing and spitting in the flames as they roasted a couple of frogs speared on sticks. Wind, icy with the promise of sleet, whipped the land. A village of about thirty wattle and daub hovels sat within calling distance. It even had a small inn-come-tavern with a roof that was almost rain-proof. There had been no glorious smell of roasting meat or drunken laughter coming from within the inn, but the beds had looked warm despite the fleas and suspicious stains on the blankets.

Sneath swiped a gnarled green finger beneath his nose, wiping snot on his breeches. 'As I always say, Clutter, coin is better in my purse than some grubbing inn keeper's. Two silvers per night! Thieving cur!'

'Should have bartered,' Clutter said. 'Given him a potion or something. Human males would give up their first born for a good aphrodisiac.'

'Give something for nothing?'

'A warm bed's not nothing.'

'How about giving me a turn at that fancy new coat of yours?' Sneath patted the thick, grey wool, tugging at it eagerly.

'Better coin in your purse than some thieving coat maker's.' Clutter pulled the hood over his face.

Sneath growled. 'You were gypped, anyway. Seen better wool on a mangy, dead goat.'

'I could eat a dead goat about now. Horns and all.'

'Who's that coming up the road?' Sneath peered between the cart's wheel spokes.

'Hopefully a bald, dead goat with big horns.'

'A good evening to you, master healers.' A woman squatted beside the cart, clutching a shawl about her head and shoulders. 'I hear tell you have potions that work miracles for very little coin.'

'That's our motto!' Sneath sprang out from under the cart, all bows and smiles.

'Whatever ails you, we have the cure.' Clutter bounced out beside his brother. 'If it's prayers you need, we have crosses blessed by the apostle Paul himself. Even have teeth and finger bones – relics from a martyr stoned to death by the Romans – if you're in desperate need.'

'Ciaran the thatcher says you healed his son!' The woman eyes were wide, haunted in her gaunt face.

'Indeed, we did!' Sneath beamed. 'A vial of our special brew and the boy was giddy with life.'

'Will you come with me? See my daughter? My husband?' The woman pointed at the village. 'We're next to the inn.'

'No point hitching up the cart for such a short journey.' Sneath patted the mule, which glared at him as though the bad weather was all his fault.

'You go. Help this fine lady,' Clutter said to his brother. 'I'll guard our wares.'

As Clutter clambered back under the cart, Sneath shot him a dour look and trailed after the woman, towards the village. By the time they reached her cottage, Sneath's boots were caked with mud and he stood a good three fingers taller than his usual four and a half feet.

'What's your name, good woman?' Sneath smiled his most handsome smile.

'Aideen.' She fumbled for the door and thrust it open, all but falling inside.

A fire smouldered in a central stone ring, the flames struggling to catch the damp timber. The only other light streamed through the open doorway, illuminating a cloud of dust, and the mildewed rushes strewn across the dirt-packed floor. Smoke hung thick amongst the soot stained rafters. The stench of sickness and damp dog fur caught in Sneath's throat. He retched.

'Sorry, I sucked in too much smoke,' he lied.

Aideen lit a tallow candle from the fire and walked to the far side of the cottage.

'They're over here.' She beckoned Sneath over.

He took the candle from her, thrusting it into the face of a bearded man who lay on a rough timber pallet. His face was slick with sweat, his eyes red and rheumy. He met Sneath's gaze with a sloppy smile, appearing more drunk than ill. Sneath peered at the man. He looked familiar. Sneath rummaged through his mind, shuffling faces and places like they were a deck of cards.

'You're the thatcher!' Sneath grinned. 'Aideen says your boy is hail and hearty thanks to my potion.'

The thatcher lurched to his feet, grabbed for Sneath but only caught a handful of air.

Not as drunk as I thought! Sneath stumbled backward and into a wall of muscle and stale, human sweat.

Aideen fled the cottage in a swirl of skirts. 'We have the cur! Call the priest!'

'Now, now!' Sneath managed a feeble chuckle. 'I'm certain there's been a misunderstanding. Did I mention there's a money-back guarantee? No questions asked. All forgiven. All forgotten.'

'Forgotten is right, you filthy, green bastard.' The thatcher lifted Sneath off the ground and shook him. 'My lad's memory is like a leaky basket since he took your poison. Pisses hisself and all. My good wife is beside herself.'

'More like the firestar is causing your son's misfortune. It's causing havoc from here to where ever.' *Oh! Good answer! I might come out of this alive and make a sale into the bargain.* 'We have a protection amulet that will shield your whole family from the curse of the firestar. Your whole village! Blessed by Bridgid herself! Or crucifixes – hand carved and sanctified!'

Shouts, screams, and loud thumps came from outside.

Oh, please don't be a troll! Sneath wailed to himself. *That's all I need! A cursed troll banging and noshing his way through town.*

Another scream.

A squeal.

That's Clutter!

A magnificent thud and explosion rocked the cottage. Brilliant blue light flared through the doorway along with the eye-watering stench of brimstone.

Oh, Clutter! Sneath hung from the thatcher's fist like a rag doll. *I could kiss you!*

The thatcher dragged Sneath outside into the rain. Blue flames engulfed the inn and smoke billowed in great stinking clouds. Townsfolk ran about calling for pails of water, coughing and cursing the two goblins. Never had Sneath enjoyed such a horrible haze before. He flapped his tunic, wafting as much smoke as he could into the thatcher's face, but the brute refused to let go. Sneath kicked and clawed and sunk his sharp fangs into the thatcher's forearm. Blood filled Sneath's mouth, hot and coppery. He would have savoured the taste if the thatcher hadn't clipped him across the back of his head.

The smoke burned Sneath's eyes, seared his nose and throat. Clutter darted from the shadows, his lovely new coat singed and smouldering. A dagger flashed in the gloom. The thatcher howled and dumped Sneath in an untidy, but grateful, heap. Clutter dragged Sneath up into a skid-sliding run and they bolted for their cart.

'Saw a mob of rather angry men heading toward the inn.' Clutter shoved Sneath up onto the seat and clambered after him. 'My warts tingled bad.' He shook his head. 'Knew we were in for trouble. I never hitched up a cart so fast. Got a nasty bite from old Muley, but it was better than what that lot had planned, I'm sure.'

Clutter snapped the reins, spurring the mule into a fast trot.

'Things are not going like we planned at all.' Sneath slumped over and examined his bruises.

Rain lashed the countryside. And, as if to rub brine into the wound, three fireballs speared through the clouds, their roar echoing long after they had vanished over the horizon.

'Still think your faerie amulet is lucky, brother?' Sneath glared at Clutter. 'Even the firestar is mocking us.'

*

After many chats about their bruises, empty coin purse and hungry bellies.

*

Sneath and Clutter perched atop their cart, digging through their miracle cures and prayers. A drizzly fog swirled around the village square, soaking everything. The sun, though high in the sky, was nothing more than a pale smudge behind a sea of dust and dark clouds.

'Good idea to set up close to the road out of town.' Clutter blew on his dusky green fingers and rubbed his hands together.

'Smart, that's me.'

'Can't fathom why the humans aren't flocking to us like they used to.' Clutter's fangs chattered. 'I've never seen the sun so dull. If I was a human, I'd be all aquiver with fear thinking some god was on a vengeance streak – especially 'cos things are getting worse.'

'Always in for bad years after the firestar sheds her skin.'

As if summoned, two smoking fireballs thundered across the morning sky, echoed throughout the hills, then disappeared.

Townsfolk pointed and cowered together, crossing their chests with shaking fingers.

'It's those damnable priests.' Sneath glared at six black-cassocked monks who stood amongst the humans, muttering about the devil and other such nonsense.

'Anyone would think we meant to do them harm.'

'I swear, I will not be chased out of town again.'

'I still have the wounds from that nasty little village last week.' Clutter touched the back of his knobbly head and winced.

'We gotta find out which towns are tainted by those prayer-mongers.' Sneath gave the monks a friendly wave. 'That way we can get on with business without their pious noses cutting into our profits.'

'Humans! You just can't trust them. Time was, when things looked bleak, they'd want protection from the Sky Gods. Now they flock to the Christians. Fickle, that's what they are.'

The townsfolk milled around all wild eyes, gaunt faces, and dressed in raggedy coats and cloaks. Many were curious, others scowled. All of them kept their coin purses well and truly closed.

One of the monks strode towards the cart, his cassock swelling like black wings on a foul wind.

'You are not welcome!' He lowered his cowl and glared at Sneath then Clutter. 'Take your evil trinkets and false promises and leave before we burn you for heresy.'

'That's a bit harsh!' Clutter spluttered, his eyes wide.

The townsfolk surrounded the cart. Unfortunately, they weren't there to purchase anything.

Sneath grinned widely. *Best look friendly.*

'Sneering will only anger us further.' The monk scanned the crowd. They nodded and murmured mean words like 'flaying' and 'hanging' and 'boiling oil'.

'We're here with open hearts to aid these poor people in such troubling times.' Clutter smiled, making certain his fangs were safely hidden behind his thin, green lips.

Sneath held up a wooden figurine that vaguely resembled a female. It wasn't his best work. Her breasts were lopsided and her legs were wonky stubs, but at least her hips were wide and round. Humans used to love figurines of the Divine Mother.

'Heathens!' cried an old man.

'Demons!' shouted a woman. 'Witchcraft! See the wicked amulets and potions they peddle.'

The townsfolk rocked the cart violently. Sneath toppled backward with a screech, landing in the box of crucifixes. He waved one over his head for the crowd to see. 'We believe! We love your god! We pray almost every day!'

'See! He brandishes an inverted cross!' The monk snatched it from Sneath and flung it into the mud. 'Jesus save us from these evil beasts.'

Clutter grabbed the reins and whipped the mule's rear so hard and so suddenly, the poor creature bucked and shot off down the road braying and snorting like a wolf was after him. Too bad the cart remained behind.

Hands – fists to be more accurate – pummelled the two goblins and dragged them from the cart.

*

Sneath scowled at the rusty cage they'd been hurled into a few hours earlier. 'Well, seems we might be in a bit of trouble.' He slumped in the corner, careful not to bump his head on the top of the cage. 'I've seen bigger baskets than this thing.'

Balls of fire slashed the night sky, closer to the earth than he had seen in centuries. Years ago, he would have been excited by such an ominous sight, imagining profit in every low-skimming star. But those days were long gone.

Villagers, harried by the monks, carted arm-loads of kindling to the town square where they piled the twigs and sticks near the stone well. Six men planted a large wooden stake in the ground and hoisted it upright.

Clutter rattled the cage bars. He pressed his face between them, wiggled, squirmed and got nowhere. 'Iron! Dirty humans used iron.'

'I hate iron,' Sneath said. 'Sucks up magic like a baby troll on his mama's tit.'

'Humans do love their metals.'

'Humans love anything that makes killing easier.'

'All that time and hard work building up our merchandise.' Clutter stared at their flaming cart parked in the middle of the village square, townsfolk all but dancing around it. 'And this is the only thing we have left.' He pulled the faerie amulet from his grubby, new coat.

'Why, by the Mother, are you still carting that around?' Sneath grabbed for the clay disc, but Clutter snatched it away.

Clutter shrugged. 'Reminds me of home. Remember the sound of frogs popping and crackling above the coals? The wonderful smell as they lightly charred? Their guts oozing. Legs crisping.'

'Good times, good times.' Sneath sighed. 'I don't suppose you have any blue fire hidden in that jacket of yours?'

'Used it all helping you escape that time.'

'Shame.'

'Rotten big shame.' Clutter shook the cage again. 'Wouldn't have worked in here, but we could have tossed it out. Those hovels over there would have gone up like a fire-hag's skirt on her birthday.'

'You reckon they'll let us go if we say we'll convert to their religion? A few prayers, a couple of confessions and we could be on our way. They'd be none the wiser and we'd be free.'

'Doubt it,' Clutter said. 'You think them monks really talk to a god? 'Cos a god would know if we lied.'

'You believe in the Mother Goddess, don't you? The Sky Gods?'

'To my dying breath.'

'Well, think how wicked we've been over the centuries. Not once has the Mother thundered out of the forest and tanned our hides like she ought. Not once have Danu or Bridgid come after us.'

'Not once!'

'I reckon the monks' god is the same. Sort of a set-and-forget god. Make something and move on.'

Soft footsteps came from the shadows. The goblins hugged their knees, arms wrapped around their heads in case another volley of stones rained down on them.

'Can't be monks,' Clutter whispered. 'They like to stomp around to show everyone how important they are.'

'Shhh!' Sneath prodded him.

A tall figure, cloaked in brown wool, peered from between the thatched roundhouses.

'Humans are so backward! Caging such vile creatures. And for what?' The figure was female, and from her tone, not in a good mood. 'Livestock perhaps?' She curled her lip. 'All gristle and bone, but too ugly for pets.'

'Strange accent.' Sneath shuffled to the edge of the cage.

'She looks human, but she's not,' Clutter said. 'Look at her eyes.'

'Not fae either,' Sneath added. 'At least no fae I've ever seen.'

The stranger edged along the closest house until she stood only a couple of paces from the cage. She squatted and held out a slender hand, palm down like she approached a wild dog.

'We won't bite you know,' Sneath snapped.

'It speaks!' Her eyes were bright green, the pupils golden slits.

'Well, of course I speak!' Sneath crossed his arms. 'We seem to be in a bit of a predicament. Any chance you could help us?'

'You have the most glorious eyes.' Clutter smiled like a fool.

Sneath elbowed Clutter, but that did not stop his brother grinning that gooey smile he always got when he saw a beautiful female.

'I only came to trade,' she said. 'Not upset the villagers.'

'They're already upset!' Sneath waggled a finger in the direction of the humans. 'At us!'

She turned and looked at the townsfolk bundling twigs around the bottom of the stake. 'Is that for you two?'

'Every stick, branch and leaf.' Clutter hung his head. 'Won't you please help us?'

'And ruin any chance I've got trading with these wretched peasants!' she eyed the goblins skeptically. 'What can you offer that these villagers can't?'

'Well, our business is in transition at this time,' Sneath said. 'But, I'm sure we can come to some sort of arrangement after we leave this confounded village.'

'I have this.' Clutter held up his amulet.

'What is it?' she reached for it, but Clutter did not hand it over.

'A genuine good luck talisman.' Sneath beamed. 'Made by genuine faeries.'

She snorted back a laugh. 'Doesn't seem to work very well.'

'You're here, aren't you,' Sneath said. 'No monks have chased you away from our cage.'

She glanced at the townsfolk. 'We're in the shadows. And they're blinded by firelight.'

'How lucky!' Sneath grinned. He ripped the amulet from Clutter, and traced the runes and symbols carved in the clay. 'Every line, every detail hand-etched by the twin faeries of High North.'

'Superstitious rot! I'll never get off this miserable planet.' With that, she strode towards the town square. She spoke to a group of women who shook their heads, their expressions grim.

Five smoking spears of fire lanced overhead, so low many of the townsfolk moaned, dropped to their knees and prayed.

The cloaked stranger threw up her hands. 'Praying won't help, you fools! They're meteorites – left over fragments from the comet. Imbeciles! This world is populated with imbeciles!'

A couple of men grabbed her by her arms and escorted her, cursing and shouting, to the outskirts of town.

'Stupid iron!' Clutter kicked the bars. 'Must be draining the talisman's luck.'

'Iron had nothing to do with it.' Sneath tossed the amulet to his brother and sagged against the cage. 'Never trust a beautiful female. Empty smiles the lot of them.'

A monk limped toward the goblins, his pallid face sombre, his hands clasped.

'Make the most of your last few hours,' the monk said. 'Anything you need to confess?'

'I am a little hungry,' Clutter said.

'And thirsty,' Sneath added.

'I told my brethren you'd not repent,' the monk said with a haughty sniff. 'Well, you die at dawn. That should ease your hunger and thirst.' He shook his head and limped back to the ever-growing pyre.

'I can't understand what we did so wrong,' Clutter said.

'Not running the moment we saw the flap of a cassock.'

'How long until sunrise?'

'Not long enough.'

Roaring fire streaked across the sky, closer than before. Closer than the goblins had ever seen. The townsfolk muttered and pointed at the fire rain. They glared at the goblins and hurried back to building the pyre.

Once they were all busy again, a tall, slender figure cloaked in brown wool edged through the shadows toward the cage.

'So, you've come back, have you?' Sneath crossed his arms and glowered.

'What do you mean?' the voice was deeper, though whether it was male or female was difficult to determine.

'Oh!' Sneath said. 'Thought you were that haughty woman who was here earlier. She was dressed like you. Tall, strange eyes.'

'And rude,' Clutter said. 'Very rude.'

'You've seen Vanin?'

'If Vanin is a cocky, rather nasty bit of work, then yes, we saw her,' Sneath said. 'How hard would it have been to open this cage and let us go? But no, too concerned with looking good for that lot.' He flicked a hand in the direction of the towns people. 'As if they're going to trade!'

'Curse her!' the stranger muttered.

'Yes, curse her very name!' Clutter clung to the bars and stared into the stranger's slitted gold eyes. 'Please save us! We're too young to burn like frogs on a stick.'

The stranger hesitated. 'I want to, I really do, but I can't. The risk of exposure is just too great. I'm sorry.' He went to move away, then stopped and smiled. 'I could, however send you help. A rather forceful kind of help that will serve both our purposes.' He patted the cage. 'Leave it with me. I'll see what I can chase up.'

And once again the goblins huddled in their cage, waiting to die.

The sky lightened as dawn approached.

'I never imagined dying in a fire,' Clutter said. 'Crackling, smoking. Legs and arms all crispy, eyes popped and oozing jelly.'

'Seems like you imagined it pretty good to me.'

'Well, that's what happens to frogs when we roast them.'

A whining roar filled the night, growing louder by the moment. Fire balls with great tails of smoke shot overhead, so many they were hard to count. A collective gasp went up from the townsfolk.

Silence.

An explosion thundered through the night. Another, louder, closer. The ground rumbled. Light, sun-bright and crackling with lightning burst upward in the distant hills. Rocks, dust and fire spewed skyward. The gaping townsfolk stared in silence, then screeched and wailed about the end of the world, about God's wrath upon the wicked. They hurtled toward Sneath and Clutter, shaking the cage, tearing at the lock.

'We didn't do it!' Clutter shouted. 'We were here, see! Locked in your cage.'

Dust and ash fluttered down on the village like bitter snow. Women howled and scooped up children, flocking to the monks, grasping at cassocks as the brothers ran in circles, praying, moaning and wringing their hands.

Another rumble, not as loud, not as distant.

Boom, boom, boom. Closer, louder.

A roar.

'Jesus, save me!' A man cried, dropping to his knees beside the cage.

'Could this day get any worse?' Sneath clutched Clutter and the both hugged the amulet between them.

Roar.

Boom, rumble, boom.

'You had to ask! I hate trolls!' Clutter groaned as a mountain of a beast lumbered into town. Taller than an oak, with skin of warty, bristly hide, the troll stomped on a roundhouse. He swooped a fist the size of an oxen through the townsfolk sending them flying.

'I like this one!' Sneath hunkered beside his brother and hoped with all his heart that the troll wouldn't see them in the cage. Perhaps iron was a good thing after all.

'Sleeping I was!' the troll roared. He pounded a roundhouse into the ground then booted another. Thatch, wood and stone exploded everywhere. 'Dreaming! Lovely it was! Warm and cosy! Then this skinny fellow with slitty gold eyes wakes me up. Get up, he says. Come out and enjoy the fire rain.'

Humans scattered, big ones, small ones, mean ones, cassocked ones all slipping and sliding in the mud, falling over one another, shouting and screaming for mercy.

What a moment! Never had Sneath wished ill on so many people with so much glee. The two goblins cowered in their cage, making themselves a small as possible.

Boom, rumble, crash. The cage bounced up and down as the troll neared. 'And then my lovely home got smashed to pieces by a great fiery rock! Cushions, candles and crystal ware falling around me like black snow and molten lava! I'll give him enjoy the fire rain when I catch up with him!'

A huge, mashed-clay face loomed above. Sneath managed a weak smile. Clutter whimpered.

'What have we here?' The troll picked up the cage and shook it causing the goblins to roll around inside. He peered at Sneath and Clutter with huge bloodshot eyes, so close they could have poked him in one. Not a wise idea considering they were so far from the ground.

'Nothing to see here,' Sneath bellowed, pointing. 'Plenty to smash out there.'

'Those humans called your mother a bumbling tree-humper!' Clutter shouted. 'And they laughed. Big, belly-wobbling laughs.'

'And that's hard when they're all like starving sticks!' Sneath clung on to the bars as the troll shook with rage.

'They never!' The troll's eyes narrowed.

'Smarter than I thought,' Clutter murmured to Sneath. 'Must be from High North.'

'You're just trying to save yourselves.' The troll jiggled the cage.

'Is it working?' Sneath clung to the bars so he wouldn't tumble on his head.

'We could sweeten the deal,' Clutter said. 'How would you like a genuine good luck amulet?'

'Made by the twins up north?' the troll eyed them shrewdly.

'The very same!' Sneath grinned, making sure he showed every fang.

'Show me,' the troll said. 'Or do I have to dig through that smouldering cart over there?'

'Ooh, he is smart,' Sneath muttered out of the side of his mouth.

Clutter whipped out the amulet, his hand shaking. He pointed at the runes then turned it over. 'See! Even has the twins' seal: a faerie foxglove, and all.'

'Give it here.' The troll held out his hand, the lines on his palm the size of small roads.

'Fae promise that you'll help us escape first,' Clutter said.

Both goblins crossed their arms, though Sneath's heart fluttered like a bird's.

The troll looked around the deserted village square. Well, deserted accept for the dead and dying. They'd been abandoned by the fleeing townsfolk. So much for the monks preaching about helping thy neighbour.

'I could just shake the cage until you fall out in a thousand pieces,' the troll said. 'One of them is bound to be the amulet.'

'Well, yes,' Sneath said, 'you could, but what if the amulet smashed on the ground because you thought it was a shoe, or a bone?'

'All that faerie magic gone.' Clutter wiggled his fingers. 'Vanished on the wind. Washed away by the rain.'

The troll frowned, his eyes moving left and right. 'All right, we have a deal.'

'Fae promise?' Sneath raised his chin. 'On at least four generations of your progeny.'

'Four!' the troll snarled. 'That's a bit rich. 'Two and we have an accord.'

'Done!' Both goblins thrust out their spindly hands, which the troll shook with two thick, leathery fingers.

With that settled, the troll tore off the lock and set the cage on the ground.

The goblins clambered out and stretched their backs and shoulders.

'Give the good troll our amulet, brother,' Sneath said. 'A deal is a deal.'

Clutter sighed and held up the clay disc. 'May it bring you as much joy and luck as it did me.'

Grinning, each tooth the size of door, the troll took the amulet and kissed it.

Sneath bowed. 'Well, if you don't mind, we'll be on our way before the humans sneak back home.'

'Don't worry,' the troll said. 'I'm awake now and frightfully hungry. I think I'll go a-hunting.'

'Those black-robed men appeared especially tasty,' Clutter said. 'May I suggest you start with them?'

The troll laughed and lumbered off. Boom, rumble, boom until the only sound was the splash of rain and the delightful groan of a few unhappy humans left to die in the town square.

'See?' Sneath clapped Clutter on the back. 'I always said that amulet was genuine and worth bringing along.'

Clutter shook his head. 'Let's go home, brother. There'll be lots of frogs to roast with all this rain.'

Dren, will you stop interfering? I know what I'm doing.

Like you did by encouraging the spread of this new religion? I get the feeling that's backfiring on you. Those villagers didn't exactly welcome you with open arms.

Shut up and stop following me. Fostering that faith seemed like a quick path to stability. The original messiah figure was a reasonable man. It's only his later followers who've been hard to—

Manipulate? Vanin, you've got to see reason. We can't—

We can. I can. Just stay out of my way, Dren, and I'll get these people where I need them to be. But only if you stop interfering.

530CE

ÉRIE (Ireland)

The Broom Star

Lynne Lumsden Green

The sky dominated Áine's existence. Most mornings she rose well before the sun to gather her cow and goats and milk them. She watched carefully as the stars faded in the morning, for it was her job to keep track of the seasons of planting and harvest. So, she was the first in the village to see the new star.

It was not a shooting star, or like anything else Áine had ever seen in the heavens. It looked like someone used silver twigs to make a whisk; a handful of straw tied together to sweep away the stellar dust. Had some god of the forge spattered molten metal across the sky?

How was it that something so lovely could make her skin crawl?

Her first instinct was to fall upon her face and plead for absolution. Instead, she clutched her shawl close and ran to fetch her athair. He would know what to do.

'Dai, Dai,' she called. He wasn't abed; he was getting ready to have his bite before heading out to feed the stock.

'Yes, my darling girl? What is the problem?' her father called back.

'You have to come see this,' she said.

Her father threw his plaid around his shoulders and joined her in the yard. Áine pointed to the new star.

'Have you ever seen anything like it?'

Her father grunted and, as Áine watched, his eyes widened and his lips thinned to grim line.

'No, croí milis, that I have not.'

Dawn washed the sky with lemon-coloured light until Áine and her father could no longer see the broom star. Birds filled the waking world with a tumult of noise, both sweet and raucous. The cow lowed, insisting on being milked and having her breakfast. A chorus of roosters crowed around the valley. The world seemed unchanged.

Áine turned to her father. 'What do you think it means?'

He scowled and shook his head. 'I can't tell you if it means anything – good or bad,' he said. 'But you and I are going straight to see Mac Daragh.'

*

The village head man was breaking his fast when they arrived at his steading. He lifted his brows in surprise when he opened the door to their respectful knocking.

Conn Mac Daragh wasn't a big man, but his stature around the village was sky high. He was known as the Stone Axe, because he could fell any man in a fight, be it a physical battle or an intellectual one – for he was also a great one for riddles. He was a man of the Old Religion, and a druid.

'Top of the morning to you, Peadar and Áine,' he said, wiping porridge from his moustache. 'May I ask what has brought you out visiting so early in the day?'

Peadar looked to his daughter. 'You'd best tell him, lass. It's your news.'

'This morning, I saw a new star. It was shaped like a broom or a whisk. It hung in the sky over the sunrise, halfway up the sky.' The girl kept the information simple and to the point.

'Did it move as you watched it?' asked Conn.

'No. It appeared to be stuck to the sky in the same manner as the rest of the stars.'

'Did it change shape or colour?'

'No. It was the very same colour as the rest of the stars.'

'What a good woman you are, to remember all this for me!' declared Conn, and Áine flushed with relief and pleasure. 'I've heard tell of these "broom" stars. They can be omens for good or for evil. It should be visible tonight, if my understanding is correct.'

He clasped Peadar's hand, and patted Áine's wrist. He said, 'I will come to your house in the middle of the night, and scan the heavens for this wonder. Does this meet with your approval?'

'I will see to it that a bowl of soup is waiting on the hearth,' said Peadar.

*

For the second night in a row the weather cooperated and no clouds stood between the watchers and the broom star. The star dominated the moonless sky.

Conn said, 'I see why Áine thought this star looked like a broom, but to me it looks more like a spear or an arrow. I've heard of these sorts of omens, and they never bring happiness on their tails.'

He looked down from the star to Peadar and Áine, his expression bleak.

'I feel a doom falling upon the world like a damp cloak dropping over a fire, snuffing out all warmth and light. We'll need to make a sacrifice,' said Conn. 'The gods demand it.'

'What will the gods ask of us? A calf?' asked Peadar. 'I have a fine black bull calf that would make the perfect sacrifice.'

Áine could see Conn did not want to face her father. A calf would not be enough. Only a human sacrifice could prevent a truly terrible crisis, and the gods had already identified their victim. As the first to see the comet, she was their chosen, for good or for ill.

Conn met their hopeful looks with an awkward shrug.

'I will have to consult with the runes,' he said. He didn't look happy. Indeed, he looked sick and grey.

Áine clutched her woollen shawl in trembling fingers, shaking from the chill of foreboding. She prayed to the gods the runes would contradict her own feelings of apprehension.

Above them, the star slashed through the diamond and velvet sky like a sword. Its presence was being noted the world over. In some places, people greeted it as an old friend. Most eyes watched the sweep of its tail with awe and fear.

*

Conn might be the Stone Axe, but flint filled Peadar's soul; axes were knapped from flint. Áine's death had been revealed in Conn's expression as the headman studied the night sky. Other fathers might give their daughters in sacrifice and be glad to do honour to the gods. Peadar had no intention of seeing his daughter's blood coat the altar stone.

Before the sun was up, Peadar set his cart behind his oxen. A person's wyrd would follow them and there was no escaping fate.

But Peadar was prepared to fight fate for his darling girl. Mallaidh, his wife, agreed it was the only course of action. Tears streaked her cheeks as she kissed Áine's forehead and waved her husband and daughter farewell.

While the broom-star still gilded the sky, Peadar took Áine away from the village.

Would the gods take revenge on the family for defying them?

*

Áine and her father spent weeks on the road, while the broom star grew bigger and brighter. The star seemed to follow their wanderings, always watching, judging, evaluating. They earned their living by taking work for a day or so at each village they passed through. Most villages needed extra hands as the year turned towards harvest time, and both Áine and Peadar were skilled and strong.

But, everywhere they travelled, the incidence of shooting stars rose dramatically; a shower of sparks calving from the broom star. As the year progressed, the blue of the day dimmed. The warmth from the sun dulled as if winter was determined to make an early claim to her domain. Crops faltered in the fields, and forests paled and withered from a lack of sunshine.

As crops failed through the autumn harvest, more and more itinerant workers took to the road. Work for Áine and Peadar grew scarce and they were turned away more often. However, a girl as pretty as Áine drew unwanted attention from the bachelors and widowers in each village and hamlet. The workers gossiped from village to village. Word spread.

One evening, as the sun drizzled honey-coloured light over the fields, Peadar was approached by the man who had hired them as haymakers.

'I want a word with you,' said Farmer Ó Gallchobhair, his manner brisk.

'Certainly, Fearchar,' said Peadar, grateful for opportunity to take a break. He wiped his sweaty hair out of his eyes.

Ó Gallchobhair laid a gentle hand on Peadar's shoulder, and said, 'There's a group of armed men moving through the countryside. This is the time of year when everyone should be too busy to make war or raids. It's said they are looking for a youngling. A girl they want for a blood-letting to appease some god or the other. Would you know anything about that?'

'Should I?' asked Peadar, trying to remain calm while his blood turned to ice water. He glanced to where Áine stooked the hay bundles he had tied.

'Well, this group will be passing this way in a day or so. I don't approve killing of children on a whim. It is too easy to misinterpret signs and portents,' said Ó Gallchobhair. 'You and your girl are upright people. Hard workers. I hate to see you go, but someone around here's bound to mention your daughter. Even if she isn't the lass they're seeking, it might be best if you made yourself scarce.'

Ó Gallchobhair looked apologetic and added, 'We don't want any trouble, see?'

'Thank you for warning us,' said Peadar, feeling ice form around his heart and the blood leave his face. 'We'll pack up and go tonight.'

'I thought you might. I can give you some coins, and rations to see you on your way, in the way of wages.'

Peadar clasped the man's arm. 'You've already paid us with this warning.'

'Don't think me so kind. I don't want to see these men causing trouble. The faster you are gone, the less likely they'll linger around here.'

Peadar and Áine were on the road before sunset.

*

Over the next weeks, they kept moving to stay ahead of the rumours that trailed in their wake; rumours of the girl who was meant to be a sacrifice. Not everyone would be as kind as Ó Gallchobhair.

Then they ran out of land.

Beside the grey sea, known as an mhuir mheann, was a strange building constructed especially for the worship of the Christian God. Neither a castle nor a great house, looked like a bit of both: a grey stone edifice with a tower filled with metal bells. The bells didn't go 'klonk, klonk' like a cow bell, or boom like the ocean waves, but sang with bold and musical voices. The holy men and women who lived in the monastery welcomed Áine and Peadar when they knocked at the gates and requested sanctuary.

Peadar took the abbot aside for a private word, while Áine wandered around the chapel. She had spent her life worshipping the gods of the sky, who controlled the seasons. She had heard of Odin, a god from over the sea like the Christian God. Odin, too, had hung from the branches of a tree – like this Jesus had been hung from a cross. Both were sacrifices. She found the idea of such suffering revolting. However, the cool cavern of the chapel, with its undecorated cross, was a haven of peace.

A plainly-dressed woman entered the chapel and approached Áine.

She said, 'I'm Naomh. I've been sent by the abbot. He wants me to tend to your needs. Do you hunger? Do you thirst? Do you wish to bathe or rest?'

'Oh. Please, I would like to wash the dust from my hands and face,' said Áine. 'I would also like to wash the dust from my throat.'

'The dust is everywhere these days,' replied Naomh. She smiled kindly at Áine and then said, 'Or are you speaking of the grit of the road.'

'I am covered in both sorts. It seems impossible to escape.'

'Well, I can arrange to shake the dust from your clothes – however temporarily – and slake your thirst,' said the woman. She gestured for Áine to follow.

Less than an hour later, Áine sat at a long wooden table in a dining hall, drinking a broth. Sitting across from her, Naomh gossiped about local events. It was here her father and the abbot found her. Peadar's expression twisted with concern.

'The abbot has heard many rumours about us,' said Peadar. 'Conn is convinced the clouding of the sun is our fault. He hunts us, so that you may be sacrificed to the god of the broom star.'

'Yes, indeed,' said the abbot. 'He believes the child must die before the broom star travels back to wherever it came from. Even now, it fades from our skies, and he grows desperate.' The abbot patted Áine on her shoulder. 'Fear not, child. We will protect you from this superstitious nonsense.'

Áine said, 'I appreciate your kindness, but I don't understand. Isn't your religion based on sacrifice?'

Both the abbot and Naomh laughed.

'Our God sacrificed His son, but He doesn't ask the same of those of His faith,' explained the abbot. 'It is because of that sacrifice we would keep you safe. One of His rules is that we should not kill.'

'We have no choice but to face Conn,' added her father, 'as we have nowhere else to run.'

*

Five days later, Conn, the Stone Axe, arrived at the porticos of the monastery. He beat his fist against the oaken planks. Behind him stood a small band of fellow druids and devout followers. All bore the marks of heavy travelling, but they didn't appear to be tired or in need of comfort; every one of them looked resolute.

'Peadar. Áine. We know you are hiding in there,' he shouted, as he pounded the doors. 'Come out! Do your duty by Nuada of the Silver Hand, and Brig, Mistress of the Grey Anvil, goddess of storms.'

The abbot popped his head out of a narrow window in the bell tower.

'Away with you,' he said. 'This is a sanctuary. Those you seek are now under the protection of our Lord God.'

'I do not recognise the authority of your toothless god,' said Conn. 'My people are of my faith, not yours. The sky gods chose Áine to join their ranks. It is an honour, and Áine insults them with her refusal. Even now, they punish us for not sending her to them.'

The abbot shook his head. 'You claim to speak for your gods? I know I speak for mine. His word is written down and very clear on the subject of murder. No killing is allowed, under any circumstances.'

'We have no time for this! Even now, the broom star fades from the sky. If you won't surrender the girl, we will come and take her by force. Let's see whose gods are more powerful!'

'We will not go back on our word,' said the abbot. Then he closed the shutters on his window.

Conn banged on the door a few more times, then turned to his companions. 'We have preparations to make before tonight. Come.'

Hidden in the bell tower, Áine watched – both horrified and fascinated – as the holy men built a pyre on a hilltop visible to the monastery. They piled wood and branches around a stake, man-high and sturdy. Then they spent a lengthy amount of time sharpening their weapons, filling the world with the shriek of stone on metal.

'You shouldn't watch,' said her father. 'Conn is trying to frighten you.'

'It's working,' replied Áine. 'Why should these good people fight? If I turn myself over to Conn, then I am the only person who must die. Who knows how many will perish if Conn attacks this place?'

'And what happens when your death doesn't change anything? What if your death is for naught? How many other sacrifices will be made?'

'Oh, Dai,' whimpered the girl, and tears tracked down her face. 'I'm so scared. I don't want to burn.'

Peadar put his arms around his daughter while she wept. 'There, there. It will never come to that. I'll not see you suffer that, even if the sun is to be snuffed out.' He stayed, holding her, even after she stopped crying.

*

As the sun dropped to the horizon, Conn and his companions formed a circle around the pyre and chanted. They sanctified the site to their gods as the broom star brightened and glittered above them. It still dominated the sky from sunset until the rising of the moon. Perhaps the ever-present dust obscured the broom star, but Áine thought the star was much smaller than it has been just weeks ago. It might be her doom, but she would still be sorry to see its beauty fade.

Áine let her gaze slide down from the broom star to the unlit pyre, and back again. The black silhouette of the men and pyre stood stark against the final red glow of the sunset. She could just hear the men's voices droning over the susurration of the waves.

The tenor of the voices altered as an eerie glow illuminated the sky, changing it from orange to purple. They cried out in surprise. The sky flared with an enormous swarm of shooting stars. A burning rain fell all around the chapel and over the hills.

One of the falling stars grew until it seemed to fill the whole of creation, turning it a stark black and white. There were shouts of horror, but they were quickly drowned out by a dragon's roar. The roar grew to a rumbling that rippled the earth like a woman shaking out a rug. Áine and Peadar cried out in terror.

The biggest giant in Éireann shouted and stamped on the ground, knocking father and daughter off their feet. White light bleached all colour from the world. Before Áine could regain her feet, a strong, hot wind buffeted her, a wind full of ash and the stench of burnt meat. It seemed safer to remain huddled on the floor beside her father.

*

An age passed before her ears stopped ringing and she could blink without being blinded with ash. She looked out onto a landscape smouldering with fire and sparks, with only the ocean a dark shadow. Smoke clouded the sky, reflecting the light from the fires below and hiding the broom star.

'Is it the end of the world?' she asked her father. 'Did Conn call down the star to destroy me?'

'Hush. Hush,' said Peadar. 'We're still here. But look to Conn's hilltop.'

The hill had disappeared. In its place was a depression glowing a deep, sinister red.

'It looks like his sky gods answered Conn, but not as he expected,' said Peadar.

The abbot stumbled up the tower stairs with several people climbing in his wake. His eyes were wild and his clothes disarrayed.

'What happened?' asked the abbot. 'Every stone in the building jumped! It's a blessing the tower didn't tumble.'

Peadar pointed out the tower window to the smoking crater. The abbot went white, then green, and then very red.

'Oh. I've never seen an actual judgement before,' he whispered. He collected himself and turned to his brethren and sistren, then announced, 'The Lord's Will be done.'

'Amen,' replied his people. As each managed to get a glimpse of the newly-made pit, they registered shock or satisfaction.

*

Daybreak revealed the true extent of the devastation; and a grey, grim, and dim daybreak it was. Smoke and the dust hid the sun. All the greenery around the crater was scorched, and every tree upon the hill flattened. A search for any trace of Conn and his companions turned up a few rags, a metal knife, and little else. The pit was full of a glassy-textured rock and little else. The hammer of the Christian God had obliterated them.

*

Áine and Peadar returned to their village, with a small escort of monks just in case there was lingering resentment towards the 'unlucky' girl and her family. They need not have worried. News got around fast. The village welcomed them back, and asked the monks to build a church. People wanted the protection of such a powerful deity.

Peadar donated land for the new church, with the full approval of his wife. With Conn, the Stone Axe, dead and gone, the village chose Peadar as their new head man. It was only right and good that he was among the first to convert to the new religion, with Áine at his side. By the time the church was built, and the village residents all baptised as Christians the dust from the comet's passing had settled and normal weather patterns resumed. The monks assured Peadar, Áine, and the villagers this was a sign of God's approval at their conversion.

One evening, not long after their conversion, Áine took a mug of ale to her father as he stood watching the sunset. The sky was a deep orange; an angry colour which would have once been seen as an omen.

'You're a good girl, my darling,' he said as he accepted the mug. He tucked her under his arm, and they both studied the sky. For a time, they were silent, while the first star came out.

'Dai, what are you looking at?' asked Áine, at last.

'It isn't what I'm looking at so much as what I'm looking for, my darling. I'm watching for the return of the broom star.'

Áine shuddered, thinking of the dead men on the hill. 'Why would you want to ever see that horrible thing?'

'If you remember, Conn mentioned there had been other broom stars,' said Peadar. 'Maybe it is just the same one, coming back again and again.'

'You fear its return?'

'No. Not anymore. But it was such a pretty sight. I wouldn't mind seeing it something like it.'

Áine smiled. 'Somehow, I don't believe Máthair would let you go a-roaming again.'

Her father sighed, thinking of his responsibilities.

'More's the pity,' he said. He grinned ruefully.

His daughter wasn't to be so easily distracted. 'Dai, are you worried that another broom star could sweep away our Christian god?'

Peadar took a mouthful of ale and savoured it, as he pondered the question. Áine remained silent while she waited for his answer.

'No,' he said. 'I don't think this Christian god, our new Lord, will ever be easily overcome. After all, it turned out the broom star was his weapon all along.'

837CE

Near Rouen, Neustria

A Maiden's Fate

Aiki Flinthart

I hadn't yet killed Remi, and that annoyed me. Seax raised, I glared at my twin – the pale mirror to my black rage – and slashed at him. Remi flinched and barely raised his shield in time to catch my blow. His return attack slapped on my kite shield but had no power. I sneered.

'Remi! Lift your arm and strike harder,' Hagen shouted across the courtyard. 'You fight like a maiden, not a man of sixteen summers! Put your whole body into it!'

I froze.

Remi blanched and his arm sagged. 'Fara!' he hissed. 'What do I do?' His sky-blue eyes widened into terror beneath the peaked metal helm.

'Keep your arm up,' I snapped, 'or Father'll come over and see it's me training with you. Then we'll both be beaten.' Sweat trickled down my back. Dust, kicked up from the dry, packed earth, clogged my nose and I resisted the urge to sneeze.

'But I just can't,' Remi whispered. 'My arm hurts. You hit me too hard. Why are you so *angry?*'

'Because it's not fair that I'm a girl and I can only train when Father's not around.' I smacked his shield and he cowered behind it.

Hagen growled. His heavy steps clomped towards us.

'Remi!' I growled. 'If you don't swing like you mean it, I swear I'll hit you so hard you'll be bruised for a month. Then Father will be the angry one.'

Remi whimpered and scraped a stray lock of blond hair from his face. His eyes flicked over my shoulder and back to me. His narrow jaw firmed. He lifted his arm and swung the wooden seax as hard as he could.

I raised my shield and blocked easily, but staggered to make the blow look more forceful. I kept my back to our father. I wore Remi's tunic and trews, and tied my long, blonde hair back with a leather thong. Unless Hagen saw my face, he should mistake me for one of Remi's usual training partners.

We exchanged a few more blows beneath Hagen's keen gaze before he grunted.

'Better, boy. But you'll never be as good as your older brothers unless you train more.' He continued muttering and strode into the servants' quarters.

Remi and I scurried away, behind the main longhouse, gusting huge sighs of pent-up breath as we ran. We collapsed in the shade of our favourite oak and exchanged horrified looks.

'That was close. Why is he back so soon?' Remi stared gloomily at the wood-and-thatch longhouse. 'He was supposed to be away negotiating for your marriage to Theodulf.' His eyes narrowed and he ripped at a piece of grass, tearing it to shreds between long, blue-veined fingers; a bard's hands, not a warrior's.

'Don't remind me,' I said, tossing my seax and shield aside. 'Maybe the negotiations went badly and Theo's father refused an unwilling bride.'

Remi sent me a cynical look. 'Neither of them care about that. Be as unwilling as you like. As long as there's a bride-price and our father gets Count Rollo's promise of men and arms next time the Danes or Emperor Louis's men come, you're marrying Theo.' He uttered a sound of frustration and jammed the tip of his wooden seax into the earth.

'And next time there's war, you'll go with Father to fight.' I leaned my head on the oak's rough bark and stared through brilliant green spring leaves at the turquoise sky.

Remi groaned. He twisted and lay down, pillowing his fair head on my thigh and crooking an elbow over his eyes.

'What are we going to do?' he whispered. 'It's not fair. I mean...you and Theo!' His slim shoulders shook and he bit his soft lips.

I sighed and stroked his long hair, so like my own in colour, but finer and softer. At sixteen summers neither of us were as tall and robust as our older brothers had been. We took after our mother: petite and slender; slow to develop. My breasts were barely fist-sized and Remi's shoulders were narrower than mine.

'I know,' I said. 'Not what I want, either. But what choice to we have? It's a daughter's lot to be sold off like cattle, and a third son's lot to be sent off to war.'

Remi sat up abruptly, his eyes made bluer by the reddening of tears. 'There *has* to be something we can do.' He stared in disgust at our wooden weapons. 'Father thinks I'm defective because I don't like to fight. Fighting just makes me...sick.'

'I know,' I repeated helplessly, drawing him into a hug. 'Don't work yourself up. We'll think of something.'

'What?' He shoved away, glaring. 'Father's been away a week and we still haven't thought of anything. Now he's back, which means you'll be married to Theo in a few weeks and I'll have to watch...'

'I don't know yet.' I stood and brushed off my trews and tunic. To the west, the sun hung low over the beech and oak forests behind our family estate. 'But we need to get cleaned up. Mother will call us in to supper and I can't go in looking like a boy.'

Remi rose, slapping at his buttocks. Dust floated, sparkling in a late ray of sunlight. 'They wouldn't even notice if you did – or if neither of us came in. We're just...just...things to dispose of. I'm going to die in a war I don't care about!'

'And I'll probably die in childbirth! Believe me, I'm happy to hear an alternative.' I glared at him and stalked away. Tears mingled with the dried sweat on my cheeks but I dashed the salt away.

*

'Fara!' Gisela, my mother, hurried towards me. She flicked her blonde plait back and wiped her hands on the grubby overtunic that protected her favourite, blue linen tunic-dress. 'Where have you been?' She didn't wait for an answer but frowned at me. 'You should have worn your blue gown, but there's no time now. The grey will have to do.' She checked my face, straightened the cream linen cloth I'd hastily thrown over my hair, then inspected my hands. 'What on earth do you do, child, to get such callouses on your hands?'

I yanked free, whipping the offending members behind my back. That Remi and I trained in swordfighting together was known only to Einhard, my father's thane. To begin with, I'd only done it because Remi was afraid of the men in Einhard's command; all big, rough louts who had no patience for a skinny, timid boy. But now I trained because I enjoyed the rush; the soaring, breathless joy that came with slipping past a shield and planting a well-placed blow on an unprotected body.

'Nevermind,' Gisela said, huffing. 'Go to the strongroom and get out the silver bowls and cups. We have guests.'

I gaped at her. 'Who?'

My mother simpered and squeezed my cheek. 'Your soon to be husband, daughter. Theodulf and his father, Count Rollo, are here for your handfasting. The wedding will be next month, when we've had time to make up the rest of your dowry and bride-chest.'

'Handfasting!' My knees sagged. 'Already! But I thought father was just negotiating.'

'Don't be so ungrateful!' Gisela fluttered thin hands to her pale cheeks, her eyes sparkling. 'It's such a good match! You'll be the next Countess of Rouen and everyone knows Count Rollo and Theodulf have King Pepin of Aquitaine's ear.'

'But…' I couldn't think of anything that would change the state of affairs. Nothing I said, or even my mother said, would carry any weight with Hagen or Count Rollo. I glanced towards the door. Poor Remi. He would be devastated.

'I don't want to hear any complaints. At least you're marrying someone you've known since you were a child. He's a good man.' Gisela passed over her keys and flipped a hand at me. 'Now, go get the silver. And tell Rosamund to broach a new mead cask. I understand Count Rollo has brought someone from the King's court with him!'

She bustled away, instructing one of the servants to lay fresh straw in the hall, fill the rushlights, and stoke the central hearth.

I slipped across the courtyard as the sun sank behind the oak forest, my heart heavier than the silver I collected. My mother was right, Theo was a good man; and a good friend. He was everything a maid ought to admire: handsome, a skilled warrior, the heir to a powerful man. But what my mother didn't know was that Theo's heart belonged to another. He couldn't love me, nor I, him.

I emerged from the storeroom, silver bowls and cups slipping from my arms as I tried to relock the door.

'Allow me,' a light, cheerful voice startled me and I almost dropped everything. Someone relieved me of two bowls but I clutched the rest to my breast and backed away.

Shadowed in early evening gloom, a tall figure loomed before me. I scurried towards the main hall; to light and family. The figure paced silently beside me. I paused as we came into a flickering pool of light cast by a wall-torch.

'Who are you?' I studied the man's face. He was taller than any man I'd ever seen, but slender and with long fingers and high, sharp cheekbones; his jaw bare of beard and as smooth as a woman's. But it was his eyes that mesmerised and terrified me. They were a blue so dark as to almost be black, but the pupils were gold, and vertical like a cat's.

I gasped and retreated. My fearful breaths clouded the cold night air…an insubstantial wall.

'My lady,' he said. 'Don't be afraid. I'm a guest of your father's. I'm here with the Count.'

'Oh.' The reply was barely adequate. I should have curtseyed but I couldn't look away from his eyes. 'What's wrong with your eyes,' I blurted. Heat burned in my cheeks and I muttered an apology, bobbing a belated curtsey.

He smiled. 'No apology necessary. I'm perfectly safe, I assure you. I was born this way.'

I plucked up courage and peered closer. 'And you can see? You're not blind?'

'Not at all.' He inclined his head. 'In fact, my night vision is better than most.' He plucked a teetering cup from my slack fingers. 'But we haven't been formally introduced. I'm Dren. And you must be Fara, daughter of the house?'

I curtseyed again. 'Yes, my lord.' The heat in my face blazed. 'I hope I haven't offended you. My mother complains that I can't control my tongue.'

'Not at all,' he repeated. 'I find it refreshing to speak with a woman as an equal in this day and age.'

I frowned. An odd turn of phrase. Women as equals? How was that possible? Men were stronger. It was natural for them to tend to warfare and heavy labour and the protection of the family. And only women could bear children, so how could there ever be equality?

A door slammed across the courtyard and I started, glancing over Dren's shoulder.

'What is *that?*' I pointed a shaking finger at the sky over the oak forest. A bowl slid to the dirt with a metallic thud. A handsbreadth above the trees, a fuzzy ball of light hovered in the lavender-dark sky. Two soft, glowing tails streaked across the sky behind it, pointing north. 'A sign from the gods!'

'You still believe in Woden and the old gods…?' Dren turned. He said nothing for a long time, but his lips pressed tightly together and his shoulders slumped. Then he straightened.

'What does it mean?' I whispered, shivering with more than cold as the spring dusk cooled into night.

'Fara? Where are…' Remi appeared by my side, gaping at the star. He clutched at my arm. 'Is it an omen? About us? It has two tails.' His voice rose towards hysteria. 'It must be about us.'

'Hardly.' Dren's amused comment broke the spiralling tension. 'It's just a piece of star-stuff, floating in the sky.'

I blinked at him. 'Floating in the sky? How can that be?'

He smiled thinly. 'Nevermind. Just believe me, it's not an omen. Not for you, at least.' He inspected Remi. 'And you must be young Remi, then? Theodulf has spoken much of you. He's fond of you both.'

Remi flushed, much as I had. I shoved a bowl into his hands to distract him.

'And we're fond of him, my lord,' I said. 'We should be getting inside.' With one more worried glance at the star, I retrieved the silver I'd dropped and towed Remi inside the hall.

'There you are!' Gisela hurried over and snatched the bowls and cups from us. She passed them to a servant with instructions to set the table. She fussed about with my hair again, then frowned at the amber and cowrie shell amulet I wore around my neck. She fingered it and chewed on her lip. 'Perhaps you shouldn't wear this, tonight.'

'Why?' I studied it. 'You gave it to me on my tenth birthday.'

'I know, but your father and the Count…they don't believe in the old gods as my family did. They're likely to…misinterpret this as a pagan sign. Best take it off. Wear the cross your father gave you, instead.'

I glared. 'There's no time to change it now.'

'Stubborn girl!' Gisela wrung her hands and glanced around the room. 'Very well. But take it off and tuck it into your purse.'

I was tempted to leave it on, in the hopes it would discourage the match, but there was no point. It would merely earn me a beating and achieve nothing. I removed it.

Belatedly remembering my manners, I turned to introduce Dren to my mother, but he had vanished. Remi was gone, too. Neither of them were anywhere in the hall. Gisela made a noise of frustration and stalked towards the head table, berating the servant laying the silver.

Theo entered and lifted a hand in greeting. I hurried over and dragged him back outside, into the cold-dark night.

'Why did you agree to this, Theo?' I gripped his wrist and glared up into his dark eyes.

He grimaced and shrugged one shoulder. 'You say that like I had a choice. Believe me, I tried. It was like arguing with a tree. You know my father.' Theo scraped thick fingers through his long, dark hair. 'Once he gets an idea in his head nothing short of a sign from God will shift it.'

I shivered and glanced over his shoulder at the bright, fuzzy star. 'Would he take that as a sign, do you think? Could we convince him it means we aren't supposed to marry?'

Theo raised a cynical brow. 'Nice thought, but he's already decided it means King Pepin will die and we'll go to war against Emperor Louis soon.' His mouth softened into a twisted smile. 'Besides, if I have to marry anyone, I'd rather it was you. At least you know me...who I am, I mean.' He lowered his eyes.

I relaxed my grip on his arm and sighed. 'We'll just have to make the best of it, I suppose. I'm just not sure how.'

He cocked his head at me and grinned. 'You'll think of something, Fara. You always do.'

Count Rollo's rough voice, lifted in querulous irritation, called Theo's name and we both jumped. Rollo emerged from the hall and spotted us. His annoyance segued into tolerant amusement. He wrapped his fur-collared cloak tighter against the cool spring evening and strolled over. His massive, dark shape blotted out the stars as he towered over me. I resisted the urge to shrink away and, instead, lifted my chin and straightened my back.

'Ah,' he said genially, 'there you two are.' He laid huge hands on our shoulders and my knees almost buckled. 'Come inside. Time we made this formal.' He winked at Theo. 'Then you two lovebirds can sneak away all you like. A handfasting might be a little old-fashioned, but it's as good as a wedding to me.'

Now it was my turn to blush. I followed, with dragging steps, into the feasting hall. I'd never thought of Theo as a husband or lover. The very idea made me cringe.

*

The handfasting passed in a blur. We said vows, bride-gifts were given to my parents. Theo gave me a heavy silver necklace with a circular pendant of sapphires. I gave him a seax, as was tradition. Afterward, I sat in miserable silence at the head table, picking at my food and avoiding Remi's mournful blue eyes. Theo smiled and laughed at the ribald jokes tossed around at our expense, but the smile slid away when no-one else watched. Under the table, his hand squeezed mine and I returned the pressure, grateful.

Before too long, the interminable feasting was over, and all that remained was for my father, his guests, and our thanes to drink themselves under the long tables until they snored with the dogs.

Gisela rose gracefully and signalled to me. I stood with alacrity, longing for the peace of my bed in the women's house.

Count Rollo glanced up and winked at me. He elbowed Theo and gave him a shove.

'Go on, boy. She'll make a man of you, I warrant. Get her with child so I can have a grandson before this damned war starts. Then you can fight at my side.'

Gisela pressed her lips together and shook her head at my father, but Hagen turned his back and grinned at Rollo. Beyond Rollo, Dren, who'd sat quietly throughout the boisterous festivities, caught my eye and sent me a sympathetic look. To his right, Remi hunched his shoulders and stared into his mead cup. He threw back his head and drained the liquid. It was his fourth or fifth cup, which worried me. He became a very lachrymose drunk with a tendency to tell his woes to anyone who'd listen. Hopefully Dren could handle him and keep him from annoying Rollo and Hagen.

Theo's smile turned forced and no longer reached his eyes. He rose from the table and extended a hand towards me. The thanes erupted into loud cheers and beat their knife-hilts on the wooden tables in a deafening cacophony. The dogs roaming loose in the room howled. Theo's jaw worked and his grip on my hand slackened.

I tightened mine and lifted my head.

'Don't you dare leave me here, Theo!' I hissed. 'You'll shame both of us and our families. Move. Now!'

He sent me a startled look and nodded. We walked, with heads high, towards the guest quarters where he was housed. Gisela led the way.

She paused outside the hut and stood before the door. She folded her arms and glared at Theo.

'If you hurt her, boy…' She wagged a finger and scowled up at him.

I fought the urge to giggle at the incongruous picture they made: the hulking warrior backing away in horror from my petite, unarmed mother.

'Mother, it's fine,' I said. 'Can you find other quarters for Rollo and Dren? They were to sleep here tonight but I'd rather we weren't disturbed.'

Gisela huffed. 'The amount they were drinking, I doubt they'll make it off the benches in the hall.' She sent one last glare at Theo before hugging me and hurrying away to her quarters.

Theo stood, shuffling his feet in the dirt. I rolled my eyes and thrust the door open, dragging him inside. I lit a rushlight with a taper from the fire, lowered the bar across the door and heaved a sigh of relief.

'Right.' I turned to face him and folded my arms. 'Now what?'

Theo goggled at me. 'Er…We're supposed to…' He made vague gestures with his hands and laughed uneasily. 'I mean…you know.'

'I know *that*, you fool,' I snapped. 'I mean what are we going to do about us…about this? You don't want to marry me and I don't want to be your wife. So, what are we going to do?'

'But…' He frowned at me and sank onto a stool. 'We're handfasted. The wedding's set for next month. What *can* we do?'

'I know. You're right. They've made up their minds, haven't they?' I groaned and dropped onto the bed, cradling my head into my hands. We sat in despondent silence a while, distant laughter and song reminding us of our new state.

'Er…' Theo cleared his throat and looked significantly at the bed. 'What do we do about…?'

I shot to my feet and brushed down my skirt. 'Nothing. But we can at least make it *look* like we did something.' I flung back the heavy, quilted covers. My mother's best linen sheets covered the straw mattress. She wasn't going to be happy. I pulled my dagger from its sheath at my hip, pricked the tip of my thumb and squeezed out a large drop of blood.

'What are you doing?' Theo appeared at my side.

I gave him a measuring look and smeared blood on the bottom sheet. 'Now they'll think I made a man of you, like Rollo said.' I pressed my lips together. 'At least the Count will stop pestering you.'

Theo glanced away, rubbing at the back of his neck. 'And when you...er...don't get with child?'

'It doesn't always happen straight away,' I said. He was an only child, his mother long dead. Clearly, he had no idea about women and I certainly wasn't going to educate him.

I frowned and glanced at the door. 'My only worry is how Remi is going to take the news tomorrow. Our parents will check the bed and everyone will know ten minutes after sunrise.'

Theo paled and studied his hands as they twisted the dagger at his hip. 'I'll talk to him. He'll understand.' He sent me an anxious, doubting look.

I laid a hand on his arm. 'I'm sorry, Theo. This isn't fair on any of us. I promise I'll try to think of a way out of this.'

His dark eyes met mine with a kind of hopeless despair that wrenched at my heart. 'There is no way, Fara. We all know it.' He shrugged and sat on the end of the bed. 'I intended to go to war with Remi. He won't last a day without me there.' He laughed bitterly. 'But even that won't happen. Not while I'm my father's only son and heir, and you're not with child. Ironic, huh? I'm stuck here, and...'

'And Remi will go to war without you,' I finished. 'And he'll die.' I glanced at the unmade, bloodied bed and swallowed. 'We could...try, I suppose?'

Theo gave a half-smile and shook his head. 'No use. I don't think of you that way. You're my sister. Remi's sister. I can't...'

He flung an arm around my shoulders. I leaned into his warmth, my body cold and heart weighted by worry. The sapphire necklace hung heavy around my throat; a beautiful slave-collar, tying me to my fate.

*

We awoke with the first grey light of dawn creeping under the door and someone thudding on the timber. I started. Theo's heavy arm lay around my waist. His body curled against mine. We were both still clothed. I shook him.

'Wake up, Theo. Someone's at the door.' I listened to the babble of voices. A horse whinnied in the courtyard. Who had a horse out of the stable at this hour of the morning?

Theo groaned and sat up, running a hand over his face. 'What's happening?'

I rose, straightened my dress and re-tied the cloth over my hair. 'It sounds like a messenger. To reach us at this hour he must have ridden through the night.'

Theo shot to his feet. 'The Danes?'

I nodded. 'Or the Emperor's army.'

*

'Silence!' Rollo thudded the hilt of his dagger on the tabletop in the great hall. Every seat was occupied and dozens more thanes stood along the walls. Every man was kitted for war, with sword, shield, dagger and lamellar armour.

I huddled along the wall behind the head table, with my mother, my eldest brother's wife and babe, and some of the thane's wives who'd come to hear the news. Gisela and I clung to each other. She hadn't even asked me about Theo, so great was her worry for her sons. Both of my older brothers stood by Hagen's side; tall, strong, raven-haired and bearing arms.

At the end of the table, Remi stood slightly apart, trembling, small and forlorn in his oversized armour. He hadn't acknowledged my greeting when we met in the hall and wouldn't even speak to Theo.

'Silence,' Rollo repeated. The arguments died away and the Count raised his cup. 'It is war, men. The messenger brought news from court. King Pepin is dead. The Emperor has announced he's giving the crown of Aquitaine to his own younger son, Charles, instead of to King Pepin's eldest boy. So, our boy-king needs every man that can be spared to march against Charles and Emperor Louis's armies.'

Hagen rose and nodded gravely to his men. 'I expect every man and boy over fifteen summers to join us. But if you're an only child with no heir or kin to work your land, you have leave to stay.' He gestured to his right. 'All of my sons will join me in the battle.'

'No!' 'No!' Theo and I spoke together.

Gisela grabbed at my arm and hushed me urgently. Hagen glared.

Count Rollo raised supercilious brows at me and laid a hand on Theo's shoulder. 'Don't fear, girl, your promised husband stays. There's no other...yet...to succeed him.'

My cheeks burned and I glanced at Remi.

'Father...' Theo sent first Remi, then me, an agonised look.

Rollo ignored him. 'Men, we leave tomorrow. Today, though...' His mouth twitched into a knowing smile. He nodded to Hagen. 'Today we celebrate!'

My mother gasped and squeezed my arm, her eyes glittering.

The Count continued. 'We've decided to hasten the wedding of our beloved children to unite our houses in this time of need. They'll be married today. This union will strengthen both houses and we will march with the king as one force! To Theodulf and Fara!' He raised his cup high and drained it. The thanes, my brothers and father did the same.

I gasped, my knees crumbling. Gisela held me up, her fingers gripping my arm so tightly my hand turned white.

Theo hastened to Remi's side and spoke urgently to him in an undertone. Remi hunched a shoulder, his face pallid and eyes huge. He shoved Theo aside. Tears coursed down Remi's thin cheeks. Theo called his name. Remi held up a hand, palm out and ran from the room, leaving Theo staring after him. I edged away from my mother and snuck out of the hall. Hagen spoke my name in angry tones. I ignored him. He could beat me all he liked, later.

'Remi!' I ran after my brother as he bolted between the buildings and headed for our oak. I caught him there, breathless, both of us crying. I grabbed his arm. He broke free and pushed me away with a cry of anger.

'Get away from me! Leave me alone.' He sank to the ground and buried his head in his arms, knees pulled up to his chest.

I dropped down beside him, bereft of words and ideas for once in my life. I wanted to reassure him; to tell him he wouldn't have to go. But I couldn't. He would leave tomorrow and I'd never see him again. My twin. My best friend. My other half. I would stay and be wife to a man who couldn't love me but as a sister. There was nothing I could do about any of it. My chest ached and my throat closed.

Clouds closed in and soft rain pattered on the leaves overhead, dripping through onto my head. We sat, unmoving, unspeaking, until the sobs wracking Remi's thin body faded to shivers and the weight around my heart crushed hope.

A footfall scuffed on the bare earth beneath the broad tree. I laid a hand on my dagger and sprang to my feet, ready to defend Remi, to fight anyone who tried to drag him from my side.

Dren raised empty hands. 'Relax, child. I'm here to help.'

I sagged against the tree trunk and laid a hand on Remi's bent head. 'How? There's no way out. I'm to marry Theodulf. Remi will go to war. That's been the fate of women and men forever. We can't change that.'

Dren shook his head. 'Where I come from, people get to choose their destiny. It's not forced upon them because of their sex.'

Remi lifted his head, staring intently at the stranger. 'You said something like that last night, when we spoke before the feast. What do you mean?'

Dren stretched out a hand and drew Remi to his feet. He stood the two of us, shoulder-to-shoulder and stepped back two paces. He looked us up and down, then nodded.

'What would you do to save your brother and get out of this marriage?' He peered into my face.

I studied Remi's drawn, miserable expression and swallowed. 'Anything, my lord.'

Approaching again, Dren took my hands and inspected them.

'You train with the sword and bow, I understand?' He quirked a grin when I hesitated. 'Remi told me last night – after several cups of good mead. Who's the better warrior?'

Remi shrugged one shoulder. 'Fara, by a long way. She could probably beat our brothers if she got the chance.'

Dren nodded. 'And do you love Theodulf?'

I grimaced. 'He's like a brother—'

'I didn't mean you, my dear girl,' Dren interrupted me. 'Remi? Do you love Theodulf?'

The blood drained from Remi's face. He shrank behind me, his eyes darting towards the great house. I laid a hand on my dagger again and interposed myself between my brother and this gold-eyed stranger who saw too much.

With a gentle smile, Dren shook his head again. 'Don't fear me, boy. As I said: my people don't segregate the sexes as yours do. All our people are equal; able to choose their own destiny; choose who they love.'

'I don't understand, my lord,' I said. 'How does loving Theo help us? Remi would be stoned if our father found out. Better he goes to war. At least that would be an honourable death,' I said bitterly.

'There's no such thing as an honourable death, child,' Dren said, his expression unutterably weary. 'There's just death.' His lips stretched in a thin smile. 'And there may come a time when you welcome it. But not right now. You both have much to live for.'

'I—'

He held up a hand. 'Just think hard about what you really want. Who you really are. Both of you. When you work that out, you'll know what to do next.' He waved towards the longhouse. 'There's no need to sacrifice anyone's happiness.'

There was a long silence. Remi and I exchanged bemused looks. Dren's mouth quirked in a lopsided smile. He bowed, turned away and disappeared into the great house.

'I don't understand,' Remi said. 'What did he mean?'

I stared after Dren and a smile pulled at my mouth for the first time in two days. I studied my hands, calloused and strong, then Remi's delicate face, so like my own. I stroked the sapphire pendant at my throat and looked again at the house. I'd expected to spend my whole life there, or somewhere just like it, raising children I didn't want to a man I didn't care for.

'I think I know what to do,' I whispered, hardly daring to voice the words, so preposterous were they.

'What?' Remi said.

'You do love, Theo, don't you?' I rounded on him.

'Of course!'

'And do you trust me?' I gripped my brother's shoulders and forced him to look me in the eye.

He nodded, but reluctance shadowed his gaze.

'Then believe me, brother, nothing happened between Theo and I last night.' I showed him my pricked thumb.

Remi's face lit up. 'You didn't…?'

I shook my head. 'I'm a maid, still. That star was an omen for us after all. Our fates are tied, but mine's not to be some man's chattel.' I tugged the necklace over my head.

'But the wedding!'

'Theo loves you, Remi. And we're about to fix this unholy mess so we both get what we want. Give me your shirt and trews.'

I clasped the sapphire bride-gift around Remi's white throat.

Vanin, please? Can't you see what you're doing? The endless wars...you're killing these people.

War drives invention and economies, Dren. You know that. War is the fastest way to bring about new technology.

No! These people deserve better than what we did to our world.

These people are nothing, Dren. It's our people who matter. Back off. There's an ambitious bastard son in Normandy who will serve my purposes excellently.

Him! No, Vanin. I'm working with someone in England. He's close to inventing flight.

Another lover? You disgust me.

Just give me time. An invasion now will disrupt everything.

You've had ample time, Dren.

1066CE

Malmsbury, England

Flight

Aiki Flinthart

'I flew once, Brother Wulfsine. Like a bird. Did I tell you?'

'Yes, Brother Eilmer,' Wulf replied. 'You did tell me. Yesterday, and the day before, and the day before that.' He knew little else about Eilmer, save that the old monk spent most of his days in this gloomy space, a converted storeroom in the west range's ground floor. Wulf tucked the rough blanket around the old man's useless legs then dragged his chair towards the door so he could watch the garden.

Eilmer scratched at his tonsured hair and ignored Wulf, as he always did. 'I'll never forget. Tried to fly from the Danes when they invaded the village. Year of our Lord, 1010. Built myself wings from wood and vellum. Climbed up in the scriptorium tower and flew off, into the sky.' He raised a parchment hand and soared it through the dank air of his cell. 'Like Daedalus. No.' His shoulders slumped. 'More like Icarus.'

'Yes, Brother,' Wulf said again. 'Your wings failed. You fell and broke both your legs. I know.'

The straw in the bed reeked of mould and urine so Wulf yanked the old mattress off and hurled it out the door, into the cloister walkway. He gagged and coughed at the stench. Hopefully Brother Kenway's illness would pass and he could return to care for the old invalid soon.

'No!' Eilmer's bushy white brows twitched together. His hand curled into a fist and smacked his chest. Dust rose from his black robe. 'My wings didn't fail. *I* failed.' Tears shimmered on his lower lids and he glared up at the heavy timber ceiling. 'I fell because I forgot to make a tail. Abbot Aelfric wouldn't let me try again.'

His gaze slid to the open door, where a sliver of spring-clear blue sky was visible past the cloister's arches and columns. One tear slipped down his creased cheek.

'No,' he whispered, 'that's not true. I fell because I lost faith in myself. I was free again and, as much as I wanted it, that frightened me. So, I hid here.'

Wulf paused. 'What do you mean, Brother? Didn't you choose to come to the abbey, either? Weren't you Called to God's service?'

'Called?' Eilmer turned sky-pale, red-rimmed eyes Wulf's way, scorn curling his thin lips. 'I was no more than six when I came here. What about you? A boy of fourteen summers knows little more than lust. Don't tell me you felt the Call?'

'No. I'd give anything to go home.' Wulf snapped his teeth shut and snatched up the broom, turning his back. Blurting out his desire to go home was stupid and pointless. If Eilmer spoke to the Abbot another punishment would follow. Wulf busied himself sweeping straw dust off the bed frame and cast about for a way to distract the old monk from asking questions.

'So why did you join the Order? And why stay?' He dragged in the new mattress and wrestled it onto the wooden pallet, rearranging blanket and pillow.

'My parents were dead. My village destroyed by the northmen. I…had nowhere else to go,' Eilmer said, his words fading into a sigh. 'Now…it's too late. I wasted my one chance at freedom and it won't come again. And when the Danes return – which they will – I'll have no way…' His jaw muscles worked and he covered his eyes briefly.

'It's been over fifty years, brother. I'm sure the northmen won't be back.' Wulf punched the pillow into place. 'I'm here because my oh-so-noble parents had no lands to give to a third son and my mother couldn't bear the disgrace of letting me do what I wanted,' he blurted. Even he was shocked at the depth of bitterness in the words. He'd prayed for humility, as the Abbott instructed, for months. Yet anger still burned a sullen torch in his stomach.

Wulf turned his back on the old man to hide the hot shame in his cheeks. His foot kicked something that clattered across the rush-strewn floor. He picked it up.

'What've you got there, boy? Give it here!'

Golden afternoon light drifted through the door on dust motes and illuminated the tiny object nestled in my palm. An exquisite carving of an eagle in full flight. No, a man with the body and wings of an eagle. Carved of a piece of oak, each feather was picked out in perfect detail, even the flight pinions, ruffled by wind; each fluttering strand of hair on the head visible; each knotted muscle smooth.

The man's face was alight with the ecstasy of one communing with God, his feathered arms outstretched like Jesus on the Cross. The oak's grain mimicked an eagle's natural colouring. Wulf half-expected the creature to flip back its wings and dig claws into his finger.

'It's beautiful,' he breathed.

'Give it here, I said!' Eilmer held out an imperious hand, grabbing at air.

Wulf blinked at him. 'But it's against the Rule to have personal possessions. I should give it to the Abbot.'

Eilmer flung the blanket aside and shoved up from his chair. He took two hasty, limping steps and snatched the figurine from Wulf's lax hand.

'It's a miracle!' Wulf whispered and crossed himself. 'You can walk again. Praise be!'

Eilmer's lean fingers caressed the grotesque. He grimaced. 'Don't be ridiculous, boy. I've always been able to walk. I just got tired of all the praying and kneeling, so I pretended I couldn't.'

Wulf gasped. 'You've been missing out on the masses, the charter readings, prayers…everything! How long?'

With an impatient shrug Eilmer tucked the little carving into his belt-pouch and peeked out the door.

'Twenty years or so.' He glared. 'I forbid you to tell anyone.'

'But, the Abbot! You must obey the Abbot.' Wulf struggled to find the words and fell back on rote. 'The Book says: *Have confidence in your leaders and submit to their authority—*'

'Oh, don't quote *Hebrews* at me, boy,' Eilmer snapped, sitting back down and flipping the blanket over his legs. 'I've been reading the Bible for seventy years. For every quote you have, I can find a contradictory one. How about Romans 12:2: *And do not be conformed to this world, but be transformed by the renewing of your mind.*' He tapped his temple with one gnarled finger. 'If God didn't wish us to think for ourselves, why did He give us a brain?'

Wulf glanced out the door and wrung his fingers together. If someone came past and heard him talking like this...His stomach growled at the thought of being put again on bread and water for two days.

A footfall scuffed outside and Brother Cuthbert loomed in the doorway. 'You done in there, Brother Wulfsine?' His dark eyes darted around the room, his lip curling.

Wulf flinched and bowed his head, hating his cowardice. 'Almost, Brother Cuthbert,' he whispered, glancing at Eilmer. The old monk's head lolled to one side, white hair mussed, eyes half-closed, a string of drool sliding from one corner of his mouth. 'Brother Eilmer just—'

'Brother Eilmer,' Cuthbert sneered, 'is a dribbling old fool who dreams of nothing but his birds and his regrets. Wipe his arse and move yours. You're to clean out the reredorter after Vespers.'

Bile rose in Wulf's throat. He'd cleaned the toilets yesterday. Today was rostered to someone else. Cuthbert's sly smile challenged him to argue. Wulf held his tongue and hunched a shoulder.

Cuthbert laughed, showing broken, blackened teeth. 'I can always come and...motivate you again.' He rubbed a hand down his inner thigh and his grin turned to a leer.

Wulf said nothing, face flaming. Cuthbert left with a chuckle.

He paused and turned back. 'I forgot.' He withdrew from his robe a folded parchment, sealed with a lump of red wax.

Wulf's heart leapt. His father's seal!

Cuthbert's grin widened. 'You know the Rule. No letters from family or friends. Your parents didn't want you. Be grateful God does.' He tore the letter into tiny pieces and crushed them in his hand.

Wulf clenched his fists, shaking in an effort not to fly at him. Cuthbert was twice Wulf's age, a full head taller and with fists of lead. He laughed again and strolled away. Bits of parchment fluttered to the ground like plucked feathers.

With a wordless cry, Wulf stalked twice about the room, tears tracking his cheeks.

Eilmer's chair creaked and Wulf spun, glaring, waiting for some wise, monkish advice to spill so he could throw it back in Eilmer's face.

'So, you can read?' Eilmer wiped off the drool and patted his hair into place.

'Yes,' Wulf said, taken aback. 'Latin and Greek. Brother Godric, our tutor at...home...' The word gathered grief and anger into a ball that lodged in his throat. 'Brother Godric taught me.'

Eilmer's mouth twisted into a wry smile. 'Read any books from the library's restricted section?'

'Er...no?'

Eilmer was silent for a moment, staring at the door, then said gruffly, 'Well, meet me up in the library tonight after you've sung Compline and the dormitory roll-call is done. I have something to show you.'

'You want me to sneak out of the dormitory to see a book?' Wulf's heart pounded.

'You look pale, boy. Afraid?' Eilmer's eyes narrowed.

Wulf hunched his shoulders. 'Five months ago, I snuck out and tried to run home. Brother Cuthbert caught me. The Abbot ordered me to silence for a week and bread-and-water for two days. Cuthbert locked me in the cells beneath the east range for three days. He...' He couldn't bring himself to tell. 'Now he watches me like a hawk and reports every mistake to the Abbot.'

'I wondered why Cuthbert made you his latest chew-toy. And he gave you that black eye you're sporting?'

'I was late for Matins.' Wulf touched the bruise.

'Don't worry.' Eilmer broke into a yellow-toothed grin. 'We won't get caught. And it'll give you something apart from home and Cuthbert to think about.'

The lure of reading something other than the Bible, or the chapters, warred with fear of incurring the Abbot's displeasure again.

Eilmer grasped Wulf's hand and squeezed it. 'Don't fret, boy. I won't let them hurt you, I promise.'

The bell rang for Vespers, its deep tones reverberating through the cold stone walls. Wulf gritted his teeth, hating the noise for the first time since he'd resigned himself to this life, five months before. The soft, obedient shuffle of feet rustled in the cloister walk outside.

'Go,' Eilmer said. 'Meet me in the library if you've still got any life burning in your belly. Wait.' His call stopped Wulf as he reached the door. 'What did you want to be, boy? What was your mother so ashamed of?'

Wulf kicked at the patterned brick floor, cheeks burning again. 'A falconer. I like birds.'

'Get along, boy.' Eilmer uttered a crack of laughter. 'You'll do.'

*

Wulf fled to the chapel to take his place in the choir. But his thoughts were on the evening ahead and his concentration faltered. With his voice yet unbroken, every mistake lilted Heavenward in the cathedral's vaulted space. Cuthbert smirked at him and Father Beorhtric, the Abbot, scowled twice in the psalms before Wulf forced himself to focus.

The few hours between Vespers and Compline passed in a blur and Wulf hurried through his duties in the reredorter and gardens. After Compline was sung, and his meal eaten, he lay in bed and stared into darkness, listening to the snores and rustlings of his dormitory mates. His eyelids drooped and the soft warmth of bed appealed more than the library's cold stone floor, or the ache in his stomach and body should he be caught and left again to Cuthbert's mercy.

But curiosity won and he slipped from under the covers. Shivering in the cool spring evening, he tiptoed between the beds and eased out of the dormitory. Stars bathed the cloister and garden in fey silvery light, brighter than usual.

The abbey lay dark and silent, save for one lantern, burning in the Abbot's study. Wulf froze as the Abbot's silhouette passed twice before the leaded-glass window. The golden glow snuffed out and only the night's frosted glimmers lit the path.

Wulf stole up the night stairs, trailing his hand along the stone wall as a guide in the darkness. At the top of the stairs, the door to the scriptorium and library stood ajar. He held his breath. The room was locked each night. Only Brother Halig, the librarian, and Father Beorhtric had keys.

Poised to flee, his heart thumping in his ears, Wulf pressed two fingertips to the wood and pushed. The door swung silently open but the library was quiet. He crept in.

'Ah. You've come, have you?' Eilmer's voice whispered. 'You source of tears to many mothers, you evil. I hate you! It's long since I saw you; but now you are more terrible, for you brandish the downfall of my country. But what more can you take from me?'

Wulf gasped and backed away. Eilmer stepped into the misshapen rectangle of white light pouring through the open west window. His gaze was fixed on something outside. Wulf glanced out the window and froze, gaping.

'What is it?' he whispered. Low above the western horizon, hung a ball of light four times the size of any star. Not the moon, yet to rise in the east. Three hazy streaks of light harnessed the star, tethering it to the sky like the reins of a celestial chariot. He crossed himself and muttered a prayer.

'An ill-omen,' Eilmer said, his voice low and harsh. 'One I'd hoped never to see again. Prayer won't help you, boy. Nothing will.'

'When did you see it before?' Wulf couldn't look away, fascinated by the way the light balanced in the night sky, motionless. Where had it come from?

'Many years ago. Nine-eighty-nine, when I was a boy of six. It boded ill then and it does, now.'

'But what does it portend, Brother? What happened last time?'

Eilmer turned a bleak look on Wulf, his face ghost-lit by the star. 'The Danes raided Malmesbury. My father died, trying to save me. They took my mother as a slave and left me to die. One of the brothers found me, half-dead, in the stream below the abbey. That's how I came to be in this place.' He limped towards the library's far end.

Wulf followed. After hearing Elmer's tale, the ache to see his father grew again in his heart and he frowned to hold back tears.

'So, what do you think this visitation means, Brother Eilmer?' he persisted. 'Is it a sign from God?'

'It means the Danes will come again,' Eilmer said. 'We need to be prepared. They sacked the Abbey in December 1010 and half our brothers died. I tried to fly away, but almost died. This time I won't be caught. The Abbot won't stop me. Look here.'

He unshielded two tallow candles on the study-table. Laid out on the oaken tabletop, was a book Wulf had never seen before. Eilmer turned a crackling page and a superb drawing of a man with outstretched arms and gilded wings shimmered in the candlelight. The man's face bore the same expression of ecstasy as Eilmer's carved figurine. Behind him, a second winged figure soared, silhouetted against the sun's brilliant yellow disc.

Eilmer pointed at the writing. 'Read. It's the story of Daedalus and Icarus.' He leaned close. 'Then, once you understand, you can help me. I can't do this alone and I'm running out of time. I know that, now.' He glanced over his shoulder at the window.

Obedient, Wulf read the story. Immersed in the trials of Daedalus and his son, he barely noticed Eilmer moving about the library, muttering to himself. As Icarus plunged into the sea and Daedalus bewailed the loss of his son, a tear dropped from Wulf's cheek to the page and blistered the parchment. He wiped it away. The old man bent over the desk and smiled.

'Will you help me, boy? When the Danes come, we'll be free. You can return to your father.'

Wulf traced the gleaming figure of Daedalus, curled around his grief, mourning his son. What had Father written in that letter Cuthbert tore up – a plea for return?

'Yes,' he whispered.

'Excellent!' Eilmer rubbed his hands together. 'I'll make you a list of what we need. You can move about more freely than I. Timber, vellum, feathers, glue, twine.'

'Where will we store everything, Brother?' The Abbot subjected the dormitory to regular bed inspections to root out any hidden personal items.

Eilmer's grin widened. 'Beorhtric gave up inspecting my room when I pretended incontinence and pissed on him. Everything will fit under my bed. Never fear, boy. You just come to my room each night after Compline. We can work until Matins. Time enough for sleep after.'

'Oh,' Wulf said. How was he supposed to function on a couple of hours between then and Prime, at dawn?

'Come, boy. Almost time for Matins, now. Get to the chapel. I'll have the list for you in the morning. We'll start tomorrow night.' Eilmer snuffed out the candles and limped to the window, staring out into the night.

Wulf slipped downstairs and regained his bed moments before the bell rang and his pious companions rose for Matins. He joined them, but his mind dwelt with the old man in the library. Was Eilmer mad? Was it insane to help him?

*

In the morning, as Wulf yawned through Prime, Brother Cuthbert's malicious eyes watched closely. During the discussion of house business, Wulf held his breath, awaiting denouncement by Cuthbert for the trip to the library, or punishment for mistakes in choir. Neither came, but fluttering disquiet still twisted Wulf's stomach into knots. After high mass and dinner at noon he arrived at Brother Eilmer's room, breathless from running the long way around the west range to avoid Cuthbert's searching gaze.

'Here, boy.' Eilmer wasted no time, but pressed a scrap of parchment and a silver coin into his hand. 'Go to Brother Iuwine, the chamberlain. Tell him: Proverbs 18:21

Wulf searched his memory. *'Life and death are in the power of the tongue.'*

'Very good, boy,' Eilmer beamed. 'Tell him I need these and if he wants my continued silence on that other matter, he'll provide them without question. Tell him I'll consider all debts paid and everything forgotten.'

The coin and list weighed heavy in Wulf's hand. Where had Eilmer got the money? What had the bluff and hearty Brother Iuwine done to put himself into Eilmer's power? A cool warning in Eilmer's blue eyes stopped the questions cold.

'Good lad. Go.' Eilmer smiled. 'When we meet in the library tonight, I'll show you some of the other Greek myths.' His eyes softened. 'The world's a wondrous place, boy. Let's discover it together, shall we?'

*

It took several weeks to gather all the supplies, for Brother Iuwine couldn't buy everything at once without alerting the Abbot to the extra expense. While waiting, Eilmer tutored Wulf using ever more exotic texts: Greek, Roman, even Persian and Moorish.

In the second week, Eilmer vanished for half an hour and emerged, dusty and triumphant, from a back room. He handed over a gilded tome that made Wulf gasp in delight: a book on falconry written by the royal falconer to King Aethelred. Eilmer chuckled and waved aside Wulf's stammering thanks and left Wulf to pour over the drawings and soak up the lore.

With each passing day, as Wulf's admiration for the old man grew, so did his fear. When he woke every morning, his heart sank and knotted his stomach. But his fear was no longer for being caught. Discovery was inevitable and he'd resigned himself to punishment.

There was no way to hide Eilmer's contraptions forever.

Wulf's fear now was for the monk, himself.

An ephemeral flame of excitement burned, incandescent, in the old man; spurring him to action, causing him to stutter as he explained his drawings of the wings. Long after the strange hairy star had vanished from the night sky, the light in Eilmer continued. It intensified as the sultry months of summer passed and he became more convinced of the need for haste.

But it was only a matter of time before the sharp-eyed Cuthbert discovered the equipment and destroyed it. Losing the wings would kill the old man this time.

*

'Autumn's here. The northmen are coming. Soon. I can feel it.' Eilmer gazed out the window to where the half-moon bathed the landscape in feeble silvery light. 'We need to test the wings, boy, and we can't do that at night.' He thumped a fist on the library table.

A book clattered from the shelves and Wulf gasped, looking towards the door.

'Oh, stop,' Eilmer said. 'We've been sneaking around for months and no-one's the wiser. Especially since you stopped yawning your head off all day. The wings are finished. We need a way to test them.' He laid a hand on Wulf's head and ruffled his hair. 'Then we can get out of here. Somewhere safe.'

'Yes, Brother,' Wulf said. He swallowed down a rush of fear and excitement, forcing himself to consider practicalities. The wings had been nothing but theory and plans for so long he half-believed they'd never be ready. Now reality intruded and all the potential problems reared their hydra-heads. 'But how can we test the wings during the day?'

Eilmer scratched at his tonsure and frowned. 'High Mass, I think. You go as usual. And when everyone's at prayer, I'll come up here.' He pointed at a low door in one corner of the library. 'I know where Brother Halig keeps the key to the roof parapet. I'll have time to test it and return before High Mass and dinner are finished.'

'But someone will see you, Brother!' Wulf waved a hand at the window. 'Malmesbury's at the base of the hill.'

'Pfah!' Eilmer dismissed the village with a flick of his fingers. 'Unlettered rustics. No-one will believe them and I'll be back in my room pretending to be a mindless fool before they can report to the Abbot.'

'Well, then…how can you be sure the wings are safe this time?' Wulf studied the hide-wrapped timber frames and the thousands of goose-feathers stitched in neat lines. His fingers still ached from needlework. 'They look so…flimsy.'

'Because I know they're safe,' Eilmer replied.

Wulf studied him dubiously from beneath his lashes, but held his tongue. Eilmer chuckled.

'You look like a terrified rabbit, Wulf. There are worse things than bread-and-water and Cuthbert's…attentions.'

'Like?'

Amusement fell away and Eilmer's face sagged. Shadows darkened beneath his eyes. 'Letting fear stop you from living.'

The bell tolled for Matins and Wulf jumped from his seat. 'I have to go!'

Eilmer nodded. 'I'll tidy up.'

Wulf stumbled down the dark stairs and skidded to a halt at the base, pressing himself against the stone wall as he tried to breathe quietly. His dorm-mates stumbled and trudged towards the church, tugging their robes straight and scrubbing at their eyes. As the last man passed, Wulf flipped his hood up and slipped into line. The man in front glanced over his shoulder. Cuthbert. His eyes narrowed and he flicked a look at the night-stairs. Wulf's heart stuttered.

After Matins and Lauds, he tossed in his bed, unable to sleep for the unanswerable questions roiling in his head. Had Cuthbert seen? Would Eilmer crash again? He was eighty-three years old! Madness for him to attempt such a feat. But Wulf couldn't miss any masses and the abbey grounds were full of people in between times. The moon wasn't full, so the wings couldn't be tested at night. There wasn't enough wind, anyway. Was he going to be responsible for Eilmer's death? Should he tell the Abbot?

*

Morning brought no relief and he struggled through the rituals and masses with his mind elsewhere. Eilmer was asleep when Wulf brought breakfast so he left it and hurried away to his duties, still uncertain.

As he sat in the back of the chapter house, waiting for Father Beorhtric to begin the discussion of house business, he glanced out the door. The sun crept higher. Every minute brought High Mass closer; Eilmer's death closer. Wulf chewed on his lip. He couldn't let Eilmer die. The old man meant too much. This was madness.

Father Beorhtric called for anyone with issues, grievances or maintenance problems to stand and report.

Wulf began to rise.

'I regret, Father...' Cuthbert's ingratiating voice intruded on the silence. 'That someone has been using the library after hours. Reading books from the restricted section.' Whispers washed around the room. He raised his voice. 'And the chamberlain's inventory shows missing items. Someone has stolen from us, brothers.'

Wulf froze, twisting his robe in his fingers.

The Abbot rose from his chair and waved the men to silence. 'These are grave accusations, Brother Cuthbert. What does the chamberlain say? Brother Iuwine?'

Iuwine stood, shifting uneasily, his jowly cheeks beet-red. He cleared his throat and cast a furious look at Cuthbert. 'It does appear, Father, that there are some…discrepancies. I'll investigate. It could be a mistake.'

Cuthbert puffed his chest out. 'Father Beorhtric, we can't waste time. If there's a thief we must search thoroughly before the goods can be disposed of in the village.'

The Abbot stroked his chin. 'Perhaps you're right, brother. Instigate a search. We'll find the culprit now, if there is a thief.'

'*Every* room, Father?' The sly look Cuthbert shot Wulf stopped his heart.

Cuthbert knew. He would search Eilmer's room and expose the old man's secret. Eilmer would be punished, his precious wings destroyed. With his dream of freedom crushed, his frail body couldn't withstand the rigors of bread-and water, or the damp cell beneath the east range.

'I did it, Father.' Wulf stood. His voice broke as he repeated the words into a stunned silence. 'I stole from the stores and I read the restricted books. I…I sold the goods back into the village so I could…pay someone to carry letters to my parents.'

A smirk flashed across Cuthbert's lips.

Beorhtric sighed and sank back into his seat. 'I'm sorry to hear that, Brother Wulfsine. I hoped you'd left the world behind and accepted God at last. Your punishment will begin immediately. A week in the solitary cell, bread-and-water for two weeks and silence for a month. You will come to me daily for prayer and further instruction. Brother—'

The side door crashed open and a village boy staggered into the chapter house, breathless and red-faced.

'My lord Abbot! I'm sorry, but there's a message from the Earl.' He waved a red-sealed paper but stayed at the door, his eyes darting around the room.

'Take it to my office, boy,' the Abbot snapped. 'Don't interrupt your betters.'

'But my lord said you must know now: Harald Hardrada of Norway has landed men in Northumbria. They march south to put Tostig Godwinson on the throne of England. And William the Bastard of Normandy has landed in Hastings. He claims the throne, too.' The boy paused, staring wide-eyed at the Abbot. 'We're at war, Father.'

The room erupted in shouts. Cries of fear echoed to the rafters. All the brothers sprang to their feet, arguing and waving their hands. Wulf edged towards the door. Eilmer needed to know. He was right: the star had foretold the coming of disaster for the king and the coming of the northmen.

'Brothers!' The Abbot's voice rang out over the babble.

Wulf bolted, for even two invasions wouldn't stop Cuthbert from meting out punishment. He reached Eilmer's cell and flung open the door.

'What ails you, boy? You're as white as death.' Eilmer sat up in bed and frowned. 'What time is it?'

'Not yet time for High Mass, brother. But there's news from London you must know.' He stammered out the message. 'You were right. The omen was right. The northmen are coming.'

'There you are you hedge-born levereter!' Cuthbert's meaty fingers wrapped around his upper arm. 'If the northmen sack the Abbey, they'll find you in the cell where you belong.'

'Brother Cuthbert!' Eilmer's call stopped Cuthbert, who turned an astonished gaze on the old man.

'What do you want, you old ceorl? This has nothing to do with you.' Cuthbert cocked his head. 'Or does it? Perhaps it's you should go to the cells?'

'What are you talking about, sirrah? What's this boy accused of?' Eilmer pulled his shoulders back and stared down his nose at Cuthbert.

'Stealing the Abbot's property and breaking into the library. Admitted it before everyone.'

Eilmer paled, his eyes fixed on Wulf. 'He admitted it! But I—'

'No!' Wulf scowled and shook his head. 'I know I've disappointed you, brother. I'm sorry. But it was important. I wanted to let my parents know…' He sucked a deep breath and willed him to understand. 'To know they were right: it's better to live your life and be free than waste it in regret. I regret nothing.'

The old monk was silent. He passed a shaking hand over his face and nodded slowly.

'You'll regret this, Brother Wulfsine.' Cuthbert giggled. His fingers tightened until the blood stopped flowing and Wulf's arm grew numb.

Eilmer opened his mouth again but Wulf sent him another fierce look. Cuthbert hauled and Wulf went, unresisting, head high. But the conviction upholding him melted beneath Cuthbert's glare, and disintegrated as the fat monk pawed at his body then slammed the door shut on the musty cell.

The key clicked in the lock and Cuthbert laughed as he strolled away.

With his back against the damp stone wall, Wulf sank to the floor and buried his head in his arms. Cold soaked through his robe and he shivered, plunged into an ocean of despair.

Eilmer would fly free. Wulf would either die in the monastery, spitted on the sword of an invader, or live out his life as Eilmer had: tied by fear to a place he detested.

*

The bell tolled for High Mass, then for Sext a while later. If Eilmer heeded the message he would be long gone now. Wulf envisaged him, soaring over the rolling hills; Daedalus, beloved of Athena, free at last, able to go anywhere and evade the northmen.

The bell tolled again. The alarm-ring, not the call to prayer. Wulf leapt to his feet. Had the northmen arrived already? Blood thudded in his ears. Footsteps clattered past the door. He pounded on the timber, demanding information, calling out for help.

At last the door opened and Father Beorthric's stern visage appeared. 'Brother Eilmer is gone. What have you done, boy? Where is he?'

Wulf shrank away. 'I don't know what you mean, Father. I've been here.'

Beorthric dragged him from the cell and pushed his back against the stone wall. 'Don't lie to me, Wulf. I read the list of stolen goods. Vellum, timber, glue, twine, feathers. Do you take me for a fool? I know what Eilmer did in his youth. The whole abbey knows he was desperate to repeat his madness. Did you help him?'

Wulf nodded. 'He wanted—'

'I don't care!' Beorthric cut him off with a wave of his hand. 'You're both idiots. He's an old cripple. He won't survive the day, even if his contraption does work. Now get out there and find him. We'll discuss your punishment when you return. Be back by dark, whether you find him or not.'

He stalked away, muttering and swearing in such foul terms Wulf never thought to hear from the mouth of an Abbot.

Without waiting, expecting a cry of 'halt', Wulf bolted for the nearest exit.

*

Outside in the warm autumn sunlight, he lifted his face to the sky and sucked a breath of clean air. To the north and east voices, lifted in desperation, called Eilmer's name. Wulf looked southwest, into the wind. If Eilmer had launched from the tower, that's where he would be headed. He picked up the skirts of his robe and ran.

Down the dusty road towards town he fled, panting as his heart pounded. At the crossroads on High Street, he paused. Last time Eilmer had crashed not far away. This time, with the tail, he would make it over the river and be free.

Wulf skirted a bread-vendor, and a furrier plying his trade from a wagon. Sidestepping a pile of steaming horse-dung, he ignored insults and laughter and ran in unseemly haste through town. Past thatch and timber houses, past the Kings Arms tavern – raucous with laughter even in the day. Breath burned in his lungs.

Cutting through a garden and hedges, he startled a pair of chickens roosting on a two-wheeled cart that leaned drunkenly against a cottage. The birds skrawked and fluttered away. Wulf raced downhill towards the riverbank. He shaded his eyes against the afternoon sun and looked skyward.

There, high above: a black dot, soaring in the sky, swooping, circling. Surely too big for a hawk? Grinning, Wulf squinted against the glare, trying to get a better view. It must be Eilmer.

Something caught his foot and he tumbled to the loamy soil and damp grass. He laughed at his clumsiness and looked back to see what tripped him.

A broken piece of timber, the tattered remains of torn white and black feathers still clinging to the ripped vellum. A few steps further,

Eilmer's wretched body lay twisted on the brilliant grass; his arms outstretched, still bound to the wings' shredded remnants. Blood matted his wild, white hair. Scattered all around, feathers drifted and fluttered across the grass, caught up by the wind and released again, carrying the dregs of an old man's dream.

Wulf crawled to Eilmer's side and cradled the old man's head. Tears dripped onto his cool skin. No breath drifted from pale lips, no heart pulsed in a still breast. He wore the tunic and hose of an ordinary peasant, a leather cap covering his tonsure. His open eyes reflected the sky: empty, blue, soulless.

Wulf stayed that way for long moments, joy shattered with the wings still tied to Eilmer's thin arms. Then a distant cry of Eilmer's name brought fear surging back. Cuthbert's voice!

Not far away, amongst the wreckage, lay a leather satchel. Wulf fetched it and scrabbled through the contents. A change of clothing, a small leather pouch, the little oak carving, and a book. He opened the pouch and gasped. Silver coins gleamed in the sunlight; a fortune.

Cuthbert's voice called Eilmer's name again, closer this time, laced with anger and impatience.

Wulf drew out the book. It was not, as he expected, the Greek mythology tome that had started Eilmer on this journey. It was the falconer's guide. Wulf hugged the book close to his chest, and bowed his head, fresh tears burning his cheeks.

Cuthbert yelled once more; strident, angry.

They would come for Eilmer. Bury him and Wulf, both, deep in the abbey. Wulf hesitated. He glanced around at the trees swaying in the wind; at the bright sky and soft clouds, the hawk wheeling overhead; at the abbey belltower, visible on the north hill behind the village.

Then he shoved the pouch, book, and the bird-man carving back into the satchel. He stripped off his black robe and stuffed it deep into a hedge. After donning the spare clothing, he dragged Eilmer's wasted frame over to the cottage. The chickens protested when he shooed them away and loaded Eilmer into the two-wheeled cart.

Wulf left four silver coins on the cottage's front stoop and grasped the cart handles. With one backward look over his shoulder at the monastery, he turned his face south.

1222CE

Near Karakorum, Mongolia

Riding the Fire Horse

DA Kelly

'If I could harness the Fire Horse…' Temujin, Genghis Khan of the Mongols, stared at the night sky. 'I would ride Eternal Heaven like a god.'

'You are a god, Khan,' Subutai said. 'To your sons, your army, your many wives. You rule our world.'

'Khan of Khans certainly. But I am no god.'

'I disagree, Khan.'

'Those who disagree with me, usually regret it.'

'I mean no disrespect, Khan. I merely point out you rule your empire as would a god.'

'You're a loyal warrior, Noyan Subutai.' Genghis rested a hand on his general's shoulder. 'One of my most trusted men. You and Noyan Muqali are my best generals and the only two whose words are not honeyed by ambition.'

'You honour me, Khan.'

'I give praise where praise is due.' Genghis shielded his eyes, watching the Fire Horse gallop westward across the night, its heart brilliant white, its tail blood red. 'He rides the heavens with a great message for me. I am sure of it. Come, Subutai, I will seek Temku's council.'

It was not a quick walk through the sprawling Mongol horde to see Temku. The shaman's gher sat on the far side of four tuman; each tuman a unit of ten thousand men. Add in their horses, wagons, livestock and circular ghers and it was more a mobile city than an invading army.

As Genghis wove his way around the ghers, with Subutai by his side, familiar sounds rose and fell in waves. Men talking and laughing, arrows thunking into grass targets, blades being sharpened, horses munching on fodder, their heads low after a day of hard riding, children playing and naks scurrying around doing the bidding of their masters.

He had built this unstoppable army. Sometimes he could not believe he had managed such a feat, but the proof lay all around him. The smell of beef and lamb, skewered and roasting on open fires floated on the icy wind, making his mouth water.

A god would not be tempted by such things.

Temku's circular gher squatted before him like a huge bull turd; the grey felt weathered, the south-facing door painted in blue and orange interlocking lines and serpentine patterns. Smoke curled from the central vent. The scent of herbs and dried camel dung gave away what fed his fire.

Genghis hesitated, his hand on the door, listening, testing his shaman's seer-sight.

'Come in, come in, Khan,' called Temku, his voice gravelly with age and too much pipe-smoke.

Genghis smiled, fleeting, tight-lipped. Only his closest noyan and his first wife Bohrte saw his softer side. To show any other face, but that of the Khan, would reveal weakness; vulnerability.

'Remain here.' Genghis slapped Subutai on the back and pushed open the horsehide door. He entered, making sure not to step on the threshold. He walked west to east around fire and sat on a pile of furs across from Temku.

'I made a dream journey this last night.' The old shaman gazed at Genghis through the flames, his eyes milk-white. 'I spoke with the great Fire Horse above.'

'If anyone can see into the Fire Horse's heart it would be you, Temku.'

'We are old friends the Fire Horse and me. Though last time we spoke his tail was not of blood, but of mare's milk and desert sand.'

'What say the Fire Horse?' Genghis leaned forward.

'That you're to gather your tuman, at least five units of ten thousand warriors and expand the Mongol Empire west.'

'A sign from the Eternal Blue. I knew it! The shaman Kokochu told truly all those years ago. The world is mine to rule.'

'You were born grasping a blood clot in your little fist, Khan. A sure sign you were destined to be a great leader. But remember, signs are often double-edged, Khan. Especially when sent from the Sky Spirits. They test us, you see. Judge if we are worthy of their attention.'

'You speak ill of the Sky Spirits! With one of their messengers cantering across the Eternal Blue? You are either brave or a fool.'

'Both.' Temku shrugged. 'Neither. I've been tested before. Many times. Lost every time.' He pointed to his blind eyes. 'But sometimes we must lose to gain what we need.'

'I shall not fail the Sky Spirits. I will do whatever it takes. Whatever I must.'

'If you think that, Khan,' Temku said with a chuckle. 'You have already lost.'

'Mind your tongue, Shaman.' Genghis Khan stood. 'Remember what happened to Teb Tengri.' He threw open the gher's door and walked into the night.

Subutai stood with Muqali and a group of warriors, sharing a bowl of airag.

'Favourable news, Khan?' Subutai and Muqali hurried over. Subutai handed Genghis the bowl.

Genghis swigged a mouthful of the fermented mares' milk, enjoying the acidic taste. 'We push westward.'

'Shaman Kokochu predicted the world was yours,' Subutai said.

Genghis nodded. 'I never doubted it. Summon the Ortoq traders. Learn all we can about the peoples of the west that we may plan the invasion. My world awaits.'

*

'I have an idea that may assure victory in the west, Khan,' Subutai said one morning as they walked among the horses.

'The Fire Horse has already spoken.' Genghis raised an eyebrow. 'You believe you know more than the Sky Spirits' messenger?'

'Never, Khan!'

Genghis did not miss a step. 'And this idea?'

'We send for a mystic. We have gathered a few into our empire over the years. I think your protection and benevolence should now be repaid.'

'Phah!' Genghis threw up one hand, startling a nearby horse. 'What would a mystic know that a shaman wouldn't?'

Subutai stroked the nervous horse's neck, calming him down. 'I have heard they deal in magic. Powerful magic beyond a shaman's wisdom.'

'Impossible!'

'Maybe so, Khan, but why take nations under your protection if we cannot harness their skills?'

Genghis pondered his words. 'Very well. Bring me one of these mystics. I shall see if they're worth my protection.'

*

Three days later, Genghis sat inside his gher, a great breast-shaped tent painted in blue and yellow swirls, and hung with colourful flags. Unlike most ghers, the Khan's sat upon the back of a huge wagon. The team of oxen used to pull the wagon grazed nearby, nuzzling the grass, chewing slowly. He liked the sound of his beasts, and the smell of his horses, just as he enjoyed the scent of a woman. He drew strength from them, and strength was vital when the weight of destiny rested on his shoulders.

A heavy knock rattled the gher's door.

Subutai. Genghis nodded his approval. The man was worth his weight in numan.

'Enter!' He settled upon a carved wooden chair covered in furs and brightly woven cloth.

Subutai pushed through the door, one arm supporting the blind shaman, Temku. Close behind followed Muqali. He held the door for a woman, her hair so grey and thin her scalp was visible, the skin mottled with age. She did not hunch as would a feeble old crone. She did not accept Subutai's arm, but hobbled west to east around the gher to stand before Genghis.

'You know our ways.' Genghis traced a matching circle in the air.

'To know one's enemy is a wise thing, Khan.'

Genghis Khan stiffened, eyeing the old woman, calculating her measure. 'I live my life by those very words. So, are you my enemy?'

'Are you my master?'

Subutai shoved her to her knees. 'You will show our Khan the respect and honour he deserves.'

'What is your name, mystic?' Genghis stood, hands on hips, chin raised.

'Most call me Xin.'

'Well, Xin.' He motioned for Subutai to help her to her feet. 'What are your gifts? Your powers? What makes you better than my shaman?'

'Can he tell you how to capture the spirit of the Fire Arrow?' She pointed skyward, the skin of her hands translucent, her veins blue and bloated. 'Because I can!'

'A woman no bigger than a child – no stronger than a newborn foal – capturing the Eternal Blue Heaven's Messenger?' Genghis laughed, the sound brittle, angry. 'Take her away. Unless...' He paused and addressed Temku. 'The Fire Arrow's spirit would make me unstoppable, would it not? Does she speak truth?'

'Khan,' Temku said, reluctance in his weathered face. 'She does not lie. But if you do as she suggests the risks are great.'

'You too know how to capture the Fire Horse's spirit?'

'I foresaw this moment, yes,' Temku said. 'But I do not know how to harness the Fire Horse. What I do know is you're approaching a living crossroads, Khan. Either path is open.'

'And yet you said nothing!'

'As I said, the risk is great. Too great.'

'Who are you to decide what I should risk? Nothing! Nothing is more important than my destiny. To shy from danger would insult our gods.'

'I am sorry, Khan. I simply wanted to protect you. Kokochu predicted the world would be yours. A precious jewel you'd rule over. But I did not see you following this mystic's path to achieve it.'

'Perhaps Kokochu was a far greater shaman than you.'

'Very likely, Khan. Forgive me.'

'So, woman.' Genghis turned to Xin. 'What do I do to capture the Fire Horse's spirit?'

'You paint it,' Xin said mildly.

*

Genghis Khan stood within his gher with Subutai, Muqali, and Temku nearby. Xin knelt before him, her gaze following his every move. A heat haze floated off the central fire stove keeping the night's chill at bay. Five carved, ivory bowls of salted tea rested on a wooden stool, one for everyone present.

'You would say you are a powerful mystic?' Genghis addressed Xin.

'Magic runs deep and strong in my family's blood.'

'Where is your family?'

'Dead and gone thanks to your warriors.'

'So, you are the last?'

'I am.'

'She seeks retribution, Khan,' Temku muttered. 'Now I see why she leads you along the wrong path.'

'I wish only that my family name lives on,' Xin said. 'But as you see, I am too old to bear any more children. By helping you claim your world, Khan, perhaps my family's name will too go down in history.'

'Honouring your ancestors,' Genghis said. 'Most worthy.'

Xin bowed her head. 'May I ask you a personal question, Khan?'

Genghis grunted approval.

Subutai loosened a dagger strapped at his waist.

Xin stared at Subutai's blade, her dark eyes glittering beneath hooded lids. 'What did your mother do with the blood clot you carried into this world?'

'You know of this?' Genghis frowned.

'Such a rare event is great news, Khan.'

'I carry it within a small ceramic vial,' Genghis said.

'You hold great magic then, Khan. A key that opens a portal between worlds.'

Genghis glared at Temku.

'The blood clot was a sign, Khan,' the shaman spluttered. 'A powerful sign from the Great Blue, but it is not magic.'

'Well, we all know signs are double-edged,' Genghis said. 'This one must be both a sign and a key.'

Temku sighed. 'You use my words against me, Khan.'

'Just as you taught me.' Genghis raised his chin. 'So, mystic, what does the blood have to do with the harnessing the Fire Horse?'

'Mix your blood-sign with the blood of your most prized stallion.'

'How much blood?'

'All of it.'

'Kill Ganbaatar?' Genghis struggled for words.

'If that is your best stallion, then yes,' Xin said. 'Use his blood to paint the Fire Arrow. Make sure you paint the most prominent stars as they appear around the Arrow. That locks this time and place within the canvas. When the spell is complete, the power of the Fire Arrow will be yours. The power will remain in the picture until the great Fire Arrow shoots across the heavens once more.' She went on to describe the rest of the ceremony.

'I may be Khan of Khans,' Genghis said, 'and the Flail of God, but I am no artist.'

'You do not need to be a gifted artist, Khan,' Xin said. 'The ritual does not require skill with a brush.'

'No, only the death of Ganbaatar.'

'A tragic loss,' Xin said. 'But if it means capturing the Fire Horse's spirit, isn't that a worthy sacrifice?'

Genghis listened then growled, angry at himself for even thinking of such a thing. Ganbaatar, with his large head, thick, strong bones and legs. His long mane and tail blowing in the wind. Never trimmed, never tamed. Genghis had sworn never to cut Ganbaatar's mane or tail. His spirit dwelled there. Cutting them would release his spark of life back up to the Eternal Blue. He was worth more than all other horses combined.

'So, I make a handle from one of Ganbaatar's bones,' Genghis said. 'And the brush from his mane and tail. The canvas from his hide.'

'Just so, Khan.'

'And recite the spell you taught my shaman.'

'Three times while walking around the painting.'

Genghis nodded.

Muqali seized the mystic, dragged back her head and cut her throat.

'Let us see how much power flows in your blood, mystic,' Genghis said as the light faded from her eyes. He glanced at Temku. 'Did you see this in one of your dream journeys?'

Muqali collect Xin's blood in a wooden bowl while Subutai shaved her head. The fine, grey hair fluttered to the woven grass matting.

'I fear you created this path alone, Khan,' Temku said.

'Would the Eternal Blue give me the world if I followed the word of a woman? A foreign woman who wishes me ill?'

'I do see the wisdom in your choice, Khan, but I fear you have chosen a dangerous route.'

'When faced with a fork in the road and you can't decide, take the third path even if it frightens you.'

*

The Fire Horse rode the heavens, his heart bright, his tail the colour of Xin's blood as it had pooled across the grass matting of Genghis's gher.

It had taken days of skinning, scraping and tanning the old mystic, but her canvas now stretched across a frame of her leg bones. The paint brush, made from one of Xin's forearm bones, and her hair had been bound together by Ganbaatar's naturally-shed mane. Genghis stirred a little blood he had taken from Ganbaatar into the mystic's skull cap. Not enough to weaken the stallion, but enough to secure the spell just in case the mystic had spoken truly. He added her congealed blood and the dried clot he had treasured for so long.

'I think it wise to start your painting, Khan,' Temku said. 'The Fire Horse rides high. His spirit lights your world, lending you all his power.'

Genghis closed his eyes, whispered a prayer to the Eternal Blue Heavens and dipped the brush into the blood. Never had he taken so much time, so much care with anything. He plotted every star, the arc of the Fire Horse just as he saw them. Though the paint was a rusty brown – not the crisp black, whites and vivid reds above – the picture mirrored the sky.

Subutai, Muqali and Temku watched on in silence. Only the buzz and clatter of the encampment, somewhere in the distance filled the still, silver-lit night.

Genghis stepped back, surveyed his work, added a pin-prick here and there of paint then, on impulse, he painted himself astride Ganbaatar onto the canvas. The depiction was crude, but the intent was clear and locked into the scene.

He sighed and put down the skull-cap, stretching his shoulders and neck. Then, slowly, he paced a circular path around the painting, reciting the spell three times. He opened himself, stretching upward, seeking a sign the spell had worked. A breeze ruffled his hair. An icy wind, too cold for this time of the year.

Then nothing.

'Is that all?' Genghis glared at Temku then at the Fire Horse.

'You expected more, Khan?'

'My wives' farts are more impressive than that!'

'Power comes in many forms, Khan. Just because there was no flash of lightning, or crack of thunder, doesn't mean the spell failed. Have patience, Khan.' Temku waved a bony finger at the Fire Horse. 'The spell must travel a great distance.'

'What think you, Temku?' Genghis grabbed the shaman's skinny arm. 'Truly? Should I have painted myself and Ganbaatar into the picture?'

Temku raised his face, blind eyes closed. 'I fear you have created a fourth path, Khan.'

'Phah! I forge my own way!' Genghis hesitated, examining the painting. 'Get me another mystic. I want to be sure the spell has worked.'

*

Genghis paced around his gher. The Fire Horse painting sat on a poplar trunk, the bone frame catching the firelight and giving the image a warmth the dead must long for. Every time he passed by the offending picture he growled and muttered.

'I fear you'll need a new mat if you keep pacing, Khan,' Temku said.

'They take too long. The Fire Horse will have moved on to fresh grazing by the time they return.'

'I am certain they travel as fast as they can, Khan. The mystic they seek will be worth the journey. The outriders said they spotted three horses heading this way, so they should be here any time.'

The door rattled with three sharp knocks.

'Ah! Subutai!' Genghis stopped pacing. 'Enter.'

Muqali and Subutai escorted a woman inside.

'Good, good,' Genghis said. 'Bring her here.'

His two noyan pushed the mystic forward, one stationed on either side.

'Her name is Gann,' Subutai said, his jaw tight, voice uneasy.

She stood as tall as a man, her eyes fierce; piercing as a golden eagle's. She scanned the gher, glossing over Genghis as if he was not there, and landed on the painting.

'Which of you killed Xin?' Gann asked. 'I taste her magic, her rage. I feel her spirit locked in that painting.'

Muqali shifted uneasily. 'I killed her.'

'You fool!' Gann laughed. 'You know not what you've done.'

'You dare ignore your Khan? Genghis Khan snarled. 'And mock a great noyan!'

'She follows you, boy.' Gann eyed Muqali, her expression now serious. 'You will not live the year.'

'You lie!' Genghis backhanded Gann. She staggered.

'Ignorance will not save you, noyan.' She touched her reddened cheek gently and glared at Genghis. 'Or you.'

'I should kill you!' Genghis Khan growled, his teeth clenched.

'I expected as much.'

'She baits you, Khan,' Temku said.

'A fool as well as a liar!' Genghis spat.

'Perhaps,' Gann said, 'but I'm not the ones bonded to an angry spirit.'

'Destroy the painting,' Subutai said. 'Burn it!'

'I don't recommend that, Khan,' Temku said. 'I fear that will make things worse.'

Genghis glowered at Gann. 'Is he right?'

The mystic remained silent, her eyes mocking.

'Make her talk!' Genghis sat on his chair, his back rigid. 'Find out everything you can about Xin and that cursed painting.'

As Subutai and Muqali dragged Gann from the Gher, she laughed and shouted, 'I shall enjoy hunting you, Genghis Khan.'

*

Alone upon a grassy rise, Genghis watched the night sky. The Fire Horse glared down at him, its heart searing white, its tail ember red. Xin's painting rested upon a pile of twigs, dried camel dung and a pouch of herbs and charms gathered by Temku to ward off evil spirits. Genghis examined the paintbrush and bowl of dried blood that had once been Xin and tossed them onto the pyre.

A flaming torch fluttered in Genghis's hand, fire dripping on the ground as he gazed out across the grasslands. Below, campfires stretched far and wide, a mirror of the sky. All of this was his to rule over.

'You said so,' he shouted at the Fire Horse.

Wind gusted around him. The torch roared and flickered.

Gann had said nothing despite the suffering she'd endured before she died. Never had he met such a fearsome female. Her courage confused him. Was her bravery blood-true? Or part of a cunning plan to erode his confidence? Either way, her threat rang in his mind. All afternoon he had struggled with what to do. Destroy the first painting and paint a second? Create another to add to the first? Sacrifice Ganbaatar and do what the first mystic instructed?

'It is not like you, my Khan.' Temku voice rose from behind. 'To second guess yourself, especially on the word of a woman.'

'I could have you dragged behind ten horses for disobeying me, Temku.' Genghis did not turn to face his shaman.

'I know you said you were not to be followed, Khan, but you have been up here since midday and still no fire. Still no new painting.'

'What if Gann spoke truly and Xin really haunts Muqali, waiting to take his life? What if burning the painting makes things worse?'

'I made a dream journey this morning, Khan, and the ancestors say the world is your jewel. That you will one day rise above all kings, Khans and emperors. It is your destiny and no one, even a mystic, can take that from you.'

Genghis nodded, huffing his acknowledgment. His breath feathered the night air. As it drifted away, he lowered the flaming torch into the kindling and set the first painting afire. The canvas scorched, sizzled and burned; the frame of bones blackened and cracked.

Silence.

A distant eagle-screech.

The wind stirred flames and smoke from the fire.

Genghis stared at the sky. His heart drummed fast; loud like one hundred horses pounding through his body.

'Nothing!' he whispered. He faced Temku with a wide grin.

'I fear you celebrate too soon, Khan.' Temku pointed at him.

'What?' Chills fizzed along Genghis's skin.

'Behind you!' Temku staggered back.

Genghis spun. 'I see nothing!'

'It's Xin! No, wait! Gann as well.'

'But I didn't make the other picture!'

'Gann is faint, Khan. Barely a wisp. But Xin… She is strong, perhaps powered by the Fire Horse. Wait! There's something else.'

'What, what is it?'

'Light shoots from the heavens, sizzling, like a fire arrow. It spears through Xin and—'

An invisible force punched into Genghis's upper gut, throwing him backwards. Pain lanced through his head, down his neck. He tumbled down the grassy rise and landed flat on his back staring up at the Fire Horse, its tail streaming out behind like blood.

A scream cut through the darkness from somewhere in the camp.

Shouts erupted, loud, confused.

Another scream, bestial, terrified.

'Ganbaatar!' Ghengis struggled to his feet. Pain crushed his heart, worming outward along his limbs. He cursed and lumbered through the darkness tripping over stones and tufts of grass. People raced about the camp, frantic, unsure, arrows nocked in bows, swords drawn, torches waving left and right searching.

Genghis did not slow, cursing and threatening anyone who got in his way. People scattered. Warriors fell in behind him, silent, swords drawn or arrows ready. Genghis neared the horses, searching for his stallion among the tossing heads and stamping hooves.

'To me, Khan,' bellowed Subutai. 'Over here! Hurry!'

Genghis pelted around the horses, dodging and weaving as they shied and jostled one another.

'Ganbaatar shows no wounds, Khan,' Subutai said.

'Herd the horses away from here,' Genghis shouted to his warriors.

As his men drove the nervous horses away from Ganbaatar, Genghis knelt beside his stallion and ran a hand along the sleek neck. The hair was soft, the flesh warm. But no pulse beat in the great throat.

'His eyes, Khan,' Subutai said. 'See his eyes.'

Genghis gently brushed Ganbattar's forelock aside. Dead, silver-white eyes gazed at him with all the beauty and chill of moonlit ice.

'What happened?' Genghis stroked Ganbaatar's velvet-soft nose.

'I don't know, Khan. We heard two screams. One from the camp, the other from the horses. I arrived to find Ganbaatar laying just as you see.'

'The other scream?'

'I'm unsure, Khan. Jebai went to investigate. I came here.'

'Find Muqali. See if he is well.'

'Khan?'

'I fear it was he who screamed.'

*

Genghis, led by Subutai, stalked into Muqali's gher to find him half-dressed and slumped on the woven grass mat.

'I am well, Khan.' Muqali clambered to his feet, swayed and stumbled.

'You lie, but I forgive you.' Genghis caught his noyan and lowered him to the ground. 'Open your eyes, look at me.'

Muqali stared at him, his eyes brown.

'You are pale, my friend.' Genghis squeezed his noyan's shoulder. Though he feared the answer, he asked, 'What happened?'

'I was readying for sleep and something tore through my guts like a fist of ice and fire. Threw me from one side of my gher to the other. And there was something else.' Muqali lowered his face.

'Yes?'

'I saw that mystic Xin standing over me. Her and that tall one, Gann.'

'Did they say anything? Do anything?'

'They just laughed, Khan. Laughed and walked through the wall.'

Genghis patted Muqali's arm. 'I will send you south, beyond the Wei River. Far from this land and the spirits that haunt it.'

'I thirst for another battle, Khan.' His words were strong, but his face remained pale and sheened with sweat.

'You have not lost a battle, my friend. It is time you finished what you started and defeat the Jin Dynasty.'

'I will not fail you.'

'I know.' Genghis turned and addressed Subutai, 'Bring Temku to my gher. He's up on the rise to the north.'

*

An eerie quiet hung over the camp of thousands. Even in the middle of the night, dogs barked, children cried, men snored. But not tonight.

'Look around, old man.' Genghis stood outside his gher with Temku kneeling before him. 'What do you see?'

'I see spirits, Khan, Three of them. Xin, Gann, and Ganbaatar.'

'He's here?'

'I don't think he has a choice. A rope of light streams down from the Great Fire Horse. It branches and connects to Xin, Ganbaatar and...' Temku bowed his head. '...you, my Khan. One more branch goes off into the night. I suspect it joins with Muqali.'

'I feel nothing! I see nothing!'

'The connection is in the spirit realm, Khan.'

'How do I cut this rope?'

'I know no other way but to die, Khan.'

'I will find another way.'

'I will seek answers from our ancestors, Khan. Harness guardian spirits to protect you.'

'I thought I already had a guardian spirit.' Genghis glared up at the Fire Horse.

'Indeed, Khan. We simply need to outwit the two mystics while pleasing the Fire Horse. I am sure he will help you fulfil your destiny.'

'I do not fear them.'

A chill raced along Genghis's neck and Xin's voice whispered, 'You should.'

*

Usually time races by, especially when leading a sea of men and horses in war. But the past year had crawled by for Genghis Khan.

Though he could not see those wretched spirits, he imagined them watching his every move. Snickering. Pointing. Mocking. Waiting.

Genghis paced outside his gher. 'Where are my riders?' he shouted to Subutai. 'It has been days!'

'There is dust on the horizon, Khan.' Subutai hurried over. 'Hopefully they have news of Muqali.'

'Gann said he would not live the year. It has been a year.'

'Perhaps setting such distance between Muqali and Xin saved him?'

'Pha!' Genghis rubbed his chest. 'I feel the pull of the fire-rope with every breath. Tethered like a yearling to a spirit no bigger than a child. To the Great Fire Horse who has long since cantered away. Why did you tell me of mystics and their evil magics? Why did I listen?'

'I am sorry, Khan.' Subutai dropped to one knee. 'My life is yours to take if that will ease your anger.'

'Get up! You're not a nak fawning to his master. You're a noyan; a great general.'

Before the day was out, three riders arrived in the camp.

Genghis elbowed his way through the crowd, Subutai at his side, pushing men away, all eager to hear news from the south. As Genghis broke free, the riders dismounted, their legs buckling beneath them, their horses lathered in foam.

One of the riders dropped to his knees. 'Noyan Mulqai is dead, my Khan. Died of sickness.'

'Not in battle?' Genghis asked.

'No, Khan,' the rider said. 'His last words were, "I have never been defeated."'

Genghis pushed through the crowd and returned to his gher. When he got there, Temku was waiting for him.

'Muqali is dead just as the mystic warned,' Genghis muttered. 'Of sickness! What of me, Temku?'

'You're forgetting the prophecy, my Khan. You will rule the world. As far as the eye can see.'

'You said I had forged a fourth path.' Genghis rubbed his face and sighed. 'Perhaps I have squandered my destiny.' He sat on his chair, but did not feel the soft furs, or the smooth-worn timber. He felt numb.

'Who is to say which path is the correct one?'

Genghis stood and stretched his shoulders. 'Make arrangements for a great ceremony to honour Muqali. And have him buried somewhere fitting. Somewhere secret so the spirits cannot haunt him.'

'We can hope, Khan.'

'Temku?'

'Yes, my Khan?'

'When I die bury me without markings. Somewhere near where I was born. And order my funeral escort to kill anyone or anything that crosses their path – to conceal my resting place.'

'A wise precaution, Khan. Anything else?'

'I can think of many things, but none to ease my aching heart. Leave me be, Temku. I should like to rest.'

*

Genghis Khan sat astride his horse, Muqali. The stallion was as magnificent as Ganbaatar. Strong, loyal, bold, and noble enough to earn the name of Genghis's long-lost noyan.

An arban of ten warriors rode behind him, arrows nocked, ready for the hunt. Subutai rode to his left, his dark eyes focused more often on Genghis than looking for gazelle.

'What ails you?' Genghis asked. 'You are like a mare with her new foal.'

'I am well, Khan. It is you that worries me. You are pale.'

'I am like a god remember? You said so yourself. Do not trouble yourself.'

'Of course, my Khan.'

Genghis straightened in the saddle, ignoring the pain in his spine. He felt every one of his sixty-five years today, especially the last five since Muqali's death. The fire cord pulled ever tighter. Xin's whispers grew ever louder, ever more ominous. A horse-shaped shimmer to Genghis's right caught his attention, but when he looked the vision disappeared.

Ganbaatar! Genghis had seen the vision often enough over the last few years to no longer doubt his eyes. He shifted in his saddle, but the pain in his back remained.

'There!' A warrior pointed. 'On the far side of those boulders. Perhaps twenty gazelle!'

With a nod from Genghis, the hunting party kicked their horses into a gallop, and the hunt began.

As he charged forth, arrow at the ready, Genghis gritted his teeth against the pain, focusing instead on the fleeing gazelle. Excitement thrilled through his veins. His heart drummed fast and loud. The sound merged with the thundering hoofs of hunted and horse. Xin's whispers and taunts were pounded into silence.

Genghis whooped. He sent Subutai a fearsome grin. Subutai laughed. His mare's black mane and tale flowed like liquid shadow. Genghis hadn't felt so young, so alive, in years. All his trouble with spirits, and the pressure of the Tangut Empire's resistance, fell away on the chill wind.

'I am a god!' he shouted. He laughed; wild, free. 'The world is my jewel!'

The gazelle speared right, racing toward a stand of trees. Genghis guided Muqali with a squeeze of his legs. Muqali turned, stumbled, collapsed, and hurled Genghis skyward. Trees, grass, boulders and summer flowers blurred, jewel-like past his vision.

Crack.

Breath whooshed from Genghis's mouth leaving ice-hot agony in his chest and whirling lights in his head.

'The Khan of Khans is but a man,' Xin whispered in his mind. 'And men die.'

Genghis wheezed in a breath. He coughed. Sucked in another. Thin, harsh and agonising.

Blue sky. Wisps of white. A bird with wings outstretched, gliding above. Darkness gnawed the edges, leaving fuzzy images. Faces perhaps.

Fizzing, roaring, and distant voices.

Black.

Blessed silence.

*

'Here, my Khan.' A gentle hand, cool, calloused from years handling reins, stroked his brow. 'Sip this. It will ease your suffering.'

Genghis peered through slitted lids. Temku, the shaman sat beside him. To his right knelt Subutai, holding a clay cup. To his left stood his son, Ogedai, and his first wife, Bohrte. Above, floating beneath the gher's domed roof, were Xin and Gann, their faces clearer than those around him. Eager. Mocking.

'Where is Ganbaatar?' He heaved himself up onto one elbow. Pain knifed through his chest. Ribs grated together, bone on raw flesh. He collapsed back onto his bedroll, coughing. Hot, salty liquid filled his mouth, spraying the blue woollen blanket with crimson droplets.

'Your horse is long dead, my Khan,' Subutai said.

'I will soon follow,' Genghis murmured. 'I feel the fire rope tearing my chest apart.'

'You have broken ribs, my husband.' Bohrte knelt beside him and squeezed his hand. 'Take some of Temku's tea. It will help you sleep so you can heal.'

'No!' Genghis swatted Bohrte's hand away. 'I see them. Those cursed mystics. They taunt me, waiting to take my soul. Can you not see them?'

'There is no one here but us, Father,' Ogedai said.

'They are here.' Temku patted Genghis's hand. 'Ganbaatar is near also. You will soon ride him across the heavens like the god you are. You will outrun the mystics, for they are but specks of stardust compared to you, my shining sun.'

'You lie, Shaman, but your heart is true.' Genghis coughed. Pain shattered him. Tears filled his eyes. 'I will die before the moon rises.'

'No, my husband!' Bohrte clutched the blanket in tight little fists.

'Why do you never listen, wife?'

'Why do you always argue, husband?' Bohrte said, her voice thick with tears.

Genghis opened his mouth to speak, but retched up dark, gravelly blood, clotted and red.

Subutai wiped away the blood, his expression forlorn, his eyes wild.

'You will hear my will!' Genghis Khan choked up frothy, red bubbles. He groaned.

'Yes, my Khan,' everyone answered.

'You will keep my death secret. I will not jeopardise the Tangut campaign. Only when we win will you spread word of my death.' Genghis struggled for breath. 'Tell many stories, so no man can say how I truly passed to the Eternal Blue Heavens. No living god dies from falling off his horse.'

'We will say that you fell in battle. Or infection from an arrow wound,' Subutai said.

Genghis shuddered in a breath. 'Temku knows what to do with my body. Ensure no one knows where I am buried. Perhaps those cursed mystics will lose my scent.'

He turned to his son. 'You will lead my Empire now, Ogedai. Make me proud! Grind the Tangut empire into dust.' He shuddered, groaning as pain carved though his chest.

The last thing he saw was Subutai's tears.

*

First was blackness.

A pinpoint of light. So bright and yet so soothing.

No pain.

No fear.

The light grew; a shower of warmth and love.

Three figures floated in the glow, neither female or male. They were just there, watching. Waiting.

The light drew him forward. He floated. Weightless.

The light intensified, pulling at his chest.

The figures floated with him.

From one he sensed love. Loyalty. A heavy sadness.

From another he sensed bitter amusement.

From the third, rage.

Genghis struggled. Turned. Looked down. Saw his body surrounded by grief. Blood smeared his mouth. Pooled on his chest. Temku did not stare at the body as the others did. He watched Genghis floating into the light, his milk-white eyes framed in leathery wrinkles.

Temku waved his cane and shouted, 'Behind you!'

'So!' The rage-filled figure loomed into view. 'I have you!'

'Xin!'

'You remember me,' she said. 'I'm flattered.'

Xin looked as alive as she had all those years ago. Beside her stood Muqali, his eyes downcast. The third figure was Gann, indistinct, blurred by light.

'Muqali!' Genghis shot forward. 'I have missed you!'

Xin yanked a strap of braided leather, its length adorned with colourful tassels. Muqali fell in behind her, bridled like a horse.

'Do not address my mount,' Xin said. 'If he even looks at you I will have him punished.'

'Muqali, you allow a woman to tame you?'

'He was mine as soon as his dagger sliced into my throat.'

'How?'

'Blood magic. And the power of the Fire Arrow.'

'You planned this?'

Xin ignored him. 'Now we are all reunited, it is time to fulfil your destiny. Never let it be said I got in the way of Genghis Khan's grand ambition.'

Genghis reached down, expecting the fire cord to be shining with life, but there was nothing. A soft wicker he had missed for so long ruffled his hair. Ganbaatar appeared from the glowing light and nuzzled Genghis's hand just as he always had, searching for a treat.

'You will ride now,' Xin said. 'Ride the Eternal Blue like a god. Ruling over the world like the Sky Spirits promised.'

Genghis went to mount Ganbaatar, but the horse vanished.

'He is mine. *Your* horse awaits on the Great Steppes of Heaven.' Xin sneered. 'Enjoy your destiny.' She flicked a dismissive hand and the light vanished.

Genghis floated in blackness once more. No, not floated, flew. The Earth grew smaller, the blue waters and golden sands swirls on a tiny insignificant ball. Great spheres, like other worlds, whipped past.

It grew cold, dark and empty.

Eternal. But not blue.

In the distance, a rocky lump of ice careened through the darkness, its tail a long, feathered dirty trail of smoke littered with rocks and gravel.

Genghis flailed, his body insubstantial as mist. Tried to stop. To return home. To the warm light. But the soaring rock loomed large. He braced himself, ready to smash into it. To shatter in a thousand pieces. Instead, it swallowed him. Genghis struggled, encased in stone. Writhing, he fought to shed the skin of rock, but he remained stuck fast. He looked around. Nothing but pinpricks of cold-white light and eternal blackness.

'What is this?'

'Your destiny!' Xin's voice filled the darkness.

*

Below, a magnificent blue and green and golden ball hung in a black sea seeded with a million stars.

A memory stirred. Fragile. So delicate the Fire Horse's Heart was afraid to touch it lest it vanish.

'Behold,' whispered a voice. The first voice the heart had heard in forever. 'Your world just as the shaman Kokochu predicted. A precious jewel for you to rule over.'

The world below did look like a precious jewel.

'Is your gift from the Eternal Blue everything you hoped for, Genghis Khan? You are higher, indeed, than all khans and emperors.'

'That was my name...' The sounds rolled around, took root and grew. 'Xin?'

The voice sneered. 'I am Gann. Xin rides the heavens atop Ganbaatar, dragging your miserable Noyan Muqali behind.'

'What have you done!'

'Fulfilled your destiny just as you wanted. Now you have eternity to ponder your choices and your destiny. And every seventy-five years you will see your precious world. See it and never step foot upon its warm sands; its cool grass. I am content now. My family and friends await me. They will be pleased by my story of the Great Fire Horse of Eternal Heaven. They love surprise endings.'

'I am sorry!' Genghis cried. 'Oh, forgive me, Muqali. I was blinded by pride. And you must pay such a terrible price. Forgive me! Temku, Subutai! Muqali! Ganbaatar! I am so sorry.'

'Too late.'

Silence.

And the Great Fire Horse's heart shattered in anguish and regret eternal.

Foretold in the Heavens

Caitlyn McPherson

'Uchimura you say? Now that is an honourable name. But do you live up to it, boy?' Lord Kenji paced the room slowly, his hands tucked into the embroidered blue silk of his sleeves. His eldest son, Ichiro, reclined on a low couch in one corner and yawned.

Kai bit his tongue, holding back a sharp retort. This was more important than pride. As ronin – wandering samurai without a Lord or clan – he could not afford to antagonise a lord of Kenji's standing. So, he simply bowed.

'With all due respect my lord, my family have been samurai for many generations. It's in my blood.' Kai said. He touched the katana at his hip: his brother's and father's before him. Both gone now. He swallowed down the pain that accompanied those memories.

'I heard two boys survived the plague, but I thought it a rumour,' the lord mused.

Lord Kenji was an older man, his hair greying; wisps escaping his topknot. The weight of years and stress dragged at his shoulders and painted shadows beneath his eyes.

'Yes, my lord,' Kai replied. 'My brother, Hiro, and I were the only survivors of our clan.'

Lord Kenji raised an eyebrow. 'And where is your brother, now?'

Kai clenched his teeth. His hand tightened around the sword hilt. 'Gone. I am the last of my clan now, my lord.' And he would die the last. The pain of his family's death was too great to ever bear again.

Hiro's final words still rang in Kai's ears. *'You gave me a reason to live, Kai. Something special to protect. Now you must find yours.'* Yet in all these years Kai had yet to find that something. So he took whatever work came his way. Tasks small or large. It didn't matter, as long as he had a reason to keep living. Something to fill his mind and push aside the memories of grief and pain.

'So…' Lord Kenji paused in his pacing and eyed Kai. 'Now you seek work with me.'

Kai bowed and waited patiently.

'Father!' Ichiro sat up straight, frowning. 'You're not actually considering this?' He waved a hand to the courtyard outside, where five armed men stood waiting. 'You have plenty of guards already. You don't need this *ronin*.' He turned the word into a sneer.

Kai studied Ichiro. Soft, pale skin that had barely been touched by the sun; delicate hands that had never known hard toil. His petulant outburst confirmed how spoilt he was.

Lord Kenji's eyes flashed with a silent warning to Ichiro. 'This is no mere unknown ronin, boy.'

Drawing himself up, Kai met Lord Kenji's eye. Lords often 'collected' samurai as a show of wealth and power and the prestigious name of the once-great Uchimura clan would certainly help Kai's plight.

Kenji nodded decisively. 'You've come at a good time Mr Uchimura. Tomorrow night is the shrine Festival celebrations. My son and I will be attending. Join us. You can be my personal guard for the evening.'

He hadn't asked if Kai wanted to accept his job proposal or not. He didn't need to. Kai nodded his understanding and bowed.

*

Visitors arrived at the temple early that morning. Some said their prayers and went without a word. Others sought out the priest or a shrine maiden, such as Akiko, for help connecting to the spirit-world. The work was taxing – long hours spent consoling the grieving, encouraging those beaten down by poverty and fear. And as the years wore on, and the temple swallowed her childhood and her youth, Akiko searched for meaning in her sacrifice. She yearned for connection. Not with the gods, but with the people. But they saw only the "maiden", not the woman. It was a lonely existence.

So, late at night when she was alone, Akiko prayed. For herself. For a life of her own. Was it so selfish? To wish for a life outside of rigid routine and servitude. A life where she might find people who cared? Someone to love? Perhaps she should just be grateful that she had not been born into a harder life. There were many worse fates in this world for women who did not hold position or marry well.

'Good morning, Akiko.'

Akiko jumped and the bells in her hairpin jingled in the silence. She bowed deeply to the Priest. 'Good morning, Elder.'

The man always looked as if a foul smell had offended his senses, even though he was quite cheerful. Maybe it was a reflection of his age?

'You seem quite occupied with your chores,' he said. 'Have you not been struck by visions today?'

Akiko shook her head. 'Sorry, Elder, but I have not.'

'I see…' He glanced up at the clear blue sky outside the temple. 'The appearance of the star with the "tail of white cloud" has made the gods and spirits restless of late. Mikoto was struck down with fever and visions this morning. Perhaps yours are yet to come.'

'Is the star a good or bad omen?' Akiko enquired.

'The gods are being unclear at this stage.' The priest frowned. 'I'm sure at the Festival tomorrow they will reveal their intent. We must focus on the preparations. We require some fresh fruit for a food offering. I need you to go into the village to get some'

'Of course, Elder.' Akiko bowed.

*

The temple stood on a hill, on the outskirts of the village. Akiko could make it there and back before the sun peaked in the sky, but there was no rush in her step. The day was too beautiful. As the wind blew leaves of red and brown from their branches, so did it banish her worries. The scent of maple and pine hung heavy in the air. Sunlight warmed her face, the cool breeze sending pleasant chills across her skin.

Since the weather was so fair, many farmers and shop owners opened small stalls in the street. A colourful crowd of merchants and villagers crammed in to the narrow street. Akiko breathed in and sighed with contentment, enjoying the sights and scents. The smell of herbs was her favourite. The temple cooks served unseasoned food so she imagined how seasoned food could taste and her mouth watered.

Like a bird, she flittered about from stall to stall, the bells in her hairpin jingling in her wake. There were so many options but only the best fruits on offer would work for the offering. Her basket of fruit grew heavy. The next stop would have to be the last. Wanting to make it count she looked around at the stalls that were left and stopped, staring.

She knew everyone in the village by sight. This man was a stranger. A young samurai with hands resting on katana and tanto; his dark eyes darting warily from person to person. He was handsome, with hair as dark as the night and the build of a warrior. But something about his eyes made Akiko shiver. Such darkness; such pain. She shouldn't have stared as long as she did but she could pray to the gods for forgiveness later.

'Miss?' the stall owner repeated.

Akiko turned back. 'I'm sorry I was looking at the autumn leaves. Don't you think they're pretty?' She sweetened her voice to hide her lie.

The man's frown disappeared. 'They pale in comparison to you, young Miss.'

Flattery was the currency of vanity and pride and Akiko made no purchase with either. Still, she gifted the owner a small smile. They exchanged coins and fruit and she headed towards the temple.

*

Kai made his way through the main street of town. Since Lord Kenji did not require his services until the following evening he wandered into the small village to get a lay of the place. The main street was crowded with merchants and peasants alike. His empty stomach stirred at the smells of fish cooking over applewood, sake, and fresh fruit. Perhaps he could find something to eat?

Kai stared at a stall selling rich, red apples. How long had it been since he had tasted an apple? They were not cheap. His mother used to buy them as a treat for the family when he and Hiro were small.

As he dug for his coin pouch a soft jingle reached his ears. His heart skipped and he spun, searching the shifting crowd. He shook his head. Ridiculous. Of course it couldn't be her. Kai's mother was the only woman he had known to wear bells like that, but she was long dead. Still, he concentrated, listening intently for the source of the sound. There! A woman in the red and white kimono of a temple maiden strolled by. He ground his teeth and turned away. The sound had ensnared him so easily.

The bells rang again, drawing his reluctant gaze back. A scarlet ribbon tied back her long, ebony hair at the nape of her neck. The taunting bells were secured into the ribbon. Her skin was moonlight pale and flawless. Her eyes were honey-brown and feathered by long, dark lashes. As she hurried away Kai was left with memories he'd rather keep buried, and disappointment. What a shame that beauty like hers was wasted on the gods.

*

That evening, Akiko sat in silent prayer at the base of the shrine.

'Up praying late again I see,' a familiar voice spoke.

Akiko turned to see the other shrine maiden, Mikoto, standing in the doorway smiling.

'It's the only time I can get some quiet,' Akiko sighed.

Mikoto laughed. 'It's quiet outside and the stars are beautiful tonight. You can even see the one with the tail too. Come see!'

Akiko followed Mikoto. Sparkling gems of all colours painted the clear sky. And the star with the tail of white cloud shone in glorious perfection. The appearance of this star was a special occurrence. Its arrival amplified the abilities of those with the gift of foresight.

'The Elder said you've been having visions?' Akiko studied her friend's profile.

'I have.' Mikoto's brown tresses swept down and she turned her face aside.

It wasn't like Mikoto to be so quiet. Something wasn't right.

'...Is anything amiss?'

Mikoto looked down at her feet. Her hands fiddled with the fabric of her sleeves. 'I...I don't know. My visions this morning...I still don't understand everything I saw but it concerns me. Have you had any visions?'

She looked at Akiko. Was that hope or concern on her face?

Akiko shook her head. 'The gods have been quiet.'

A soft breeze blew and both women shivered in its wake.

'It's late. Let's sleep and see what the gods bring tomorrow?' Akiko suggested.

Mikoto glanced apprehensively up at the star and nodded.

*

The following evening Kai accompanied Lord Kenji to the temple. The festival was to commence after sunset so they arrived just as the sun kissed the horizon. The red torii gate towered overhead, marking the beginning of sacred grounds. Kai and Lord Kenji bowed then mounted the stone stairway to the temple.

The smell of incense and offerings burning wafted through the temple grounds. The two men washed their hands at the basin and entered the temple. A babble of voices reached Kai's ears as they entered the crowded area.

Lord Kenji's son, Ichiro, was supposed to accompany them, but he'd stayed home claiming illness. Kai couldn't help but wonder if it was all a farce by the pampered son to avoid the festivities. Kai didn't blame him. He, too, did not enjoy festivities such as this. But for Lord Kenji's request, he would not have attended. The gods had abandoned his family. He would give them nothing more than contempt. At least this festival would be over quickly.

A bell tinkled softly. There she was again. The woman who had danced in the back of his mind since he saw her yesterday. He frowned, shoving thoughts of her aside. He couldn't afford to be distracted by such things. Yet as she, and a maiden with brown hair, glided to the front of the temple Kai's eyes and thoughts wandered back to her.

The crowd fell silent. The atmosphere thickened with anticipation as the women readied themselves for the ceremonial *miko kagura* dance. The strum of *koto* strings echoed across the grounds, signalling the start. Following in time, the maidens took their first steps, dipping, bowing and sweeping their arms in precise and purposeful movements.

The music grew as the dance became more complex. Soft trills of flutes and the steady beat of taiko drums accompanied the priest's chanting. The temple maidens raised their ribbons, sweeping, twirling, hypnotic, never missing a beat. All eyes were on them but Kai saw only the maiden with the bells.

He caught the fall out of the corner of his eye. The maiden with brown hair collapsed. People cried out in alarm. The spell over the crowd broke.

'Mikoto!' the maiden with the bells called, running to her fallen companion.

A few men rushed over to the maidens and the crowd broke into hushed whispers. Looks of confusion flickered across every face.

The Priest rose from the maiden's side and called for everyone's attention. 'The gods are pleased! They have come upon our maiden and gifted her with visions in this hour of worship. This is a good omen!'

The crowd broke into a jubilant cheer. Kai grimaced. Nothing more than livestock following their herder. Lord Kenji clapped but Kai did not join in. He watched instead as the maiden with the bells accompanied the others away. Her eyes were wide, her cheek pale. He didn't need to be a superstitious man to see that something was amiss.

*

Was this really a good omen? Clearly the gods could not wait to pass this message on. The temple servants laid Mikoto on her bed. Her breathing was strained, her skin clammy with sweat.

'Mikoto?'

Her only response was to moan and toss in her bed.

'Mikoto? Can you hear me?'

Mikoto's eyes fluttered open. '…A-Akiko?'

'I'm here.' Akiko squeezed her friend's hand.

'You're safe? Thank the gods' Mikoto murmured.

Akiko frowned. 'What do you mean by that?'

Fear clouded Mikoto's eyes. 'My vision…In my vision I saw you. You were inside the temple…Lord Kenji was there too, and a samurai. D-death …everything was painted in blood! Oh gods Akiko! So much blood!'

Akiko's stomach turned.

'That's why you haven't been having any visions!' Mikoto clutched Akiko's hand. 'You can never foresee your own future, but I have seen yours!'

Akiko rose from her knees. 'If that's true then I must go and warn Lord Kenji and the samurai.'

'No! If you do you might die!' Mikoto grasped tighter at her hand.

'The gods gave us this warning for a reason. If there are people's lives at risk I must try and save them, Mikoto!' Akiko wrenched her hand free. 'Besides you didn't see me die, right? It's a warning not a prophecy.'

Akiko didn't wait. She hurried to the door pausing at the threshold to look back at Mikoto's tear-streaked face. 'Pray for me.'

*

The Festival petered out with the abrupt ending of the *miko kagura* dance. The last prayers said, the crowds dispersed and returned to their homes. Lord Kenji, however, headed inside the temple. Kai followed. Maybe he wanted to pay his respects before leaving?

They stepped inside.

'My Lord!'

Lord Kenji paused. The maiden with the bells rushed towards them.

She bowed, breathless. 'Lord Kenji. Forgive me but there has been a vision of your future. I believe you're in danger.'

Lord Kenji quirked an eyebrow. 'What sort of danger?'

'Mortal.' She glanced fearfully around the quiet room. 'We must leave this place!'

The Lord chuckled. 'This is a temple, my dear. No gods-fearing man would touch me in here.'

'My lord, please. You must listen to me!' She laid a slender hand on his wrist.

'Enough.' He shook her hand off and drew himself up. 'I do not answer to the whims of a woman. I shall leave when I'm ready. I wish to speak with the Priest. Summon him.'

The maiden's eyes briefly flickered to Kai. Their depths held determination as well as fear. Did she think he could sway Kenji? He had as little power as she to convince him. She must have realised the futility of the appeal, for her eyes returned to the ground and she bowed. She might be determined, but she was smart enough to hold her tongue. The tension in Kai's shoulders eased.

The maiden made her way towards the door. With her hand on the panel, her body tensed. She turned back, fear in her eyes. Kai didn't need to ask why. He, too, recognised the heavy footfalls of armoured men marching across the courtyard outside, and the clang of metal weapons. Whoever these newcomers were, they were no peasants.

Kai stood protectively in front of Lord Kenji and the maiden. His right hand hovered over the hilt of his katana; ready for the first sign of trouble.

Outside, the priest cried out, 'Put down your weapons! This is sacred ground!'

A short pause in the marching. One man yelled a battle cry. The sound of steel slicing flesh cut off the priest's cry of fear. The maiden gasped in horror. Lord Kenji swallowed and eyed the door, his face pale. But Kai poised himself for battle.

The door burst open. The first intruder ran into the temple, sword high, ready to strike. Kai drew and unleashed his katana. The glint of steel gave way to a spray of red. A muffled gurgle, then a thud and the intruder fell to the floor.

At the door, a band of eight men took one look at their fallen comrade and then at Kai. They charged forward, faces contorted with snarls of rage. Kai turned aside, katana slicing into an unprotected back. He snatched out his tanto and blocked a strike at his head. Attack, block, counter. The metallic clang of clashing steel sang in the cold night. He swung, stabbed, and drew his blade across an exposed throat. A man cried out for his severed arm before his head followed suit. Kai was no longer a man with a sword, but force of nature.

*

Akiko froze. The young samurai confronted each opponent with an unearthly grace and skill. But still more armed men entered the room, replacing their fallen comrades. Akiko feared this was a battle he couldn't win. She wasn't about to stay to find out.

'Follow me!' she hissed at Lord Kenji, and ran towards the back of the room. She revealed a door, disguised in the timber panelling.

Akiko and Lord Kenji slipped into the next room and out another door to the gardens. Cloud covered the moon, making it difficult to see where they were going. But Akiko had walked these grounds for half her life, so she went by feel and memory. An old broom leant against a nearby wall. Akiko grabbed it. It wouldn't do much good against a steel blade if they were caught, but it was better than nothing.

In the darkness, Kenji's heavy footfalls were loud on the autumn leaves. The bell in her hair jingled. She discarded the hairpin and drew the lord onto bare ground.

The clash of weapons and shouts of men rang out from within the temple. An unfamiliar voice called for the attackers to search for Lord Kenji in the grounds. Akiko clutched the broom close. Their attackers would undoubtedly kill her, too. But where to hide?

Footsteps crunched somewhere to the left. They had to move, and quickly. Akiko grabbed Lord Kenji's kimono sleeve and guided him further into the dark gardens.

*

Yanking the katana from his opponent's chest, Kai was rewarded with an anguished cry. The man slumped to the floor with the rest of his comrades. Blood pooled on the tatami and spattered the timber walls. But not a single drop was his. An overwhelming sense of victory filled Kai as he assessed his handiwork.

He flicked his katana to remove the blood then turned to reassure Lord Kenji and the maiden. They were gone, but where? Kai spotted the hidden door, still ajar, and made his way through. The door led from the back of the temple, into the extensive grounds out back.

Kai's foot brushed something that tinkled. Picking up the little bells, Kai cursed. How was he supposed to protect them if they'd run off? And where were they now? More attackers stalked the grounds, brashly confident in their noisy search, hacking at bushes and thrusting weapons into every hiding place. He'd just have to pray that Kenji and the maiden stayed alive until he found them.

*

Akiko shrank into the darkness of the tiny shrine and held her breath. Beside her, Kenji stilled. A dark form filled the doorway, silhouetted in the cool moonlight. A torch flared. She flinched. The intruder gave a cry of satisfaction and snatched a fistful of Kenji's hair.

'Found him! Here!' he yelled. 'Cowering behind a woman.' His companions responded with laughter.

'No!' Akiko cried out, tugging at the lord's arm. 'Let him be!'

Her protest was useless. Lord Kenji let out a pained grunt as he was dragged from their hiding place by his hair.

The lord struggled against the man with more ferocity than expected of an elderly man. He thrashed and kicked his captor in the shin. Their attacker let out a yelp but kept his hold on Lord Kenji.

Akiko leapt and swung the broom into the unprotected back of the soldier's head. There was a sickening crack and the broom handle exploded into a firework of splinters. The man crumpled like rice paper. Kenji staggered free.

Akiko stared in horror. Moonlight filtered through the trees and illuminated the body at her feet. A shard of wood protruded from the base of his skull. Blood flowed from the wound and stained the white pebble path into scarlet. The soldier's eyes stared blankly back at her.

*

A cry of triumph ahead alerted Kai. Lord Kenji and the maiden had been found. Kai followed the sound. Two more soldiers tramped through the gardens, headed towards their companion and his captives.

A scream sent a chill through his blood. The temple maiden's voice. Kai ran. He caught the two soldiers and cut them down before they could raise the alarm. He sprinted past their lifeless bodies and skidded to a halt before a small, secluded shrine.

Lord Kenji and the maiden stood in the shadows nearby. Their attacker lay dead, a shard of wood embedded in his skull. Lord Kenji trembled, his hair in wild disarray, mouth opening and closing like a landed fish. The maiden clung to a tree and wept helplessly. The broken stump of a broomstick hung from her hand.

'I killed him...I-I killed him.' She choked down sobs and sank to the ground. Her face was ghost-pale in the moonlight and she stared at the bloodied stick in her hand.

Guilt clawed through Kai's gut. It was his role to protect them. The maiden's hands were soiled with the life of another; something that could never be wiped clean. But they did not have time to dwell on such things.

'We can't stay here. There could be more men,' he whispered

The maiden sniffed and rose on wobbly legs. Kai offered her a steadying a hand. Her fingers gripped his and she looked up at him. Tears drowned her dark eyes. A strange sensation tugged at his stomach. He wanted to make those tears disappear.

'You'll be alright. I'm here now,' he murmured.

She nodded, took a shaky step, then collapsed. Kai caught her before she hit the ground. Her clothing was spattered in blood but she didn't seem to be injured. She had simply fainted. Kai gathered her into his arms. Her body was so small and warm against his. Focus! They had to keep moving. Kai jerked his head at Lord Kenji.

'Let's go, my lord.'

*

Akiko woke and struggled to dispel the fog clouding her mind. She lifted her head. She was inside Mikoto's quarters. An *andon* lantern flickered dimly in one corner and cast a dim glow over Lord Kenji and Mikoto, who slept on pallets against the walls. The young Samurai sat beside Akiko, his back against the wall, facing the door. He was cleaning his blade. He paused when she sat up, his dark eyes locking onto hers.

The murderous attack came flooding back and she inhaled sharply at the onslaught of memory. Tears welled but she bit her lip and clenched her eyes shut.

'You did what you had to do. If you didn't, you would be dead.' The Samurai's voice was soft and reassuring.

Akiko didn't trust herself to respond. If she tried to brave even a single word, her voice would shatter and break. He was right. She had acted in self-defence, but that didn't stop the sickness in her stomach when she remembered the dead man lying on the ground.

She had spilled blood and was tainted forever. Her heart gave way to the anguish and the tears flowed freely.

The young samurai shifted closer and pulled her into a comforting embrace. She should have fought against his touch, but she was too weary and broken. She gave in to the warmth and safety his arms offered. He continued to hold her even after she'd stopped crying.

'What's your name?' he asked breaking the silence.

'Akiko.' She sniffed.

He shifted as he dug for something in a bag hanging from his *hwa-obi*. He offered the object to her on his open palm. 'I believe you dropped this, Akiko'

Akiko stared in bewilderment. It was her hairpin with the bells. 'T-thank you…' She paused. She didn't know his name.

'Kai. Kai Uchimura,' he said.

She gingerly accepted her hairpin and a pleasant tingle ran through her as her fingers brushed his palm. 'Thank you, Kai,' she whispered looking up into his dark eyes.

His lips pressed together. He snatched his hand back and turned away with a frown. An uncomfortable quiet fell between them and Akiko's heart sank. Why the sudden change? He had been warm and comforting just moments before. Was it something she'd done?

She shifted, attempting to create some space between their bodies. But Kai turned back to her and she froze. He looked uneasy and unsure. Kai's gaze shifted from her to the hairpin.

'I have to know. Why the bells?'

'Why?' Akiko raised the hairpin to eye-level and twirled it in her fingers. The bells made a small jingle. 'The gods follow the calls of bells. It means they're always near, wherever I go.'

He frowned again. Not at her but at the hairpin. His gaze darkened; his fists clenched. But why? She didn't have the courage to ask.

'You still believe in such things? Even after tonight?' His words were strangely cold.

Akiko stared into the flame of the lantern. 'I do. I am certain they are looking after me. Especially after tonight.'

Kai eyed her sceptically. 'And why is that?'

'Because they sent you.'

Kai's frown disappeared and his gaze softened. Feeling the heat rise to her cheeks, she turned aside. But Kai touched his fingers under her chin and lifted it. Akiko hadn't expected him to be so gentle. Her heart fluttered and goosepimples danced across her skin. He leant closer, his eyes fixed on hers. Her lips parted in anticipation.

*

The sound of her bells had drawn him to her like a moth to the flame. But was he ready to fly into that flame and burn? Everyone he'd ever loved had been ripped away from him. Why would she be any different? Doubt plagued him and he pulled away.

'I'm sorry. Akiko. I...' His excuses died before they passed his lips.

Akiko's honey brown eyes held nothing but innocent confusion and his chest tightened. He gently pushed her aside. He couldn't think straight when she was close. Maybe he should go outside and get some fresh air?

'Did I do something wrong?' Akiko asked.

She sounded hurt. Guilt clawed at him. The last thing he wanted was to hurt her. Why was he doing this to himself? To her?

'No…' He let the word hang in the air unsure of what else to say. 'You should go back to sleep.'

'Are you going to sleep?'

'No.' He stared at the door. There had been no sounds of soldiers for many hours. 'I have to keep watch.'

'Then I shall stay up with you and keep you company.'

She gazed up at Kai and lifted her chin, silently challenging him to rebuke her. He should have done just that, but his curiosity got the better of him.

'Why?'

Akiko took his hand gently between hers. He tried to pull free but she held on. She brushed her thumbs against the back of his hand and looked him steadily in the eyes.

'Because I don't want you to be lonely.'

He was speechless. Akiko's words sent shock rippling through him. The armour fell away and his reservations crumbled. He couldn't fight it anymore. He wanted her. He cupped her face and leaned in until their lips met.

The kiss was slow and gentle. Kai savoured the sweet taste of her soft lips and drowned. He snaked an arm around her waist and drew her close. He felt every ragged breath she took between their kiss. Could she feel his heart hammering?

The sound of shuffling broke them apart. Lord Kenji had moved in his sleep. Kai dropped back to reality. Was he mad? Even if he took the risk of opening his heart to Akiko, what would their future look like? She was a temple maiden, married to the gods.

Maybe he would burn in the fires of *Jigoku* for falling for her. The corners of his mouth twitched. Antagonising the gods in such a way was an amusing thought. Looking back down at Akiko, he kissed her forehead. She smiled and rested her head against his shoulder.

The lantern flickered, the wick nearly finished. Soon the sun would rise, and bring with it a new day. And for the first time in a long time, Kai wouldn't face it alone.

*

Akiko clutched Kai's hand as they left Mikoto's room at dawn. The bodies of the fallen lay strewn in bloody death throughout the temple grounds. The priest, some of the musicians, and the intruders. Over twenty of the attackers lay across the compound where Kai had cut them down. Akiko shuddered and looked away. Lord Kenji laid a hand on Kai's shoulder in rough gratitude.

As they arrived in the village Lord Kenji sought out the village headman to track down the person responsible for the attack. It didn't take long for the investigations to bear fruit. Lord Kenji returned to his home and ordered Kai to his side.

A guard stood outside the heavy timber door.

'Move aside,' Lord Kenji snarled. The guard looked hesitantly to the door. Kai drew his sword, the slither of metal on wood loud. The guard swallowed and bowed. The door slid aside and Lord Kenji stalked in, Kai close behind. Akiko trailed them quietly.

'Father!?' Ichiro's voice went up an octave. His eyes widened and his jaw dropped.

'What is the meaning of this?' Lord Kenji demanded, waving a hand at his son. Ichiro occupied the lord's traditional seat. A spread of delicacies lay on the lacquered table before him.

Ichiro shied away from his father, eyes darting around the room.

'W-w-what do you mean?'

'Your plot to have me killed last night! You've already told the people I'm dead and named yourself Lord!'

Ichiro rose from the seat and drew himself up. He faced his father in open rebellion 'I *am* Lord now! The priest assured me that the star with the tail was a sign of my divine appointment.'

Lord Kenji's face purpled with rage. 'You are not Lord! Not so long as I draw breath!' He paced away, the rage fizzling to hurt as he eyed his son. 'How could you commit such treachery!'

'How? How!?' Ichiro clicked his tongue 'You say I'm your heir but what will I be the Lord of by the time you finally kick the dust? You rule with too soft a hand. Our lands are being taken by the Himoto clan in the north. You should have stepped down when I asked you. You left me no choice!'

'And you leave me with no choice. Guards!'

Two of Lord Kenji's guards, who'd been waiting outside, entered at his call.

The panic returned to Ichiro's eyes. 'You can't!' He backed away from their grasp. 'I am Lord! Cease this at once!'

The guards ignored Ichiro and grabbed him. Ichiro squirmed and yelled abuse, but they dragged him away. He would await Lord Kenji's judgement. Akiko's heart ached. Such a betrayal would leave a deep wound. Lord Kenji took a shaky breath and faced her and Kai.

'I owe you both my life. Thank you.' He bowed to Kai. 'I will see to it that you are both handsomely rewarded. And I would ask you, Kai, to stay on as my personal guard.'

Kai's face lit up. He bowed deeply. 'I'm honoured, my lord.'

Kenji nodded. 'I have much to do to clean up after this mess. Assist the temple maiden then return to your duties, here.' He waved them away.

They bowed and left the Lord in peace. By unspoken agreement, they turned away from the path to the temple and headed towards the village. Akiko lifted her face. The sun warmed her skin, but not nearly as much as the excitement blooming in her chest. Kai took long strides and she had to skip to keep up. He hadn't said a word all morning. Akiko couldn't bring herself to break the spell between them.

Kai halted abruptly outside the village. His face was a blank mask. 'What will you do now the priest is dead?'

Akiko paused. What would she do now? Another priest would be sent and she'd be able to return to the temple. But did she want to? Akiko looked at Kai and the answer was simple. No, she did not want to return. She was done with the temple. There was truly only one thing in this world she wanted above all else: to stay by Kai's side.

The gods had brought them together. Carved him into her soul and written him in the heavens. The connection she'd always sought. She would follow him into death if that's what it meant to be with him.

'I'm going to resign from the temple,' she finally answered.

Kai turned to face her, brows lifted. 'Can you do that? Aren't you married to the gods?'

He stared at her intently. Akiko looked down at her garments still covered in dirt and speckled with blood. 'I'm tainted now, so the marriage is nullified.'

Silence fell upon them and Akiko played at the fabric of her sleeve to ease her nerves.

'So, you would be free to marry whoever you wanted then?' He sounded unsure yet hopeful.

She smiled. One little word gave her such joy. It opened her up to a world of new possibilities and a freedom she'd never known.

'Yes.'

Kai saw the world anew. Such was the effect of Akiko's revelation. She was free from her role as a shrine maiden. Hiro's last words echoed again in his mind.

'You gave me a reason to live, gave me something special to protect. Now you must find yours.'

Kai finally understood Hiro's meaning. He had found someone to protect. Not some lord to fight and die for. But someone special he could *live* for: Akiko.

His path had crossed with hers and now their lives were inextricably joined.

For better or for worse, only the future could tell.

1531CE
Somewhere on the Mediterranean Sea

Marvel of the Stars

Jo Seysener

'Would you keep this infernal boat still!' Peter Apian-Bennewitz griped, balancing on one leg and gripping his tripod tightly. A soft snort drifted down from the quarterdeck. The deck lurched again. Peter took several stumbling steps. The ship pitched forward. He bumped into a sailor, who flinched away, crossed himself, and muttered a curse.

The telescope Peter clutched dropped to the hardwood deck, hit with a smack that made the scientist wince, and rolled, tinkling, towards the gunwales. Peter chased it across the deck. Sailors' laughter mingled with gasps, curses, and a few well-aimed kicks at the suspicious instrument. Peter slipped on freshly-applied decking oil and plunged headfirst into a pile of mops and wooden buckets.

His precious telescope – a gift from Charles V, Holy Roman Emperor no less – zigzagged its way through the clutter of ropes and straight over the side. Peter uttered a sharp cry, slipped again, and planted his face firmly into the mop's soggy tentacles.

A cheer sounded. Peter lifted his damp face. A golden halo of curls rose above the side of the ship, followed by a cherubic face bearing a cheeky grin. The young boy shimmied onto the deck, telescope in one small hand and paintbrush in the other.

He waved both enthusiastically and let loose a torrent of words Peter could only partially understand. Droplets of white paint spattered crew and deck alike, causing an uproar of shouts and creative insults. The tiny sailor made his way through the crowd and, with a small bow, presented the telescope. Peter sat up, not bothering to brush off the dripping tendrils clinging to his shoulder.

'Thankyou.'

The boy smiled and bowed again, still chattering away. Peter caught a scatter of recognisable words mixed into the pigeon language that evolved between sailors and ports. A steady rhythm of bootsteps diverted his attention. The Captain descended from the quarterdeck.

The Captain was not a young man, though he regularly assured the officers that he had been, once. Not too long ago, either. Dark eyes studied Peter, who understood how the minute beings he tried to observe beneath his lens felt.

'Is it broken, then?' The Captain's voice was surprisingly soft, though he could bellow through a gale.

Peter gingerly shook the telescope, listening for the ominous tinkle. His chin came up. He met the Captain's ironic gaze. Then Peter's hand tilted downwards. The sound of glass sliding on metal froze the half-smile on his mouth. The Captain's lip curled and he walked away, a small bounce in his step. Peter groaned. He would never get to view this blasted comet and prove his theory!

'I'll fix it for you.'

Peter wheeled about. A small head of sun-bleached curls bobbed at navel level. The young sailor who had recovered his telescope spoke.

'I-if I c-c-can, that is, sir.' Angelic blue eyes gazed at Peter. 'I have an Uncle, well, he's not really an uncle, he was just a friend of me Pa's, but he, um, he used ta show me how to fit glass, not grind it, you know, he used to do them 'ard bits but fit the glass, well, if you have any spare, sir, I'll give it a go.'

'Your Uncle used to grind glass and make...spectacles? No, no not your Uncle, your Pa's friend, that's it isn't it?' Peter corrected himself as the cherub's mouth opened.

'Yep. Pa's mate. He could help them old folk see better. Some young ones too, I reckon. He let me wind the wire round about and fix it with them tiny screws, then polish the glass up 'til it was clear as...well, as, clear as glass? Erm, anyway, does it have a spare one? A lens I mean?' The boy gazed at Peter in great curiosity.

'Well, I don't know if it has a spare one, Master...?' Peter lifted a brow.

'Baker.' He sketched a quick little bow. 'Matthew Baker.'

Peter glanced over his shoulder to see the Captain observing the exchange. The Captain gestured the boy away, his eyes on Peter the entire time.

'Mister Apian,' he said, 'you be careful with that boy. He lost his father young and we're his family now, right here. I don't care if the bloody Pope insisted you board my ship—'

'Emperor. Charles V, Holy Roman Emperor—'

'—but I will not have you pushing your ludicrous ideas on our young men! Men brought up to be sailors, not cosmologists chasing bloody comets!' The Captain snorted derisively. 'Do you know who his father was? He's named after him and you don't even know, do you?'

Peter shook his head, angst tightening his chest.

'Matthew Baker was a famous shipwright. Built this very ship. Not that you'd care about that, Mister Apian.' He prodded Peter's shoulder. 'Her Majesty might want you here, to keep in with Rome, but this is still my ship! If I hear you giving that boy any funny ideas...' Glaring, the Captain turned on his heel and left Peter standing alone.

*

A low whistle drew his attention. Matthew waited at the hatch. Peter followed him down into the muggy darkness. It didn't seem to matter how frigid the air was above decks, beneath the air was always stale and still. The effect of men and animals living in close quarters. Matthew followed Peter into his cabin. Peter laid the telescope on a small bench nailed to the wall, and picked up a cylindrical leather case, fiddling with the straps.

'You're not afraid of touching a devil's instrument then?' Peter asked wryly. 'Not scared you'll be possessed?'

Little Matthew shook his head. 'No, sir.'

'Well then, let us see if the Holy Roman Emperor saw fit to supply me with spares, Master Baker.' The end of the tube popped open. Peter delicately inclined the case over his bunk. Nothing fell out, and the two shared a glance.

'If I may, sir?' Matthew reached for the case. His slid a thin arm in all the way to his armpit. With a pull that sent him halfway across the cabin, he emerged, holding a small leather pouch. Ginning, he tossed it to Peter, who caught it with a panicked gasp. Peter carefully unfolded the pouch to reveal two smooth, rounded lenses. He smiled. Matthew pulled a thin tool from his waistband.

The two worked quietly in the beginning, passing small wires and other parts, speaking only when necessary. Slowly, and with many a covert glance, Matthew began to ask questions: what was it like in Rome; to meet the Emperor? What was an Emperor V, anyway? Which famous people had Peter met? Had he met the Queen? Why was the telescope on a ship that moved constantly? Why did the Captain call him a 'mad Bastard'? Peter smiled and answered the boy's questions as best he could.

'What's a cosmo-oologist?' Matthew leaned towards the lantern hanging above him and twisted a wire through two small holes in the brass casing to secure the outer lens.

'I'm not supposed to be "giving you ideas", young Matthew. According to the Captain,' Peter answered, rubbing the lens with a cloth.

'Pfft. I'm on a ship, sir. A ship full of sailors who teach me how to swear and which whore to pick at each port. I'm thirteen next birthday, sir.'

'Good God, are you really?' Peter stared at the boy, taking in his small stature and thin arms. 'Very well then, Matthew Baker who is nearly thirteen years old, I shall tell you what the study of Cosmology is.

'Cosmology is more than just the study of our universe, the Cosmos,' began Peter with a sweeping arc of his hand. 'It incorporates an understanding of all our known sciences, plus astronomy of course – the study of our stars. Cosmology is the study of an object in space and its relativity to everything in the universe. Like the Sun to our moon, or a far-off star. To grasp all this, though, one must have learned mathematics and geometrics, cartography, chemistry, physics, and philosophy. I personally favour the works of Ptolemy, but others are not so convinced…'

Mathew watched him, wide-eyed.

Peter shrugged. 'I've written a book. Plotted the cosmos as far as we can see. Well, for now, anyway. And that, Master Baker, is why I am here!' He smiled and stood tall, bumping his head on a low hanging deck beam.

Matthew nodded eagerly. 'Why, sir? What's why you're here?'

'You shall see in the next few days, Matthew. Very soon, we shall all see.'

*

Wilson went cross-eyed watching the dark liquid slosh within the bottle. Up, down, up…down. The rum moved at a slightly slower rate than the ship's sway. He imagined a tiny ship within the bottle, meandering above the waves, before sinking, swallowed. Wilson's head canted to the side, with a pop that would cause a crick in his neck tomorrow. He sang a little tune and picked out the stars through the mist hanging low over the gunwales.

Thirty degrees off the horizon, a small sun burned, tiny at first, then steadily brighter; a demon red glow. An omen of doom for the ship! Befuddled, but not insane, Wilson hesitated. For sure the Captain would give him the old Cat for stealing rum, and for being drunk on duty, if he rang the bell. He eyed the demon-glow again and swore. Stumbling, he tottered toward the bell, grasped the bell rope and pulled with all his might.

The clang reverberated through the quiet night. Sailors spewed forth from the ship's guts, most barefoot and with clothing in disarray. Some brandished weapons – whatever had been nearest to them as they dashed for the ladders. Wilson bellowed, gesturing frantically to the sun glowing through the fog. Gasps and cries arose in a terrified fervour. The Captain paced the deck with soft bootsteps, lips pursed and a deep frown etched into his harsh features.

Peter Apain's head, his mouth agape, popped out of the hatch. He stared at the crowd clustered around Wilson, who still had his arm in the air.

'Well, well,' said Peter, smiling. 'What's happening here?' He climbed onto the deck.

The sailors stared at him. Peter's eyes followed along Wilson's arm into the sky and paused at the spectacle before him.

'Well,' he whispered. He spun in wide circles with his arms stretched out, face turned upward. He took a great, shuddering breath and let out a whoop of laughter, which bubbled on and on. Wilson and the crew stood frozen, watching the mad man cackle and prance. Echoes of his laughter bounced back, distorted by the mist.

The Captain cleared his throat.

*

Peter stopped his dance and looked around at the mixture of fear and resentment on the faces of the crew.

'This…this is…it's… Oh, you didn't think…you think…?' Peter stumbled through several thoughts at once. 'This isn't a-a-a hellspawn,' he cried. 'This is a comet! My comet,' he whispered. 'Isn't it Captain? This is what I'm here for.'

The Captain's face remained frozen. The crew slowly turned to face him, their attention divided between Peter and the Captain.

'Yes, Mister Apian, this is what you're here for.' The Captain hawked and turned on his heel. 'We should all get a good night's rest now so you can chase your blasted comet tomorrow. Mister Wilson, you'll report to me in the morning.' He threw this last over his shoulder and stalked off in the direction of his cabin, pausing only to have a quiet word in the ear of his first mate.

The sailors dispersed, with malevolent backward looks at Peter. The mate enlisted a sailor and they collected Wilson, who was frozen with an expression of fear.

Peter stayed on deck, gazing up into the heavens. The sky began to lighten. Peter returned once to his cabin to retrieve some writing materials.

*

Something nudged Peter's shoulder. A voice whispered in his ear.

'Sir,' Matthew murmured. 'Sir, please, you need to get up now.' He jostled again and this time Peter cracked his eyes open. Matthew tilted his head. 'You must be cold and sore lying there, please get up before the Captain comes out.'

Peter sat up, rubbing a hand over his face. He squinted at Matthew, then grinned and tousled Matthew's hair.

Matthew grinned in return. 'This is it, isn't it, sir? What you said you needed the telescope for?'

Peter nodded and opened his mouth. He was cut off by a cry from above.

'Land!'

A snort came from a nearby deckhand. 'That's not land. There's not enough of it to *be* land!' A few sailors laughed.

A thump beside Peter made him jump. He stared at a pair of black boots.

'Your rock, Mister Apian,' said the Captain.

*

Several hours later, Peter clambered gingerly down a swaying ladder into the tiniest boat he had ever seen. The little boat bobbed ominously, yet Peter managed to safely ensconce himself behind the sailor manning the oars, with Matthew in the front. Salty water rained in droplets down Peter's neck with each stroke of the oars. The little rock in the middle of the sea grew nearer.

A sharp crack, followed by a cry, echoed over the waves. Peter twisted around. On the ship, sailors gathered in a knot on the deck. Another crack, another cry. Peter faced forward again. Matthew turned away, looking to the rock formation ahead. His slim shoulders shook with shuddering breaths. Even the oarsman's face was grim. Peter focused on the rugged black stone and soon he and Matthew were slowly clambering up the only scalable incline. The sailor cursed while he searched for a safe place to secure the tender.

At the top, the rock strata was sheared off, creating a flat area. Peter set up his telescope there, measuring angles and making adjustments. Matthew held his precious star charts and notes for safe keeping in the blustery winds. Shadows lengthened as dusk settled over the little island.

'What are you looking for?' asked Matthew. Both the young sailor and the scientist wore their warmest garb and had wrapped themselves in blankets against the sharp night air.

'I'm observing the comet, Master Baker,' began Peter. 'I've watched it from four different parts of the world, now. The comet's tail… Come, see through here…' He led Matthew, still clutching rumpled papers, over to the eye piece.

'See, the comet has a rounded head, followed by a long arc, ending in a point? That's the tail.' He shifted Matthew aside and put his own eye back to the telescope. 'Yes! The tail points backwards now, away from our sun! Whatever approach the comet is on, the tail points away from the sun. It seems to be dragging sometimes in a backwards-rearing arc. Perhaps in an attempt to avoid our great solar giant!'

Matthew nodded enthusiastically. 'Where does the comet come from?' he asked. 'Is it alive, then?'

'Oh no. Dear me, no!' laughed Peter. 'Though it does rather look like it, doesn't it?' Peter tilted his head, trying to see the comet as the sailors viewed it: a fearsome and unknown thing sighted on a foggy night when miles from anywhere in an old ship. No wonder they were superstitious fools.

Peter glanced sideways at Matthew and, in what would undoubtedly cause him an enormous amount of trouble in the near future, launched into a monologue on the comet and its purported origins; adding in his theories of radial waves. Matthew fell asleep and it took Peter a while to notice. He stayed up and observed the comet as long as he could, then he, too, succumbed to sleep and curled up next to the boy.

*

In the morning, he spent the return dinghy trip telling Matthew what he'd noted about the comet. Matthew yawned and pointed out his own handiwork – fresh signwriting on the bow of the ship. *'Marvel'* it read in neat white lettering.

When they reached the *Marvel,* the oarsman held the bottom of the ladder while Matthew climbed up quickly and disappeared over the side. Eager to catch him, Peter shot up the ladder and rolled clumsily onto the deck. The morning sun beat down and droplets of sweat gathered in the hollow of his shoulder before creating a small cascade over his collarbone.

Hand raised, finger extended and mouth gaping open to continue his teachings, Peter froze before the sullen silence pervading the deck of ship. Several men scrubbed at a dark stain beneath an overhanging beam from which frayed ropes dangled. Faces turned towards him showed open hostility. Peter weaved silently around the crew and, with quickened steps, found his way to his cabin.

*

Peter, Matthew, and their boatman spent the next few nights in a nocturnal cycle: rowing to the islet in the late afternoon, spending their nights on the blustery rock to observe the comet, and returning to the ship as the sun rose each morning. During those days, Peter tried to engage several of the crew, but found few of them responsive. The worst came when he enquired about Wilson, and was met only with scowls and undisguised anger. So Peter retired to his cabin, and stayed there.

A tired Matthew brought him food he said he had taken from Cook under the pretence that it was for himself. On the third afternoon of his self-imposed isolation, Peter decided fresh air was more important to his health than avoiding the crew's animosity. He stumbled up onto the sunlit deck. The glare blinded him briefly. A familiar soft cough startled him. He turned to greet the Captain, whose face wore a deeper scowl than usual.

'Must you go against every command I issue you, Mister Apian?' he growled. 'The boy has been spouting off all sorts of scientific nonsense. Things that have no place on my ship. Mark my word, you'll cause problems,' he grumbled. 'He'll spend no further time with you. As soon as we reach our next continental port, you'll be off-loaded.' His lips compressed into a thin line and he stalked away. His crewmen closed the path behind him.

Peter sighed. There were so many good men who thought in the same backwards way. How could he make the Captain see how valuable his science was?

He walked forward across the deck, stretching his legs. The seamen, scrubbing at decks and tidying ropes, muttered as he passed.

'…heard four months ago – Portugal flattened out like God smashed Sodom and Gomorrah…'

'…earthquake, killed half the town!'

'…and that comet; red as a devil comin' to burn us all!'

Peter breathed deeply of the sea air, his shoulders slumping. Finishing his pilgrimage to the bow he prepared to face the sailors on his return journey. He paused. There was a still heaviness in the air; a quality that hinted at a not so far off storm. There. Dark clouds loomed behind his rock, moving with a wind only the heavens could feel.

Shouts raised the alarm. The figures on the quarterdeck shaded their eyes and strained to see the cause. Rigging was hastily manhandled and sails trimmed to orders as a squally wind blew up. The ship began to rock in the swell. Storm clouds blotted out the sun. Peter stumbled and grasped the ropes dangling from a mast. The ship swayed and his feet slipped from under him.

Rain pelted the sailors, who rushed about securing loose items. Lightning flashed and thunder cracked overhead. Peter gasped. The ship had swung around to face his rock. Too near. It no longer looked friendly. Peter clutched at the ropes. How frail the ship was in relation to the rugged islet.

Wind gusted across the deck sending two crewmen crashing into Peter's mast. One lay still, water splashing over him, his head lolling. Peter hooked a foot around the sailor's leg. Rain and seawater stung his eyes and Peter tilted his head down to protect his face.

The rain eased. Thunder boomed, muted now. Peter looked about. The squall had moved off as fast as it had materialised. The sea settled into a sullen, grey-green roll. Peter wiped the moisture from his eyes with numb, shaky hands. He sloshed towards his cabin and crashed into a bulky sailor, who seemed intent on staring him down. Peter stammered his apologies, moving around the mountain only to find a wall of men, glowering at him and muttering darkly to one another.

Peter stood, fixed. On the quarterdeck, the Captain's penetrating gaze swept the men. Peter shivered, lost on his little section of bare wooden boards, saturated and sticky with salt water. The large sailor knocked him heavily aside.

Mutters turned to angry cries.

'Walks right up on deck, right the bow of the ship! Then...'

'It's 'is fault, it is!'

'Not natural, 'im. That ungodly scope-thing.'

A whisper. 'Jonas.'

Peter froze, looking from one seaman to the next. A mob was the world's most dangerous creature. A waft of cold air stroked the nape of Peter's neck. A sailor wearing a deep scowl stared at him. Flecks of white salt crystals gathered in the creases of the sailor's bloodshot eyes. Mutters, like a chant, swirled. Hands closed around Peter's arms; hauled him sideways. Peter stumbled several steps across the deck, feet tangled in a coil of rope. Panic strangled a cry in his throat.

A bell-like sound echoed around the ship, across the open sea. Crewmen halted, then milled in confusion.

'Sirens.'

'Mermaids,' they cried.

'That rock 'e was on, them sirens sing from it!'

'They'll drown us, sink the ship!'

'Take 'im back. Send 'im back to 'em!'

For a moment, silence reigned. Then the deck creaked. The ship shuddered and moved without a wind. A single, gentle bump. Up, down. A sigh ran through the crew. As one, the crowd shuffled across the deck, dragging Peter with them. The deck tilted. His steps became laboured. The deck rose, as though a mountain grew beneath the ship. Ropes uncoiled into thin snakes, slithering down to the sea. Buckets and crates tumbled past him to collect in a pile against the gunwales. Sailors screamed and scrabbled for handholds.

With a mighty yawn, the ship arced back into the sea, slamming into the water with a resounding splash. Peter tumbled to the deck, drenched in salt water. Spluttering, he splashed across the deck to locate Matthew, finding him beneath a bucket and part of a ripped sail. He set the boy on his feet.

Again, came the sound attributed to the sirens, but close this time, so much closer. Peter peered into the water. Beneath the ship glided an enormous white shape. A giant, black eye gazed back at him, then the huge beast rolled and dove. His stomach clenched in fear, until a sailor's shout broke the silence.

'Kraken!'

Peter spun about, his momentary fear eradicated by disbelief. Demons, sirens, mermaids, and now krakens? The superstitions held by the seamen astounded him. He snorted, patted Matthew on the head, and swiped at the salt water still dripping into his eyes.

Still chuckling, Peter began to collect the small items that had been displaced during the almost biblical upheaval. He straightened, and stilled. Seamen clustered in a semi-circle around him, gazes fixed. Bemused, Peter sighed. Not again, surely?

A shout came from below decks.

'Water! We're takin' on water down here! Capt'n, we need to find land. We're going to sink!' With a well-timed, ominous groan, the ship creaked and shuddered. Snapping sounds crackled through the still air and crewmen grabbed for their nearest support.

'He calls 'em.' An old sailor edged forward, pointing at Peter. 'He calls 'em all, to eat us and break the ship!'

Peter huffed. Where was that damned Captain when he was needed? Couldn't the old bugger see there were more important things going on here?

'Listen here, these are none of your krakens or sirens or, or whathaveyous.' Peter pointed over the side of the ship. 'This is just a—'

A little cry behind him stopped his heart and choked his breath. Very carefully, so as not to startle anyone, he turned around. The huge crewman held Matthew, with a rope tied about his tiny waist, half lifted over the gunwales.

'Put him down.' A soft voice called down the length of the deck. Heads swivelled to the Captain as he paced steadily towards the mob. 'Now.'

'Capt'n, we can't,' spoke the little old sailor, pointing at Peter. 'He's made Matthew 'is familiar. We gets him off this ship, sir, an we'll be free. We'll be safe!' The crew all grumbled in agreement. Matthew swore and kicked at his captor. Peter held his breath.

An exasperated sound escaped the Captain.

'Blast you, Apian, I warned you,' the Captain growled, never taking his eyes from his crew. 'Now they think that if they toss the boy overboard to these "spirits", we'll all be safe! You and your blasted comet….' He drew in a sharp breath and expelled it, fixing his gaze on the sailors knotted before him.

'Now see here,' the Captain began. 'You! Canners. You release that boy now, or I swear you'll be wishing for port by the end of the day! And you, Perkins, back off! Now!' The Captain's roar echoed over the sea. 'You can lynch someone later. Right now, we have to get to land or we'll all join the damned kraken.'

'But that's just it, sir,' cried the old man, 'we won't make it to land with 'im aboard.'

The Captain glared at him. 'Is it to be mutiny, then?'

That should do it. Relieved to have someone take charge of the situation, Peter relaxed. But there was no change in the sailors' resolute expressions. The Captain continued his tirade, promising retribution and hellfire for those disobeying his command. Matthew's head disappeared beneath the railing. The ship creaked again, settling lower in the water.

'You have to throw me in.'

The sailors froze and the Captain's head snapped sideways. Peter gulped and firmed his gaze. He had to make this believable.

'It's me the kraken wants,' he continued, swallowing his fear. He held his gaze steadily on the sailors, searching for inspiration. 'It won't stop for the boy. Just me. Me and my telescope. Send away the sirens too. No mermaids, not today.' He stopped, planting his feet apart with his hands on his hips.

The ship creaked and groaned. Water gurgled belowdecks. The sailors muttered and nodded. Matthew's head reappeared over the railing and the boy was placed back on the deck. His eyes were wide and he clutched his arms, shivering.

Peter nodded to him and looked back at the crew. 'Well?'

Matthew's rope was released and fell to the deck. The Captain growled. Peter stepped forward. Eager hands grabbed his upper arms. He stepped up onto the railing. Someone pressed the telescope, in its case, into his hand. The old sailor must have moved fast to get to and from his cabin so quickly. Peter smiled wryly. One of the sailors holding his arms looked at him askance.

A muttering rose from amongst the crew. Several crewmen grumbled, milling about uncertainly. Peter blocked it all out. He took a deep breath of the salted air and sent a brief prayer to heaven. Perhaps drowning would be a quick process. Probably not. He'd be able to send a longer one on the way down. Peter teetered on the rail, waiting for someone to shove him over the side.

Poised upon his pedestal, Peter began to feel rather silly. Well, if they were going to take their time about it…He unstrapped the telescope from its case and let the case drop – theatrically – into the water.

The ship creaked ominously. Shouts from belowdecks took on a note of panic. The sailors crossed themselves. They advanced on him.

Peter steeled himself. One last look at his comet, then. He turned the telescope to the sky. The sun was still too bright. He couldn't spot the orb burning in the heavens. He sighed and dropped the telescope down to the horizon; the sea.

A shimmer of light, there, in the distance. He steadied the telescope with his other hand.

Peter smiled.

'Land,' he yelled.

The Captain launched himself to the rail, squinting against the glare. 'I see nothing!'

Peter handed over his telescope. The Captain hesitated, then peered through it. He lowered the tube, raised it, and lowered it again.

'I'll be damned,' he muttered. The Captain raised his voice. 'He's right. There's land. If we keep pumping the bilges we'll make it.'

Peter gazed about the crew. They stared back. For a breath, not a soul aboard moved. Then one of the sailors nearest him raised an arm. Peter braced himself, preparing for the cold immersion into depths of the sea below. A hand took his wrist. Another gripped his other arm, and another, pulling him back to the deck.

Peter looked about, completely nonplussed. He sought out Mathew. Were they sacrificing the boy again, instead? No, there he was, wrapped in a blanket, nestled at the Captain's feet. The crew scattered, raising sail and manning the bilges as the ship got underway.

The Captain gave his customary snort, his lips curved in a half smile. He returned the telescope.

'The men have decided your…scientific method…is a worthy talisman against the assorted mythical creatures assailing us today.' The half-smile grew to full capacity. 'Although that has a great deal to do with your spotting land at an opportune moment. I didn't think you had it in you, Mister Apian. You're safe.' He clapped Peter on the shoulder. Peter stumbled sideways on watery knees. 'So's the boy,' the Captain added.

Peter looked down at Matthew, now asleep at the Captain's feet.

'I have three of my own, Captain,' he said. 'Four, if my wife is safely delivered of the next by now.' He grinned at the Captain, who snorted derisively.

'Join me later, Mister Apian,' the Captain said. 'I have some fine cigars.'

Peter bowed. 'I would be honoured, sir.'

'And perhaps I won't offload you at the next port, after all,' the Captain said, glancing at the telescope. 'Especially if you can lay your hands on one of those, for me.'

The Captain slapped him on the back again and, this time, Peter's knees didn't buckle.

Vanin, where are you?

Does it matter?

Did you hear the message from the biocom?

Of course I did, you fool, Dren. It doesn't matter.

But they got our beacon. They'll send help.

Not soon enough. The message said they're evacuating the home world. It could be another millennium before they reach us. My goal hasn't changed. I just need to get to the new colony, instead.

But you're driving these people at a rate this world can't sustain. And the leaking crion particles are affecting their genome: those goblin-like creatures we met, and now there's a mother and daughter in—

Your daughter?

Don't be ridiculous, Van. Envy doesn't become you. Besides, we're incompatible species.

How can you stand *to be so close to them?*

How can you have lived amongst them for so long and not care about their welfare? They're not so different from us. C'mon. You're better than this.

...I can't, Dren.

Why?

If I let myself get involved I'll never get home. My people are more important. They have to be.

1682CE

Sagore, Bavaria

The Firestone

Belinda Messer

'But, Father,' Sarcha said, 'why must we move to Elsenfeld?' She twisted her apron in her hands. 'We've lived in Sagore all of my life. I was born in this house. Mother loved this—'

'Don't!' Ezekiel held up a work-roughened hand and frowned. 'Don't bring your mother into this, Sarcha.' His shoulders sagged and he sat at the wooden dining table he'd made sixteen years before, when Sarcha was born. 'If she were here, things would be very different – but she's not.' He swallowed and looked away.

Sarcha held her breath and stirred the pot over the fire. How she longed for her father to speak of her mother, Ellan. He'd all but forbidden the mention of her name after the cart accident, five years ago. Hope that he would continue to speak made Sarcha's heart pound.

'Father,' she tried again, 'haven't I always done everything you asked? I do my lessons, I cook and clean for us. I'm well-behaved and not the least bit of trouble for you.' She pushed aside a pang of guilt. No, now was not the time tell him about the tiny ginger kitten, hidden in her room.

He scraped his fingers though silvering hair and grimaced. 'You're a good daughter, Sarcha. Clever and kind. I only want what's best for you. We'll move to Elsenfeld where a bright girl like you will have a better future.'

'But it's a whole day's ride away!' Sarcha prodded angrily at the hearth fire, causing smoke to puff into the room. If only he would understand how lonely she was. 'You already make me stay away from everyone in Sagore. People like Maryim and her son, Lark, who loved and respected Mama—' She gulped as he glared at her.

Ezekiel rose. His head almost touched the timber-beamed ceiling. His face reddened. 'You will not speak Maryim's name again. I forbade you to see her after Ellan died and my order stands.'

'But, Father,' she protested, 'Maryim was Mama's best friend. Lark was my best friend – before he went to apprentice with his uncle, in Elsenfeld. And I heard he's back now. Why do you hate them so much? What did they do? I've just so many questions.' Her voice quivered with frustration.

'No.' Ezekiel slammed a fist on the table and turned away. 'I don't want to quarrel with you. Stay away from that woman, and her son. It's for your own good.'

She brushed away a tear. She couldn't bear for him to see her cry. If she ever wanted him to listen, he must see her as a mature woman, not a child.

'Off to bed now, Sarcha.' He dismissed her with the flick of his hand. 'I have to work on that special cart order. It's to be ready for pickup tomorrow afternoon.'

Sarcha swallowed down resentment. There was no point in arguing when he got like this. Ever since Ellan's death, her father had hidden his emotions away and not even his daughter could reach them. More tears slipped down her cheeks. She wiped them away and trudged up to her croft bedroom. The tallow candle in her hand dripped hot, like her tears.

*

Sarcha slipped into her room and closed the door quickly. Rogan emerged from beneath her bed and stretched, yawning. He trotted over and rubbed his fluffy little body against Sarcha's leg. She smiled and gathered the tiny kitten into her arms, cradling him close. He began to purr and she sighed.

'What's the point, Rogan?' she said. 'Father won't listen. And we definitely can't tell him about you. He's gets so cold and distant when he's mad. I can't stand it. He wasn't always this way'. She nuzzled the purring kitten and placed the candle on the little timber table Ezekiel had made for her fifth birthday. She looked around her beloved room. The knitted blanket her mother had made. The much-worn, cushioned chair beneath the shuttered window.

Her father had built this house with his bare hands. How could he want to leave? Why did he forbid her from seeing Maryim and Lark? Did Maryim know something about the Firestone? Or her mother's ability to see others' fates?

She sank onto the bed and set Rogan down. He curled up against her leg. Sarcha reached into her bodice and drew out her mother's Firestone. Five years ago, when Ellan had first given Sarcha the Firestone, it had been too hot to hold. Now it was cool and smooth. The pearl-white, oval stone nestled in her palm and gleamed in the candlelight.

Tonight, it seemed to tingle softly. Just as it had when she found Rogan, yesterday, in her favourite spot by the stream. And again, last night, when she'd lain in bed watching the bright, new fuzzy star shining through her bedroom window.

'Do you think Father hates Maryim because of this, Rogan?' Sarcha stroked the kitten and stared at the Firestone. 'And because of the Sight it gave to Mother?' The kitten mewed softly. 'Can I tell you a secret not even Father knows, Rogan?' Sarcha whispered. 'Mother gave this to me the day before she died. She said it gave the women in our family the Sight. That it's been handed down from mother to daughter since forever. She said I should keep it hidden and never tell anyone, not even Father.'

Rogan kneaded at her leg with his sharp little claws.

'And I have the Sight, too,' Sarcha added, breathless. 'Sometimes I practice seeing things about people's lives, just as Mother used to. I want to use it like she did – to help people. I don't understand why I have to hide it from Father, though. Unless...' She stared at the kitten, who licked her fingers.

'Do you think that maybe that's what their big argument was about, the night before Mother died?' She petted the kitten again. 'I remember them yelling. Something about not going to Elsenfeld just for material for the dress Maryim was making. And when I went downstairs, Mother was writing a letter. She tucked it away when I came in. She looked so sad. And she cried as she hugged me so tightly.'

Sarcha bit her lip, unable to see through the tears clouding her eyes. 'She told me again to keep the Firestone hidden. Maybe she foresaw her own death, Rogan. Maybe that's why Father doesn't want me to see Maryim. Because Mother went to Elsenfeld for

Maryim's sewing supplies. I *wish* he would talk to me! I'm not a child anymore.'

She rose and went to the window, clutching the stone close to her breast. Easing the shutters wide open, she stared into the glittering sky and breathed in the soft spring air. Since her mother died, she'd felt a strange comfort looking at the stars. The fuzzy star was there again, tonight. Even brighter. It's tail even longer.

'Incredible,' she whispered. 'What can it mean, Rogan?' A falling star arced across the sky. The tingling from the stone grew stronger for a moment and she gasped.

The kitten ignored her, cleaning one paw intently.

'I think…Yes. I'm going to see Maryim tomorrow, Rogan' Sarcha said, holding the stone tight in her fist. The tingling grew stronger, as if to agree with tomorrow's intention. 'I miss spending time at her house, like I did with Mother. Watching Maryim sew pretty dresses for the ladies in town. Listening to her and Mother talk. And I can't leave Sagore not knowing for sure why Father won't let me see her. And…' Her cheeks warmed and she smiled. 'I want to see Lark again. I miss him, too.'

Sarcha closed the shutters to prevent Rogan escaping, changed into her nightdress and tucked the stone into the bodice. She fell asleep with the kitten curled against her back, the stone tingling on her chest and a smile on her lips at the thought of seeing her best friend once more.

*

Sarcha spread warm jam on two pieces of fresh-baked bread and placed them on the table. Ezekiel poured the morning coffee and added a dash of milk to each mug.

He cleared his throat. 'I've been thinking.' He took a bite of bread and chewed it slowly. 'Perhaps you should stay home from your lessons today. There's a great deal to do here before we go. A few weeks off between now and finding a new teacher in Elsenfeld won't hurt.'

'But, Father!' Sarcha's heart thudded. She had to go into town today. It was her last chance to see Maryim and Lark. 'I…I have books to pick up and I must say goodbye to my tutor and my friends. Please, let me go one more day?'

He frowned and tore his bread into small pieces. 'Very well. But *only* to school, mind you! Nowhere else.'

'Yes, Father,' she said grudgingly with the guilt rising like bile in her throat.

'Good girl.' He nodded. 'This new customer is paying good money for the cart he's picking up this afternoon. Maybe I can buy you some new schoolbooks when we move.' Sarcha had been asking for new books for a year. It was his way of making it up to her.

*

'Goodbye, Father,' Sarcha called as she closed the heavy door at the entrance to her home. She swung her book satchel over her shoulder and walked down the garden path. Looking back for a moment, she studied her childhood home. The dark wooden window shutters and white-painted timber walls, two tall chimneys stacked high beside her bedroom croft with its little square window.

Ezekiel was in his workshop – out the back and out of sight. Sarcha picked up her pace anyway, took a left turn for town and continued until she was far out of eyesight. Her heart was heavy at the thought of lying to her father, but he'd left her no choice. The decision was made. She had to see Maryim and Lark.

She rounded the corner of the bakery and stepped right into the hustle and bustle of the villagers setting up their carts for the day to sell their wares. The scent of baking bread made her mouth water.

She waved away a flower-seller and wrinkled her nose at the smell of the fishmonger's stall. Steel on steel rang out from the blacksmith's forge and Sarcha nodded in greeting as she walked by, her head in a cloud, thinking about what she'd say to Maryim.

Someone bumped into her shoulder and Sarcha jumped.

'Excuse me, miss,' the woman said. The wriggling toddler on her hip wailed. Sarcha stumbled over a loose cobblestone and lost her balance sending the contents of the closest cart and herself tumbling on to the ground. Piles of folded linen and skeins of coloured wool spilled onto the road.

'I am sorry, sir,' Sarcha said standing and dusting her plain grey dress off. 'I mean ma'am.' She blushed.

Sunlight glinted red on the lady stall-holder's hair. The lady was ever the beauty Sarcha remembered. Fine lines danced around her smiling brown eyes.

'Maryim!' Sarcha smiled.

'Are you hurt, sweetheart?' Maryim asked as the two embraced.

Sarcha shook her head. She was thrilled to have found Maryim. 'I'm fine. I was actually looking for you.' She picked up the yarn and small trinkets that had fallen. An old and delicate silver needle case caught her eye. She gathered it up.

Sarcha's Firestone came to life, tingling against her skin under her bodice. She "read" the little case. Sarcha was still learning to control the Sight so she just saw a glimpse of Maryim stitching a beautiful, green woollen gown. Sarcha sighed and plucked at her old grey gown. How she would love a dress that colour. But all her dresses were made by a very proper and dull tailor in Elsenfeld, now.

'Sarcha?' Maryim held out a hand.

Sarcha shook her head and the vision faded. 'I'm sorry. Here you go.' She handed Maryim the pretty case and the other trinkets from the ground.

Maryim nodded in thanks and placed her wares back into position. 'What did you see?' Her gentle eyes glimmered with a hint of mischief.

Sarcha gasped. Her hand flew to her bodice. She'd never told anyone about the stone or her Sight. How did Maryim know?

'It's alright, Sarcha,' Maryim whispered. 'I know.' She smiled warmly and pulled Sarcha into another embrace. 'Never mind, sweetheart. I'm just so happy to see you. And look at you, almost grown and a woman now!'

Sarcha's heart soared. How she longed for someone to recognise she wasn't a child anymore.

'But these clothes,' Maryim added with a tut, 'will not do at all.' She snatched up her measuring strings. Within a minute Maryim had wrapped, marked and cut them around Sarcha's bust, waist and hips, gathering Sarcha's exact dimensions.

'I...' Maryim spoke around the measuring string clenched in her teeth. 'Am going to make you a dress today whilst you are in lessons. That's where you are off to now, isn't it?'

Sarcha beamed at the thought of a beautiful new dress and nodded eagerly.

'And that way,' Maryim added, returning her smile, 'I'll see you again when you pick it up in this afternoon. There.' Maryim packed away her tools and glanced beneath her long lashes at Sarcha. 'And perhaps I'll find out why you came to see me?'

Sarcha nodded. Perhaps, if she found out why Ezekiel so hated Maryim, she might also discover why he wanted to move away. And maybe find a way to change his mind.

'Miss Kyla?' Sarcha spoke over the giggles of the younger girls. The class was split into two groups. The younger girls learned the basics of how to read and write, while the older girls learned from books filled with numbers, history, astronomy, plants and the like. 'Did you see how bright the fire-star was last night?'

The girls quietened and looked up, wide-eyed. The class had discussed the strange star the previous day.

'Yes, I did,' Miss Kyla said. She plucked a thick and heavy book off the shelf.

Many of the young girls raised their hands. She listened patiently while they chattered about last night's sighting. Lifting the book for the class to see the hand drawn images, she turned the pages.

'Hmm, let me see,' she murmured. 'This is from an old monastery in France. The monks kept records of the star movements. I think I remember seeing a drawing in here about a slow-burning star. Aah. Here it is.' Kyla turned the book around to show the class.

Sarcha studied the drawing. It looked like the same star she had witnessed outside her window last night, and the previous night. Miss Kyla read the text out loud. She explained that some thought the blazing star reappeared in the skies every seventy-five years. The monks recorded seeing the star in both 1531 and 1607.

'Miss, this is the year 1682!' one of the children exclaimed.

'Yes. Well done. So perhaps it's the same star again.' Kyla beamed.

'May I see the book'? Sarcha asked. She wanted to hold it and see if she could get a vibration from the book. She wasn't entirely sure if the Sight would work as she would be "reading" an author's text about the star, not the star itself.

Kyla passed the book over. Sarcha checked to make sure no-one was watching, then placed her hand on the drawing. The Firestone began to vibrate inside her bodice. In the trance, Sarcha normally saw clear images play out in her mind. This reading was a far different experience. Heat and brilliant light overwhelmed her thoughts. She hissed and snatched her hand away. Her classmates turned to look.

Sarcha apologised for the distraction, feigning an insect bite on her hand. Her hand stung and the Firestone tingled strongly. There must be a connection between her stone and the star. But what?

With her mother gone, there was only one way to find out. She felt sure, somehow, Maryim would be the key to unlocking the truth about many things, including the Firestone. Today after lessons was her only chance to find out before she and Ezekiel packed up and were gone from this town forever.

*

Sarcha squared her shoulders and swallowed. She raised a hand and knocked gently on the great wooden door. A lizard scampered down the old door and she jumped. It vanished into the overgrown bushes around the front of Maryim's cottage. The front yard, once blooming with flowers, was now full of weeds. Perhaps, with Lark away for so long serving his apprenticeship, Maryim couldn't care for the house on her own.

Maryim opened the door. With a welcoming smile, she invited Sarcha to come inside.

'Excuse the mess.' Maryim blushed as they stepped over an oversized satchel blocking the entrance. 'You can see Lark is back. I must have asked him to move this great big pack ten times this week'. She shook her head and used her heel to push the pack aside.

Sarcha didn't mind. She was just so happy to be in this home once more, even if it was to be her last visit.

'Ezekiel is the messy one in our home.' Sarcha immediately regretted speaking his name.

Maryim smiled and touched Sarcha's shoulder reassuringly.

'He's a good man, love. You're free to mention his name here. I'm just sorry we weren't able to get along after your mother—'

The back door swung open and a whoosh of fresh spring air burst into the kitchen.

'Afternoon, ladies.' A tall young man appeared, his broad shoulders almost filling the doorway. His warm brown eyes gleamed as they alighted on Sarcha. He leant on the handle of his pick axe and grinned at her. A lock of dark hair fell across his eyes and he flicked it aside.

'Lark!' Sarcha blushed and lowered her gaze modestly. 'Welcome home!' He had changed so much. Lark had been a tall, lanky boy with a quick smile and ready laugh five years before. Now he was simply the most handsome man Sarcha had ever seen.

Maryim had the good sense to join the conversation after the cat took Sarcha's tongue and left her a staring mute.

'Good, Lark, I was hoping you'd take a break from the yard and have a mug of coffee with us.'

'Of course, Ma.' Lark leaned the axe outside of the door and came inside. He reached past Sarcha to fetch the mugs from their hooks, near the hearth. His arm brushed hers. It was all she could do not to jump as an image flashed in her head; just a fraction of Lark's future. She saw him married and playing with a child, here in this house. She saw him teaching a young, fair-haired girl to ride a pony; even felt the love he would have for his family.

Sarcha emerged from the trance. Sadness weighed down her heart. His future would be without her. He would marry some other girl and have that family. She was moving away. The Firestone tingled. She opened her eyes. Hopefully they'd only been closed for a second. Lark stood close to her, three mugs in hand, his familiar and beautiful face tilted, eyes full of wonder.

'Are you alright?' He grinned.

Sarcha nodded, giddy at his proximity. She recovered and took the mugs from him.

A smile flickered over Maryim's face as she sat down and accepted a mug.

'I'm just happy you're home,' Sarcha said briskly. 'For Maryim's sake, of course. She needs your help.' She had missed him terribly over the years, especially with her mother gone. Lark had tried to see her. Ezekiel had sent him away many times. Then Lark had moved away to apprentice on his uncle's farm.

'Oh yes,' Lark said, his eyes twinkling. 'For Ma's sake. Of course.'

*

After drinking his coffee, Lark returned to work in the garden and Maryim produced the dress she'd made for Sarcha.

'Lark was looking forward to seeing you when I mentioned you were coming by today,' Maryim said as she tightened the lacing at the back of Sarcha's new dress. The seamstress stood back, looked at her work of art and clapped her slender hands together with a smile.

'You look simply bewitching, Sarcha. The very picture of your mother.'

Sarcha felt a surge of excitement looking down at the emerald green wool dress. She twirled to see the hem flitter about her heels. The gown was unlike any of the simple dresses Ezekiel had ordered for her in Elsenfeld. It made Sarcha feel sophisticated and womanly, fitting to her figure perfectly.

'I can't pay you today, I have no money with me…'

'Nonsense, girl.' Maryim tutted at Sarcha with a shake of her head. 'It's a gift. Your mother would have wanted me to make it for you.'

'Mother…yes.' Sarcha touched the bodice of her new dress, where the Firestone lay safe. How did she ask Maryim about her mother?

'Come sit down,' Maryim said. 'I have something for you.' She led Sarcha to one of the two, winged chairs near the window, where the light was brightest. Maryim rummaged through a wooden trunk next to her chair and handed Sarcha a rolled-up piece of parchment.

'On the night before Ellan died, she came to me terribly upset.' Maryim clasped her hands together tightly. 'She gave me that letter. For you.'

Sarcha stared at the paper and blinked back hot tears. She was finally going to talk about her mother with somebody who knew her closely.

'You see, darling,' Maryim continued, 'Ellan knew there was going to be an accident. I assume Ezekiel told you?'

Sarcha shook her head. 'He's never told me anything! But I guessed she must have known.' A tear spilled and Sarcha wiped it away with the palm of her hand. She held the parchment gently, half-afraid to open it.

Maryim touched her knee. 'Your mother gave you something, didn't she?'

Sarcha had done exactly as her mother had told her and kept the amulet a secret. She couldn't bring herself to answer Maryim. Talking about the Firestone felt like a betrayal of her mother's trust.

'I know she did,' Maryim said. 'It's alright. You don't have to tell me.' She sighed and looked pensively at the paper in Sarcha's hand. 'Your mother and Ezekiel had a terrible row the night before the accident. Ellan asked Ezekiel to give this to you when you were grown. He became very upset when he couldn't convince Ellan to change her plans to go to Elsenfeld the next morning. So Ellan decided I should give this to you.'

'But,' Sarcha said. 'He loved her so. How could he spend their last night together in an argument?'

Maryim pressed her lips together and looked away, her cheek pale. 'Ezekiel blames the Sight for her accident. And he blames me for Ellan's plans to buy material for a new dress that day.'

Sarcha touched her bodice protectively. Maryim *did* know! How?

'Ellan was my dearest friend, Sarcha,' Maryim said sadly. 'We grew up together. I've always known about her visions. But does Ezekiel know you have it; the Sight?'

Sarcha shook her head.

'This is why Ezekiel hasn't talked to me in all these years.' Maryim pointed to the parchment. 'He was furious that I wouldn't destroy it. He didn't want the Sight for you, Sarcha. He didn't want you to die, like Ellan. He's never accepted her death, or that she chose to go when she could have stayed home.'

'But *why?*' Sarcha whispered. 'Why did she go? Why did she leave us?'

Betrayal was a rock in her heart. How could her mother have chosen to die? And how could her father have kept her away from Maryim, the very person that could have helped her through these difficult years?

Maryim gathered Sarcha into a gentle hug. 'Because the visions are always true, my dear. No matter how you try to avoid them, you can't. Ellan knew that. She had no choice, really. Ezekiel didn't believe her.'

Tears slid down Sarcha's cheeks. All of these years. Had her father been looking for signs she had her mother's gift? Was that why he was so strict with her? If only he'd opened up and spoken of his fears. Perhaps they could have comforted each other and she could have made him understand how wonderful the Sight was; how much it connected her to Ellan.

Sarcha stared at the parchment, still in her hand. This must be the very same letter her mother had tucked away, the night before her death. Shaking, Sarcha carefully opened the letter and read the contents.

My sweet girl

I want you to know that you have made me the proudest mother.

Watching you grow has shown me so much true joy that it pains me I am to leave tomorrow. I wish that I could be there to show you the way, but I know you are a strong and mindful child who will do well, even without my guidance.

The treasure I gave to you is yours alone. It will show the sight only to you. The visions will sometimes be overwhelming, but you must learn to use it wisely. Help people. Make the world a better place. That has always been the duty of the women in our family. When the time comes you will do as I have done and pass the amulet down to your own daughter.

I imagine you wonder where the stone came from. Earth is not its birthplace. Think Night. Think Bright. You know the origin, don't you darling girl?

I will love you and your father always.

Your mother

Ellan

'The fire-star,' Sarcha whispered. 'Thank you, Maryim. This means the world to me. My mother loved you terribly, and Lark too.' She embraced Maryim warmly, both of them crying now.

Sarcha sighed. 'I just wish there were a way for you to make amends with father. He's taking us away from Sagore and I want to stay. I want to stay so much it hurts.'

'But why does he want to leave?' Maryim frowned.

'I think,' Sarcha said, stroking the parchment, 'he's trying to protect me from the Sight. From this. From what you know.'

'What will you do?' Maryim glanced out the window. 'I don't want you to leave, either.'

Lark swung his axe just outside. He sang a song in his rich, deep voice; soothing and strong. But Lark was destined to have a beautiful family and Sarcha was destined to leave Sagore.

She shook her head and swallowed. 'I don't know. Father is so hard to talk to. He just won't listen. I know he loves me, but he shuts himself away and I can't reach him. I don't think anything will change his mind.'

'I'm so sorry, darling,' Maryim said. 'I wish I could help. We'll miss you.'

The two ladies walked to the front door and embraced one last time.

'Thank you so much, Maryim.' Sarcha brushed away fresh tears and forced words through her tight throat. 'For the dress, as well. I'll cherish it.' She had lost her mother, Maryim, and Lark in one fell swoop. She couldn't bear to lose them again.

'It's my pleasure.' Maryim stroked Sarcha's cheek. 'I know we'll see each other again. I only hope it will be sooner rather than later.'

Sarcha turned and ran, clutching the parchment, sobbing.

*

Arriving home far later than expected, Sarcha opened the heavy wooden door and peeked inside.

'Thank God! You're home!' Ezekiel strode towards her, frowning darkly. 'Where have you been all afternoon? I've been worried sick!' His eyes fell on her new attire and his brows lifted.

Sarcha was about to answer when movement under the table caught her eye. She inhaled in surprise and looked quickly away.

'I'm sorry I'm late, Father,' she said. The sleepy-eyed kitten wandered out from underneath the table and straight over to Sarcha. She scooped Rogan up and tut-tutted in his ear. He purred and snuggled into her arms.

'About this too.' She nodded towards the cat. 'He found me by the stream. He needed me…and I needed him.'

Ezekiel said nothing, only scowled at her and the cat.

Sarcha's heart thudded. Was he very angry? She swallowed and lifted her chin, clutching Rogan close. 'Father, I've been to see Maryim and Lark today. That's why I'm late. And I'm *not* sorry I went. I needed to see them. To talk about Mother. Because you never would.'

Ezekiel's frown deepened. He folded his arms. The tense silence stretched out. Sarcha trembled. Then his broad shoulders slumped and he heaved a sigh. He strode across the room and for the first time she noticed him limping with age.

'But I *am* sorry, my girl.' Ezekiel took her in his arms. 'I'm sorry you felt you had to sneak away to see her.'

'You're…you're not mad at me?' Sarcha whispered, staring up at him.

'I'm not mad,' he said. 'I've tried to put off this day as long as I could. But I knew you'd find your way there one day. And this?' He plucked at the exquisitely-stitched sleeve. 'It's really beautiful on you. Did Maryim make it?'

Sarcha nodded. Joy surged in her breast at his approval. 'She did. And she gave me something else.'

'I see,' he said solemnly.

'You know what it is, don't you Father?'

Ezekiel nodded, tears shimmering in his eyes. 'Sarcha, I'm sorry I couldn't do as your mother asked. I just couldn't. Losing her nearly destroyed me. And I had you to worry about. The last thing I wanted was the Sight for you too.' He paused and scrubbed a hand through his hair. 'Do you have it now – the Sight?' He searched her face.

She gulped. 'I've…always had it, Father. Mother gave me the Firestone before she…died. I'm sorry I hid it from you. But you wouldn't talk to me about her and I was so lonely. It was like I had a tiny piece of her, all to myself. I was afraid you'd take it away.'

Ezekiel sighed and nodded. He threaded his fingers through hers. They leaned their heads together.

'Well then,' Ezekiel said, his smile sad. 'We'll get through this, won't we, girl?'

Sarcha sniffed and beamed. He stroked her hair and scratched Rogan, still curled in her arms, behind the ear. The kitten batted at Ezekiel's finger and Sarcha giggled.

There was a soft knock at the door. Ezekiel wiped his eyes. He stood straight and fixed his mussed shirt.

'This'll be the man I was telling you about this morning. Here to pick up his cart.'

Sarcha put Rogan down and turned towards the hearth to start dinner. Ezekiel opened the front door. The Firestone buzzed fiercely, hot against her skin.

'Good Afternoon, Ezekiel, sir.' A deep, amused voice spoke from outside.

Sarcha gasped and spun to face the door. The Firestone's heat seemed to burn in her cheeks.

'My name is Lark. I'm here to pick up a new cart ordered by my uncle.' He handed Ezekiel a heavy purse.

Ezekiel looked him up and down, hefting the purse in one hand. 'Young Lark, eh? You've grown, lad.' He sent a sly look back over his shoulder at Sarcha. 'Cart's out back. Anything else I can do for you?'

Lark snatched the woollen cap from his head and held it between his hands. 'I would like to see Sarcha…if at all possible, sir. Is she here?'

Sarcha's heart skipped a beat as her father moved aside and waved her forward. Sarcha stepped into the light. Lark's mouth fell open. She spread her beautiful green skirts and dipped a curtsy.

Lark shut his mouth and cleared his throat. 'Hello, Sarcha.' He took her hand and brought it to his lips. His eyes gleamed. 'Were you really going to go without saying goodbye?'

This time when the Sight came, Sarcha saw her own future laid out. There she was, lazing by the very same stream she and her mother had loved, all those years before; the stream where she'd found Rogan, yesterday. She wasn't alone. Beside her on the grass reclined Lark, older and even more handsome. Love and trust lay close between them. She saw herself sit up. A child called out. A fair-haired little girl with Ellan's hazel eyes and Lark's joyous grin. She saw herself stand up and reply, 'I'm coming, Ellan, my darling daughter.'

She emerged from the trance to find Lark smiling down at her, still holding her hand. A few steps away, Ezekiel chuckled.

'I don't think you have to worry about her saying goodbye, young man. I don't think we're going anywhere in a hurry.'

238BCE – 1758CE
Florence, Tuscany

Adventure of a Lifetime

Georgia Willis

My head rolled gently across the ground. My little mouth formed an 'O' of surprise.

Dead.

Again.

Sighing, I walked away from my body. It never paid to watch what animals and insects did after the soul left – a lesson I learnt quickly the first time I died.

Hades stood a few steps away, looking smug. 'Not going to mope over yourself this time?'

Scowling, I looked back at my dust-covered, fallen form. My head lay a few feet from the rest of me, unrecognisable in the dirt and blood.

'That makes three,' he said. 'Fail my challenge twice more and your soul is mine.'

'Have I told you I hate you?' I snapped. 'And this stupid cave.'

He grinned. I shook my head and made my way back through the cave – the same way I'd come when I was alive. I'd made it through two previous sets of booby traps only to break a trip wire and set off two horizontal saw blades, one in front and one behind. If I hadn't jumped backwards, I would have been fine. Three booby-traps, three deaths. And Hades was right, if I died twice more he would own my soul, and I would never reach the Elysian Fields.

*

238BCE

Somewhere near Faesulae, Roman Republic

My first family were Greek merchants. On a fateful summers day, while we travelled between towns selling our wares, I convinced my parents to stop for lunch. A man in the previous town had told me of a cave. A cave said to hold some sort of treasure. But everyone who entered, vanished. Naturally, this piqued my curiosity. I wanted to see this cave. However, I neglected to tell my over-cautious parents. Instead, as a savvy merchant's daughter, I convinced my father to stop for lunch. Alas, before the water had even boiled for our lunch time stew, bandits swarmed out from the trees and took from us all we had – including our lives.

Hades found me not long after the bandits had moved on. Both my parents had entered his realm and I wasn't far behind. I lay dying on the dirt road when he wandered through. He asked where Persephone was and I laughed at him. I knew who he was and the irony of him searching for his lost loved one, when mine lay slaughtered around me was almost too much.

Lightning shot through his silvery eyes and he sneered. I expected him to be angry, to cast me into Tartarus to forever be punished. Instead, he poked a long, pale finger into the hole in my chest, making me gasp.

'Did you know you're related to Persephone?' he said, drawing his finger out. His expression turned from cold arrogance to morbid curiosity. I had neither the strength nor inclination to answer him. What did it matter now? I would be dead soon.

'I have a deal for you, dear girl,' he said, running the bloodied finger down my cheek. 'I'll give you five opportunities to complete a task I set for you. Five lifetimes. If you succeed I'll allow your soul safe and speedy passage to the Elysian Fields. If you fail, I'll own your soul and you'll live beside me in place of...in place of Persephone.'

'And if I choose neither?' I gurgled, struggling to stay conscious.

He tilted his head, his pale lips straining against the gathering storm in his eyes. An arrogant smile washed across his face. 'If you choose neither you, and the rest of your family here, will be stuck on the wrong side of the River Styx.' He pointed at my dead parents.

'Unless you think someone will give you a proper burial once I'm done hiding your bodies.' His shark-like teeth gleamed in the fading light. He waited for me to answer, but all I managed was a single tear. He walked over to my mother. Dragging her by the ankle, he headed into the forest.

'Wait!' I cried.

He hauled my mother's body back and towered above me.

'If I do this, they both go to the Elysian Fields,' I whispered looking at the broken form of the woman who had birthed me. He tilted his head to the side.

'Or there's no deal,' I finished.

Hades snorted and looked to the heavens. The sky turned a faint pinkish-orange, signalling the end of the day. A streak of hazy white light appeared on the dusk-darkened horizon.

'What's your name?' he asked.

'Halley,' I replied, more blood spilling from my lips to join the ever-growing pool around me.

'By the hairy star that flies above us, I agree to your terms,' he said, releasing my mother. 'Now all you have to do is find my Persephone.' His sharp eyes shot down to me. 'If you fail, you won't be the only one to feel my wrath.' He vanished, leaving me to die.

*

I arrived at the river Styx. My parents already awaited me on Charon's boat. The ferry man held out his hand for coin, but I hadn't been buried with coins on my eyelids. I splayed out my empty hands. His face contorted in a snarl. With a strange barking noise, he ushered me onto the ferry. Other souls, moaning and screaming, tried to climb aboard, but Charon pushed off from the shore. The unlucky souls fell into the river Styx, which consumed them.

My mother and father looked at me sadly, but none of us dared to speak. The boat neared the opposite shore. This might be the last I ever saw my parents. I darted across the deck, causing it to rock on the ghostly water. Charon grunted and muttered something to himself. I flung my arms around my mother. Her increasingly-transparent arms wrapped around me. The large – albeit faint – hands of my father fell on my shoulders. *Be strong*, he had always told me when I was scared. Now, as my parents faded away, I took those words to heart.

The boat hit the shore with a thud, and my parents barely gave me a second look as they glided through the gates guarded by the great three-headed beast, Cerberus. Charon grunted and I followed them. Cerberus placed a paw, much larger than I, down before me. I cried out to my mother, but she continued on without hesitating. The closest fanged head leant down and sniffed me. It growled softly, making the ground shiver. I froze, trying not to draw any more heads towards me. The middle head glanced at me and gave a short bark. The third head, the one furthest from me, whined sadly and looked away.

A man, wearing a toga and crown, appeared from where my parents had disappeared. Cerberus's first head still watched me, its dark blue eyes narrowed. The man, who I recognized from the many paintings and carvings in the Temple of Hades, was the former King Aiakos. He usually presided over the fate of newly arrived souls.

I took a few quick steps towards him and cast a dubious look back at Cerberus. The beast made no move to follow and I sighed in relief. Aiakos barely registered my presence and turned away. I hurried after him, into an empty grey desert covered in an eerie white fog.

Aiakos guided me to a much narrower river than the Styx. The name was on the tip of my tongue, but something kept me from grasping it. Perhaps this was the river that made you forget; the one whose water and mist consumed everything from dreams to memories. The thick wet mist swelled up from the river's lapping waters, clung to my skin and clouded my eyes. Aiakos all but vanished. The longer we walked, the more I forgot about myself and why I followed this man.

My mouth was so dry that my lips cracked and the coppery taste of blood on my tongue was the only liquid I could savour. The river gurgled beside me. How long had we been walking? Maybe I would stop, just for a second, and quench my thirst. No! I needed to resist eating or drinking here, especially from the river Lethe. That was it! The Lethe. With a clenched jaw and much agony of willpower, I trudged along the bank.

The fog keeping my mind dull dissipated as we neared another, much larger, river. This one seemed to flow in two directions. It must be the Acheron. As we approached, Aiakos muttered under his breath,

'Huh. Maybe there is hope for us, yet.'

A tall, familiar figure stood by the edge. Hades waited for me. Tendrils of the river Lethe, still clinging to my mind, stole the question I had for Aiakos before it reached my lips. I walked towards Hades. Memories of my parents flooded back. Grief overwhelmed me.

Hades smiled, ignoring my distress.

'You resisted. Well done. I'm not surprised though. You do have a...prestigious heritage.' His smile turned smug then he frowned. 'Why are you crying?'

He shrugged before I found the words to speak, grabbed me by the shoulders and threw me towards the Acheron. Hitting the water knocked the air from my lungs. Gasping and spluttering, I struggled to keep my head in the clear as the current dragged me from Hades's domain. I lost sight everything except the black, swirling water. I tried to scream but water filled my mouth. The Acheron dragged me down.

*

111BCE

Somewhere near Florence, The Roman Republic

I woke as a small child, with a new set of parents. My childish brain suppressed the horrors of my former death, turning them into a story; a dream half-forgotten.

The next twenty years were pleasant, if dull. My parents were well-to-do Roman merchants, so our home was comfortable. My family betrothed me to an eligible bachelor, recently returned from the war with the Greeks.

I fell in love with him at our first meeting. He looked brutal: muscles bulging out his clothes, covered in scars and healing wounds. But I saw past all that to the kind-hearted soul within. Together we would have the perfect life. Having a husband and a home of my own to run would have to be enough of an adventure to satiate my restlessness.

I married not long after my twenty-second birthday and produced an heir – a beautiful baby boy, Caelius, not a year later. My parents were thrilled, as was my husband. But, a few months after the birth, I began having horrid dreams: of bandits and massacres, of drowning in a river, and a monstrous three-headed beast. Most bizarrely, I dreamt of Hades, a god not even from the pantheon of my own religion.

My husband took me to a healer, but the man knew of no cure for nightmares and dreams. He suggested it could be a strange reaction to the birth of my child. I stopped telling my husband of the dreams after that. But I wrote them down and studied them, trying to divine their meaning. They became more vivid as time wore on. Soon, I didn't know if I was Roman or Greek.

The night before my twenty-fourth birthday, I woke from yet another dream, where I wandered a grey dusty desert following a bored man who walked no logical path. I sat at my husband's desk with my little book. Lighting a well-used candle, I wrote down my latest dream. One day I would tell them as stories to Caelius. The candle flickered, nearing its end as I finished my writings. I checked on my baby boy. He slept peacefully in his crib, wrapped in woollen blankets. I strolled into the gardens, by the little stream, letting the cool breeze soothe my aching head.

I often sat by the soothing waters, under the shade of an aging oak tree, while I was pregnant. I sat there now and admired the starlight that bounced off the flowing water. Looking to the heavens I spotted the white fuzzy blob that had appeared a few days ago and was ever so slowly inching across the sky. A sign from the gods perhaps? I shivered. Even in these peaceful surroundings, uneasiness crept up my back. Someone watched me. I rose and headed home to my husband.

A shadowy figure appeared and pushed me backwards into the courtyard. I screamed. Moonlight bathed the figure. I knew my cry fell on deaf ears.

Hades stood before me just as smug as in my dream. Tears flowed down my face.

The dreams were real.

He stepped forward as I scampered back. 'You will find my beloved Persephone.' He prodded my chest with a sharp-nailed finger. 'And you will do so before the hairy star leaves these Earthly Skies, or your new little family will follow the last.' Grinning, he disappeared in a swirl of grey smoke. His words and snide laughter hung in the air.

There was no way out of a deal with a god, not if I wanted my loving husband and beautiful baby to live past the next moon. I wrote a letter to my husband and son telling them I had to leave for their own safety. I kissed my sweet child goodbye and, like a thief, I stole away before the sun found me.

As I trudged away from my home, more memories returned. My feet headed towards the fateful road where I died one hundred and fifty years before. When I arrived, no hint of my tragedy remained. It was a plain dirt road, worn with use and dotted with weeds. The trees closest to the spot seemed to bend away as if frightened by what they had witnessed. I sat where I had drawn my last, agonised breath and replayed my first meeting with Hades. Something told me the treasure-cave I'd wanted to investigate was the place to start my search for Persephone.

Shivering, I headed into the forest. The cave was so covered in vines I almost missed it. Scraps of torn clothing and remnants of bones littering the ground indicated I was in the right spot. More bone fragments marked the entrance with a dull white path that crunched beneath my feet. The sheer quantity of bone had me concerned. Hopefully it was just for show. Otherwise, Persephone ate people and I was in trouble.

I cleared the vines away, leaving the entrance open for a fast escape. Grey afternoon light filtered a few steps into the darkness. I crept along the bony path. Faint light spots illuminated the ground twenty steps or so inside the cave. The cave roof must have collapsed, allowing beams of light in.

I inched towards them. The ground shifted beneath me. I froze. My heart thudded in my chest. I felt around my feet. One foot had pushed a stone deeper into the earth. I shook my head, smiling to myself. What harm could a sunken stone do?

I stepped forward. The ground gave way. I plunged deep into darkness.

*

I willed my body to move, but my arms and legs were dead weight. I couldn't force my eyes to turn. A beetle crawled across my mouth. Even that torment wasn't enough to make me shift.

'What are you doing?' Hades stepped forward. 'Don't you understand you're dead?' He laughed.

I looked down at my body, impaled on stakes at the bottom of a pit. Tears streaked down my transparent face as his words sank in. A crescendo of rushing water roared around me. I headed towards the sound, more by compulsion than choice.

*

1507CE

Florence, Tuscany

My second attempt to find Persephone started out much the same way. I wandered through the grey desert following Aiakos, then along the treacherous river Lethe, to where Hades threw me back to be reincarnated. This time I was born during the reign of the Medici family. But I won't bother going into much detail about this incarnation. Suffice to say, after an uneventful childhood, turning twenty-three and having the dreams start again made my monotonous life rather thrilling.

Of course, that changed on my twenty-fourth birthday when I realised the dreams were real. Hades demanded I find Persephone. I headed to the cave to find her. I easily jumped the pit and headed for the little beams of light that seemed so inviting. Oh, how wrong I was.

I stepped into the light.

Arrows launched out of the wall and skewered me.

This time I didn't bother waiting for Charon to snarl at me before climbing on his boat. Nor did I let Cerberus's growling frighten me. By the time Aiakos lead me to the Archeon, where Hades stood, I was so angry I didn't wait for Hades to throw me into the river. I dove in. This was getting ridiculous.

1682CE

Florence, Tuscany

My third attempt came in 1682, once more in Florence. The dreams began again when I turned twenty-three. Again, Hades appeared when the comet appeared in the night sky. Again he gave me my task: find Persephone.

This time anger flooded back along with the memories. I didn't sneak out. I stormed out of my house, ignoring my family's protests. The cave would not beat me again. I jumped the pit with ease. Carefully, I approached the light and, waved a stick through. Three arrows shot out of holes in the rock and smashed upon the opposite wall. Just in case, I edged around the beams without breaking them. I sighed with relief as I came to the other side of the trap unscathed.

I swept the stick from side to side across the ground, finding loose stones and other debris. When the stick got caught on something, I lifted it over. My foot followed the stick. Something pressed against my ankle. The pressure broke with an almost-silent twang. A buzzing noise filled the cavern. Bits of dirt and stone burst forth from the wall. I leapt backward. My head rolled away. The blade blurred past.

*

For the fourth time, I stood in front of Cerberus. The first head continued to glare at me. This time I planted my hands on my hips and glared back.

'Aiakos,' I said, as he approached, impassive as ever,

'Come with me,' he replied turning on his heel.

I stomped after him. The soft grey dust kicked up in puffy little clouds around our feet. I'm sure we were both tired of this long, arduous walk.

'Aiakos?'

He ignored me and continued.

'Aiakos!' I stopped walking. He continued for ten paces before he stopped and looked behind. Shrugging nonchalantly, he headed off once more and disappeared.

He would come back.

I waited. Time passed. Had he left me here in this empty wilderness of grey dirt and fog? Anxiety got the better of me and I followed his footprints.

'Aiakos! Hades!' Panic rose in my chest. I was trapped in a sea of fog and dirt. Was the fog getting thicker? Would I wander lost for all eternity?

A figure emerged in the distance. I ran towards it. Anything was better than being trapped here, alone. I ran, and ran, but the figure eluded me. My foot caught on something in the dirt. Arms flailing, I tripped and hit the ground hard, adding a plume of dust to the fog. I blinked; once, twice. My eyelids were strangely heavy.

I woke with a pounding head. Reaching up I pressed a hand to the sore spot on the side of my head. My hand came back covered in blood. I was dead, damn it! Why was there pain and blood in the afterlife? Grumbling, I looked down to see what I'd tripped over. A small, white, spherical stone. And another near my face, covered in blood, protruded from the ground. Typical. Nothing but dirt everywhere and I found the only rock. No, two. Lucky me.

'Are you coming?' a bored voice said.

I scrambled to my feet. 'Aiakos!'

'Next time you stop, I will not come find you. Understand?' he said curtly. I nodded

Soon after, we came to the Lethe, and then to the Acheron, where Hades waited. He frowned.

'Where have you been?'

'Sightseeing,' I snapped. 'But it's dull here and I still hate you.'

He snarled, grabbed my arm and hurled me into the river. I cough and spluttered as the river swallowed me once more.

*

1734CE

Florence, Tuscany

Once more I was born to a merchant family, one that was both prosperous and forward-thinking. My father, having only one child, gave me an education. By adolescence I was well versed in literacy and numeracy, and could keep track of my aging father's books.

My father arranged a marriage for me to a man who understood he would be the face of the business, and I would be the brains. It was a strange concept, but I had a knack for business, and my father knew it.

On my twenty-third birthday I began to dream. At first, I put the dreams of ancient gods down to all the books I had read. But the dreams continued. I told my father, who decided I was too stressed, and offered to take back some of my workload.

Soon after I realised I was pregnant. My whole family was overjoyed, for I had begun to wonder if I was barren. The dreams, however, didn't stop. I dreamt of oblong stones covered in blood, of buzzing saws, and of a figure standing in fog. Perhaps the stress and the dreams contributed to Livia's early birth. She was sickly to begin with, but soon began to thrive.

On the night of my twenty-fourth birthday, I was feeding Livia, when the floorboards behind me creaked. I whirled, holding my child close to my chest. A shadowy figure stepped forward. He seemed familiar.

'Another one?' he mused as he moved into the candle light.

'Hades.' I whispered. 'Not again!'

'Yes, you do always seem to know me, don't you, my child?' He sniggered and drew down the blanket to see my little girl.

'She has your looks,' he said. Then his sharp eyes caught mine. 'This is your second-last attempt, Halley. Find my Persephone, or I will take this family from you as I have the others. You have till the comet flees these dreary blue skies.'

He disappeared, leaving me to sink to the ground. My small baby began to fuss in my arms.

Before the morning mists had cleared, I saddled a horse and left my home in search of a myth. My dreams had shown me where to seek, only a day's ride away. The journey was both fearful and boring. I jumped at every unexpected noise. When I got to the worn stretch of road I had died on so many years ago, I sighed. I was determined to make it out of the cave alive, so I unsaddled – but loosely tied – my horse.

I crept into the cave, found the pit and leapt over. Determination gave me power over the resounding fear in my head. I edged around the lights. Carefully I stepped over the cracks that held the blades. Nothing happened.

Letting out a sigh of relief, I shuffled forward, hands outstretched, feet feeling the way. My hand touched a smooth wooden surface that gave no clues to its purpose.

Being able to see in the dark would be so useful. In the dreams, I'd been able to see. When I was dead, anyway. Why couldn't I see now? The answer seemed both obvious, and wrong. I blinked a few times, straining my eyes in the dark, willing the shapes to appear. Slowly the black hole lightened. The cave contents became visible: the loosened stones from the blades, my headless skeleton, my bony skull not far away. They appeared in a haze, as if a full moon shone in the cave with me.

I looked to my wooden obstacle. It was a door. Smooth, round, white hinges held the arched wooden panel in place. Where the handle should have been, was a notch in the wood. I traced the notch with my fingers and pressed the button inside. The door clicked and groaned open. I pushed it further, wary of more traps.

Inside was an empty room, dark and spider-webbed. Disheartened, I entered. Perhaps something could point me towards Persephone. As soon as I crossed the threshold the room changed. I gasped, confronted by a well-lit room with a bed, and a desk and even a small book case. A man sat staring at the floor intently.

'Hello?' I ventured, preparing to run if he attacked. His head shot up, his eyes clouded with confusion.

'Who are you?' His eyes narrowed.

'My name is Halley...' I said, shuffling back towards the door.

He leapt from the bed. Joy lit up his face.

'It's really you, isn't it?' he whispered. 'Persephone said you'd come for me!' His eyes filled with tears.

'Who are you?' I asked, my hand clutching at the door and ready to slam it shut on him.

'I'm your son!' The man faltered when I shook my head. I had only Livia. I frowned. Something tugged at the back of my mind.

'You must remember me.' He stretched out a hand. 'You gave birth to me in father's villa. Father said you used to sit along the river bank and sing to me while I was in your womb. There was a great oak tree you used to sit next to!'

Memories returned. Tears brimmed my eyes.

'Caelius?' I asked, half hoping, half fearing.

His face shone. 'Yes, Mother! It is me!'

He looked so much like his father. I embraced him and we both cried, out of joy, and over the disaster our lives had been.

'How are you still alive?' I asked.

He raised his brows. 'I'm your son.'

'Not helpful. I don't understand,' I said, searching his face.

'You're Halley, the Goddess of Adventurers.'

I stared blankly.

He frowned and pointed to himself. 'I'm therefore a demigod. I don't have a normal human lifespan.'

I waited for him to laugh. When he didn't, I did. There was no way I was a goddess. He remained serious. My laughter died. He removed a piece of parchment from the small bookcase, and handed it to me.

'When I was but twenty summers old I found the little notebook you used to write your dreams in. When I realised you had left a map in it, I thought I would follow and see if I could find you.' He looked away, his shoulders slumping. 'I found the old road you described, but you were gone. I was about to leave when a woman approached me.' His gazed returned, an odd fire burning within it. His face contorted bitterly.

'She asked who I was looking for. When I told her about you, she said she could help. She brought me here and told me to wait. She said one day you would come. And she gave me this letter for you.'

It read:

My dearest Halley,

I am sorry for the little trick I played on you, but all those years ago your father and I made a bet. We wagered that you, the Goddess of Adventurers, would not be able to find me within five human life times. Your father wasn't allowed to help you, but he had the advantage, as you could use your powers. So, I replaced your drink with water from the river Lethe.

On my latest visit, I found this boy who claims to be your son. He's certainly a demi god. He has promised to wait for you. Anyway, I suspect this is either your last or second last attempt at finding me, so tell your father I have won. I get to be queen of the underworld without his meddling presence for the next thousand years.

Love always, your mother,
Persephone.

I looked at Caelius.

'Have you read this?' I whispered.

He nodded. 'Only every day since I have waited here.'

'Is she insane?' I waved the paper in his face.

He shrugged. 'They're gods, what do you expect? Sanity isn't high on their priorities.'

We sat in silence for a time. I was unsure what I should do. I was a goddess. One who didn't remember being divine. And my son was a demigod.

'Is it normal to hate both your parents?' I asked, Caelius shrugged and looked away. A pang of guilt followed by righteous hate soared through my heart.

I straightened. I'd had enough of these games.

'What are you going to do?' Caelius eyed me apprehensively.

'Fix this once and for all,' I snapped. 'HADES! Get up here! Now!' When he didn't appear, I stalked out of the cosy room and into the dark cave. I continued yelling, demanding he appear. Grey smoke fizzled around my feet. I rounded on him. I was glad Caelius had stayed in the room.

'You're my father?!'

He smirked and inclined his head.

I shoved the scroll at him. His face contorted into a snarl as he read it. Once finished, he grabbed my wrist and the cloud of grey smoke took us.

I landed on the marble ground of Hades palace. At first, I was disoriented, but soon the palace began to feel familiar. Hopefully Caelius wouldn't wait for me to return. I might not be able to.

'I told you to find her, Halley,' he snapped scrunching up Persephone's letter and brandishing it in my face. 'I told you to find her or your families would suffer!'

I paced the floor, hands fisted at my side, resisting the urge to punch him. This was all about a bet made over a thousand years ago? I had been made a pawn in a very cruel game, played out of the boredom of the gods.

'Halley!' Hades bellowed.

I blinked, startled. I had not been listening. His liquid silver eyes were stained red with rage. That meant trouble. What was I, a lowly human, going to do against a god? But I wasn't a lowly human. I straightened my spine. I was a *goddess*. I just couldn't remember being one. So far, the only power I had was seeing in the dark, and that was not going to help me now. Hades was still glaring at me.

I had an idea.

'So, Persephone gets to rule the underworld if she wins. What do you get if you win?' I asked, proud my voice didn't catch on any of my words. He seemed to calm down slightly.

'Persephone would give you her Springtime powers for the next thousand years. She would stay by my side while you did her job,' he replied. 'Not that I really want her here. She meddles.'

Neither of them wanted the other to win, out of sheer spite. I didn't want either of them to win because it would be a disaster for both the underworld and Earth. Persephone would turn the underworld into a springtime heaven, destroying the balance between the Elysian fields and Tartarus. And if Hades kept the goddess of springtime from her duty, that would be worse. Even if I were to temporarily take over, I barely knew who I was. How was I supposed to make spring happen? Earth would surely suffer.

Was there a third option?

Oh! What if *I* won?

'I can find Persephone within this lifetime,' I said, lifting my chin.

Hades narrowed his eyes at me.

'But,' I continued, one finger raised, 'I have a new proposition. When I find her, she will drink from the river Lethe. Then she'll spend four lifetimes living amongst the humans and unaware of her heritage.' I held up a hand when Hades opened his mouth. 'And, only during the period of time the comet flies in the Earthly skies will you be able to visit her. Those are my terms. Your alternative is to let her win.'

I folded my arms and glared at him. Hades looked at me with a mix of anger and pride.

A mournful howl sounded outside. I spotted Cerberus, who stood next to the great gates separating the river lands from Hades's palace.

'And,' I added, 'when I return to Earth to live out this latest incarnation, with my husband and daughter, Cerberus is coming with me. He needs a break.'

'So, this is revenge because we made a bet?' Hades said, his expression weary.

'No,' I snapped. 'Because you both stole who I am from me, time after time after time. And you not only made me suffer the loss of several sets of parents, but also the loss of my husbands and my child.' I prodded him in the chest. 'You were both cruel and childish. You'll agree to my terms. Then you'll get to see just what it's like to lose the one you love, and watch her have a family without you. And she'll know the punishment of losing who she is, just as I did.'

'And Cerberus?' he asked, almost sounding amused.

'He…' I wasn't sure why I had asked for that, but I seemed to be on a roll. 'He'll make a good adventuring companion.'

Hades shook his head. 'Lose my queen or my Kingdom…' He sighed. 'Fine, you have your deal, daughter. So where is my Persephone?'

Cunning glinted in his silver eyes. If I didn't know where she was, my deal would go out the window. But I knew. Definitely. I turned aside. The memory was like a word stuck on the tip of my tongue. The realisation was just out of reach.

I considered all the clues: the cave, and my son, and the letter. The letter said that Persephone *visited* the small magical cave. And Hades obviously didn't know about it, otherwise he would know about Caelius. So, if Persephone made that room to hide from Hades, perhaps she had another.

I thought about the door to the magical room: the solid oak; the hidden handle catch; the rounded white hinges. Maybe the doorway lead to another place. Something tugged at the back of my mind. I grinned.

'I'll find her before the comet leaves the Earthly Skies,' I said. 'But can I borrow Cerberus?' Was that pushing my luck?

'Fine.' He dismissed me with a wave. 'But the comet will no longer be visible in two hours, Halley, so be quick or our deal is off. And I'll make sure all your numerous families pay the price of failure, while you watch.'

I glared. 'I still hate you, you know.'

He smiled.

I ran out of the palace to Cerberus. The one head who had ignored me on all my previous visits looked up as I approached.

'Cerberus!' I cried, grinning, He hesitated for a second before barking happily. I vaguely remembered playing with him as a child, here in the palace. Cerberus was only one who paid me any real attention, or cared for my wellbeing. Hugging a dog whose nose is bigger than your head, is a very awkward and wet affair. But he seemed to enjoy it. The middle head watched me, uninterested. The angry head growled.

'I'm sorry I left you. And I'm sorry I didn't remember you, but it wasn't my fault. Persephone made me drink from the Lethe. I...' I looked away, tears in my eyes. The pain I had caused him was written on all three faces.

'I need your help,' I whispered, unsure if he would. The three heads looked at one another, then the head I had hugged licked a long line from my hand to my face. I laughed. At least one head seemed to forgive me.

'Out there somewhere...' I waved in the direction of the empty greyness, '...are two little stones. One of them has my blood on it. Do you think you could find it?'

The friendly head tilted and gave an inquiring little growl. It turned to the others. After a debate, which consisted of barking growling and a small tantrum from the head that wanted to eat me, the friendly head nodded. He crouched so I could climb up onto his neck. And then we were off. Travelling by dog was so much faster.

*

We found the two white stones, one now stained rust-brown. I jumped off Cerberus's neck. I brushed dirt from around the bloodied stone, and grinned when I found a straight edge of something solid. I worked quickly making my way around the arched door. I laughed when I found the notched handle and button. The lock clicked and the grey dust around the door shivered.

I tugged on the handle, but it was far too heavy. Cerberus whined, I shuffled backwards and indicated for him to try. He curled his giant claws around the edge of the door and heaved. Dust shifted and the ancient wood groaned. Cerberus growled all three heads in unison. The muscles in his foreleg bulged. The wood warped. The middle head bit into the edge of the door. A sharp splintering sound cracked the silence. I jumped. Cerberus fell backwards with half a door in his mouth.

The middle head looked at the other two heads, both of which now stared intently at the oversized stick. The angry head growled. All three chomped at the board. Another growl from the angry head followed. Each head tried to steal the prize from the other two. At least he wouldn't run away while I was retrieving Persephone.

There was just enough room for me to slip through the broken door. I tiptoed down the stairs, dreading the idea of more traps. I opened another door, this one made of thick oak. The passageway became brighter. The sweet scent of lavender flower and fresh water wafted to my nose. I rounded the corner. My mother lay sprawled on a couch, sipping wine, eating grapes, and twirling flowers in her fingers. Daisies were threaded through her long, dark hair. She didn't spot me at first.

'Mother,' I said.

She jumped, then composed herself. Surprise, anger, and contempt all crossed her face.

'How did you find me?'

'Well, it was a bit of an adventure,' I replied, not wanting to talk about my ordeal.

The same cunning look I had seen in Hades eyes now crossed hers.

'How about we make a deal?' she said slyly, putting down her grapes and flowers.

'If you come upstairs with me, I'll think about it.' I turned to leave.

'How stupid do you think I am?' she asked, just a little too pleasantly.

'You don't want me to answer that. I can't see you enjoying the answer.'

She snorted and screwed up her perfect nose.

'Well,' I said, 'I need some air. We can talk when I come back down. Maybe we can work something out. I'm in no rush.' I shrugged. Would she take the bait?

'That sounds wonderful,' she replied, smiling smugly. My parents were so self-absorbed. She probably couldn't even imagine I would try to trick her.

'You'll be here when I return?' I asked. Would she run and ruin everything?

'If you're gone less than five minutes,' she said turning back to her grapes.

I nodded and walked out of sight. Then I ran, not for the first time that day, to find Cerberus. I climbed out of the broken door and his heads shot up to stare at me. I whispered in the friendly head's ear. He nodded and they headed back towards Hades's palace, while I climbed back into the passageway. I had to stall my mother.

She grinned malevolently at me.

'Excellent, my dear. Now, how should we get down to business?' she asked, patting the spot beside her. I ignored her gesture. I was close enough to my conniving mother.

'First, I'd like to know how you travelled between this world and Earth. And how you met my son. And how you stayed so well hidden?' I exclaimed, trying to sound awe-inspired.

The easiest way to keep a god preoccupied was to flatter them. Her eyes lit up.

'Well, they are all very good questions, my dear Halley.' She swept a gleaming lock of dark hair from her pale forehead. 'I first met your son when I travelled back to Earth for the Spring, a lifetime ago,' she said, and winked. 'He was wandering lost on a little dirt road, clutching a worn old book.' She pointed to an old leather-bound book discarded on the floor.

'Dull read.' Her eye showing a hint of spite.

I held my tongue. I needed to keep her here.

'When he said he was looking for you I was surprised. My only grandchild! How could you not have told me?' She smiled mockingly.

I gritted my teeth but said nothing.

'I felt sorry for him, so I took him to the cave to wait for you with my letter.' She looked puzzled. 'You did find him? He did give it to you, didn't he?'

I nodded, trying not to let my anger show on my face. I vowed to give her little satisfaction.

'Excellent. It is so hard to find good help these days.' She sighed, taking a small rose from a bush at her side and breathing in its sweet perfume. 'But now I have a question for you, my dear. How did you find me?'

'I fell over on top of your door,' I replied.

'You fell over it?' she asked, her brow furrowing. Then she laughed; a genuine, bright little collection of notes. 'Well, perhaps I shall bury my door better next time!'

Hades brushed past me, invisible. My mother continued to laugh at my misfortune. The wine in her glass rippled as something dripped into it.

'May I have a drink from your wine, mother? I'm ever so thirsty after this difficult task of finding you,' I asked. Gods hated sharing.

She snatched up the glass and downed the contents, grinning at me when she had finished.

'What wine?' she replied, giggling.

Hades appeared in the centre of the room. Persephone gasped, and turned venomous eyes towards me.

'You lost, my love,' Hades crowed, taking the glass from her hand.

'No, I will not lose to you!' She shot to her feet, fists clenched.

Hades snorted. 'Actually, we both lost – to our daughter.' He explained my terms.

Persephone's jaw dropped. She glared at me. 'Oooh, I think I hate you.'

'I believe I agree, my dear,' Hades said.

I grinned at them.

Persephone's eyes clouded. The water of the Lethe worked its magic.

'Leave this place, Halley,' Hades muttered. 'Take Cerberus if you must, but do not return anytime in the next millennium. Do you understand?' He didn't look at me.

'Who are you? Where am I?' My mother's confusion seemed to enrage Hades further. His silver eyes gleamed red. I needed to get out fast before he turned on me.

I ran back up the passage and out the doors, to where Cerberus waited.

'Want to come to Earth for a holiday?' I asked the middle head.

The heads eyed each other. Then the middle head lowered enough for me to climb on. Cerberus galloped for the Acheron river and the way out of the underworld. He leapt into the water. It wasn't as scary this time. For one, I was riding on the back of a fanged life boat; for another, I knew who I was now. And I was going home to my daughter, my son, and at least one of my families.

Darkness surrounded us. Cerberus whimpered just before the river swallowed us both.

I laughed.

We're so close, Dren. I can taste it.

What, the death? The slavery and poverty? I'm done, Vanin. I've tried for two thousand years to bring you to your senses. You're a fool.

And you're a fool if you think the opinion of an Orange would sway me. That sort of weak thinking is what got our people into trouble in the first place. It's up to me and my family to save us. I'm the only one who can.

No, Van. You and the other Primary families were the problem on our home planet, exactly as you are here. You think you have the right to destroy a whole world to satisfy your personal ambition.

The ambition to guide our people to safety and prosperity can hardly be called 'personal'.

You're beyond redemption, Van. It's clear I can't stop you. You've put this world on an irreversible path. You've taught these people to place no value on their biosphere and no value on life...I only hope you can sleep at night.

1835CE
Richmond, Virginia

A Life Worth Saving

Melanie Sienkiewicz

A gust of wind blew through the great oak. The storm tugged at crimson leaves that held tight to branches rattling against the parlour window. Sarah threw a log in the hearth and poked at the fire. Smoke mixed with dust and fell on frames atop the cheap, secondhand bureau.

Sarah's gaze settled on Samuel's portrait. Endless hours spent cradling the frame had worn the silver plating to black. It didn't matter how long she stared at his face, she still saw his swaddled body, stiff in the cot. His eyes had been blue, like hers.

Next to Samuel, a smaller frame held an image of Sarah's mother. Two people she'd never known, side by side. Their loss, and that of the three little souls she'd carried but never known, tugged at Sarah's heart. More than anything, she wanted a family with John, but how much more heartache could she bear?

She stared out the window, into the storm-grey afternoon. One of the slaves from the Anderson's farm stumbled past, carrying a child, wrapped in a tattered shawl. The woman's bare brown arms were almost pale in the chill autumn wind. The child's wail was thin and faint.

Sarah watched her out of sight. There was always the old slave-woman across the river. Growing up, she'd heard the slaves talk of the old lady who spoke with the dead; who knew things no-one could possibly know. If anyone could give her answers – the assurance she desired – perhaps it was Nanny Rose. Was she still alive?

The door knob turned and Sarah jumped. She set the picture frame back on the bureau and turned to face her husband.

'There you are, my love.' John smiled.

'John!' Sarah's cheeks warmed under his pleased scrutiny. 'I thought you'd left for work already.'

A look of concern crossed his face. 'Are you feeling alright?'

Sarah brushed a blond curl behind her ear. 'Yes, yes. I'm fine. Just a bit chilly.' She rubbed her hands together and held them towards the fire.

John took his seat by the hearth and ran thick fingers through his dark moustache.

'Aren't you going to be late?' she asked.

'I have a meeting this afternoon. I wanted to prepare. But I thought I'd see if you need anything in town, before I go.'

Sarah sat in her own chair. 'Oh? What's the meeting for?'

'I don't want to get ahead of myself,' John said, 'but this deal could make a difference. To the business…to us?'

She studied her hands. 'Actually, there's something I need to discuss with you. About our finances, I mean.'

'Oh.' John straightened. 'Of course. What is it?'

'It seems Mr Jones told Millie that he…well, it's just…'

John tilted his head. 'What's Mr Jones said now?'

Sarah dropped her gaze. 'He won't let Millie place anything more on the account. Not unless the bill is settled.'

His face closed up. 'Oh.' He cleared his throat. 'Not to worry. I'll sort it out with old man Jones.'

'John—'

'I'd better go.' He stood. 'Don't want to be late.'

'John, there's something else,' she said in a hurry as he strode towards the door.

He looked back, brows raised.

'I'd like to try again,' she blurted. 'For another baby, I mean.' She glanced at Samuel's portrait.

'Ah.' John shifted on his feet and frowned. 'Are you sure? It's only been a few months. Maybe we should wait.' He tugged down his jacket.

'But—'

John stared back, his dark eyes haunted. 'We will, I promise. We just need time.'

Sarah shot to her feet and clasped his arm. 'Please, John? You know how much it means to me. How much I want children.'

He searched her face and sighed. 'I do know, my love. I'm just worried.' He kissed her cheek. 'I almost lost you once. Then Samuel. I don't know…'

'It'll be different, John,' she said, breathless. 'I'm sure it will.'

John hung his head. 'Very well.' He spun on his heel and walked out the door.

Sarah's eyes flicked around the room and settled on Samuel's picture. Her heart ached. Would there ever be more than an image behind the glass? She absently chewed at her nails. The woman the help spoke of in hushed tones: Rose. Maybe she should pay this Rose a visit. Just for reassurance. No harm in that.

*

Walking up the path towards the cabin, Sarah shivered and pulled her cloak tight. Once lush trees stood bare, gnarled branches exposed for all to see. Winter wasn't far away.

Sarah climbed the dilapidated stairs, placing her feet carefully. The gaps in the floorboards were big enough to lose a shoe. She raised a fist to knock against a door warped by half a century of sunsets. But her hand hung mid-air. If she entered this house, there was no going back. The answers she sought may not be what she wished to hear. And then what?

Before she could decide either way, the door opened. In the skewed frame stood a small lady, skin the colour of coffee.

Sarah jumped. 'Oh!'

'Come on in.' Her voice was gravelly, but her tone welcoming. The old woman opened the door further, and Sarah shivered as she looked into the woman's opaque eyes.

'Oh, uh…I don't have an appointment,' Sarah stammered.

'But you're here, ain't you?' The woman smiled and exposed gaps in her yellowed teeth. She patted at her halo of wiry, salted hair.

'Well, yes—'

'Then you'd better come in.'

'Yes, of course. Are you Rose?' She offered her gloved hand. 'I'm Sarah.'

'I know.'

Sarah's brow creased. 'Have we met before?'

'Why don't you come in, out of the cold, missus?'

Sarah edged past the woman. Her eyes darted around the interior of the small cabin. The floor groaned under their feet, and Sarah ducked to avoid a rabbit's foot dangling from the rafters. Her chest tightened. Star anise burnt in the hearth, and the smell of smoky liquorice filled the air.

'Please.' The old woman indicated a wooden table. 'Sit.'

Sarah paused and blinked several times. Her eyes gradually adjusted to the dim light thrown by the single candle set on the table. She sat and took several measured breaths. 'Excuse me, Miss...Rose?'

'Nanny Rose, they all call me.'

Sarah fiddled with the cord on her belt-pouch. Should she bring out a coin? 'Miss...Nanny Rose. How does this—'

'It's the spirit's will, missus.' Rose spoke with authority. 'There's no use you asking. They'll talk if they want.'

Sarah closed her mouth and clasped her gloved hands in her lap. She sat stiffly on the edge of the seat.

Rose's brow creased and she nodded. 'Your mama. It was important to her that you survived.'

Sarah drew a sharp intake of breath. 'What do you mean?'

Rose stared straight ahead, her face unreadable. 'She knew the risk of having a breach-baby, but believed it was worth it. That you were worth it, even though she paid a heavy price.'

Sarah's lips parted, but nothing came out. Only family knew that her mother had died giving birth to Sarah in a breach birth. How could this old crone know?

'And yes.' Rose inclined her head. 'For you there's another. And this one will survive.'

'Really?' Sarah couldn't stop the smile that stretched her mouth wide. Nothing else Rose had said mattered now.

'Spirits ain't never wrong' Rose nodded emphatically.

Sarah placed a coin on the table. 'Thank you!' she breathed. Excitement hammered her heart against her ribs.

'Wait!' Rose's face clouded over. 'There's more you need to know.'

'What?' Sarah frowned. 'You see something.'

Rose held up a hand. 'There's a powerful wrong threatens this land, missus. Your boy'll help it change.'

'A boy?' Tears welled in her eyes. She covered her mouth. 'Are you sure?'

'Yes, missus. He'll arrive as the Comet appears in the sky—'

'But he'll survive?' Hope flickered in her heart and she leaned forward, breathless. 'You promise?' Was the old woman just saying what was expected? Sunlight streamed across the table and the coin glinted. Sarah's shoulders sagged. Of course she was. No-one could be certain. Childbirth was dangerous. She couldn't afford to get her hopes up too high. The disappointment was too bitter.

'Yes, missus,' Rose repeated. 'The child will survive.' She shifted in her seat. 'Miss Sarah, this boy…He's important to the nation. His'll be a life worth saving.'

Sarah steeled her heart. Coming here had been a mistake. This woman was nothing but a charlatan. She clearly wanted more money and thought predicting a great future for the child would open Sarah's purse again.

'Of course,' she said stiffly, 'all children are important to our great—'

'No!' Rose cried.

The chair scraped against the floor as Sarah jolted back. 'I should—'

'I'm sorry to scare you, missus.' Rose's eyes fell. 'You're important in this, too. Yours is a life worth living. But it's important you understand how much this boy means.'

'Of course.' Sarah's voice trembled.

'A law will pass.' Rose nodded. 'One meant to stop folks advertising and talkin' of rebellion.'

'I'm afraid I don't understand what this has to do with me.' Sarah lifted her chin and pressed her lips tight.

'You doubt my words. You need a sign,' Rose said. 'To believe what I say is true about your son. So watch. When spring comes, you'll have a sign. You mark my words, missus.'

'I'm sorry,' Sarah stammered. She began to rise. This was madness. 'But I—'

Rose held her hand up. 'Many struggle to hold on to faith. Many don't believe and don't listen – and regret it later. But when you see this law written; when you read the words banning freedom. You'll know I speak the truth. And you'll know what I tell you about your son is also true.'

Sarah's heart skipped. She hesitated. She should leave. Shouldn't listen to this nonsense. But she didn't. 'What about him?'

'Your son.' Rose stared at Sarah. 'He'll help end my people's plight. He'll help end slavery. Your mother is here. She's telling me this. Telling me you both must live to help our people.'

'My mother!' Trembling with anger and fear, Sarah jumped up. 'That's a hateful thing to do! You're twisting things. Trying to manipulate me in to joining your rebellion by promising my child will live if he leads your people! How could you?'

The old woman said nothing. Her lined mouth pursed but she merely shook her head and sighed.

Sarah uttered noise of frustration and fled into the cold afternoon with tears stinging her eyes.

*

The visit out to the cabin rattled Sarah's nerves. For several days she couldn't look at her mother's picture. And several weeks passed before she was able to put the meeting out of her mind. But as Christmas approached, the memory faded and all her focus shifted to preparing for the festive season.

*

Dim, grey winter-light shone behind the curtains and woke Sarah. Her eyes stung, and she blinked several times. Smoke hazed the bedroom. Millie must have crept in to light the hearth fire. Sarah stretched a leg out to feel for John, and nudged him.

'Merry Christmas,' she whispered in his ear.

John rolled to face her, his eyes still closed. 'Merry Christmas.' He smiled.

The bed bounced slightly as Sarah sat up and pulled her robe around her. 'Wonder if there's anything in the stockings?'

'I'm sure you won't try and guess what's in there while you wait for me to come down,' John teased.

Sarah headed out the door onto the landing. Her slippers scuffed against the wooden floor. 'I'd never dream of doing such a thing!'

She entered the parlour and silently thanked Millie for waking early and getting the fire ready there, too. She pulled the heavy drapes back and smiled. A thick white blanket covered the trees and fields. Sarah stood for a moment and enjoyed the pristine landscape.

'It's beautiful, isn't it.' John whispered in her ear.

'Oh! I didn't hear you.'

John pulled her close and kissed her gently. 'Merry Christmas, my love.'

'Shall we exchange gifts?' she said.

'You're even more impatient than I remember.' He laughed.

She grabbed his hand and pulled him towards the hearth. 'I really can't wait much longer to give you mine.'

'Now I'm intrigued.'

'Shall I open mine first?' She unhooked her stocking.

John settled back in his chair. 'Well, it seems so.'

Sarah reached down into her stocking and pulled out a small tightly-wrapped package. Her hands tore at the paper impatiently. 'Oh. John!' she cried. 'It's beautiful.' She turned the pendent and touched the small sapphire that hung from the silver chain.

'It matches your eyes.'

She passed the chain to John and pulled her hair aside. 'You shouldn't have,' she said.

John admired the small pendant around her neck. 'You deserve it.'

Sarah kissed the top of his head. 'Now it's your turn.'

He took the stocking that she held out for him. 'Goodness, I'm not sure what to expect.' He pulled out a small box. His fingers picked at the twine, undid the knot, and lifted the lid. He peeled a sheet of tissue away and lifted a small pair of woollen booties.

John held the booties up, his brow creased. 'I don't understand—'

'I'm pregnant.' She beamed.

John flung his arms around Sarah and buried his face in her hair. 'What a wonderful surprise.' He drew back and kissed her, but his eyes held a hint of worry.

She touched his cheek. 'It will be alright, I promise.'

'How can you be sure?' His fingers crushed hers.

Rose's wrinkled face flashed into her thoughts and Sarah shivered. But she put on a determined smile for John's sake.

'Because I'll make it alright.'

*

Sarah sat back against the chair and waited for John to join her. She drew a deep breath and inhaled the sweet smell of spring as it wafted in through the open window. In the garden, the first daffodils pushed their heads through the soil in sharp, green spikes. A red-breasted robin sang merrily amongst the oak's green buds.

'Morning, dear.' She smiled at John as he joined her at the breakfast table.

John folded his paper and smiled. 'Good morning, my love. How are you feeling?'

Sarah picked up a small knife and buttered her bread. 'The nausea has passed now, finally!'

He patted her hand. 'You look positively radiant.'

She smiled. 'What's in the news today?' She nodded at the paper.

'Hmm, not much.' John sipped his coffee. 'But I think I'll have to have a word to Robert about that apprentice of his.'

'Oh, why?'

'I know there's a difference of opinion in these parts about the slaves.' John pulled at a sheet of paper. 'But putting these pamphlets around is going a little too far.'

Sarah drew a sharp intake of air. An image of two negro girls, their heads bowed confronted her. The word 'Stolen!' jumped off the page. Underneath, it urged people to attend a meeting, to discuss the abolition of slavery.

'I don't understand...' Sarah's brow creased. 'How does Robert's apprentice have anything to do with this?'

'He's a sympathiser.' John waved the pamphlet. 'Of the slave rebellion. Must be if he's spreading these pamphlets around.'

'Well, yes…but…' The visit with Rose rushed through Sarah's mind. Spring, she'd said, would bring a sign. No, she'd talked about a law. This was a pamphlet about the rebellion, not the law against it. Rose was just a crazy old woman sowing dissent.

'Don't you worry about it,' John reassured her.

'Oh, no…I was just—'

John shoved the pamphlet back into the paper. 'It'll soon be illegal anyway, that sort of thing.'

'What do you mean?'

'Look.' He pointed to a small by-line on the front page: *Georgia Enacts Death Penalty for All Publications that Encourage Slave Rebellion.*

Sarah's stomach lurched. The law Rose had mentioned! It was true. Sarah laid a protective hand on her belly. Did that mean her son really was destined to help free the slaves? How could that be?

John's voice intruded on her thoughts. 'It won't be long before they bring that law here.' His brow knitted. 'Which is precisely what I'll be telling Robert. His apprentice needs to watch himself.'

Sarah fixed her gaze on the tablecloth and flicked at a small pile of crumbs. 'It's not right, though,' she whispered, her mind still turning Rose's words over.

He shifted in his chair and ran a thick finger around the rim of his cup. 'Slavery?' He asked without looking up.

'Mmm.' She sat straighter and waited for John to meet her eye. 'You never agreed with your father's way of treating them.'

John looked down at his hands. 'No, I didn't.'

'In fact, you made a point of saying to me, when we married, that we weren't going to have any slaves.' She tipped her head. 'Just help you said. Paid help.'

His eyes filled with doubt. 'Yes.'

'I think,' she said, certainty growing, 'there's a great many of us that know slavery isn't right, but we're too darned scared to speak out.'

He placed his hand over Sarah's and squeezed it gently. 'I think that's about the measure of it, isn't it?'

'It's wrong that we, and others like us, just sit around and hope someone else will make it all right, isn't it?' She stroked her stomach. A faint flutter of movement rewarded her.

John stood and tucked the paper under his arm. 'It is wrong, my dear. I know.' His brow furrowed. 'But what can we do about it? We can't get involved, Sarah. It's too dangerous. For you and the baby, especially.'

Sarah nodded. John closed the door behind him. At first, when Rose had said she would have a son, and that he would live, she'd been filled with joy. Yet the woman's insistence that he was important…to the nation's survival…it just seemed fanciful. But the pamphlet…that newspaper article… Could there be any truth in the old woman?

*

The cloying heat of summer filled the air. Morning was the only decent time of day for a walk to stretch her legs. Sarah latched the gate and walked down the path, smiling as the birds chirped and danced around the branches. She turned the corner and the cicada's song started. It buzzed in Sarah's head. The song of summer; a knell to short lives and impending deaths.

The slaves in Mr Bennett's fields were out already, harvesting the crop. Sarah stopped and watched a man in front. His strong arms glistened as he raised the scythe and swung it through the corn stalks. His shirt was already soaked. He straightened and arched his back, then mopped at his brow.

'What you doin' boy?' James Bennett's voice bellowed.

Sarah crept behind a large tree trunk. A whip cracked through the air. Her heart thumped. She pressed up against the trunk and peeked around the side.

Mr Bennett stood over the young man, turning the whip in circles through the grass like a snake. 'You ain't stoppin' less I say so.'

'Yessir.' The young man stammered.

Mr Bennett brought his arm down and the strap lashed the slave. 'Get up boy!'

The slave stumbled as he tried to stand. Mr Bennett struck again. *Crack!* Sarah stiffened and her cheek scraped against the gnarled trunk.

The young man lifted the scythe high and winced. Bright red weals striped his back. Mr Bennett stalked away, muttering.

Sarah stumbled back from the tree. Her shoe caught on the roots and she almost fell. She laid a protective hand on her swollen stomach and struggled upright. The baby kicked her ribs. Her heel stuck between the roots and she tugged at it, her heart racing. Her shoe dislodged in a shower of leaves. A folded piece of paper fluttered free. *Georgia Enacts Death Penalty...* She snatched it up and flattened it. *...for All Publications that Encourage Slave Rebellion.* The article John had shown her months before. She crushed the paper in her hand and hurried home.

Sarah eyed the oak outside. Its branches were laden with acorns. The leaves had begun their transition, not long now before summer gave way to autumn. She chewed a mouthful of blueberry pie slowly. The baby pressed on her stomach.

'I can't manage another bite!' She laughed, pushing the plate away. 'Do you want it?'

'I shouldn't.' John leant back against his chair and mopped his chin with a napkin. 'That was a delicious dinner.' He raised a brow and considered the food left on Sarah's plate.

'You know you want it,' Sarah teased and handed her plate over.

'It is good pie,' he admitted. 'Oh. Mother asked if she could drop off some blankets she's made for the baby.'

'Yes, absolutely—' She gasped and gripped her stomach.

John jumped from his chair and rushed to her side. 'What's wrong?'

'Oh…' she bent over. 'Ahhh…' Sarah's heart filled with fear. 'All of a sudden…I just felt this awful pulling at my side.'

He helped her rise. 'Come and sit over here.' His face clouded with concern. 'It's too early, isn't it?'

She nodded, groaning.

He guided her to the parlour and helped her onto the settee. 'Perhaps you should raise your legs?' He fussed around her, plumping cushions. 'How are you feeling now?'

Sarah wiped at the tears rolling down her cheeks. 'The discomfort has gone, but it feels tight.' Her chest rose as she sobbed. 'I'm scared, John…I can't lose another.'

John perched on the edge of the settee. 'Shhh.' He soothed. 'I'll call for your midwife.'

'I don't have one.' Her voice was barely a whisper.

His eyes widened. 'What do you mean?'

Fresh tears brimmed. 'We couldn't afford it...'

John stroked a stray lock of hair from her brow and shook his head. 'Oh love, no. You and the baby...there's no price too high. Surely it's not too late to call for the midwife?'

'You could try Ruth Kelly.' Sarah sniffed. 'She's only down the road, but she's—'

'Sarah.' He raised his hand. 'Please, let me worry about the cost. Right now, you and the baby are all that matters. I'm going to call around quickly, see if she can look in on you now. I'll only be a few minutes.'

'I'll be fine.' She grabbed his arm. 'Thank you.'

A few minutes later John's voice echoed down the hall. 'I appreciate you coming around on such short notice.'

'Not at all.' Ruth's tone was all business. 'It's what I do.'

The door burst open and John smiled reassuringly at Sarah. 'I ran into Mrs Kelly just as I entered the street.'

Sarah winced as her belly hardened once more. Ruth ran her weathered hands over Sarah's belly. 'Hmmm.'

Sarah stiffened. 'Something's wrong, isn't it?'

The midwife stepped back and briskly brushed down the front of her plain, black gown. Her small, dark eyes remained fixed to Sarah's stomach. 'Well...he's breach. But there's time to turn.' She looked at Sarah directly for the first time. 'Lord knows I've seen them turn right up to the end. Hurts like the devil, mind you.' Ruth shook her head and gave a wintry little smile.

Sarah swallowed and twisted her skirt in her fingers. 'I don't understand. Will everything be alright? My...my mother died giving birth to me. I was breach.'

'Now, now. Don't you go getting yourself in a state. Like I said. Most of them turn. With a little help, sometimes.' Ruth pulled a well-worn notebook out of her leather satchel and made some notes. 'It won't be long now. The best thing you can do is rest. She stuffed the book back into the satchel and folded her hands across her lean stomach. 'I'll be back next week.'

'Thank you.' Sarah called out as Ruth pulled the door behind her.

John sat on the edge of the settee and stroked her hair. 'Do you feel better now?'

Sarah jumped and laughed in relief. 'He's moving again!' She placed John's hand on her stomach. 'There! Did you feel it?'

John's eyes glistened. 'Yes!'

Sarah ran her fingers through John's thick hair. 'Sweetheart—'

'Mmm?'

'I'm…it's just…I'm scared.'

He looked up. 'Oh, my love, it's normal to be nervous. I am, too.'

'I know it's silly.' Her voice trembled. 'I just…My mother. And Samuel. And the other babies. I won't lose another one, John. I can't.'

John took her hand and held it tight. 'I'm not going to let anything happen to you, or our baby.'

Sarah lay her head in his lap. Something scratched against her cheek. 'What's that?' She sat up and pointed at a piece of paper protruding from John's pocket.

'This?' He pulled out the scrap of paper. 'Ruth wrote down an elixir for you.'

Sarah's throat went dry.

'Are you alright?' John's voice rose sharply.

She pointed at the paper. 'It's the pamphlet,' she whispered.

'What do you mean?'

'There.' She pointed once more.

He turned the paper over in his hand and raised a brow.

A chill went up her spine. It had been months since she'd seen that pamphlet.

'Ruth must've torn up some old papers.' He shrugged. 'To write on. She probably didn't even realise.'

The hair on her arms tingled. 'No, I suppose you're right.' Rose's words returned: *believe what I say is true.* Sarah struggled for breath and calm. Did she dare believe? Believe that her son would survive; that he would one day be great? She shivered and leaned into John, afraid.

*

The last weeks of Sarah's pregnancy were full of discomfort. She was breathless all the time. Her back ached and her ankles were the size of oranges. In the first week of August, she lay in bed for hours before she fell into a restless sleep. She tossed and turned, unable to find comfort. She slid out from under the covers, donned her robe and waddled downstairs to the parlour.

The fire had burned down, but the embers glowed red in the dark. Sarah tugged the curtains aside until the moonlight shone through. Standing at the window, she shivered. Her eyes caught a soft glow. Unsure of what she'd seen, she blinked and focused once more. The sky was glowing! The comet, just as Rose had said it would be.

The ache in her back intensified. Sarah gasped. Pain gripped her stomach, and her smile faded. Wetness flooded down her legs. It was time.

She made her way upstairs as quickly as she could, gripping the rail with each step. 'John!' she yelled. 'The baby's coming.' Another contraction rippled across her belly and she bent over, gasping.

John appeared at the bedroom door, hair dishevelled, a lamp in one hand. 'Now?'

'Yes. Now!' she said through gritted teeth.

He ran towards the stairs, then back again, his eyes wild. 'Get into bed. I'll fetch help.' He kissed her cheek and gripped her hand as she groaned.

When he left, Sarah eased herself into bed and concentrated on her breath. The pain was worse this time. Worse than it had been with Samuel. Panic seized her and she bit back a sob.

Her ears pricked to the sound of unfamiliar steps on the timber floor. 'Ruth?'

'Sshh, child.' Ruth's voice soothed. 'I'm here.' Low voices muttered and John scurried out of the room again. Millie appeared, still in her nightgown, carrying a steaming copper kettle. Ruth directed her to boil more water and bring linen.

Sarah cried out as a contraction tore through her body. 'Ruth! I can't see you. Where's John?'

Ruth appeared at the bottom of the bed. She wiped her hands briskly on a towel and tied an apron around her waist. 'I'm here. You're ready, Sarah. I'll tell you to push in a minute. Do you want John in here?'

Sarah nodded and fell back on her pillows. Her hair stuck to her face and sweat soaked her nightgown. She screamed as the pain began again. So much worse than with Samuel. What was wrong? It shouldn't be like this. The second baby was supposed to be easier. She sucked a sobbing breath.

'Alright, now – push,' Ruth demanded.

Sarah bore down, as hard as she could. 'John?' She panted. He grabbed her hand and squeezed.

'I'm here.'

'It hurts so much!'

'I know. I'm sorry,' he murmured. His face was pale and he swallowed hard. His brave smile wavered as he glanced at Ruth's set face.

'The baby's stuck,' Ruth said, her voice low.

'What's wrong with my baby?' Sarah's cry ended on a scream as another contraction seized her.

'No!' Ruth said. 'Don't push, Sarah. I have to try and turn him. He's still breach.' She pressed the heels of her hands into Sarah's stomach, massaging and pushing.

'Breach?' Sarah raised her head when the pain eased and sought Ruth. 'You said he would turn.'

'I know what I said, young lady,' Ruth said shortly. 'And most of the time they do. Yours didn't. I can't turn him, either, so we have to work quickly if we're going to save you.'

'What do you mean? You have to help him!' Sarah tried to kick at Ruth but the midwife held her ankles.

Ruth exchanged a grim look with John. Sarah groaned as the pain came once more and the room darkened.

A hand stroked at her brow. 'There now.' A familiar voice soothed.

Sarah's eyes fluttered, it was an effort to keep them open. 'John?'

'Yes, my love.' He kissed her cheek softly. 'I'm here.'

She touched his cheek. 'I'm so tired.'

Tears welled in his eyes. 'Sweetheart?'

'Mmm?'

'The baby's stuck.' He cleared his throat. 'Ruth says you can't keep going.'

'No!' A contraction hit and she cried out, clutching at his hand until he winced.

'Listen to me love. There'll be others.'

Sobs racked Sarah's body. 'No John. You don't understand—'

'I'm sorry, Mister John,' Ruth said abruptly. 'But we can't wait any longer.'

'No! You don't understand…' Sarah turned her head side to side, looking for support. John stared back, his eyes shadowed by fear.

Ruth looked sternly down at Sarah. 'Now, you listen to me. This baby's got to come out, one way or another.' She brandished a sharp metal hook. 'If he doesn't come out you'll both die.'

'Sweetheart, please,' John begged. 'Let Ruth do what she has to.'

'No!' she cried. 'No! No! You can't kill him!'

'Hold her, Mr John.' Ruth bent down, her face bleak. 'Just don't look, Sarah. They'll be more. But not if I don't act now.'

Sarah fell against her pillows and sobbed. Her hand grasped her belly as a fresh wave of contractions tore at her insides.

'Wait.' She called out. Nanny Rose's words echoed in the delirium of her mind. *Believe. He will survive. He'll help end slavery. A life worth saving.*

Ruth looked up impatiently. 'There's no time for delay, Sarah.'

'No. Please.' Her strength had faded. Everything Rose had predicted had come true so far. Sarah gathered her will. She just had to believe. To have faith. It was an effort to speak. 'John…this boy…he has to—'

'I haven't got time for this nonsense.' Ruth waved her off and turned back to fixing Sarah's legs in position.

'No!' Sarah shrieked. Ruth looked up, eyes wide, mouth agape.

'But, Sarah,' John said, 'this was how your mother died. I can't lose you—'

She clenched her teeth and dug her nails into his hand. 'I will *not*. I'm not my mother and this child *will* live. Because I *say* he will. Because I *know* he will.' She glared at Ruth. 'Try to turn him again.'

The midwife hesitated.

'Do it!' Sarah snapped.

'You're mad.' Ruth huffed. 'There'll be no-one left to save in a minute.'

'You've heard my wife,' John said, drawing himself up. 'She's adamant that this baby will be born. I fear her heart will be inconsolable if I say otherwise.'

'Have faith.' Sarah ground out through gritted teeth.

Ruth threw her hands in the air. 'Very well.'

The midwife positioned herself on a small wooden stool at the bottom of the bed. John held Sarah's hand as she bit down hard on a leather strap. Ruth's hands worked her belly, and Sarah screamed with the pain. Her insides were torn and falling out. The agony peaked, unbearable, unendurable.

Piercing wails filled the room as the first grey light of dawn crept under the curtains.

Ruth breathed a sigh. 'It's a bloody miracle, it is.'

Tears streamed down Sarah's face. 'Is he alright?'

'He's beautiful.' John kissed his wife.

'You've got yourself a real tough one there,' Ruth said to John as she cleaned up and dealt with the afterbirth.

'Yes, he's quite the fighter.' John beamed.

'No.' Ruth nodded at Sarah. 'I meant this one.'

His brushed his hand against Sarah's cheek. His eyes glowed with pride. 'Yes. She had an unshakeable faith.'

Once Ruth was satisfied that Sarah was stable, she left the new parents to enjoy their son.

'Thank you,' Sarah whispered. 'For believing me.'

'There was a look in your eye…I've never seen it before.' John shook his head.

She inhaled the baby's sweet smell. Her gaze flicked to the dresser, where she'd placed her mother's picture days before. Silly really, but it was Sarah's way to have her here. Something about the picture caught her attention.

'John, could you pass me that painting of Mother?'

He handed the frame over. A puzzled look crossed his face.

Sarah held the frame close, her breath fogged the glass. How had she not seen it before? There, behind her mother. The artist had painted Rose.

'John?' Her voice quivered. 'Do you know that old lady living in the cabin over the river? The little one on the Curtis's farm?'

He frowned thoughtfully. 'What lady? That cabin's been empty for years.'

'Nanny Rose…she lives there,' Sarah stammered.

'No love, she died. Must be about ten years ago now.'

She shook her head. 'You must be thinking of the wrong person. I saw her, went to her house and—'

'Shh,' he soothed. 'What does it matter, anyway?'

'I…I suppose it doesn't,' she lied, and studied the tiny red-cheeked face poking out of the bundle in her arms.

John looked down on his wife and son. 'Thank God you fought to save him.' He said with a catch in his voice.

Sarah held her baby's soft head against her cheek and whispered. 'Yes, and now you will save the lives of many.'

1910CE
9th April, Mercia, The Isles

A Window on Wonder

Susan Ruth

The patient, Valdin Blake, was fortunate enough to have a bed in a side room off the crowded main ward of a Northern hospital. Blake welcomed the peace and privacy this afforded, especially as he felt self-conscious about his injuries.

'It's not as if I was wounded in battle like most of the others here. The South didn't do for me, as it did for them,' Blake said to his friend, Felix Skryker, who was putting up a telescope at the large window beside his bed. 'I wasn't paying attention to where I was going. I tripped in the dark. Then fell headlong down a flight of stone steps, like the fool that I am.'

Skryker glanced at him and smiled. 'It could have happened to anyone. It was an accident.'

'But it didn't happen to anyone, Felix. It happened to me, just two nights ago. Now I'm laid up in a military hospital with a broken leg and three cracked ribs for no good reason. I'm of no use to anyone here. I should be working. I've got patients who need me. We have so many casualties at present.'

'Certainly. But you're stuck here for a while longer. Once you're back on your feet you'll feel better.'

'On crutches.' There was an angry note in Blake's voice. He glanced at the window. His room was on the third floor of the hospital and the curtains were pulled back, giving onto a wide, dark night-time skyscape. 'And how I'm to be expected to use that star-glass you're fiddling with, Sol Invictus alone knows. I'm doomed not to see this wretched comet of yours, after all. I was going out to look for it when I had the accident. We can put that down to its malefic influence, that's for sure.'

'There is no malefic influence. That's just superstition.'

'Hah! I know that, Felix. Stop being so damned reasonable!'

Skryker turned from his telescope again and grinned at Blake. 'People are already getting unreasonable about the Great Comet in this visitation.' He bent to look in the eyepiece of the instrument, testing it and adjusting the setting. 'And it's still not visible to the naked eye. You'll have a good view from this window, when the comet gets a little closer. Until then, you can look at it through the star-glass. Are you able to get out of bed yet?'

Blake shook his head, indicating his situation with a feeble wave of an arm. His left leg was in plaster and set at a forty-five degree angle by a system of pulleys and counter-balancing weights. 'No, I'm still in traction for a few more days. You're wasting your time, Felix, trying to cheer me up. I swear I'm beyond redemption at present. I know I'm being unreasonable too.'

Skryker reached into the kit-bag he had brought with him, taking out a pair of field glasses and setting them on the side of the bed within Blake's reach. 'You can use these to look at the Great Comet, if you wish. They will give you a good general view from your bed there. You have only to turn your head and look out through the window. By my reckoning, we'll have our first clear sighting of the comet this time tomorrow. You're well-placed to see it.'

'Gramercie,' said Blake between clenched teeth. Right now, he really cared very little any more for the imminent appearance in the heavens of the Great Comet. He laid his hand on the field glasses. 'Put these on the cupboard for me, Felix. I'll wait until I can see this wonder with my own eyes.'

Skryker's grey-green eyes lit up. 'And see it you will. And very soon, for you have a window on wonder here.' He rose and brushed down his fleece-lined flying jacket. 'Well, I'll be going now. I'm expected at the Observatory Tower at Valerian College tonight. We're making some sightings of the comet with the Cassini star-glass, and there are tests to be done on the gases in the tail.' Before the outbreak of the Civil War, Skryker had been an astronomer at Valerian College. 'I'll come back around this time tomorrow.' He transferred the binoculars to the bedside cabinet.

'I'll look forward to it,' said Blake with studied politeness, closing his eyes. He heard his friend say *Well met* and pick up his kit-bag. Listening to the retreating footsteps, he gave a half-choked-down sigh of relief. He wanted to be left to enjoy his self-pity in solitary splendour, not to waste his time on astronomical frivolities.

Then his growing despondency came up against his almost-buried sense of fair-mindedness. He should feel grateful his friend had seen fit to visit him rather than be so thankless and impolite.

Hearing another footfall, he opened his eyes. Perhaps Skryker had returned and he could apologise for being so abrupt. Then his heart sank within his aching breast.

A man stood on the threshold of his room, coming forward as if certain of his welcome. 'I heard that you had a visitor, so I thought I would come and see you myself. This is a very bad business. And all down to this daemon star everyone is talking about.'

Blake wished almost anyone else had come to see him. 'Messire Rampling. Unfortunately, it's all down to my not looking where I was going, pure and simple.' Rampling was a distant cousin. Blake had been brought up to be formal with the older man.

Donatiss Rampling was a tall, thin individual in his sixties with wispy grey hair and a pale, lined face. He wore long, dark grey robes and had the silver Earth disc of his order at his breast. He was a senior cleric in the church dedicated to Sol Invictus, the solar deity of the state religion of The Isles.

The coming of the Civil War, which had split The Isles, had also rent apart the church and all its attendant offices. But Rampling, accustomed to power, was always quick to take the slightest opportunity to foster the church in this Northern fastness. The Isles might be divided but, as Rampling saw it, he was still a big fish – albeit in a smaller pond.

Blake wondered what he was doing here. He did not customarily attend the hospital in any religious capacity. He was too important for that. And their relationship was not close.

Messire Rampling smiled an unctuous smile and came further into the room. He drew up a chair to the bed and sat down. 'I heard you had gone out looking for this daemon star. And that it caused you to take a tumble.' He had a beautiful voice, deep-toned and musical, compelling and convincing.

Despite this, Blake held his ground. 'I fell in the dark. It was an accident.'

The smile broadened. 'You can be honest with me, my dear boy. The daemon star is a harbinger of doom. Everyone knows that. It always has been and always will be. It's an affront to the good order of Sol Invictus. The sooner people accept that the better. I mean, here you are helpless now and wounded under its dark influence. You need looking after. The sooner this thing comes and goes, the better it will be for everyone.'

'I didn't even see the Great Comet,' said Blake. 'It's not yet visible to the naked eye, apparently. And I fell two nights ago.'

'But it's coming. The daemon star's up there in the sky, making its baleful influence felt.' Rampling glanced across at the open curtains and the telescope. He made a reverence to Sol Invictus: hand to heart, to brow, and to mouth. He rose, drawing the curtains closed with a snap and turning the star-glass around ungently. 'That friend of yours goes too far. This is an instrument of the devil.' He manipulated the body of the telescope on its tripod so the opening was pointing to the ground.

'It's a star-glass!'

'Exactly.' Rampling sat down, staring at Blake with over-bright eyes. 'An instrument of the devil, I say. A tool of heretics and dissidents.'

Blake stirred uncomfortably, his breathing laboured and painful from his cracked ribs. He glanced at his bedside clock. Still three-quarters of an hour to go before he was due to take his next dose of painkillers. If only Rampling would leave so he could rest as peacefully as possible while he waited for the nurse to arrive.

But Rampling was now talking on a subject dear to his heart, his musical voice rising and strong. 'As soon as I heard what had happened, I knew I must come to you, my dear boy. This veneration of the daemon star is little better than heresy. And that young man who was with you... Felix Skryker he calls himself now... Well, he was born a Sheldon, and everyone knows about the Sheldonian Heresy.'

And with that he was away on a history of heresy in The Isles and the place in it of the seventeenth-century astronomer, Richard Sheldon, who wrote that Sol Invictus, the deity, was in fact just an ordinary star, one among many. There had been a famous trial, and eventually Sheldon had been forced to recant or face execution.

Listening to that enthralling voice, a critical part of Blake still wondered why Rampling had come. Heresy was a recurrent issue in The Isles and there had been recent, equally-famous trials, but given the Civil War, the topic had faded somewhat from the public mind. People had more pressing matters to think of: the enormous numbers of war dead on both sides, the even greater count of injured, the shortages and economic dislocation...

Rampling continued. 'And then those people at Valerian College, those so-called astronomers and astrophysicists – it's rightly called the Dark Faculty, I say – well, we all know they're nothing but a lot of heretics. They foster the taint of blasphemy. And this Felix Skryker used to work there. He is one of them.'

Blake was beginning to see the light. Rampling was making a power play. By describing the Great Comet as a daemon star, and by attacking those who were interested in it and its progress, the cleric was hoping to revive the waning power of the Congregation of Believers, his bailiwick in the church. Blake sighed. This was hardly a battle that he wanted – or needed – to fight now.

He almost resented Skryker for having brought the star-glass in the first place. Ordinarily, he would have been delighted to observe the comet. He stared at the drawn curtains. Skryker had left them open. Rampling had closed them. There was a choice to be made here. Which did he prefer?

This question on his mind, Blake lay in his place, enduring the unwanted presence, trying to find a comfortable spot. The beautiful voice had lost its allure.

A long half-hour later, Messire Rampling had finally gone. A very punctilious nurse arrived with his medication and, with one narrow glance at Blake's face, declared that visiting time was over for the night. At first Rampling demurred, saying he was there by invitation, but the nurse stared at him, a militant gleam in her eye.

'The patient needs to sleep, good sir. He needs time to heal. You must leave, good sir, and return during visiting hours.'

Grumbling, Rampling complied, rising in a flurry of grey robes and staring down at Blake. 'I will come back tomorrow night. You'll be needing me, I think, lying here helpless under the influence of the daemon star and Sol Invictus alone knows what – or who – else.'

Weary, Blake made no reply to this, merely bidding the older man a civil goodnight and looking anxiously at the nurse.

She gave him his painkillers, holding the tumbler of water to his mouth as he swallowed. Then she straightened his disordered pyjamas and helped him use the bedpan. Once he was under the covers again, she glanced around the room and turned down the light until it shone with a gentle glow.

'I'll be in during the night, Doctor Blake. If you need me, just ring the bell.'

With that she gave a small, satisfied smile and left the room, drawing the door part shut behind her.

She left the curtains very properly closed.

Blake did not know whether to be glad or sorry.

*

Felix Skryker returned as promised on the following evening. He came in with a smile, taking a book out of a paper bag as he did so.

'This might be more suitable than a star-glass, or even binoculars.' He held the book up so Blake might see the garish cover of a white cat in a tuxedo and a red hat, under a full moon. 'The woman in the book-shop assured me it was light and amusing. And all the rage, too.'

'Gramercie,' said Blake automatically, trying to smile. He did not really want a book either, the very act of holding it would tax his cracked ribs. But it would be impolite to say so.

'I hope you find it entertaining,' Skryker said, a tentative note in his voice.

Blake glanced around. A nurse had made the room up for the night. The curtains were drawn and the overhead light switched off, with the bedside lamp providing a gentle illumination. The star-glass on its tripod was as Rampling had left it: down-turned and awry. Neither the nurses nor the orderly earlier had touched it. The binoculars were still on the bedside cabinet, but now tidied away and out of reach.

Having pulled up a chair, Skryker sat down by the bed. For long seconds, he said nothing. Skryker must have noticed both the closed curtains and the telescope. Blake sought for something to say to fill the awkward silence.

Skryker was before him, his voice gentle as he laid the book on the bed. 'I hope you can manage this. It's mainly short pieces – articles and stories, in the main. I could read aloud to you, if you'd like.'

Blake shook his head, cursing his friend for being so fair-minded. He glanced at the star-glass which seemed to dominate the room. Should he mention it?

Skryker smiled, chatting vaguely about the book as he folded up the paper bag and slipped it into his pocket. 'If you don't like this, of course, I can always change it for something else. There's a new thriller out by that author you like, Seabert Oliver. I saw it in the shop. But it's been out a while, and I thought you might already have a copy.'

Blake took a ragged breath, wincing as he did so. 'I had a visitor last night. Some sort of enemy of yours, Felix.'

'Yes?'

'Messire Donatiss Rampling. He's a distant relative, more's the pity.'

'Ah...' Skryker frowned, his face briefly darkening. 'Rampling of the Congregation of Believers. I'm in his black books. He doesn't like my flying concern. Try not to let it bother you. You must concentrate on getting your strength back. Rampling is just trying to make his presence felt. The Congregation of Believers is a bit of a backwater since the coming of the Civil War.'

Trying to ease himself, Blake shook his head again and regretted it. 'He called the Great Comet a daemon star. He wouldn't stop talking about how it's a messenger from the devil.'

Skryker burst out laughing. 'He's probably not alone in that thought. But it's a very outdated attitude. More than likely, Messire Rampling still thinks the Earth's flat and that the star Sol revolves around it; rising in the east and setting in the west and travelling through the underworld during the night.'

'Whatever he thinks, he closed the curtains, and he turned the star-glass down so I wouldn't feel the malefic influence of the comet.'

The laughter left Skryker's eyes. 'And have the curtains been like that all day?'

'No, they were open during daylight. The nurse closed them when it got dark.'

'Do you want to see if the comet's there?'

'Not really. Not tonight, Felix. I've rather lost interest in the comet since the accident.' Blake fiddled with the edge of his sheet.

'Very well.' Skryker's voice was noncommittal, but his eyes were full of understanding. 'You can't get out of bed anyway, so the star-glass is of no use to you. And it's of no use to anyone else either in the way that Rampling left it. Shall I take it away?'

Having succeeded in getting what he wanted, Blake instantly changed his mind. 'No, leave it, pray. I'll only be rigged up to this contraption for a few days. They talk of letting me sit up properly, soon. I'll see if I can use it then. The comet will be here for a while, you said. There's plenty of time for me to look at it later.' He tried a smile: weak and wavering, but the best he could manage. 'Why not read me one of these stories, Felix, I'd like that.'

Skryker reached for the book, checked the table of contents, and found the page he wanted. 'The woman in the shop recommended this one.'

Blake lay back on his pillows, his eyes closed, listening to his friend's voice. Ordinarily, the story would have made him roar with laughter, but tonight he was hard to please. The pain in his leg grew and his attention wavered. Perhaps he should feign sleep so Skryker would leave.

When Skryker was done, Blake opened his eyes briefly. 'Gramercie. I think I'll nod off soon.'

'I'll say goodnight then. I'll come again tomorrow, at the same time.' Skryker put the book on the bedside cabinet by the field glasses, but within Blake's reach. 'Well met, old friend. Rest peacefully. I hope you feel easier in the morning.'

Skryker left with a quick smile and another quiet *well met.*

A minute or so later, Messire Rampling hurried into Blake's room. 'I thought he would never go. You must be tired out, my dear boy.'

'I'm a little weary, I must admit,' said Blake, hoping Rampling would take the hint. 'I've had a number of visitors already today.'

Rampling looked about the room approvingly. His eyes lingered on the drawn curtains and the down-turned star-glass. 'I see you are not risking the rays of the daemon star tonight.'

This helped make Blake's mind up. 'I'll look for the Great Comet tomorrow. It should be visible from my window then.' He tried – and failed – to reach for the binoculars on the bedside cabinet. They were too far away.

With a shake of the head, Rampling sat down. 'You mustn't risk it, my dear boy. Look at the trouble the daemon star has already caused you. And all down to the influence of that very dangerous young man, I'll be bound. It was his words that sent you in search of this thing in the first place. You should keep away from him.'

'What do you have against Felix Skryker?'

Rampling drew the skirts of his robes about him, as if Skryker was still in the room and he wished to avoid contamination. 'He's steeped in heresy, that one. And he draws others into blasphemous thought with his soft and coaxing words.'

'Really? I'd have thought he was too busy for that.'

'Busy? What does he have to keep him busy?' Rampling's lip curled. 'Why, he's not even a fighter for the cause. He has no real loyalty to the North, it's all just feigned.'

This was at the heart of it: Skryker's maverick undertaking in the Civil War. Blake eyed Rampling coolly. 'Skryker fights on neither side, he's loyal to The Isles itself. He always has been. He's made no secret of it. He got this crazy flying venture of his off the ground, and he works for the betterment of both sides in the Civil War. I never thought he would manage it. But he has, so far.'

Skryker operated a small, private air force of like-minded compatriots. They delivered medicines to besieged hospitals, repaired beacon lights, rescued hostages, and sent back-channel messages to both the North and the South. This was a precarious operation and he needed all the support he could get.

'Aye, but he will come to grief one of these days, your fine friend, and it won't be long away. He's a heretic, first, last, and always. A creature of Valerian College. You had best steer clear of him, my dear boy. Forswear this daemon star and look to the light of Sol Invictus. That is the way of true salvation – the only sure way.' Rampling stared at Blake, his eyes alight with certainty, his voice compelling.

Blake shifted on his pillows, trying to find a comfortable position. There appeared to be little that he could say in reply. Trying to defend his friend would only further antagonise Rampling. He took advantage of a short pause to redirect Rampling's thoughts.

'Why do you link the Great Comet with heresy? The comet orbits the star Sol. Surely it's another of the wonders of Sol Invictus?'

'That thing is a creature of the night. It's linked with disaster and ill-omens, we all know that. The daemon star may be fair to look upon, but at heart it is foul, as with so many of the devil's trickeries. Look at what it did to you, my dear boy. Look at your predicament.' He waved at Blake's immobilised form.

Rampling was starting to repeat himself. His tones were now less than captivating, and every attempt by Blake to counter him led to the same few thoughts on heresy and blasphemy. He spoke at length on those topics as one who was in love with his own beautiful voice. In the end, Blake welcomed the early advent of his nurse with his night-time medication. As on the previous evening, she quickly saw Rampling off.

Having finally said goodnight to his unwelcome caller and after enduring his nurse's patient ministrations, Blake lay back in his bed and turned his head to stare at his window. Skryker had called it a window on wonder. Was the comet finally visible to the naked eye? What was hidden behind those closed curtains? He was on a battleground of Rampling's making, and his own ill temper had made him spurn his friend's advances. Did he really want to look at the comet? Some primitive part of him blamed it for his troubles and was relieved he could not see it, lest some new disaster happened.

Sleep was a long while in coming.

*

Blake passed an indifferent day, very much at odds with himself for not proving to be a better patient. His leg ached, the simple act of breathing was a hardship, and his significant bruising made any position uncomfortable. He had painkillers to take the edge off the discomfort, but was reluctant to become dependent upon them. His treating doctor, a colleague, told him he was a fool.

Felix Skryker came with the evening, as promised. Again, the curtains were firmly drawn and the star-glass still downturned. Skryker did not mention either. He also failed to talk about the comet, instead keeping up a gentle chat about mutual friends and their doings. Out-manoeuvred, Blake's uncertain temper rose.

'Cut the gossip, pray, Felix. Tell me why Messire Rampling has it in for you. And why he's seen fit to involve me.'

A frown clouded Skryker's open face. 'I'm sorry he's done that, and I'm even sorrier that you're lying here at his mercy. Rampling wants to save you from my bad influence. He's a kinsman, and I assume he thinks he's acting in your best interests. I'm too much of a free spirit for his liking – an affront to his tidy outlook on life. And he resents what I do in the Civil War.'

'And your involvement with Valerian College.'

'There is that. Rampling's made a field of conflict here and, for good or ill, you're a warrior on it.'

Blake frowned in turn. 'I didn't ask for this, Felix. I didn't ask for any of it. Not to be lying here helpless while that man carries on about heresy. He might be some sort of relation, but we've never been close. I didn't ask for him to come here like this, as if he's out to save my soul.'

'No, you never asked for this battle.' Skryker glanced briefly at the drawn curtains. 'But it has come to you nevertheless, and when you're least expecting it. You'll need to make your mind up where you stand, or you'll never be rid of Rampling. I'll do what I can to help, but you're his preferred target at present.'

'Why does he want to have the Great Comet deemed heretical?'

'Because he can. He's obsessed with heresy. It's his field of influence and the centre of his power at the Congregation of Believers. From there he can govern on heresy and matters of church doctrine. Heresy comes in waves in The Isles, sometimes it's powerful, sometimes not so much. But people aren't talking about it at the moment. They have the war on their minds.'

Skryker rose and paced the room. Blake gave a wry smile at seeing his friend so energised.

'The Great Comet's popularly linked with misfortune and bad luck. I've no doubt people will talk about the comet, but I don't think they'll be relating it to heresy.' Skryker stopped by the closed window. 'Rampling will talk about heresy, though, if he can get anyone to listen to him. He's seeking to restore the Congregation of Believer's influence, and the Great Comet's a prime opportunity.' He shifted to the downturned star-glass and shoved his hand in his coat pockets.

'Gramercie, Felix, you talk a lot of sense. I thought that, myself. He's making a power play, and I've let him get under my skin, haven't I?'

'You're trapped here. You can't escape any of us who come visiting.' There was a pause and Skryker coloured. 'Do you want me to go?'

'Not yet. Tell me about the Great Comet, pray.'

Skryker smiled, his eyes lighting up. 'With pleasure. Far from being an emissary of the devil, the comet is a gift of Sol Invictus. For most of its orbit, the comet is far distant from the star, Sol. It's no more than a conglomeration of rock and ice hurtling through space on its path. That conglomerate is called the nucleus. Usually, it's quite invisible in the darkness of space.' Skryker grinned. He made a fist, and then thrust his arm through the air in a slow curving move. 'It travels from out past Neptune to a spot between Venus and Mercury. When it gets close to Sol, the action of sunlight starts to affect it.'

'How?'

'Volatile gases in the conglomerate evaporate under the influence of light and heat. A cloud – the coma – forms around the rocky nucleus. Then, in the solar wind of our star, the dust and gases of the coma light up and a trailing tail appears. The dust reflects sunlight, and shows as a white tail. Gases fluoresce and give off a blue light, forming a second tail.' Skryker's fist unclenched, and he spread his hands wide. 'As I said, the comet as we see it is a wonder of Sol Invictus. It comes to life under the influence of sunlight.' He paused and smiled wryly. 'I could go on, but I don't want to tire you. I'll leave it there.'

'Gramercie, old friend. You've given me a lot to think about. It's always good to get the scientific perspective. Especially when I have Rampling going on about devils and whatnot.'

Skryker stood with his back to the window. 'I must be going. I'll bid you well met, and wish you a quiet night.'

Blake grimaced. 'I've no doubt Rampling will be along soon. So, the comet is a gift of Sol Invictus? I will remember that, Felix, and use it to counter him.'

'Excellent.' Skryker grinned, then turned towards the door, waving over his shoulder.

'Wait, Felix,' Blake called.

Skryker whirled around.

Blake glanced at the closed curtains. 'Is the Great Comet visible tonight?'

'Yes, but not in its full glory yet. You'll need to wait a little while for it to get closer.'

'Then... Open the curtains, pray. I want to see out of my window on wonder. I want to see the Great Comet. Where are those binoculars?'

Skryker took the field glasses from the cabinet, handing them over with a bow. Then he flung the curtains wide.

Blake stared.

A few minutes later, after realigning the star-glass, Skryker had gone and Blake lay back on his pillows, his head turned to one side, staring out of his window. The Great Comet lay revealed before him. Skryker had told him he would have an even more spectacular view in the nights to come as the comet drew still nearer. Even so, Blake could already identify the vivid point of the nucleus, with the nebulous coma bright about it, and then the diffuse and ephemeral parti-coloured tail, white and blue.

He stared at the magnificent sight, revelling in his new-found knowledge. He now had a scientific point of view with which to counter Rampling's weight of superstition and negativity. This was no fairy-tale or groundless nonsense. This was a true and real marvel which gripped both heart and mind.

Even more, he had a window on wonder, and what he could see was all due to the light of Sol Invictus.

1910CE

Mercia, The Isles

The End of the World Party

Susan Ruth

AN END OF THE WORLD PARTY
WILL BE HELD
FROM 10 O'CLOCK
ON THE NIGHT OF MAY 19
AT THE DISUSED WIMBERIE ORATORY
TO MARK PASSAGE THROUGH THE TAIL
OF THE GREAT COMET
Fancy Dress Desirable
P.S.: Be assured the world will not
come to an end that night,
but it's a good enough reason for a party,
is it not?

*

No-one quite knew when the notion of End of the World parties in The Isles first originated, but it predated the Civil War that had torn the country asunder and which was now in its third year. There was, in fact, little to celebrate. Neither North nor South seemed capable of winning the conflict, and neither side would give in. More and more resources and troops were being poured into the war effort. Casualties were immense and economic suffering dire. The appearance of a comet, especially one with a reputation for bringing disaster in its wake, came as just another blow to the worn-out citizens of Mercia and Alba.

The news that there were poisonous gases in the tail of the Great Comet only added insult to injury. It certainly enlivened the End of the World party being held at the disused Wimberie Oratory in southern Mercia, where the first costumed and masked guests were gathering on the ground floor of the tower.

'I bought some comet pills,' said the young woman dressed as Columbine, taking a phial from the front of her costume. 'They were on sale in Deva.'

'And were they expensive?' This was the host of the party, Felix Skryker. He was unmasked and in evening wear.

'I'm not going to tell you,' said Columbine. 'I view them as an investment.'

'I imagine they're just sugar pills,' said Skryker. 'You'll come to no harm.'

'But there's cyanogen in the tail of that comet. That's cyanide gas. I read it in the newspaper.'

'In infinitesimal amounts. I took a flight machine up this afternoon and I'm still here.' Skryker was a flyer with a very small private air force.

A Plague Doctor, robed and with a long-beaked mask, joined in the conversation. 'But what will happen when we actually pass through the tail? That's what I want to know.'

Skryker consulted his watch. 'We're passing through the tail even now...'

Columbine gave a shriek and opened her phial to shake out a pill.

'…but I shall say again, the levels of poisonous gases are negligible. The whole tail, which is made up of gas molecules and fine dust particles, is estimated to fit in—'

'—A portmanteau,' finished the Plague Doctor, sounding the *R* and rolling out the last syllable thrillingly. 'I read the article too, Felix, and what I want to know is what type of suitcase it is – an overnight bag or a steamer trunk, there's all sorts – and who's doing the packing? I swear my mother got half the house into a trunk when she went to Hesperia before the war.'

Skryker smiled, his grey-green eyes lighting up. He said nothing.

A number of other guests joined them: a Ballerina with an open pink umbrella; a Monk, and a Gypsy wearing dark mirrored glasses; and three Heian Gentlemen, each carrying an umbrella with a shiny coating.

'What's this?' asked the Plague Doctor, pointing to the reflective umbrellas.

The First Heian Gentleman spoke for all. He brandished his umbrella, rotating it so the silvery surface glimmered. 'This is to turn back any sunlight that refracts through the comet's tail. I hope I have that right…'

Gentlemen Number Two and Number Three nodded, turning their parasols in unison.

'The rays of the sun could be concentrated, like a burning-glass. We all might go up in flames.' The First Heian Gentleman looked askance at the Ballerina's fantastically-decorated and lacquered paper umbrella. 'Is that flimsy thing wise?'

The Ballerina shrugged. 'It's to protect me from the gases. I'm not altogether convinced that the tail of that comet will fit into a suitcase of any size. I mean it's millions of miles long and it's shining. There's something up there.' She raised her umbrella on high to indicate *up*.

'The gas is fluorescing in the action of sunlight,' said Skryker. Before the war he had been an astronomer and knew about such things.

'It's dark, Felix. There is no sun, it's night-time,' said the Ballerina. 'That comet is as long as a third of the sky, and we're passing through the tail tonight. I can't be sensible about it.'

'Nothing will happen, believe me.'

'What if the comet hits us?' Columbine asked.

'It's not going to hit us,' said Skryker. 'It's too far away. In fact, it's more than fifty million miles away. The moon is less than a quarter of a million miles distant from us.'

'The moon, you say, then what about the tides?' This was the First Heian Gentleman, his voice full of foreboding. 'They say in Hesperia that the Pacific will empty into the Atlantic, such will be the effect of the comet.'

'That will not occur. It's never happened before when the comet came close. The tides are under the influence of the moon's gravitational pull as they always have been. The Great Comet's nowhere near as big as the moon. The head of the comet's only about ten miles long and five miles wide. The tides won't be affected. Besides, we're well inland here, so there's nothing to worry about. Anyway, let's go outside, shall we? The main party will be in the marquee, there's drinks there and food, and music. I have telescopes set up as well to observe the head of the comet, and field glasses for those who want a more general view.'

But the guests were more inclined to stay under cover to discuss the possible ending of the world as they knew it, and less interested in looking at the celestial visitor at the heart of all the panicked rumours.

Skryker decided to leave them to it for the time being, and greet the rest of his visitors in the large marquee erected in the grounds of the old Wimberie Oratory. He also wanted to check on the two telescopes he had borrowed from the Dark Faculty at the University of Deva. Skryker had once been a Fellow of Valerian College, but that was before the Civil War. He owned a telescope of his own, of course, but he wanted to make a proper display for his guests. All three instruments were now trained on the peanut-shaped nucleus of the Great Comet.

As he hurried out through the doorway of the tower he almost tripped over a form lying face down halfway onto the path in front of him. He stooped and shook the person's shoulders.

'Are you alright, my friend? You really can't stay here. You'll have people walking over you very soon. Let me help you up.'

There was no answer.

Skryker shook the figure more firmly. He – for it appeared to be a he – lay partly on the path, and partly on the grass beside it. A way-lamp cast a little light. Skryker lifted the figure's arm.

Again, no response.

Then, hearing his name called, he looked up in relief.

'Ah, there you are, Felix. People are starting to arrive now and I didn't want to let any more through this way. I know the tower's dangerous and you don't want too many there.' This was Skryker's friend, Allan Lawrence, an Akkadian physician with a shock of red hair and a goatee beard. He too wore evening dress and was without a mask. 'What's the matter here? It's very early in the night for someone to be passed out from too much alcohol. Let me take a look.'

Lawrence squatted down beside Skryker and examined the recumbent figure.

For some time, he said nothing.

'Help me turn him over, pray, so I can get a better look.'

Skryker assisted his friend in laying the figure on its back. The individual was not in costume, but wore an ordinary daytime business suit.

'He's dead,' said Lawrence. 'But I think you knew that already.'

'Yes.' Skryker's voice was bleak and toneless. 'How did he die?'

'He appears to have fallen from a height.'

Skryker felt shock well up inside him. He turned to stare up at the stone tower looming above them. 'From up there?' He shuddered. 'Then someone's world has come to an end tonight.'

*

The Wimberie Minster was an oratory built for the worship of Sol Invictus, the solar deity of the state religion of The Isles. The building was now disused because local salt workings had undermined the foundations of the tower and caused it to lean at a precarious angle. A restoration project had been interrupted by the Civil War between North and South. Accordingly, the place was declared off limits to the public.

By rights, Skryker was trespassing by holding his party here, but he had a key. As he planned that the festivities themselves would take place in the marquee near the ornamental gate, he hadn't thought much about the tower.

'Should we move him?' Skryker asked Lawrence, studying the dead man's body. 'We could put him in the vestry.'

'No, not yet. We must let the constabulary know, and they'll want to see how and where he was found. I only turned him over in the hope of finding a pulse. I should probably have followed my first instinct and left him how he was.'

'Beeston can go and find a constable.' This was Skryker's driver, who tonight acted as doorman. 'He'll go into Deva if necessary, if the local officers are not experienced enough, or senior enough.'

'I'll stay here for now,' said Lawrence. 'You go and talk to Beeston. And see if you can bring something to cover this poor soul with. And a torch as well so that I can examine him better. Bring my bag from the carriage too, if you would. I'll need that.'

Without a word Skryker headed off up the path and towards the gate.

It was some few minutes before he returned, and in that time Lawrence had not been disturbed in his vigil beside the dead man. Skryker came back with two wait-staffers, a man and a woman.

'These two are medics and they will wait with him until the constables arrive, Allan. Here's your bag too.' Skryker handed the medical case over.

'Gramercie. This man's not long dead, but there are a few checks I want to make. Just give me a little time here. Why don't you go and ask if any of the others saw him? The ones who went into the tower to find you will have to have walked along here. I'll join you there when I'm finished.'

'Let me see him before I go. The light here isn't very good, but he did look a little familiar.'

'He has an invitation anyway,' said Lawrence, who had been feeling in the man's outer pockets. He handed it to Skryker, then motioned to the male medic to shine the torch into the dead man's face. His upper body had landed on the grass rather than the path and was not badly disfigured. 'Do you know him?'

'No. But I think I saw him earlier in the day when I brought the *Sunlight* in to land at Woodhall.' This was Skryker's nearby estate where his private air flight was based. 'He was hanging around the airfield. It's not exactly private, but neither is it public, so I asked him what he was doing there. He said he was looking for work, and that he knew a bit about mechanics. I told him to come back tomorrow and have a chat to Beeston. I was in a hurry to get the telescopes set up and I neglected to get his name.'

'I'll check his inside pockets. He should have his identity papers on him.'

'Gramercie. I'll let you get on, then.'

Skryker straightened up and took a moment to look at the comet above him. They were passing through the tail now, but there was no visible sign of this happening. He could see no bright radiance about him, just the great streak of silvery light across the sky, alien and essentially removed from the mundane world below.

*

'There's been an accident,' Skryker said baldly to the masked and costumed people still talking in the oratory tower. 'Someone has fallen from the top of the tower here.'

Everyone fell silent and, in unison, peered upwards.

'Here?' said Columbine. 'But there's only us here, Felix, there's been no-one else.' She stopped suddenly, her mouth open, and stared fixedly at the space above her.

'That's quite a fall from up there. The tower's high,' said the Plague Doctor. 'I assume you're about to tell us if whoever it is has survived.'

'It's a man, and he lies dead on the footpath outside. I found him when I left you before. Allan Lawrence is examining him even now, so I'd like you to stay here until he gives us the all-clear. I've sent for a constable to attend. There may be questions for you later. For the moment, I have a couple of my own.'

'Well, I didn't see anyone lying around outside,' said the Plague Doctor.

All three Heian Gentlemen shook their heads.

'It's the comet,' said the Gypsy breathlessly, shaking out her skirts as if to distance herself from tragedy. 'I knew something bad would happen, and it has.'

The Ballerina shivered and closed her pink umbrella with a snap. 'Someone's world has ended,' she said, unconsciously echoing Skryker. With her free hand she made a reverence to Sol Invictus, touching chest and brow and mouth. 'May his soul rest in peace.'

'Who is it?' This was the First Heian Gentleman, talking again for all three, but with the air of someone who did not want to know.

'No-one I know. A stranger. I think he was at Woodhall earlier, asking if there was any work. He is of average height and build, dark-haired and thin-faced. If it was the man I saw this morning, he's probably a Southerner. He spoke with a London accent, an educated one, but London nonetheless. He's not in costume, but is wearing day clothes, a dark grey suit with a white shirt and a red-and-blue-striped tie.'

Columbine gasped. 'I said there was no-one else here, but there was someone. I think I saw him not so very long ago. He was on the path outside as I came down to find you, Felix. I got here early, remember?'

'I remember. Did you talk to him?'

'Only briefly. He was asking about the way up to the top of the tower,' said Columbine.

'But didn't Felix say it was locked?' The Plague Doctor turned to Skryker. 'We went up there yesterday to have a look around, you and I. You were going to put the telescopes up there, but we decided there wasn't enough room and they should go near the marquee.'

'And I wanted people concentrating on the Great Comet rather than worrying if the tower was going to collapse.' Skryker felt in his pocket and took out a keyring with a number of ornately-headed keys. 'I'm sure I locked up after us.'

'You did,' said the Plague Doctor. 'I saw you with the keys in your hand. At the time I was wondering how old they were. That's how I remember.' He shivered and peered upwards once more, his fantastically beaked mask quivering. 'I hope Allan Lawrence isn't long, I'd like to go now.'

'He'll be here as soon as he can.' Skryker turned to Columbine. 'Did you see where this man went?'

'He seemed to know his way about the oratory here, but only from the outside. That's why he was asking about the way up the tower. I think he'd been here before, though. He went round by the side of the tower towards the main door.' Columbine pointed to the corner of the room where there was an exit into the oratory proper.

A single staircase went up to the top of the Wimberie Minster tower. Access to it was either via the main entry to the oratory itself, or internally from the ground floor of the tower where they were gathered now, through the doorway to which Columbine was pointing. The vestry and an accompanying office were situated off this larger room, which was itself entered via a side door that gave directly onto the footpath where Skryker had discovered the body.

'Well, he didn't come this way,' said Skryker. 'I would have seen him if he had.' He glanced around. 'Did anyone else see a stranger here?'

All except Columbine shook their heads.

'And you saw no-one collapsed on the path?'

A chorus of *noes* followed.

'I came straight in search of you, Felix,' said the Plague Doctor. 'I was wondering if you needed help with setting up the telescopes, and I bumped into Angalia here outside the door.' He gestured towards the Columbine, pronouncing her name with a hard *G*, as in *gala*, as was the way in The Isles. 'I must have just missed this stranger.'

'Yes, you did,' said Columbine. 'He had already gone round the corner to the main door when you arrived. I got to thinking about the comet then, and I forgot about him until just now when Felix described him to us. Poor man, he must have gone straight up the tower and then fallen.'

'Or was pushed,' said the First Heian Gentleman in doom-laden tones. 'How do we know he wasn't meeting somebody at the top of the tower?'

'We don't,' said Skryker, 'but it seems unlikely.' He glanced around at the others. 'Was there anyone else around?'

There was another chorus of *noes*.

'Gramercie. I saw no-one apart from us here either. I wish I knew how this man got up to the top of the tower. There must be other keys to the place. I certainly haven't let the ones I have out of my hands.'

'He wanted to know about you, Felix.' This was Columbine again, all in a rush. 'He wanted to know about Woodhall and flying and what you did and how many flight machines you had.'

'That was quite some conversation,' said the Plague Doctor. 'What did you say?'

Columbine shrugged. 'I said nothing, of course. I know that Felix likes to be private about Woodhall.'

Skryker led a somewhat precarious existence, refusing to fight for either North or South in the Civil War but campaigning, as he said, for the better spirit of both. He had organised a small private air flight out of Woodhall with like-minded compatriots and they flew missions of mercy to both sides, delivering medicines to blockaded hospitals, repairing beacon lights, exchanging hostages, and delivering back-channel messages. To date the madcap enterprise had succeeded.

'Who in the South would want to know about you, Felix?' This was the Monk, who up to now had been silent.

'You always ask the right question, Solbert,' said the Plague Doctor, turning to the Monk and then to Skryker. 'Yes, Felix, who wants to know about you?'

'The Southern security forces are very interested in what I do, but I fear my secrets are probably already known. There's not much to hide, after all.'

The Monk spoke again. 'But the Southern spies might like to have an up-to-date report on what's actually happening at Woodhall. You say this man was hanging around the airfield earlier. Perhaps he was after intelligence.'

'Well, I didn't push him off the top of the tower,' said Skryker, getting to the point.

'We know that,' said Columbine. 'I came straight here and spoke to you after seeing the stranger walk around to the main door of the oratory. That may have taken half a minute. Then everyone else came. You, at least, are in the clear, Felix.'

'Gramercie,' said Skryker ironically. 'There is something odd about the stranger.' He felt in his coat pocket. 'Allan found that he had an invitation to our party here.' He scanned the piece of light card once, and then a second time. 'This is a forgery! Now why is that?'

'He must have really wanted the pleasure of our company,' said the Ballerina, opening her umbrella once more. 'How do you know the invitation's a forgery?'

'I finished it with these words: *be assured the world will not come to an end that night, but it's a good enough reason for a party, is it not?* I wrote *is it not* out in full, as separate words. But on here…' Skryker waved the invitation. '*Is it not* is written as *isn't it*, as a contraction. This is a forgery.'

'He wanted to get close to you, Felix, and hadn't the nerve to just come along and chance it.' This was the Monk again. 'I tell you, this man was a spy for the South.'

At that point Allan Lawrence came into the room. He had heard this latter exchange and nodded at the Monk. 'I think you might be right, Solly. Felix, I found a sheaf of notes about you in the man's inside coat pocket. Quite detailed notes as well, with descriptions of Woodhall and the airfield. And I also found picklocks on him.'

'That may have been how he got into the tower,' said Skryker. 'I was worrying that I might have left the place unlocked.'

'You didn't! I told you you didn't! Why does no-one believe me?' The Plague Doctor's voice grew agitated.

'I believe you,' said Skryker soothingly. He looked at the others. 'Why don't you lot join the main party? Allan and I will take a look at the top of the tower. Stay around though, the constables may want to talk to you. Especially you, Angalia, as you seem to have been the last to see our stranger.' He smiled at Columbine.

She managed a half-smile in response. 'I saw him, and now he's dead.' She stared around at the others. 'And that's all! Why are you staring at me like that?'

'No-one suspects you for a moment, Galia,' said Skryker. 'He must have fallen while we were standing here talking about the comet.'

'That only makes it worse, somehow.'

The Gypsy spoke, huddling in her shawl. 'I said something bad would happen tonight, and I was right.'

*

Once up on the roof of the Wimberie Oratory tower, Skryker spared a moment for the original reason why they were all there: the Great Comet. The celestial visitor streaked across a full third of the sky, from the bright point of the nucleus to the diffuse radiance of the streaming tail.

'What might you say, my friend, if you could talk? What might you have seen?'

'And here speaks the man with a doctorate in astronomy!'

'Allow me to be a little fanciful, Allan. I'm still shocked from almost falling over a dead body. Take care now, this whole place is on a lean, although we tend not to notice it when we're up here. Our minds play tricks on us. The path is below us, down there, see.' Skryker led the way across the roof to a low parapet on the northern side. 'Our friend must have been standing about here.'

'Yes, this looks to be the right spot,' said Lawrence hastily as he tried – and failed – to look down. He inched away from the wall, mopping his brow with a white handkerchief. 'And the question is, did he fall or was he pushed?'

'Is there any way you can tell from the disposition of the body?' Skryker peered over the edge at the covered shape and the attendant medics below. 'I wish we could move him. It seems scandalous to leave him just lying there.'

'We could bring him in to the vestry if the local constables haven't arrived when we get back down.'

'That would be good.' Skryker moved carefully about the roof with his torch, scanning along the parapet line on the northern side and inspecting the stone edging. 'There are no obvious clues as to what happened, Allan. Nothing to go on. No suspicious marks. I can't even see any footprints. Maybe it will be different come daylight.'

Lawrence looked up at the Great Comet, following its trailing length across the sky. 'You're right, Felix. If only the comet could talk.'

'But it can't. And it's up to us to try to make sense of what happened here tonight. Did you find his identity card?'

Moving back a little further from the edge, Lawrence shook his head. 'Not in his outer clothes, no. He was very interested in you, though. I told you about the papers in his pocket.'

'So you did. Was there anything to say why he might have come up here?'

'There was the invitation.'

'That was a forgery.' Skryker explained.

Lawrence gave a low whistle. 'It seems a lot of trouble to go to, doesn't it? He might just as well have donned costume and mask. There's quite a crowd here tonight, no-one would have been the wiser.' Music, laughter and merry voices drifted up from the illuminated marquee.

'He wasn't to know that, I think, or maybe he'd nothing suitable to hand. Anyway, we seem to have a last sighting and an approximate time.' Skryker told Lawrence about Columbine's encounter with the stranger.

'That would fit,' said Lawrence. 'He was not long dead when we found him. It's hard to be precise with short times, of course, but I think he died less than two hours ago.'

Skryker glanced at the illuminated dial of his watch. 'It's getting on for midnight now, and the party was due to start at ten o'clock. Angalia Reeve was one of the very first to arrive. I checked with Beeston before he left and he saw her come through the gate a bit before ten. He told her that I was still in the tower and she came down to find me. She saw the stranger outside the oratory about then. She said he was looking for the way up the tower. There was no-one with him then.'

'And he had picklocks to open the door. That would seem to argue that he came up here alone.'

'Unless he met someone at the front door and let them in.'

'There is that,' Lawrence conceded. He gave a heavy sigh. 'We simply don't know, do we? Oh, there was something else, Felix. He had an article about the comet in his pocket too. A scientific article, not one of these sensational, panicky things that are all the go at the moment.'

'Maybe he just came up here hoping for a better view.'

'Perhaps.' Lawrence glanced about, then pointed to the northern edge above the path. 'This is the side with the lean, isn't it?'

'Yes, we make allowances for it when we're up here, and tend not to notice what the true situation is.'

'So, if he stepped up onto the parapet he might just have slipped and gone over by mistake?'

'It's possible. Unless someone came up with him and pushed him over.'

'And Angalia Reeve is in the clear?'

'Yes, we know when she arrived. Beeston can vouch for her, as I said. And I know what time she was talking to me. I checked my watch to see about passing through the tail of the comet. More importantly, there was no body lying there on the pathway when Solly and the others came down. He must have fallen after that, while we were inside talking together, and you were stopping anyone else coming down here. You didn't say if there was anything about the way the body lay that would make you think he fell of his own accord or was pushed.'

'He was lying close to the wall, as you saw. It's hard to decide. There's nothing obvious about how he lay to say exactly what happened. Except that he fell from a height.' Lawrence stepped away gingerly from the parapet. 'I don't know if it was deliberate or not. All I know is that he's a stranger and he was interested in you. He made quite an effort to be here tonight, and now he has fallen to his death.'

'What happened to the notes about me?'

'I put them back in his pocket. I imagine you can see them later when the constables arrive. He was gathering information about you, though. There was a detailed description of you – he must have seen you close up, or been told about you by someone who knows you. He had your eye colour, grey-green, and that you have dark hair, and you wear it long and tied at the nape of your neck.'

Skryker peered over the edge of the tower once more; he was a mountaineer as well as a pilot and had no fear of heights, unlike Lawrence who now stood fixedly in the middle of the paved roof. He climbed nimbly up onto the parapet, feeling the stone under his feet.

'Felix! For the love of Sol Invictus, get down!'

With a wry laugh Skryker complied, returning to where his friend stood, shaking from head to foot. 'Look up, Allan, look at the comet. That will ground you.'

'No, it won't!'

'Look at it, and concentrate. The Great Comet has a highly elliptical orbit and travels from beyond Neptune to a spot somewhere between Venus and Mercury, where it is at present. It's travelling at more than a hundred and fifty thousand miles per hour.'

'Felix!'

'Is the giddiness passing? I could go on.' Skryker reached an arm about Lawrence's shoulders.

Lawrence shivered. 'Pray don't, not for me. Save the technicalities until we're back down. The only thing that will ground me is the earth beneath my feet. Can we go now? There's nothing up here to show if someone pushed the stranger over or if he fell all by himself. No handy clues. And I'd like to move the body inside, I think.'

Skryker led the way to the staircase down.

'I think he fell, Allan,' he said, shining his torch on the stone steps. 'It would be easy enough to make a mistake of judgement on that edge up there, the stone-work is a little rough in places. I think he might have climbed up to get an even better look at the comet and then went over. Mind you, I can't prove it.'

'Sol Invictus help me. I got dizzy up there myself and I was right in the middle.'

'On the other hand, if he did meet with foul play, we have to think of who and why; and why meet up at the top of the Wimberie Minster tower of all places? And none of the others saw a second stranger. It's possible there was someone, of course, but I doubt we're looking for a killer.' Skryker turned back to play the torch beam at Lawrence's feet on the stair. 'Take it slowly. The authorities haven't arrived yet, there was no sign of them down there. There's no rush.'

A few minutes later they were at the foot of the tower. Skryker took a hip flask from his pocket and unfastened it.

'Drink. It's aqua vitae. It will steady you.'

Lawrence drank, then wiped the lip of the flask before handing it back. 'Gramercie. You're right, it would be a strange place for a rendezvous. And why would someone want to kill our stranger?'

'I'm the most obvious person with a motive if he was a spy for the South, which is starting to seem rather likely,' said Skryker. 'Only I didn't do it, and I had no idea he was even here tonight or that he was taking notes about me.'

'Besides, you have an alibi, Felix. There's Angalia, and Solly, and all the others to vouch for you.'

'So there is. Yes.' Skryker locked the door behind them, testing it to check that it was secure. 'There will be a proper investigation, and then it will be up to a jury at a coroner's inquest to decide. I expect the coroner will hear all the evidence. And ask all the right questions to help the jury come to a decision.'

'You could be right. Although I think I'd argue in favour of accidental death after seeing you on that edge up there.'

The two friends moved around the side of the tower towards the pathway where the dead man lay, now decently covered with a white cloth. The two medics sprang to attention.

'None of that, pray,' said Skryker, with a wave of his arm. 'At ease now. The authorities should be here soon, I hope, and then we can move him out of the way.'

'We have let no-one by, my lord.'

'Gramercie.' Skryker turned to Lawrence. 'We should leave him here, for form's sake if nothing else, even though I don't like it.'

'I think there's someone coming now, Felix. We should be able to move him soon.'

Skryker nodded, but let Lawrence do the honours with the body and the local constable, who quickly said he would have to wait for the higher-ups from Deva to arrive. Skryker's eyes went involuntarily to the Great Comet. He knew more than most about the physical make-up and actions of the celestial visitor, but some primitive part of him was in awe of the apparition and its doom-laden reputation.

He glanced at the constable examining the body and suppressed a shiver. The stranger had wanted to come to his party badly enough to forge an invitation. Now he was dead. Cause of death would be for the jury at a coronial inquest to determine. An inquest where he would have to appear as a witness.

Meanwhile the Great Comet moved on, following its own path back to the stars, remote and entirely alien.

*

'Well, that would appear to be that,' said Felix Skryker. It was some two months after the End of the World party, and he was in the library at Woodhall talking to Allan Lawrence on the evening of the inquest. They had both given evidence into the stranger's death.

'The coroner's jury returned an open verdict today,' said Lawrence. 'You were expecting that, Felix, weren't you?'

Skryker handed his friend a glass of aqua vitae and then sat down opposite him, his own drink in his hand. 'Yes, they decided they couldn't rule in or out accident, foul play, or even suicide. There simply wasn't enough evidence to go on, despite the investigation that was made. I don't see how they could have found otherwise. But the verdict leaves possibilities open. I still think it was an accidental death myself, even though we can't prove anything for certain one way or another.'

'I agree with you,' said Lawrence. 'He was interested in the Great Comet, he had that scientific article in his pocket, and he wanted a better view. So he went up the tower by himself and didn't take into account the lean. Accidental death. As you say, we can't prove any of it.'

'There was no sign anyone else was up on top of the tower with him,' Skryker added. 'The detective constables certainly found no trace in daylight. No useful footprints, or clues. No sign of a second stranger about. And there was no evidence that anyone at the party other than Angalia Reeve either met our man or followed him. Everyone else is accounted for.'

'Including you.'

Skryker smiled. Two zealous jurors had come up with a theory that if the stranger was gathering intelligence on him, then Skryker himself might have had a motive to kill him. 'Only I provided myself with an alibi all unknowing. I was accounted for less than a minute after Angalia Reeve last saw him. Still, they did their best to make a case. But the coroner was having none of it, so I'm in the clear.'

'As is Angalia herself.'

'Yes, the times ruled her out too, as we knew they would. She couldn't have done it.'

'At least we have a name for the stranger now.'

Skryker nodded. 'Petriss Pettigrew, of St Aldgate's in London.'

'And he had concealed his papers in his shoe, of all places. I only checked his pockets. I shall know better next time.' Lawrence shuddered. 'Only I hope there is no next time.'

'It was a shock, wasn't it, finding him like that? There we were, having an End of the World party to celebrate passing through the tail of the Great Comet, and someone's world did come to an end. It was a tragedy.' Skryker sipped his aqua vitae. 'A tragedy.' His voice was gentle.

'It's frustrating, though, not knowing for sure what happened to him.'

'But we can't force a meaning when there's so few definite facts to go on. He wanted to go up the tower. He was found dead at the foot of it, with injuries showing he'd fallen from a height. That's all we really have.'

'And so it was an open verdict in the end.' Lawrence reached for the decanter to pour more aqua vitae.

'Yes. We don't have to agree with it, though, do we? We can chalk it down to accidental death between ourselves.'

Lawrence gave a wry smile. 'It's better than thinking there's an uncaught killer around.'

'There is no killer.'

'No, I expect not, which is good to know.' Lawrence sipped his drink. 'And now the comet has gone.'

'Yes, it's on its way back to Neptune. The Great Comet will return again, but not in our lifetime, Allan. There'll be other comets to see, though perhaps not as spectacular as this one, but glorious nevertheless.' Skryker raised his glass. 'To the stars.'

Lawrence did likewise. 'To the stars, Felix.'

I have someone, Dren!

What are you talking about?

I've found four women with the kind of minds I need. I'm so close to getting the ship repaired and getting us home!

Home to what, Vanin? Do you really think that, after two thousand years, our people will be the same? Don't you think they'll have changed, even if you haven't?

Why would they? They will always need a Prime to lead them, Dren. You've lived here too long, amongst these ephemeral creatures. They change quickly because they die quickly. They break your heart time and again and you keep championing them. Our people are more resilient.

You mean more resistant. In two thousand years these people have reached a level of technology it took ours twenty thousand to achieve.

Because of me!

You flatter yourself, Vanin. They're smarter than you give them credit for. But you've corrupted them and I fear for their future.

You have no vision, Dren. You ran from our homeworld when things got difficult, just as you ran from me when things got challenging, here.

Maybe you're right, Van. But I certainly can't see a happy result for your vision.

I'm your Prime, Dren. I know what's best for us.

I know you think you do, Van.

You're a fool.

So you've said.

1830-1986CE
London, Great Britain

Reason's Light

Lynne Lumsden Green

Matters that vexed the minds of ancient seers,
And for our learned doctors often led
To loud and vain contention, now are seen
In reason's light, the clouds of ignorance
Dispelled at last by science. Those on whom
Delusion cast its gloomy pall of doubt,
Upborne now on the wings that genius lends,
May penetrate the mansions of the gods
And scale the heights of heaven.

Excerpt of 'Ode to Newton' by Edmond Halley (1687)

*

1830CE

Clara crushed her letter into a ball and tossed it into the fireplace, where it ignited with a crackle and flared into orange and green flames, before being reduced to a handful of black ash. On any other day, it would have seemed a brave and defiant gesture. Not today.

Outside, in the garden, the sunlight was so perfectly crisp and golden that the thrumming of the bees could be mistaken for the vibration of the air. The breeze was warm and redolent of roses and lilies. Hilda's various house cats slept in cuddlesome nooks and crannies around the crowded parlour. A glorious lunch adorned the table; pots of tea, chocolate and coffee all steamed with promises of luscious caffeine.

Yet the mood around the table was not cheerful, not in the slightest.

'Well, I don't want to be the one to say, "I told you so",' said Clara, 'but I wasn't expecting a different outcome to our requests for membership.' She made no effort to hide the bitterness in her words.

Her ex-husband would be smug when she went to visit the children and he heard about this. He'd cited her scientific work as one of the causes for their divorce, and publicly declared her 'unwomanly' in court. *'A woman's brain is unsuited to natural philosophy and mathematics,'* was one of his ruder comments. He had gone on to say, *'I am worried that her obsession with rocks means more to her than caring for her children.'* The court had agreed with him.

Well, they were wrong. Clara glared at the burning letter. Women were finally gaining admittance to the learned societies of Britain. In 1829, the founding of the Zoological Society of London had seen women Fellows admitted from its inception. This had given the four women sitting around the table encouragement to try for admission to the Royal Society of London. All four women had received official replies from the Royal Society.

Clara's was now smouldering in the fireplace.

She met the gazes of her three friends and colleagues. Beatrice, a brilliant chemist and engineer; Lucy and Hilda, both astronomers, mathematicians and physicists beyond par. And Clara's own achievements chemistry and geology were not inconsiderable, even if she were being modest. They had studied hard all their lives; written and published papers at their own expense; proven over and over their expertise. Yet the monstrous regiment of men running British academia considered all four to be nothing more than a damned nuisance.

So much talent, so much education, so much genius, thwarted by the stupidity of fussy old men who could not see past gender.

Beatrice, who scandalised polite society by wearing men's clothing, took a flask out of her pocket and poured a slug of gin into her teacup. She held the flask up and said, 'Well, at least my studies of chemistry have a practical use, even if the Royal Society won't admit me. Does anyone else want a splash of comfort?'

The sombre mood lightened. There was a chorus of 'Please,' and the other women held out their cups.

'It is a rather smug letter,' said Clara, after a sip of tea and gin. She nibbled on a macaroon without really tasting it. 'Apart from changing our names, it's very nearly the same letter copied out four times.'

'I was hoping that the Duke of Sussex would be more amenable than that Davies Gilbert, but no such luck,' said Lucy, sighing. With restless hands, she smoothed the dark grey silk of her rather severe gown. 'He is one of those men who believes there's a connection between the faith of religion and the rationality of science. As a religious man, he probably supports only the traditional roles for women.'

'Then why did God give me a brain if he didn't want me to use it?' demanded Clara.

Beatrice leant over and patted her cousin's hand. 'I don't believe for a second that she doesn't want us to use our gifts, Clara. What a waste that would be.' She smiled and her blue eyes vanished in a mass of creases.

Lucy stuck her nose into the air and tutted. In a gruff voice, to mimic an old man, she said, 'How dare a group of women gain an education in mathematics and natural philosophy? Why didn't their brains melt?' She sniffed, shifted the toolbelt that hung – in place of a chatelaine – around her hips, and sipped gin-laced tea from rose-patterned porcelain.

Hilda buttered a scone, while looking pensively out the window. She said, 'It is a pity we can't force those men to take us seriously. If only we could do something so splendid they would have to acknowledge us.'

Lucy brightened. 'Rub their noses in it, so to speak?' A tabby cat leapt into her lap and she scratched it absently behind the ears.

Hilda nodded. 'Yes. Discover something truly bizarre or invent something well beyond their expectations.' She sat back in the chintz-covered chair, fanning herself gently with her rejection letter. A lazy smile tugged at the corners of her mouth, as if she contemplated the humiliation of those bombastic old men.

'I like it,' said Clara. 'We can make them look petty and stupid for not accepting us into the Royal Society.'

'But what would be great enough? As it is, any man with our accomplishments would be feted with awards and medals,' Beatrice pointed out, tugging at a lock of grey hair that had fallen from her haphazardly-pinned coiffure. 'Look at Lucy's mathematical formula for the three-body problem. Completely superior to using Lagrangian points for finding a solution. And completely ignored.'

Lucy smiled, but it was a tight, dry smile with little humour in it. 'Being ignored is far worse than being criticized or refuted. How do you fight against an absence of opposition?'

'Yes,' said Clara. 'It's like trying to walk against a strong wind: tiring and struggling for each tiny step forward.'

'So...' Hilda tapped her fingers on her lips. 'To make them sit up and take notice, we'd have to do something that would make news everywhere. A discovery or invention so big that nothing else could compete with it.'

Lucy said, 'Well, we could discover a new planet. Alexis Bouvard's astronomical tables of the orbit of Uranus hints at another planet. And John Herschel mentioned in his last letter that he saw something strangely like a planet in the right area.'

'Hah! He just wants to follow in his father's footsteps,' said Clara.

'And he could probably lay a claim to finding it if we did locate it, because of that letter,' said Hilda.

'Hmmm. But I do think something related to astronomy would get attention,' said Beatrice. 'But it can't just be finding a new planet or a new star. It needs to be bigger than that.'

'More dramatic?' suggested Lucy.

'Less passive,' said Beatrice. 'Even a pirate can find treasure. I'd like to see us make an important achievement. And, it would be nice if it was a project we could all contribute to, so that we can all share in the glory.'

'That seems to be a knotty problem,' said Hilda, 'since we don't all work in the same fields.'

'Then we must get creative,' Beatrice replied.

Silence fell as the women contemplated the challenge. Clara stirred lemon into her tea. Beatrice ate an egg salad sandwich. Hilda sipped her tea.

Lucy held out her teacup. 'More of that rotgut of yours, please Bea. I need rocket fuel for my brain if I'm going to think of something extraordinary.'

'That's it!' Clara sat up straight, her breath catching in her throat. 'You're a genius, Lucy!'

'Well, I know that,' Lucy replied, lifting dark brows, 'but how, particularly?'

'Hilda,' Clara said, 'I remember you telling me about a comet coming in a few years.'

'Yes. Halley's Comet. It's due in 1835, during the autumn. It should be visible in the sky around September and October.'

'So…five years away?' asked Clara.

'Yes.' Hilda consumed her third scone and licked jam from her fingers. 'But how on Earth can that be of use to us?

'That's just it,' Clara smiled delightedly and again met the eyes of the other women. 'Not on Earth at all. Why don't we capture the comet with a rocket?'

'Capture the comet!' Beatrice snatched Clara's teacup away. 'No more for you!'

Clara laughed and leaned forward. 'No, I'm serious. Beatrice and Lucy can make the fuel and build the rocket. Hilda can do the calculations to have the rocket and the comet meet up. I can organise and handle the planning, implementation, and coordination of the details.'

'Capture a comet? How big are they?' asked Beatrice. She handed the teacup back, after adding a fresh splash of gin.

'I don't know if that's even possible,' exclaimed Hilda.

'Well, if it's too big,' Clara conceded, 'maybe we can at least get samples and images to prove we've been there. *That* would show them!'

Lucy sat, wide-eyed and mouth agape for a moment, then she slammed her hand on the table. 'Brilliant! Utterly brilliant! That's exactly what we need to make those fusty old men take us seriously. Right, Clara's come up with the concept. Now we have to start planning.'

*

1835CE

Hilda was still bent over her calculations, even though it was so late at night it was very nearly dawn. Her head ached, but she was worrying at the quandary of communicating with the rocket was once in flight. They had settled on a panel of coloured lights on the rocket, but there was still no way for the team on the ground to communicate with the rocket's pilot once she soared too high to be seen. Once in the air, she would be left to depend upon her own resources.

It had fallen to Clara to be the pilot. The stresses of the rocket launch would be too harsh on the older bodies of Lucy and Beatrice, and Hilda's weight was too heavy for the initial and crucial fight against Earth's gravity.

Hilda had argued that the pilot should be a mathematician or a physicist, such as herself or Lucy. If the rocket got into trouble, they might figure a way out of their difficulties. Clara pointed out that the main worry with the rocket was it exploding…and no expert in anything could survive that. Then Hilda took Clara aside for a frank discussion about Clara's children. They needed their mother. Clara turned stubborn, though her eyes had filled with tears. Her husband, she'd said, had custody of the children. The best she could do was make them proud. Hilda gave up trying to convince her.

In the past five years, Clara had been allowed only supervised Christmas visits with her children. On those occasions, she had been treated as if she presented a considerable danger to them. Hilda supposed their father was worried Clara's independence and vivid intellect might contaminate them in some manner. He wanted obedient children. There was talk in the papers of his remarrying. Clara pretended not to care. She had committed all her energies to the rocket, but she wasn't fooling anyone, least of all her friends.

Hilda looked up from her desk, into the pre-dawn grey light and studied their rocket. It was quite beautiful, in the way that good engineering was always satisfying. The last, faint moonlight glinted off the tower of rivets, polished brass plates, and thick quartz windows.

Now, it stood in an empty field in Sheffield; outside the cottage they'd hired in the country, to hide their work from the world. But, in just a few days, it would be tested in the vacuum of space. It was a testimony to all four women that it existed at all.

Though much of the design was based around William Congreve's rockets, Beatrice had incorporated something of the submarine into its structure, as well as every safety device she could imagine. To allow for the rocket's return to Earth, she had included parachutes, designed by French inventor, Claude Ruggieri. Hilda wasn't too confident of the concept of the parachute, even with plenty of testing.

However, there came a point when one just had to take it on faith that the design would work. The real test would be a successful return to Earth.

Beatrice's talented sons and daughters had assisted in the rocket's construction. It had been a truly family project. Without all that help, the project would never have been finished on schedule. Five years seemed a long time when they started, but it had flown past.

There were only three days until the launch to meet with the comet. Beatrice and Lucy insisted the rocket had to be named, for luck. Something other than 'the rocket', particularly since that was Stephenson's name for his steam-powered locomotive. So, the three other women referred to their invention as 'Sophia', which meant 'wisdom' in Greek. Sometimes they spoke her name in loving tones; sometimes after swearing in frustration at her.

But how could a rocket be wise? Hilda preferred to call her 'Saraswati'. She was, after all, the product of intellect.

'Good morning, Hilda,' said Beatrice, strolling into the workshop. 'Want to come out with me to look at the comet before the sun comes up?'

Hilda stretched and yawned. Blushes of pink and grey crept along the eastern horizon. She had been up all night.

'Yes. I would like that very much,' she said, and pushed herself away from her desk. Her legs were stiff and she nearly toppled over. Beatrice caught her and helped her regain balance.

'Here, Hildie, you didn't work through the night again?' asked Beatrice. 'You're a silly old thing. Let's get you some breakfast.'

'No, not yet,' protested Hilda. 'I really do want to see the comet.'

'Righto,' said Beatrice. 'But then I'm making you eat something. We need you thinking straight, today of all days.'

They collected a shawl for Hilda and a jacket for Beatrice, then sauntered into the garden. Hilda breathed the chill dawn air, fresh with dew and the spicy smell of damp leaves. They gazed up at the sky. As a child, Hilda had thought a comet would be like a bigger and better version of a falling star; a bright scratch frozen across the night sky. What she hadn't expected was how beautiful the comet was. Some giant finger had crushed a large star against the dome of obsidian and then smeared it, leaving a glittering trail. How had comets become "harbingers of doom" when they looked like fairy dust and sequins?

The cold made her eyes water, and the comet blurred.

'The world will remember us, won't they?' she whispered.

'Oh yes,' Beatrice said firmly. 'Our descendants for the next two hundred years will look back at our achievements and be proud.'

*

1835CE

The nucleus of the comet surprised Clara. She'd expected something like a glowing diamond, not a dull hunk of caliginous ice and rock. After nearly being blinded by the luminous tail, Halley's comet itself was both a relief and a disappointment. She wiped away moisture condensing on the porthole and took another look.

She smiled. She really was here. Five years of preparation and worry had paid off. If only the others were here, too. She would take copious notes, images and samples. How the stuffed-shirt men of the Royal Society would squirm when the evidence of this trip was presented to them. Clara allowed herself a beatific moment imagining a scenario where every arrogant slight and sneer was redeemed by the mass humiliation of the male scientists.

A warning buzzer reminded her that she had work to do. Her rocket was in its final approach to perihelion in relation to the comet, and was finally inside the coma. Things were about to get tricky as she manoeuvred into position to take samples. Around her the nucleus flickered with white and blue light, similar to the shimmering curtains of the aurora.

The shifting light of coma created strange shadows in her capsule, which – in turn – caused a few problems. She pressed the wrong button, swore in an unladylike fashion, and corrected the mistake. The dial indicating velocity blurred before her eyes. She rubbed the dial, then her eyes, and frowned. Was there something amiss with her eyes? Her clumsiness and blurred vision was disconcerting. Once the samples were safely aboard, she needed to make a series of carefully-timed booster shots to turn the rocket around and return to Earth. Miss one, and she wasn't going home.

Perhaps the dancing lights were causing her maladroitness, as well as the headache and nausea. The unwashed smell of her body after six days in a tiny compartment made her queasy; she had hoped she would get used to it.

Space flight was…much less glamorous than she had hoped. To think she had fought to risk her life, and live in her own stench for days on end. She glanced out the porthole again and smiled. No, it was worth it. A woman scientist was not only the first in space, but the first to see a comet up close. Winning wasn't everything, of course. It did beat coming in second and never having the opportunity to view of the stars through the veils of the Comet's coma.

Clara shook herself. Enough daydreaming. She needed to take a daguerreotype of the phenomenon, or Beatrice would never forgive her. Her camera was a modified Camera Obscura. Bea had spent hours teaching her the proper techniques for its use.

It was bulky and difficult to use in the cramped space. She struggled to set up the camera in time to get her shot. Hopefully the flickering light wouldn't blur the details of the image. There was no way of knowing if image captured through the thick porthole would come out clearly. Not until she returned to Earth.

As a back-up, Clara drew lots of sketches and took copious notes. Her fingers ached from constant use in the biting cold. She flexed her fingers and frowned. Arthritis? It had never bothered her before. Must be the cold. All her bones ached. She made a note in her journal. The next rocket needed better insulation. In full sun it was hot, but bearable. In the comet's shadow, she was freezing.

As her capsule swept past the black ice of the comet, the motion stirred up more nausea. She gritted her teeth and swallowed. Motion sickness. Well, it was only to be expected, with the weightlessness and all.

The comet nucleus loomed in her porthole; massive, brooding, intimidating – and strangely beautiful. With nothing to give her any reference for size, it seemed larger than the Moon, which she had passed three days before.

But the comet's texture did not resemble the Moon, even though it had impact craters and hills. The surface was never still, volcanoes of dust or gas vented and fragments broke away, spinning past the rocket.

The nucleus was rough and irregular, several spheroids mashed together. It didn't appear that the journey around the sun had sanded away the contours of the comet. Hilda was going to be disappointed. She had theorized that the comet would be smooth and bullet-shaped.

Clara hit a button on her panel, taking care that it was the correct one. A series of vacuum tubes opened in the skin of the rocket. A warning light flashed, blinding in the dark cabin. She frowned. The sampling tube wasn't closing properly. If it didn't seal soon she'd lose all the samples. Her heart fluttered as she pressed at a sequence of buttons and flipped a manual override switch. She couldn't come all this way and not get the gas samples to prove it.

For a heart-stopping moment, nothing happened. Then the warning light blinked out and the dials showed the tubes were sealed. Clara slumped in her seat. With luck, she had taken samples of the comet's gases. Beatrice's goal was to provide undeniable evidence of the visit to the comet.

She checked her pocket watch. Nearly time for the first boost that would turn the rocket for home.

Just as she needed to be her most alert, nausea brought a sour taste to her mouth and the persistent headache throbbed with a gathering intensity. She scratched at her skin and grimaced. Her arm was covered in reddish blotches. The ache in her bones spread to the rest of her body. Her fingers trembled, and she couldn't tell if it was from the burning cold or not.

She took a sip of water, to fight the nausea. Her hand shook so much she cracked the edge of the copper flask against her teeth. One of her eyeteeth fell out. It floated away, trailing tiny droplets of blood. Clara looked at it in horror. She reached for it. Her shaking hand knocked it away, to bounce around the cabin. Something was very wrong.

A bell went off, reminding her to push a button that would set off one of her sequence of return-to-Earth rockets. As she pushed it, a blood blister formed under her fingernail. The rocket juddered to life, turning with ponderous grace. The stars wheeled past, fuzzy through the coma.

She squinted through the porthole, but the glowing coma obscured the bright blue pearl of Earth. How she wished it was visible. She wanted very much to go home. She wanted to see her friends; fight for her children; change the world.

Another bell went off, and Clara struggled to press the correct button. Or was that sound one of the buzzer telling her to imprint more images on photographic plates? Was she making the right choice? Her thoughts seemed as fuzzy as the comet's tail. What was wrong with her?

It was cold. So cold. Her limbs dragged and ached, even without gravity. Even lifting her head was an effort. Perhaps if she just slept a little while.

When the next bell went, Clara shook off a light doze and managed to press the button. Well, a button. Just to be sure, she pressed a couple of others and was comforted by the shuddering that indicated a sudden change of direction. As the rocket swerved, Clara floated away from the panel. Helpless, she drifted down to the floor, pressed there by centrifugal forces. She struggled for a moment, and then gave herself over to the motion of the thrust.

She wanted so much to be home and in her own bed, with a cup of strong tea. Or having lunch with her fellow scientists. How thrilled they would be when she returned. Better yet, she wanted to be tucked in with her children, reading them a story. No. That's right. Their father had taken them from her in the divorce. But they knew she'd be home, one day. They would be so proud.

She closed her eyes, dreaming of her darlings.

*

The little space vehicle spun out of control. Caught in the gravitation of the comet, the marvel of engineering and vision was soon just another gem in the glittering trail.

*

1986CE

Sophie rose to make her announcement at the press conference. The sea of expectant faces confronted her. Some looked plain bored.

Some eager, clearly hoping for real news from space. Something as important as confirming life on Mars and Titan. Well, they weren't going to be disappointed. She swallowed and tucked a stray lock of blonde hair behind one ear.

'Hello everyone,' said Sophie. 'As you know, it's been quite a race between many countries to get close to Halley's Comet. The Armada, you journos have called it. Well, I'm pleased to announce our probe has arrived first!'

She waited for the excited murmurs to die down. 'The probe has been sending us back detailed images of the comet.' She touched a remote and the screen behind her filled with an image of the comet's nucleus – a potato-shaped blob of black ice and rock. She smiled at the murmur of disappointment that swept the room. 'Most are rather dull if you're not a scientist.' Laughter. 'But this is one image we've isolated from a series of photographs we received yesterday.'

There flashed up a picture of a rocket, pitted and covered in ice.

The was a series of gasps and sighs around the room. A babble of speculation arose. Three journalists raised their hands.

'Now,' Sophie continued. 'There's no record of a rocket lost in the vicinity of the comet. However, we suspect this rocket is of human origins, because of its shape and construction. We're sending a second unmanned probe to investigate further. With luck, we might be able to salvage the vehicle.'

Another image appeared, taken from a different angle. It revealed how curiously old-fashioned the rocket was, with its rivets and plates, and its quaintly rounded portholes. Jules Verne might have imagined a rocket like this.

'There is a strong possibility this is an elaborate fraud,' warned Sophie. 'Of course, if it's not, it could have far-reaching implications for the history of space travel.'

Every arm in the place shot up.

'I am now throwing the meeting open to questions.'

It took Sophie an hour to answer all of them.

*

She did her best to answer politely, but she was exhausted when the last of the journalists left the conference room.

'Coffee?' asked her best buddy, Carol. 'I was lurking at the back of the hall. You handled the media well. Glad that was you, not me out there, though.'

'Coffee! Oh yes, please!' replied Sophie. 'I was nearly ready to scream if anyone else asked me who the rocket belonged to. What part of "we don't know" did they not understand?'

Back in Sophie's office, Carol made them both a cuppa and opened a packet of chocolate-chip cookies. Sophie rolled her shoulders and shook out her hands, as she paced around the room.

The public scrutiny of her Halley's Comet research wasn't going away any time soon. This press conference would be the first of many. It was a pity so much of her time was spent on marketing and politics, and not doing proper science research. Still, the discovery of the rocket meant she would have no trouble with funding for the rest of her career. As the tension finally drained away, she sat down at her desk and tidied a pile of papers to clear space for the cookies.

Carol sat down across from her. 'I think you can guarantee the rocket will be leading all the news reports for the next day or so.'

'Probably longer. Everyone loves a good mystery,' said Sophie, and took a sip of coffee.

Carol laughed and said, 'Too true! This is one of the best! Mysterious space vehicles. Possible aliens. Explorers from the outer planets.'

Sophie flinched. 'Aliens? Not you too, Carol? You've seen the photos.'

'Just yanking your chain,' said Carol, and took a bite from a cookie. Her grey eyes gleamed.

'I'm not a toilet.'

Carol laughed again, nearly choking on her cookie. It took her a minute or so to clear the crumbs from her throat.

Sophie took sips of coffee to wash away the lingering irritation. Then she asked, 'Did I ever tell you why I joined the space programme?'

Carol shook her head. 'A deep desire to work with patronising misogynists? Because it couldn't have been for the fame or riches. Though – I guess – you are famous now.'

Sophie accorded that a faint smile. 'Family history claims that my four times great-grandmother flew a rocket to Halley's Comet in 1835, and never came back.' Sophie stared pensively at the grainy photo of the rocket. 'I grew up thinking that all women should be rocket scientists – particularly since my proud daddy named me after her rocket.'

Carol spluttered her coffee. 'Pardon? 1835! Are you kidding?'

'I never really believed those claims. But now I have to give them some credence.'

'Seriously? Why have you *never* mentioned this before?' Carol was miffed, Sophie could tell.

'I'm sorry,' she said, 'but honestly, would you have believed me? I still don't believe it.'

'No,' Carol said, her head cocked so she could see the photo. 'I guess I don't either. There's no way they had the technology to launch a rocket in that era.'

'That's what I always thought. My great-umpteen grandmother always kept a journal. I inherited a couple of them just a few years ago,' said Sophie. 'I couldn't wait to read about my adventurous Clara. I discovered the truth was not that exciting. She lost her children when she left her husband. Back in those days, men had all the rights and entitlements. He wouldn't let her visit with them. She was bitter for a while, and then she put all her energy into her "project" with her friends. I thought she went a little insane – a rocket to chase a comet? And when she went missing in 1835, I assumed she committed suicide.'

'How awful.'

'I know,' Sophie said. She tapped the photo. 'But look at this. Brass. Rivets. Those ridiculous fins that look like something out of an old sci-fi movie.' She lifted her eyes to Carol's. 'It's exactly as she described. What if they really did it?'

The women were silent awhile, nibbling cookies and staring at the impossible image.

'So,' Carol said finally, 'what if that rocket really is the one your great-grandma flew? What then?'

'Then...' Sophie grimaced and shrugged. 'I hope we leave it there. What a mausoleum!'

Carol glanced up to the ceiling, as if she could see through the upper floor and the roof of the building, and then bypass the millions of kilometres to the icy capsule trailing behind the comet. Her expression sobered, and she considered the dregs of her coffee.

She said, 'It would be so lonely. If it was me, I'd rather be with my family, here on Earth.'

'Yes...' Sophie said dubiously. 'She did talk a lot about how much it would mean to her friends and her children if she made it back. They must have been incredibly disappointed.'

'Y'think?' Carol said, with just hint of dryness. She added, 'What about you? How will you feel?'

Sophie sipped her cooling coffee and considered the question. 'I'll be both relieved and horrified if it turns out she is in that rocket. I mean, my ancestress, my role model, was the very first person in space! And I thought she was a mad woman, raving on.' She took another gulp of coffee. She made a face. 'I'll feel like I've somehow let her down – let all the pioneering female scientists down – by not believing, I guess. After all, we've faced some patronising idiots, but what they stood up against...what she sacrificed so we could work as equals in this field...'

Carol picked up the photo. 'You couldn't have known the truth.'

'Well, we'll discover the truth soon enough.' Sophie smiled and nodded at the image. 'It may be that Clara was a better role model than I ever realised. I owe it to her – to that team of four inspiring women – to find out.'

1986CE
Brisbane, Australia

Rocket Boy

Jo Sparrow

Bailey sent his racing-red BMX skidding across the concrete floor of the garage. He threw his school bag hard against the blonde bricks of the house and jogged to the kitchen door. His father's red Holden stood in the driveway. Bailey grinned. He had big plans with Dad tonight. They'd be viewing the 1986 passing of Halley's Comet with the school's astronomy club. A renowned astronomer would also present Bailey with a prize for his winning school paper about the comet. He was beyond excited.

He'd stuck the excursion note to the fridge door a week earlier to give his father ample warning and had reminded him every day since. Certain his father would cancel, Bailey had kept his excitement in check until he arrived home that afternoon and saw the car. Only now did he allow himself a moment of cautious optimism. Maybe this time Dad would keep his promise.

Bailey was an arm's length away from the kitchen door when a shattering smash, followed by his mother's primal wail, stopped him cold. His Adidas shoes transformed from bouncy rubber to concrete blocks. The cortisol and adrenalin cocktail that had settled after his Evil Knievel ride home, soared again. Tension travelled through his neck and shoulders like an invading parasite and colonized in his head.

It was a safety zone day and protective wear would be required.

From the age of six, Bailey wished for an end to these days; whenever he cracked a chicken's wishbone, spotted a shooting star, or blew out birthday candles. Ten years of unfulfilled wishes…ten years of escalating drama between his parents. They fought most days, each more destructive and wounding than the last.

He was a statue, still less than a metre from the open kitchen door leading into the fray. Closing his eyes, he sought to settle himself. The distant hum of traffic was only just discernible over the sound of Sesame Street on the television inside. Filling his lungs deeply, the pungent scent of freshly-chopped onion and coffee brewing in the percolator caught in his throat. His heartbeat slowed enough for him to prepare.

He was entering a hostile environment, one where oxygen was scarce and the ground so devoid of nutrients that only weeds grew. Bailey had discovered, after his tenth birthday, that in order to survive and thrive at home, he must wear a protective spacesuit when entering such environments – a bespoke suit, like the ones NASA astronauts wore. He squinted his eyes tight in concentration and hummed. When he opened them, the suit materialised.

Lifting one leg at a time, Bailey slid the heavy weave of nylon, spandex and Dacron up his legs and torso. As it reached his ribcage, his body lightened…floated, even. He pressed a button on each moon-boot, countering the loss of gravity, and was safely secured to the floor. Sliding his arms into the sleeves, he clipped the tab clasps around his neck with a flourish.

He pulled the helmet, with its golden reflective mirror, over his shaggy hair and turned it an inch clockwise until it locked into place. The transformation was complete. He was Bailey no more. He was now Rocket Boy, and all vulnerable parts were hidden from harm. He was in complete control over how much of the tempestuous atmosphere would penetrate his suit.

Protected as he was, Rocket Boy was still nervous about making contact with terra firma in Planet Kitchen. He needed to make immediate assessments and decide if it was too dangerous to land. There had been other occurrences…times when instead of digging in, he'd shouted inside his helmet *ABORT MISSION, ABORT MISSION* and run for his bike.

Every landing had three goals, and they never changed:

Calm them down

Separate them

Live to fight another day.

Bailey breathed deeply, a Darth Vadar-like sound signalling the entry of oxygen and exit of carbon dioxide. He clumped through the kitchen door onto foreign dust and chunks of rock. Leaning carefully so as not to tip over, he collected a rock. Ceramic and painted glossy white with segments of blue and orange geometric pattern…the same as the family's dinner plates.

One finger hovering over the ABORT button on his chest plate, Rocket Boy surveyed and assessed the terrain. He flicked his thumb and a small keypad and screen rose up from his sleeve. He hit the SWOT analysis button and began typing in Strengths, Weakness, Opportunities and Threats.

Planet Kitchen SWOT Report

Present: Captain Mum (Janice), Commander Dad (Robert) and, behind a rock wall, First Mate Meg (Sister, age 4).

Strengths: No physical injuries.

Floor covered in debris – nothing expensive or dangerous visible or broken.

Everyone accounted for and present (or is this a threat?)

Weakness: Captain Mum slumped on floor near sink. Upset – head in hands.

Commander Dad leaning, shoulders hunched, head stooped low over breakfast bench.

Meg has the TV blaring Sesame Street (I hope she hasn't heard everything. She is too young for a spacesuit)

Opportunities: Fanned out between Commander Dad's hands are a bundle of $50 notes – at least one thousand dollars.

Threats: Next to the money is a TAB (Totalisator Agency Board) ticket.

While the report captured valuable data, it failed to calculate navigation options. All technology Rocket Boy tried to that point failed to deliver the answers he needed. Data analysis was entirely up to him.

Rocket Boy's boots crunched the broken moon-rocks. Commander Dad looked up from the kitchen bench. His blue eyes – so like Rocket Boy's own – held nothing but dullness. His latest faux pas had dipped a paintbrush in a tin of matt-finish-shame and painted over the gloss. This was one part of the terrain Rocket Boy needed no report to understand. Whatever had occurred in Planet Kitchen before his arrival was most certainly Commander Dad's fault. His father seemed powerless to resist endlessly repeating the same follies.

'Hey, mate,' Commander Dad said, flushing deep red. 'How was your day?'

Rocket Boy nodded. Should he walk straight through the kitchen and check on his sister or engage with his parents immediately? It was surprising to find Commander Dad in Planet Kitchen at all at that time of the day. His father was usually an apparition, fleeting and travelling at the speed of light through his life. Even though Dad was around every day, it was rare to find him halted, tethered, connected and willing to engage on any topic not horseracing...as he was today, in the kitchen. Like Halley's Comet, Commander Dad was a burning ball of trouble leaving only a bright, insubstantial tail for his family to grapple with.

A garbled sob from the floor under the sink drew Rocket Boy's attention back to Planet Kitchen and to Captain Mum.

'It's bad enough that you spend every cent we earn on your bloody horses! But to involve our son...Christ, what are you thinking?' said Captain Mum.

Her fingers, buried deep in her long blonde hair, scratched mindlessly at her scalp. Her blotchy face appeared only for the seconds it took her to spew venom at Commander Dad, then she dropped her forehead to rest on her knees again. Rocket Boy swallowed. Captain Mum's cheeks shone with tears and mucus and her pants had giant wet patches on the knees.

What had he done? How was he involved? Blood drained from his head. The conversation he'd had with his parents before leaving for school that morning came back to him. His father had had a big win at the track previous day. How big Rocket Boy didn't know, but even the biggest win couldn't make up for the thousands

Commander Dad lost on the racetrack every month. Captain Mum had been in a good mood as she'd had money for groceries for a change and Commander Dad was still giddy from his win.

'Here, son,' his father had said, motioning for Bailey to join him at the kitchen bench. He'd had the race guide smoothed out in front of him with red circles, crosses and dashes marked beside various horses. 'Here's twenty dollars...pick three horses and I'll put a trifecta on for you. You can have anything you win.'

Bailey heard the breath catch in his mother's throat and caught her biting her lip and frowning. Her unspoken words were clear in her expression. *Don't start my son gambling. Don't let him feel the triumph of a win. Let him only see the heartbreak that comes with the inevitable losses.* She whispered those words to him, prayer-like every night of his life before she went to bed...when he appeared to be sleeping. But she'd kept silent that morning, and to keep the peace, so did he. He'd picked three horses.

1. Halley's Wish (on the nose)
2. Wicked Games (for second)
3. Promise Me (to complete the trifecta)

Something must have happened in that race.

Standing in the kitchen, Rocket Boy pressed the Turbo button on his chest plate and the oxygen returned to his lungs. He breathed deeply and looked at the fan of toxic fifty-dollar notes and the winning TAB ticket.

He'd won.

That's when the meteor shower hit him straight in the stomach. Small, molten particles and marble-sized rocks flew through the door and pelted his suit, stinging his tender skin underneath. They sizzled as they evaporated the humid layer coating the suit. A low heat penetrated, but stopped short of burning him. He didn't step back or collapse, instead he held his arms behind him and leaned into the shower...a show of risky defiance born from years of survival.

'You picked well mate. You won.' Commander Father cut short his brave stand. He held the fan of notes in his fist, and offered them to Rocket Boy...seemingly oblivious of how disrespectful the action was. 'Halley's Wish didn't just win; he was four lengths in front of the pack! There's twelve hundred there.'

'No, I didn't win...we all lost,' Rocket Boy mumbled under his helmet. He took the money, shoving it into a pocket on the front of his suit without counting or looking at it. He'd slip the money into Captain Mum's dressing gown pocket later, when things died down...her purse wasn't a safe zone.

'Just get out!' Captain Mum reignited her attack. 'Why don't you just piss off already and leave us alone before you wreck every...little...thing.' She stopped sobbing and crumbled like a broken bird, knees and wings askew...squatting on an alien planet that she'd crash landed on, not a home of her own choosing.

Rocket Boy thought of the mission. He'd achieved step one, things were calmer now; just his appearance seemed to slow them down. It was time for step two, to separate them so they could all live to fight another day. But Bailey, hiding underneath Rocket Boy's suit, wasn't sure about the final part of his mission anymore. Maybe they'd all be better off if things stopped at step two – separation. If his parents just split up, perhaps a cloud of peace would fall over the planet. But, for now, he concentrated on separating them so he could get to his comet viewing.

Rocket Boy rested one gloved hand on his father's shoulder, lightly digging his fingers in to get his attention and pressed the comms button on his chest with the other hand. 'Why don't we go now?' he suggested, nodding.

Commander Dad mirrored his nod, a brown curl falling over his forehead. 'Sure. See you in the car.' He left. The car door opened and engine ignited.

With the outside pressure reading vastly reduced, Rocket Boy shuffled over to his mother and held out his hand. Her fingers slipped into his palm and she gripped him tight. He pulled her up, broken shards of ceramic scraped under her thongs.

'I'm sorry, Bail. I don't know what to do,' she said.

The helmet nodded up and down in reassurance. Rocket Boy knew this. When he was younger, he used to get angry with his mother for constantly nagging and fighting with Commander Dad. *Why can't she just leave him alone?* That was before he'd noticed the mound of bills next to the phone growing into a mountain, and before he'd taken on the role of gatekeeper between his parents and the bank.

I'm not here, his mother would mouth every time the phone rang. He'd become quite adept at making up excuses for why his parents never replied to John from the bank's messages. *Errr, my Grandma has been sick,* or *my sister was in hospital,* or *she definitely called you back...I'm sure she'll be home soon.* As his responsibilities and knowledge grew, so did understanding of his mother's anger, and resentment of his father's addiction.

Why hadn't all the begging calls to grandparents for money shamed Commander Dad out of his love of the gamble? There was no "rock bottom" where his father was concerned. There was always a plan – another horse to make them rich, or moneymaking opportunity to see them retire in luxury. Always too good to be true.

The atmosphere cleared and Rocket Boy removed his helmet. Pressure hissed out as he turned it counter-clockwise and a sandy curl tumbled down over his own forehead. He was Bailey again. His mother wiped tears from her cheeks with the palm of her hand and turned back to the chopping board to finish prepping the ingredients for Apricot Chicken. The onion she'd cut earlier was still pungent, but had lost its tearful sting.

'We're going to the school now, Mum. For the comet watching night. Do you want me to clean this up first?' he said, indicating the broken fragments of plate all over the floor. 'Will you be okay?'

'Yeah, love. I'll clean it up. You go on. I'll keep some of this for you to heat up when you get home.' She wiped the curl out of his eyes. 'You'll be needing that cut. I'll make an appointment for tomorrow afternoon.'

Bailey nodded and dodged the pieces of broken plate as he made his way to the lounge room to see his sister before he left.

'Bay! Bay!' his sister shouted, not moving from in front of the blaring television.

'Hey, Princess Meg,' he said, ruffling her curls. 'You okay?'

Meg's eyes darted towards the kitchen and then returned to Bailey and he knew she'd heard the entire argument but, like him, there was nothing to say.

'See you later, alligator!' he said, heading to his bedroom to collect his backpack and grab a hoodie.

'In a while, crocodile,' she mumbled back, her attention already returned to the television.

Bailey raced to his room. Students were to set up the telescopes in ten minutes, before the prize presentation and a sausage sizzle. He grabbed the backpack he'd stashed in his bedroom. It was bursting with binoculars, Poppas and packets of chips.

Bailey raced out to the garage, peeling off his spacesuit and hanging it near the kitchen door. He jogged to his father's car and sat in the passenger seat. The V8 engine roared and throbbed under his legs as his Dad clunked the car into reverse and backed out of the driveway. The kitchen door grew smaller, until it disappeared.

*

Despite the afternoon tension, the bounce returned to Bailey's Adidas shoes in anticipation of sharing a once in a lifetime experience with his father. He basked in the dangerously-warm glow of his father's tail, enjoying the rare event of having a comet burning brightly next to him. It wasn't cool to show excitement as a teen, but Bailey couldn't wipe the goofy smile off his face.

'Can I put the radio on?' Bailey pushed the on/off button as he asked.

'Sure.'

He turned the dial from the racing station to Triple M, which was churning out space-themed songs to celebrate the comet's passing. *Venus,* by Bananarama, blasted through the car and even his father tapped his fingers on the steering wheel in rhythm to the music.

Bailey was so absorbed in the moment, he only registered where they were when the car lunged to a stop. There were no Astronomy Club friends carrying telescopes and eskies down to the oval, only abandoned shopping trolleys and the golden arches of a fast food restaurant.

'Dad?' he said. 'Why are we at the shops? We'll be late!'

'Come in with me. You're turning out to be my lucky charm,' his father said.

'What?'

'You still got that money in your pocket?'

Bailey glanced from his father to the shops. The car was parked in front of a green and white, fluorescent TAB sign. Clutched in his father's hand was the trots guide. They weren't going to the comet viewing at all.

All noise left the car, replaced by an eerie nothingness. Bailey's father's mouth moved, but no sound emerged. They were in a space-like vacuum. Gasping, Bailey reached into the back seat to grab his suit and helmet. No! He'd left them at home. He was unprotected and vulnerable. And he wasn't Rocket Boy...only Bailey. He'd gambled on his father and lost again.

He spotted the meteor shower returning over the roof of the TAB and knew he was defenceless against it. He stretched his arms behind him and leaned into it.

So, are you ready, Vanin?

Almost. The 1986 orbit excited too much attention, but this time the world's watching the new Mars colony. My little project is barely registering on the newsfeeds.

And you have what's needed to repair the ship?

Easily, Dren. Do you still doubt me?

...

You'll be returning with me, Dren.

I'm...not certain. There's someone here...

There's always someone here you care about, Dren. What about our people? Don't you care about them anymore?

...

Well, you know where I'll be, when the time comes. We're launching from the Australian site. Be there, or stay here. I don't care.

I know, Van.

2160CE
Melbourne, Australia

Fractured

Melanie Sienkiewicz

Helen paused in the doorway of the study. The crack was spreading. It was barely noticeable nine months ago when Tom stood fidgeting before her, suggesting a break; a temporary separation. How had she never seen the flaw before that day?

Floorboards creaked as she walked to her desk and sank into a leather chair. The monitor on the corner of the desk illuminated and a reminder flashed: *Call Mum.*

The growing pile of books beside the desk threatened to topple as Helen placed a package on top. She bought them for her mother. Claire loved the feel of paper between her hands in this age of virtual everything. But work was hectic; there had been no time to visit. It'd be quicker to get a courier to deliver the books.

Helen called out to her Smart Automated Machine. 'SAM, arrange for a package to be delivered to Claire please.'

'Yes, Helen.' SAM's calm voice filtered through the study. 'Placing request now.'

She wrapped freshly-manicured fingers around her mug and gazed out at the ever-changing cityscape through the floor-to-ceiling window. The sound of a siren in the distance pierced the stillness of the apartment. Helen closed her eyes, savouring the taste of hot coffee.

'Incoming request from an unidentified number, do you accept?' SAM's voice broke through.

Helen gulped down her drink. 'Yes SAM, thanks.'

'Connecting now.'

'Helen speaking.'

'Hi.'

'Shit!' Helen flinched and hot liquid spilt down the front of her silk blouse.

'Look, I realise you may not want to talk, but—'

'No, no. Oh, God. Hang on, Tom. Can you just give me a minute?' Helen hit the mute button. Snatching at the scarf around her neck, she patted her blouse dry.

There was no point; she'd have to change. She hurried into the bedroom, stripped off the blouse and drew on a fresh one. Tossing the scarf and shirt into the laundry, Helen took a deep breath. 'Reinstate the call please, SAM.'

'Unmuting comms now,' SAM replied.

'You there?' Helen tugged at her blouse.

'I am. Was beginning to wonder if you'd forgotten me, though.'

Helen pictured Tom behind his desk, if that's where he was. The creases around his blue eyes would deepen as he tried to figure out what she was up to. 'Sorry, I just...' she searched the room, devoid of embellishments, for an explanation. 'I knocked over Mum's books.'

'You still ordering those in for her? She won't use the e-reader you bought her?'

'Yeah, you know how she loves clinging to the past.' Helen smiled and rummaged in a desk drawer for her powder compact.

'Maybe your Mum's just trying to feel as if she's still a part of a simpler world? I kind of admire her for that.'

'Mmm.' Helen murmured distractedly as she dabbed on powder and ran signature red lipstick over her lips – the colour Tom had always complimented.

'So, you still think you need a device in your hand, to be in touch—'

'Oh yes,' Helen laughed. 'How could I forget: you think our tech-filled world isolates us from each other.' Checking her appearance in the small mirror, she smoothed a few errant hairs back into their low bun.

'It can,' Tom replied, sounding sombre.

'Jesus, Tom!' Helen snapped as she threw her compact down. 'It's always the same argument with you. Why can't you see how fortunate we are to live in a world where most cancers are preventable, life expectancy is well over a hundred—'

'Yes,' he responded with his usual, irritating calm, 'but what's the point if you aren't actually *with* those around you?'

'Oh Tom, for goodness sake!' Helen sighed. 'We've never been more in touch. You only have to speak and your in-home comm responds. You can search, buy and have anything delivered within hours.'

'Mmm, that's my point. Where's the interaction with others?'

'Why, if you don't have to?'

Tom groaned and the sound filled the study. Helen pictured him rubbing at his temple the way he did whenever they hit an impasse. She bit her lip and frustration ebbed. Thirty years together and it was still the same argument. Helen had fallen in love with his sensitivity, and Tom with her independence. Yet that's where the cracks in their relationship first set in.

'Anyway,' Tom continued, 'I'm sure you're busy, so I'll get to the point of why I called.'

'Oh, yes,' Helen raised her brow. 'Is it about that box of your stuff? I'm sorry. I haven't been around for your guy to come and get it. But I'm in town for a few days now, so anytime you want to send him around.'

'No, that's not it.'

'Oh.' Sitting back in her chair, Helen tucked a stray hair behind her ear as she waited for Tom to continue.

'I, um…I was just wondering. God, Helen, I feel horrible saying this. My lawyer says they're still waiting for the papers.'

The reality of their separation hit her right in the gut – again. Helen slumped in her chair.

The sound of Tom's voice continued to fill the study, but the words made no sense. Helen hadn't yet been able to accept the finality of those papers.

'Sorry Tom, can you say that last bit again. You dropped out.'

A heavy sigh came down the line before he spoke. 'You got them, didn't you?'

'What, the papers?' Helen glanced at the stack of books. The envelope from his lawyer lay buried beneath. The arrival of that envelope had come as a shock. How had they come to this point? Yes, she'd missed a few of the counselling sessions she'd agreed to, but it seemed ridiculous to see a professional just to talk. She was willing, of course, but work was unrelenting. Surely Tom understood?

'I just figured…since the counselling didn't work out…'

Tom's comment stung.

'Helen—'

'No. Of course,' she said through gritted teeth

'So, if that's what we want, I think it's best we tie this up. Don't you? It's the only way for us to move forward.'

Helen bristled. She yanked the envelope out from underneath her mother's books. How ironic that in this age, lawyers still used paper. If they'd been electronic, she'd have no excuse for the delay.

'Fine, Tom. You know I've been out of town, otherwise I would've had the papers to the lawyers by now. Consider it done.'

An awkward silence fell for a moment before Tom spoke. 'Right, well I guess that's it then. I'll um…speak to you later?'

'Sure,' Helen snapped.

'Ok, well—'

Helen slapped the disconnect button.

Tears welled in her eyes and threatened to fall. Blinking them back, the moment receded, but not before a stray drop fell, landing on the papers, right where she'd signed her name the day they arrived. In brushing it aside, the ink smudged.

'Damn it!' Helen hurled the papers across her desk.

Moving away, she stood in front of the wall-screen.

'TV on,' she commanded SAM.

'Would you like to watch the morning news? SAM responded, his voice mellow and calming.

'Yes please, SAM.'

The screen lit up and the male anchor caught Helen's attention as he introduced the next story.

'Next we're crossing live to Shannon,' his commanding tone told the audience, 'where she's been talking with some of the early birds staking out their vantage point for Halley's Comet tomorrow night.'

'Thanks, Rick.' A perky blond with perfect white teeth flashed up on the screen. 'Halley's comet returns every seventy-five years. It last came by in 1986, and now here we are in 2061, awaiting it again. Let's hear from some of the families hunting for the best spot to catch a glimpse of Halley's Comet tomorrow night.'

The reporter asked a family why they were there and Helen shook her head. Wasn't it obvious? The woman's cheerful disposition grated, especially her smile – it never faltered as she spoke. Helen screwed up her nose at the larger-than-life image. Not a blonde hair out of place; perfect makeup. So young. Even in a world where fifty-five looked like thirty used to half a century before, the woman's youth made every bone in Helen's body ache. Not for the first time, Helen regretted allowing her gym membership to lapse. Would Tom replace her with something like that?

'Now it's back to you, Rick,' the blonde presenter said, wrapping up her segment.

Rick appeared back up on screen. 'Thanks Shannon. And remember folks, we'll be crossing live tomorrow when Halley's Comet appears for the first time.'

Something the presenter said tickled in the recesses of Helen's mind. What was she forgetting? Her eye fell on the pile of books. Crap! Mum! The comet. She wanted to see it. When they spoke last, Claire mentioned something about seeing Halley's Comet back in 1986.

'SAM, call Claire,' Helen instructed.

A pang of guilt struck. She shouldn't have let work distract her. Her mother was important too. Helen walked back to her desk and waited for her mother to answer. She opened a drawer and swept the legal papers in. Tom said they should move forward, and so she would – by not allowing this situation to continually paralyse her. She'd return the papers when she was good and ready.

The sound of the call attempting to connect stopped, and Helen cocked her head. Silence filled the room.

'Mum?'

'Yes?'

'You alright? You don't sound ok.'

'I just—'

'Mum, you there?'

The light on Helen's keyboard went dark, indicating the connection was lost.

SAM's voice cut in. 'Helen, your webinar commences in thirty minutes.'

'Thank you, SAM.' Helen tapped at her keyboard, retrieving notes for the upcoming meeting.

'SAM, call Claire again please.'

The sound of her mother's voicemail filled the room. Helen disconnected without leaving a message. She tapped her wristband. Frustration mounted. This webinar was vital.

But last month the manager of Clair's apartment complex had called. He'd found Claire collapsed on the back porch. Helen had pleaded with her mother to consider an assisted living facility, but Claire refused. What if she'd had another fall?

Helen tried to call one more time. No answer.

'Damn it! SAM, cancel my webinar and have the elevator brought up. I'll need my vehicle brought around also,' Helen commanded, snatching her keys up.

'The elevator is on its way, arriving in sixty seconds. The vehicle has been called. There will be an approximate thirty second delay between your arrival in the foyer and the vehicle.'

'Thanks, SAM.'

*

The elevator doors closed and Helen sagged against the wall. Claire was ninety-three now, yet she steadfastly rejected the technology Helen lived by. Molecular nonobots that repaired damage on a cellular level were widely used, but Claire dismissed such advances as unnatural.

The smartcar drew up and Helen's voice trembled as she requested a route to her mother's address. Once outside Claire's unit, she ran up the path. Knocking on the door, she called out,

'Mum! Are you there?' Helen tried the handle. It turned and the door opened. 'Mum!'

'Goodness, what's all this fuss about?' Claire's voice drifted down the hall.

The door squeaked shut. 'You gave me a fright.' Helen said, trying to catch her breath.

'You're actually here.'

'Oh God!' Helen jumped.

Claire raised her brow, feigning mock surprise. She pulled the bedroom door shut behind her and limped down the hall. The sound of her cane bounced off the tiled floor. 'Let's sit down, shall we.' Claire chuckled as she brushed past Helen. 'You can tell me what got you so wound up that you came out from behind your screens.'

'Well, for a start, you appearing out of nowhere and startling me,' Helen muttered as she followed her mother. 'And not answering the phone!'

'I did answer.' Claire eased onto a well-worn sofa and patted the seat next to her. Helen complied, nestling in beside her mother. She ran her hands over the worn floral fabric on the arm of the seat.

'You've had this for years Mum, isn't it time you bought a new one?'

'Why would I? It does its job perfectly well, not everything has to be new and flash you know. Now, what's going on? One minute you're calling, and the next you're banging down my door!'

'You sounded as if you were in some sort of distress when I called. I panicked.'

Claire patted her daughter's hand. 'I hardly got a chance to talk before the call cut out. I think the battery died.'

'See.' Helen said, exasperated. 'It's what I always say: why can't you at least fit your home out with smart technology? Everybody else does it.'

'I'm sorry love. Did you try to call back? I'm in the middle of a fabulous book. I guess I just got distracted.'

Helen ran her eye over the bookcase that engulfed one half of her mother's sitting room. The shelves bowed under the weight of actual, paper books. Framed photos and an assortment of trinkets filled an entire shelf. The eclectic style of décor was in stark contrast with hers. Helen opened her mouth to respond, but caught her breath as a photo, taken the day she married Tom, stared back at her.

'Is something bothering you, dear? You haven't been yourself for a while now.'

Helen rose from the sofa. 'How about I make us a tea?'

'That sounds nice. Then I can tell you my news.'

Helen returned several minutes later with two steaming mugs.

'So?' Helen prompted as she set their cups down on a set of nesting tables that had belonged to her grandmother.

'Well,' Claire began and then paused, fiddling with the pearls around her neck. 'I've been corresponding with someone for a while.'

'Oh?' Helen stared at her mother. The call with Tom reverberated in her head.

Claire blushed. 'It's an old friend. From a very long time ago. I was just a young girl when we met – the night I saw Halley's Comet, actually.'

'What were you...eighteen or something?' Helen asked, trying to focus on what her mother was saying.

'Yes, that's right. Peter's his name. We kept company for several years.' Claire picked at a stray thread on the pleat of her tweed skirt.

'You mean you dated?'

'Oh, Helen, don't sound so surprised.'

'No, it's just…funny, I guess. To imagine you before.'

'I was young once you know. Don't let the white hair fool you! Yes, we dated. He was very special.' Claire's cheeks, etched deep with wrinkles, flushed deeper pink.

'So, what happened? Who contacted who?'

'Peter wrote to me,' Claire's lips twitched into a secret smile. 'Eight weeks ago, now. He said a story in the news about Halley's Comet's arrival got him thinking. He wondered what had happened to me.'

'I bet that was a surprise.' Helen brightened, welcoming the distraction. 'Does he still have feelings for you? Do you have feelings for him?'

Claire's fingers travelled back up to her pearls. 'He's ill, and I think he's doing what people my age do: casting an eye back over their life and making amends.'

'Tell me about him,' Helen said. 'I'm intrigued.'

'Oh my goodness,' Claire began, soft brown eyes glistening. 'You know how it is to be in love. But we were young, and eventually real life took over. He was offered a job overseas. I didn't want to leave what was familiar to me. I wanted him to choose me; stay here.' Claire held her daughter's stare and went on. 'I realise now that all relationships require compromise. On both sides.'

'Why couldn't you find a compromise?' Helen's jaw tightened.

'Because I was obstinate.' Claire looked directly at Helen a moment before continuing. 'Losing him is my biggest regret.'

Helen always knew her parents were a poor match. Their divorce had been a relief to everyone in the family. Now it made sense why Claire had never met anyone else.

'Does he want to see you?'

'Funny you should ask. He wondered if we might see the comet together. A second chance, he said.'

'That's sweet.' Helen swallowed down a lump in her throat.

Claire squeezed her daughter's hand. 'You alright love? You look sad.'

'Mum, there's something I need to tell you.'

'Is it about Tom?'

'How did you know?' Helen's stomach clenched.

Claire smiled. 'It's not hard to sense something's wrong if you know a person well enough. I also bumped into him last week at the market.'

'Funny. He never mentioned it to me.'

'How could he, if you don't speak to one another.'

'Why, what did he say?' Helen demanded.

'Oh love, it's not what people say that matters, it's what they don't say you need to pay attention to.'

Helen shifted back into the corner of the sofa, hugging one of Claire's tapestry cushions to her chest. 'Did he tell you he's seen a lawyer?'

'Yes. But you two should talk. Face to face.'

Helen shook her head.

'Love, I know it was difficult for you once your father remarried. You've had a wall up ever since he met that woman.'

'It was years ago, Mum.'

'Your father should never have said he loved her more.'

Helen picked intently at a loose thread on the cushion. 'It's in the past now.'

'Mmm. But you're still guarded. Especially with those closest to you.' Claire said pointedly.

'Nothing wrong with protecting yourself.'

'Oh, sweetheart.' Claire sighed. 'Love is a risk.'

The loose thread snapped off in Helen's fingers.

'That reminds me.' Claire leant on her cane and levered up from the sofa. 'I've been meaning to give you something.' Shuffling towards the bookcase, Claire's knees crackled. 'I found it a while ago, when I was cleaning out my cupboards.'

'Here, let me help you.' Helen came up behind Claire.

Claire batted Helen's arm away and extracted an envelope tucked between two books, 'For goodness sake, I'm not as frail as you seem to think!'

'Sorry,' Helen said, throwing her arms up as she took a step back.

Claire faced Helen, her wrinkled fingers curled tight over a small envelope.

'What's that?' Helen pointed.

'It's your wedding vows.' Claire handed over the envelope. 'I thought I'd included them in the album I made you all those years ago, but I guess not. Seemed almost symbolic, stumbling across it as your silver anniversary approaches.'

Helen snatched the envelope out of her mother's hand and shoved it into the pocket of her pants. 'Yeah, well forgive me for not feeling the sentiment right now.'

'You know, Helen, I'm sure Tom would welcome an opportunity to try and work things out.'

'Just leave it Mum!' Helen picked up their mugs and marched towards the kitchen.

The sound of china clinking echoed through the unit.

'Be careful.' Claire called out. 'I like those mugs.'

'So, about that comet, do you still want me to take you...' Helen stopped abruptly in the doorway. Claire was holding the photo of Helen and Tom.

'Yes, please. I'd love you to meet Peter,' Claire replied. 'Perhaps then you can see what lost opportunity looks like.'

*

Helen helped Claire out the smartcar. 'Lead the way, Mum.'

With barely a nod, Claire walked towards a corner of the field. 'This is it. This is where we stood, back in '86.'

Helen surveyed the landscape. People everywhere busied themselves setting up for the night's event. A young couple waved a packet of biscuits in front of their son, coaxing him to be still. Beside them, two young girls weaved in and out between their parents, chasing one another. The ground was a sea of clashing-coloured picnic rugs, and the smell of barbequed meat wafted through the air. Further down the field, amateur astronomers prepared their telescopes while others admired the impressive instruments.

'I had no idea how seriously people took this event.'

'Oh yes, it's quite a thing.' Claire nodded, her mouth lifting in a reminiscent smile. 'It was the same in '86: people as far as the eye could see.'

'What time did Peter say he'd be here?' Helen tapped at her wrist band.

'Seven. What's the time now?'

'Just a minute after. But you saw the carpark, it's getting busy.'

'I'm so nervous,' Claire said as she fiddled with the top button on her pale pink cardigan.

Helen placed an arm around her mother. 'You look beautiful!'

'I think I see him!' Claire cried. She lifted a hand, then frowned. 'But it can't be, he's too young. Goodness how it looks like him, though.'

The two women watched as a figure headed in their direction

'He's way too young. But the crowd's in the other direction. I wonder why he's coming over here?' Helen whispered.

As the man approached, Claire gasped.

'Mum! What's wrong?' Helen glanced back and forth between the man and her mother.

'It can't be. Peter?' Claire's voice trembled.

The man drew up in front of them. His blue sweater hugged broad shoulders and salt-and-pepper hair framed a chiselled face. 'I'm sorry if I've startled you.'

'No, it's not that,' replied Helen. 'We're just waiting for someone.'

'It wouldn't be for Peter Hamilton, would it?'

Helen stood protectively in front of Claire. 'Yes, it is. Who're you, and how do you know why we're here?'

The creases around the man's grey eyes deepened as he smiled and extended a hand to Helen. 'Forgive me. I'm his son, Jack.'

Claire stepped out from behind Helen. 'That's why you looked so familiar. Oh my, you're just like him!' Claire's eyes brightened.

'Yes, I'm told that often,' Jack smiled sadly.

'I've forgotten my manners. I'm Claire, and this is my daughter, Helen.'

'Lovely to meet you.' Jack's grip enveloped Claire's frail hand.

Holding on to him, she looked up, eyes wide, and smiled expectantly. 'So, where is he, then?'

'I, uh—'

Claire waved a dismissive hand in the air. 'I thought it might be too much for him in his condition to walk over here.'

'I'm afraid I have some news—'

'Oh dear, he couldn't make it?' The smile on her face faded.

'No. He died two days ago.'

Claire's face crumpled and a sob racked her small frame. Helen caught her mother as she sagged, trembling, with one hand over her heart. She helped Claire over to a bench and Jack followed.

'I'm terribly sorry, I meant no harm.'

Claire sat hunched, sobbing silently.

'I'm sorry. About your father.' Helen said, watching her mother anxiously.

'Thank you. I'd hoped he would last, but I'm afraid this last week he suddenly deteriorated.'

Claire's voice broke in. 'It was kind of you to still come tonight.'

'Oh, no. Of course.' Jack's brow furrowed as he watched Claire. 'I knew he was going to meet you here. He never stopped thinking of you. I wanted to fulfil his wish, as best I could.' He indicated the corner of the bench. 'May I?'

'Of course.' Helen replied, swapping to the other side so he could sit next to Claire.

'I found out about you when I was a young man.' Jack went on. 'I was going through a patch in my own marriage. Dad used your relationship as an example of the need to communicate. He and my mother had already divorced. Nothing dramatic, just not meant to be. Dad told me how he regretted leaving you, or at least not trying harder.'

Claire looked at Helen. 'Oh, no Jack. It was my fault. I shouldn't have been so unwilling to compromise.'

Jack shook his head and went on, 'I asked Dad back then why he never tried to find you. He said he heard you were married and had a child. Then, in these last few weeks, he told me he'd finally plucked up the courage to write to you.'

'Yes.' Claire smiled.

'He was going to tell you that you were the love of his life,' Jack said. 'I felt you should know that.'

Claire stared off into the distance, her face blank. Helen waited, her heart aching. What might have happened if Peter had tried to find her mother years ago?

The sound of Jack clearing his throat broke the silence. 'Claire, I'm sorry. It all happened so quick in the end. But he wanted you to know he never stopped loving you. It gave him great peace when I said I'd come and find you.'

'I'm glad you did.' Claire said. Her smile was strained. 'Really. It's just a shock.'

The commotion from down the field reminded them why the crowd was there. The sun's glow faded below the horizon and timid early stars glimmered in the purpling sky. Helen pulled her coat tight around her as a chill filled the air.

'It's coming!' Excited voices carried over to where they sat. 'I see it!' someone squealed.

Jack stood. 'If you'll excuse me, I wanted to see the comet. For Dad, you understand.'

Claire grabbed the corner of Jack's coat. 'Stay. Please.'

Jack nodded and sat back down. Claire took his hand. They sat in silence, hands entwined, waiting for the comet to grow to full brightness.

Loneliness engulfed Helen as she tried to ignore the bittersweet moment of intimacy occurring beside her. Nearly a year had passed since she'd last shared a bed with her husband. The indent of Tom's body was forged in the mattress, but the feel of him next to her was a fading memory.

Jack stirred and cleared his throat.

'Thank you,' Claire said again.

'You're most welcome.' He stood, and Claire pressed his hand against her cheek.

'Please.' There was a catch in her voice. 'May I ask where he's buried?'

'Of course. He's at the old cemetery, on the hill.' Jack turned to Helen, 'You know the one?'

'Yes.' Helen nodded. 'We'll go next week.'

*

'Sure you're up to this?'

'No,' Claire replied on a sigh, 'but I need to do it, regardless.'

Helen led the way towards Peter's grave, gravel crunching under their shoes as they headed down the cemetery path. Perched high above the city, the graveyard afforded commanding views of distant skyscrapers. Not that a view mattered much to the inhabitants.

Headstones in varying stages of dilapidation filled nearly every inch of space, each telling their own story. Helen glanced at the names as they walked past, noting their loving inscriptions. Husbands lay with wives, encased under marble that had slowly started to crack. Yet they lay together, forever.

After several minutes she found a makeshift cross with Peter's name on it, marking the spot. Claire let out a soft cry, and Helen went to her mother's side. They remained still, huddled together with their heads bowed for several minutes before Claire broke the silence.

'Don't let this happen to you.'

'Mum! What on Earth is that supposed to mean?'

Claire clasped Helen's hand. 'Love, please listen. Don't you think I wish it wasn't too late? He's my biggest regret.'

Helen looked off into the distance, desperate to avoid her mother's stare.

'I've had to make peace with that now.' Claire stood in front of Helen, forcing her to make eye contact. 'And I wouldn't have you, would I? But you're as stubborn as I was. If you're not careful he'll slip through your fingers, too.'

Helen fiddled with the strap on her bag.

Claire went on. 'You know, love…Halley's comet. Not many people see it twice; get a second chance if you like.'

Helen's brow furrowed. 'Yes, Mum, I know. But what's that got to do with anything here?'

'I missed my second chance.' Tears glistened in Claire's eyes. 'We didn't try hard enough. But it doesn't have to be the same for you. It's not too late.'

Helen turned aside and rummaged in her bag. Her hands found the smooth metal device and she pulled it out.

'Helen!'

'What?' The notification showed she'd missed three calls from work. Damn! 'How long do you want to stay here?' Helen scrolled through her messages.

Claire stared at her daughter a moment. Her shoulders slumped. She placed a small bunch of flowers on top of the freshly turned earth.

'We can go,' she said.

*

Sinking back into her seat inside the vehicle, Helen spoke to the navigation unit, 'Plan trip to Claire's home.'

'Route programmed,' the car's audio responded as the engine hummed to life.

'I almost forgot,' Helen said. 'I have some more books for you. They're in the back. Remember them when you get out.'

'No love. I won't forget something that matters to me.'

*

Helen watched her mother wave and close the door to her unit.

The visit to Peter's grave left Helen drained.

'Find the nearest bottleshop,' she instructed the car's navigation. What kind of wine should she buy? Ah, yes. A nice light red; something she and Tom had discovered on a trip through Tuscany.

As Helen entered her apartment, she threw her bag on the hall stand and headed down the narrow hall to the kitchen. Finding a glass, she went straight for the couch and fell into the oversized cushions. She poured a generous glass of the ruby liquid and savoured the deep berry aromas as it burned the back of her throat. Alone at last, thoughts lurking at the edge of her mind all day surged to the forefront. Life with Tom.

Remorse sat with Helen, as she acknowledged the role she had played in deconstructing their happiness. Throughout their marriage she had isolated herself from Tom. But she'd been powerless to stop herself. She'd always had a tendency to withdraw from those around her, and her love of gadgets had made it easy. Of course she had driven him away. She couldn't blame him. All he ever wanted was for her to open up to him.

The apartment suddenly felt cold, and Helen tugged at a soft ivory throw. The smell of Tom on the cashmere invaded her nostrils. Tossing the blanket aside, Helen went to her study. There was no smell of him here.

The freshly plastered patch caught Helen's eye as she entered the room. He'd been then – the building manager. The crack was gone, and all that remained was to touch up the paint. Was it really that easy?

A soft glow emanated from the monitor on her desk. Helen drifted over. Absently checking her in-box, she felt around in her pocket for a tissue. Her hand brushed against crumpled paper. The envelope she'd stuffed in her pocket while at her mother's house last week.

That night, all those years ago, came into view. It had started with Helen teasing Tom about writing their wedding vows.

'No-one says they're going to obey their husband anymore.'

'You wouldn't be the woman I want to marry if you did.' Tom's blue eyes smiled lovingly at her.

With a heavy heart, Helen pulled the envelope from her pocket and broke the seal. Sliding the paper out, her words jumped out...*to find time, every day, to be together and talk.* She'd jokingly included that line. Tom was so passionate about it: that they always make time to talk to each other. She'd laughed. *Of course they would talk. What sort of marriage would it be otherwise!* Yet it was the one vow she'd failed to keep.

What if she'd made time all those months ago and gone to see someone with him?

'SAM,' Helen called out.

'Yes, Helen?'

'My mother. She's so old school. She lets herself feel.'

'A feeling is an emotion or opinion. I require specific direction.'

Helen placed the envelope on the desk. Her hand ran continuously over the paper, smoothing out the creases. 'Alright. Call Tom.'

'Calling Tom.'

'No! Cancel call!' Helen stood abruptly. Her heart pounded.

'Request cancelled.' SAM's smooth voice responded.

'Crap.' Helen muttered, pacing between the window and her desk. The room closed in on her and she grabbed the chair, collapsing into it. She reached trembling hands out for her tablet and swiped impatiently at the screen, trying to wake the device. When the screen remained blank she tossed it on her desk. The envelope fluttered slightly.

'SAM, call Tom.'

After a moment his voice filled her study, 'Hello? Helen, is that you?'

'Oh, hi Tom.' Helen replied as she ran sweaty palms down the front of her pants.

'You ok?' Tom asked. 'You sound a bit...drunk.'

Blushing, Helen straightened in her seat, 'I don't know about drunk, but I have been enjoying some of that wine we used to get. Remember?'

Tom's voice filtered softly through the room. 'Yes, I do.'

'Listen Tom, I just wanted to say...' The reality of the moment took hold, and Helen's resolve cracked. Seeing the envelope on her desk she went on, 'I'm sorry.'

Several moments passed. 'Tom? Are you there?'

'Yes. I'm here. Helen, why now? Why are you telling me this now?'

'God, Tom! I know I've messed up. I'm not asking you for another chance, but—'

'Is that what you want, another chance?'

It was hard to read his tone. Was he punishing her or genuinely asking how she felt? Too late now. Might as well lay all her cards out.

'Maybe,' she went on. 'I don't know. I took Mum to see Halley's Comet.'

'I'm not sure what that has to do with any of this,' Tom said.

'Yeah, I didn't either. Until now. She got a letter from an old admirer.' Helen clutched the envelope against her chest.

'Oh?'

'Mmm. You were right, you know.' Helen let out a deep breath.

'Right about what?'

'About Mum – people – wanting to be with each another. The old flame...they didn't communicate well. A lifetime later he got back in touch with her. But it was too late. He died before they could meet.'

'Geez, Helen, I'm sorry to hear that. But I don't understand what any of that has to do with us?'

Helen opened the scrunched note. 'I was at Mum's last week and she handed me an envelope.'

'You're not making a lot of sense right now. Are you ok?'

Helen wiped her nose on the sleeve of her sweater. 'I'm not very good at this.'

'At what?'

'Any of it. Being with someone. Talking.' She held her breath, waiting for Tom's response.

'Is that what you want. To talk?' he said quietly.

'Yes. If it's not too late.' Helen fiddled with her ponytail, smoothing fine strands back into place. 'I realise now. All these years. I thought I was protecting myself, and all I was doing was pushing you away.'

Tom drew a long, slow breath and then let it out. 'Well, why don't you start by telling me more about your mother's friend.' He paused. 'Then I can make sure our story ends differently.'

Helen's heart skipped a beat. 'What about dinner? I could fill you in then.'

'Sounds good.'

'You know,' Helen said smiling as tears spilled down her cheeks. 'Mum pointed out that Halley won't be coming by again for me.'

'Mmm. I guess we don't all get a second shot.'

'No, we don't.' Helen said, tucking the slip of paper back into the envelope. She glanced at the patched crack in the wall. It was still rough. Some work was still needed in order to smooth it out. But at least the repairs had begun.

2160CE

Near Roma, Australia

And When We Return

Pt II

Aiki Flinthart

'Dren,' Vanin said, neutrally. She nodded as I joined her in the observation lounge.

'Vanin.' I leaned on the railing and stared through tinted glass at the launchpad. The rocket was a sleek, white needle pointing skyward. Beneath it lay bare concrete, grey and cracked. Beyond the launch site, the vast, red-dust Australian landscape shimmered and baked under the white mid-winter sun. Heat hazed the blocky outlines of Roma city on the eastern horizon.

'Everything ready?' I asked. The sharp silence between us made me uncomfortable. We hadn't spoken in months and before that, decades. There was little left to say. I hadn't seen Vanin for over two hundred years. Earth was a big planet, even with the advent of atmo-skimming low-orbit transports.

I looked sideways. She hadn't changed much. She'd let slip the illusion of human-ness and stood at the picture window in her true form; still female though her resting-green skin was tinged brown with age. Her hair was now pale, mist-blue, rather than the cobalt of youth, but her back was straight and her chin lifted as she stared at the culmination of two thousand years of effort. No regrets. No pity for humankind. Still that unquenchable drive.

'Was it worth it, Van?' I gestured at the arid, salt-crusted plains around the launch site. 'You've brought this world to the level of technology we need to get back. But have you stopped to look at what's happened to the planet to get to this point?'

She turned cool green eyes on me and her mouth lifted in a distant smile. 'So? We don't need this planet as a colony. Our people have found one. What does it matter? Besides, as you said – humans are resourceful. They'll recover the world.'

'Maybe,' I said.

'You've worked yourself into a position of trust...Prime Minister.' Van turned the title into a sneer. 'Taught them the right steps. The seedbanks, the cryo-freeze DNA banks.' She pointed northeast, to where a geodesic dome glittered in the sunlight. 'And the Habitats are protecting key ecosystems until the solar shield's completed and global warming's reduced. The Mars colony is successful, too.' Her smile turned bitter. 'They certainly won't die out in a hurry.'

I sighed and scrubbed a hand over my head. My human-form shift was yet in place. Reflected in the window, my hand touched the greying hair on a human businessman.

Vanin's fingers gripped mine on the rail and I flinched. Her eyes glittered.

'Can't you see, Dren? I've done it.' She flung an arm towards the rocket. 'By this time tomorrow we'll be back in our ship. We can repair the drive and be on our way home!' A beatific dream of homecoming slid over her face.

I pulled free of her touch. 'We haven't heard from our people on the colony world, Van. We don't even know—'

'We do know.' She cut me off with a sharp gesture of denial. 'We got the signal from the colony when they started the homing beacon for us, remember?'

'But that was four hundred years ago, Van,' I said gently.

She swiped a hand over her face and paced a few steps away, her eyes fixed on the rocket. 'They'd have a lot to do. Rescuing us wouldn't be a priority. Setting up the colony would.'

'Rescuing the Prime Blue not a priority?' I managed to suppress a laugh but not the sarcasm. 'Could it be you're not as vital as you thought?'

Her claws extended and she rounded on me with green eyes ablaze and skin flushed to match the dirty-blue sky. 'Sneer if you like, Dren, but when I get back my people will celebrate for a year. *They* want Prime rule. I'm still female and can bear a child.'

I straightened and cocked my head. 'Have you considered what you'll do if you get there and find the colony has failed? If they're all dead? Or they don't want Primes to rule any more. Or a dozen other possibilities that might make your obsession pointless.'

'Yes.' She turned back to the launch site.

'And?'

Her smile held genuine puzzlement. She waved a hand towards the distant city, hazed by pollution and glinting in the remorseless sun.

'I'll return, of course! The humans have come far, but these people still need me.'

'Ah.' I slid my hands into my pockets and looked away.

'You're coming with me, Dren.' It was an order from my Prime and, even after all these years apart, the tone was difficult to resist.

I gazed at her with pity. 'No. I'm not. Strangely enough, I care for these people.'

Disgust flickered across her face. 'Yes, you've grown attached to a few over the years, haven't you?' She shuddered. 'I don't see how you could. Or how you can stand losing them when they die. They lead such short lives.'

'Death is part of life. It hurts, but they're worth loving.' I glanced at the digital display on the window. 'But don't let me keep you. Almost launch time. Your chariot awaits, Prime.' I raised my voice. 'SAM, order the transport to the ground floor door. Captain Vanin is ready to depart.'

'Yes, Prime Minister Drencovic,' responded the building's automatic control system.

Van returned my steady regard with scorn. 'You always were soft, Dren. I'll tell them you died on this forsaken planet. No one will come for you.'

I bowed. 'I expect nothing less. Goodbye, Van.'

She spun on her heel and shifted into her latest human form: a young, female astronaut in an Australian Space Administration dusty green uniform. The elevator opened and dignitaries from the city hurried in to watch the liftoff. I moved aside and took a less central position at the window. Vanin disappeared into the elevator without looking back. Moments later, a support vehicle raced towards the rocket.

The rocket's ion-drive thrummed to life. Subsonic. Nothing more than a faint tremor through my feet and chest. An ache in my back teeth. And a different sort of ache tightened my throat. There were times I wished our species could cry. For me. For her. For the Earth and for Haos.

I withdrew a hand from my pocket and looked at the small, black plastic object resting in my palm. The blue-lit button in the centre glowed, tempting me. I hesitated.

On the window-display, the count began: a discreet ticking of numbers down from ten. The chatter around me settled into whispers and murmurs. Champagne glasses clinked elegantly. Coffee, that rarity from the highlands of Nepal, was passed around and sipped with reverence.

A rumble through the ground signalled liftoff.

I stroked the glowing button with a thumb and sighed as the rocket rose majestically into the sky.

I waited. It continued to spear towards the stratosphere. I'd been deluding myself to think she would change her mind.

When the rocket was the merest dot against the vast blue, I pressed the button.

A silent spark on high. A shower, spraying bright fireworks against the ceiling of the world. Gouts of billowing smoke and fire; cosmic dust. Gasps of horror from my fellow onlookers. Fingers pointed at trails of white smoke spiralling back to Earth. Returning to the surface, forever.

If they found enough debris to study, investigations would show a faulty regulator caused the ion engine to explode.

I tucked the remote back into my pocket and turned away, heart-heavy.

Then I went home, to one day choose my manner of death amongst people I loved, on a colony world I'd discovered – and might yet be able to save.

About the Authors

Megan Badger is an award-winning Brisbane-based author of speculative fiction. She has been published in sirens call magazine and Veronica Literary magazine. Nicknamed macabre Meg by her friends she has a fascination with the dark and mysterious sides of human experience. Megan has a BFA in creative and professional writing

Aiki Flinthart lives in Brisbane. She has published a popular YA fantasy series *80AD* and has two fantasy trilogies (*The Kalima Chronicles; Shadows)* due for publication in 2018. She has a BSc (Hons), runs a business full time with her husband and son, and practices various martial arts and musical instruments in what little spare time exists between that and writing.

Website: **www.aikiflinthart.com**

Twitter: @aikiflinthart

Facebook: **https://www.facebook.com/aiki.flinthart**

Ted Johnson writes mostly non-fiction, amusing anecdotal stories about family, plus the occasional foray into fiction. Every year or so, God tries to destroy Brisbane. Her persecution results in extended power outages. And there's not much to do by candle-light except dig in and write. Just write.

DA Kelly writes dark, gritty fantasy stories. She can't help it. Magic, fairies, and dragons make life exciting. Since she lives in a small Qld town, where nothing fantastical ever happens, she has to make it up. She's currently working on a dark fantasty trilogy of novels, *The Little Clock of Sorrow*.

Website: dakellyfantasybooks.com

Twitter: @dakellyauthor

Facebook: https://www.facebook.com/dakellyauthor

Lynne Lumsden Green has twin bachelor degrees in both Science and the Arts, giving her the balance between rationality and creativity. She spent fifteen years as the Science Queen for HarperCollins Voyager Online. These days, she captains the Writing Race for the Australian Writers Marketplace on Facebook and volunteers at the Queensland Writers Centre, when not writing. You can find her blog at: https://cogpunksteamscribe.wordpress.com/

Caitlyn McPherson is an emerging writer who has studied Children's picture book writing & creative writing through the Australian and Queensland Writers Centres. She's dabbling in the romance genre for this anthology.

Belinda Messer is a children's book author with a penchant for writing books on topics that matter. Sex education, IVF, and grief have all received their own book titles (*21st Century Guide to the Birds and the Bees, An IVF Story, On the Wings of a Butterfly*) and in 2018 her new book, *Australia Rules,* will be published. In the mean time she's working on a women's fiction novel and a beautiful children's bedtime story.

Website: **www.belindamessercreative.com.au**
Facebook: **https://www.facebook.com/Belmesser11**
Instagram: **https://www.instagram.com/belmesser11/**

Susan Ruth loves to tell stories. She writes historical fiction set in England in the seventeenth and eighteenth centuries. She is also the author of the *Chronicles of Deva*, a fantasy sequence set in an alternative Britain in the early years of the twentieth century during a time of civil war. Her new novels, *Minister of State Security* and *Flight of the Queen,* will be available in 2018.

Jo Seysener is an emerging author who's always loved to write. She prefers to pen dystopian and YA fiction, but is also working on her first illustrated children's book. She lives in Brisbane with her family, two dogs and nine chickens.

Melanie Sienkiewicz grew up in Melbourne, now happily resides in Brisbane. She writes contemporary fiction, and is currently working on her first novel. She draws on her Arts and Politics degree for inspiration and her family – human and fur – for support (when they're not driving her mad) as she scribbles about the fascinating world of human relationships.

Dr Jo Sparrow has worked as a professional writer for seventeen years. She published a non-fiction book with Amherst Media in New York (2007) and has been published in newspapers and magazine in Australia and internationally. Jo has degrees in journalism, public relations and holds a Doctorate of Creative Arts (Creative Writing). She also serves on the management committee of the Queensland Writers Centre.

Georgia Willis is an avid reader, and emerging author writing in the fantasy genre. Born and bred in Brisbane, she lives with her crazy dog and numerous fish. She is a member of a newly formed writers group and is enjoying the interaction with other authors.

www.ingramcontent.com/pod-product-compliance
Lightning Source LLC
Chambersburg PA
CBHW030646120726
47905CB00001B/85